D0886686

PRIDE AND PREJUDICE
AND ZOMBIES

DAWN OF THE
DREADFULS

BY STEVE HOCKENSMITH

ILLUSTRATIONS BY PATRICK ARRASMITH

QUIRK BOOKS
PHILADELPHIA

Library of Congress Cataloging in Publication Number: 2009943659

ISBN: 978-1-59474-454-9

Printed in Canada

Typeset in Bembo and Mrs. Eaves

Cover design and zombification by Doogie Horner
Cover art courtesy the Bridgeman Art Library International Ltd.
Interior illustrations by Patrick Arrasmith
Production management by John J. McGurk

Distributed in North America by Chronicle Books
680 Second Street
San Francisco, CA 94107

10 9 8 7 6 5 4

Quirk Books
215 Church Street
Philadelphia, PA 19106
www.irreference.com
www.quirkbooks.com

LIST OF ILLUSTRATIONS

For Jane.
We kid because we love.

CHAPTER 1

WALKING OUT in the middle of a funeral would be, of course, bad form. So attempting to walk out on one's own was beyond the pale.

When the service began, Mr. Ford was as well behaved as any corpse could be expected to be. In fact, he lay stretched out on the bier looking almost as stiff and expressionless in death as he had in life, and Oscar Bennet, gazing upon his not-so-dearly departed neighbor, could but think to himself, *You lucky sod.*

It was Mr. Bennet who longed to escape the church then, and the black oblivion of death seemed infinitely preferable to the torments he was suffering. At the pulpit, the Reverend Mr. Cummings was reading (and reading and reading and reading) from the *Book of Common Prayer* with all the verve and passion of a man mumbling in his sleep, while the pews were filled with statues—the good people of Meryton, Hertfordshire, competing to see who could remain motionless the longest while wearing the most somber look of solemnity.

This contest had long since been forfeited by one party in particular: Mr. Bennet's. Mrs. Bennet couldn't resist sharing her (insufficiently) whispered appraisal of the casket's handles and plaque. ("Brass? For shame! Why, Mrs. Morrison had gold last week, and her people don't have two guineas to rub together.") Lydia and Kitty, the youngest of the Bennets' five daughters, were ever erupting into titters for reasons known only to themselves. Meanwhile, the middle daughter, fourteen-year-old Mary, insisted on loudly shushing her giggling sisters no matter how many times her reproaches were ignored, for she considered herself second only to the Reverend Mr. Cummings—and perhaps Christ Himself—as Meryton's foremost arbiter of virtue.

At least the Bennets' eldest, Jane, was as serene and sweet countenanced as ever, even if her dress was a trifle heavy on décolletage for a funeral. ("Display, my dear, display!" Mrs. Bennet had harped at her that morning. "Lord Lumpley might be there!") And, of course, Mr. Bennet knew he need fear no embarrassment from Elizabeth, second to Jane in age and beauty but first in spirit and wit. He leaned forward to look down the pew at her, his favorite—and found her gaping at the front of the church, a look of horror on her face.

Mr. Bennet followed her line of sight. What he saw was a luxury, hard won and now so easily taken for granted: a man about to be buried with his head still on his shoulders.

That head, though—wasn't there more of a loll to the left to it now? Weren't the lips drawn more taut, and the eyelids less so? In fact, weren't those eyes even now beginning to—

Yes. Yes, they were.

Mr. Bennet felt an icy cold inside him where there should have been fire, and his tingling fingers fumbled for the hilt of a sword that wasn't there.

Mr. Ford sat up and opened his eyes.

The first person to leap into action was Mrs. Bennet. Unfortunately, the action she leapt to was shrieking loud enough to wake the dead (presuming any in the vicinity were still sleeping) and wrapping herself around her husband with force sufficient to snap a man with less backbone in two.

"Get a hold of yourself, woman!" Mr. Bennet said.

She merely maintained her hold on *him*, though, her redoubled howls sparking Kitty and Lydia to similar hysterics.

At the front of the church, Mrs. Ford staggered to her feet and started toward the bier.

"Martin!" she cried. "Martin, my beloved, you're alive!"

"I think not, Madam!" Mr. Bennet called out (while placing a firm hand over his wife's mouth). "If someone would restrain the lady, please!"

Most of the congregation was busy screeching or fleeing or both at once, yet a few hardy souls managed to grab Mrs. Ford before she could shower her newly returned husband with kisses.

"Thank you!" Mr. Bennet said.

He spent the next moments trying to disentangle himself from his wife's clutches. When he found he couldn't, he simply stepped sideways into the aisle, dragging her with him.

"I will be walking that way, Mrs. Bennet." He jerked his head at Mr. Ford, who was struggling to haul himself out of his casket. "If you choose to join me, so be it."

Mrs. Bennet let go and, after carefully checking to make sure Jane was still behind her, swooned backward into her eldest daughter's arms.

"Get her out of here," Mr. Bennet told Jane. "Lydia and Kitty, as well."

He turned his attention then to the next two girls down the pew: Elizabeth and Mary. The latter was deep in conversation with her younger sisters.

"The dreadfuls have returned!" Kitty screamed.

"Calm yourself, sister," Mary said, her voice dead. She was either keeping a cool head or had retreated into catatonia, it was hard to tell which. "We should not be hasty in our judgments."

"Hasty? *Hasty?*" Lydia pointed at the very *un*dead Mr. Ford. "He's sitting up in his coffin!"

Mary stared back at her blankly. "We don't know he's a dreadful, though."

But Elizabeth did know. Mr. Bennet could see it in her eyes—because now she was staring at *him*.

She didn't grasp the whole truth of it. How could she, when he'd been forced to keep it from her for so long? Yet this much would be obvious to a clear-thinking, level-headed girl like her: The dreadfuls *had* returned, and there was more to be done about it than scream. More her father intended to do.

What she couldn't have guessed—couldn't have possibly dreamed—was that she herself would be part of the doing.

"Elizabeth," Mr. Bennet said. "Mary. If you would come with me, please."

And he turned away and started toward the altar.

Toward the *zombie*.

CHAPTER 2

AT FIRST, it wasn't just difficult for Elizabeth to follow her father. It was impossible.

With her mother aswoon at one end of the pew and Kitty and Lydia shrieking hysterically at the other, both paths to the aisle were blocked. Elizabeth and Jane couldn't induce them to any movement more gainful than mere flailing, and eventually Mary resorted to a sobering slap across Kitty's cheek. The gambit actually paid off to this extent: Kitty stopped screaming and tried to slap her back.

A moan from the front of the church broke up the tussle. It started low, almost literally so, as if bubbling up from the depths of the earth, a distant wail from Hell itself. Then it built to a high, piercing howl that rattled glass and emptied bladders all through the chapel. It was a cry that hadn't been heard in Hertfordshire for years, yet nearly everyone there knew what it was.

The zombie wail.

The mourners shot for the doors like a great black arrow, and with miraculous speed Mrs. Bennet regained her footing and found the strength to join them in flight. Jane went with her, but not before pausing for a doleful glance back at Elizabeth and Mary, who were holding their ground in the aisle even as Kitty and Lydia and a host of other parishioners poured around them.

Elizabeth could go after her father now. But would she? Should she, when reason surely said to flee, and fast?

The debate raged for all of a second.

Run! said Fear.

Obey, said Duty.

And then a third voice chimed in, one Elizabeth didn't even recognize at first, so well trained were proper young ladies in ignoring it. The voice of Self.

Oh, go on, it said. *You know you've always wondered. . . .*

Elizabeth turned toward the front of the church, facing the throng rushing at and past her, and began walking against the flow. Each face flying by looked more terror stricken than the last. Yet when Elizabeth felt their panic worming its way inside her, threatening to infect her, she simply willed herself to stop seeing them. Everyone and everything merged into a great, dark blur, so much so that she didn't even notice when her Aunt Philips flashed past, crying, "Lizzy, what are you doing? This way! *This way!*"

Elizabeth didn't let herself truly see again until she was almost at the end of the aisle. She looked back, wondering if Mary had come, too, and found her younger sister right behind her, so close that her steps brushed the hem of Elizabeth's skirts.

Elizabeth felt such relief she actually smiled. It was a compliment Mary wasn't willing to accept.

"I was simply following you," she said.

When Elizabeth looked ahead again, she saw her father watching them from beside the bier. He wasn't smiling, though there was a curl to his lip and a gleam in his eye that suggested droll satisfaction, as when he and she shared a private joke at her mother's expense. Only three other people had dared gather with him near (but not *too* near) the casket: Mrs. Ford; her brother, Mr. Elliot; and the Reverend Mr. Cummings.

Of course, Mr. Ford was there, as well, but he didn't count as "other people" anymore.

"Come closer, girls. He won't bite," Mr. Bennet said. "Not so long as you stay out of range."

With slow, uncertain steps, Elizabeth and Mary joined their father. Mr. Ford turned toward them as they approached, watching with empty eyes. It comforted Elizabeth somewhat that the expression seemed so familiar: Mr. Ford never had been the friendliest of her neighbors, hoarding his small store of cheer for those more likely to bring him business.

He'd been the village apothecary all Elizabeth's life, building up a reputation thereabouts for both humorless competence and a heavy thumb upon the scales. Two days before, he'd bent down to retrieve a stray ha'penny from the road and was promptly run over by a joy-riding Lord Lumpley, who'd been momentarily blinded by a smiling milkmaid. All might have been well if His Lordship hadn't circled his cabriolet to see what he'd hit (and get another look at the girl), compounding Mr. Ford's minor scrapes and bruises with a most *un*minor severing of the legs.

"Oh, Martin, my precious Martin!" Mrs. Ford sobbed, and Mr. Elliot had to hold tight to keep her from squeezing her husband to her heaving bosom. "To think we almost buried you alive!"

Her precious Martin merely turned his vacant gaze her way for a moment before returning to the task at hand: trying to heft his trunk up out of the casket. He would have met with immediate success had he simply loosened his pants, thus freeing himself of the literal deadweight of his amputated legs, but this was beyond his now nonexistent powers of reasoning.

"My dear Mrs. Ford," Mr. Bennet said, "I'm afraid the only thing premature about this particular burial is that it was almost conducted with

IT WAS A CRY THAT HADN'T BEEN HEARD IN HERTFORDSHIRE FOR YEARS.

your husband's head still attached."

"No!" Mrs. Ford cried. "He was just sleeping! Unconscious! Cataleptic! He's better now!"

Drawn by the sound of the woman's distress, the creature in the coffin began making lazy swipes at her with its long, stiff arms.

"Urrrrrrrrrrr," it said.

"See! He recognizes me!" Mrs. Ford exclaimed. "Yes, darling, it's me! Your Sarah!"

"Oh, for heaven's sake," Mr. Bennet sighed. "All he recognizes is an easy meal." He turned to Mr. Elliot. "Might it not be best if you were to remove the lady?"

"Yes . . . yes, certainly," Mr. Elliot muttered with a quick nod. He was obviously anxious to remove himself, first and foremost, yet he managed to tug his sister along as he made his eager escape up the aisle.

"Maaaaarrrrrrrrtiiiiiiiinnnnnnnnn!" howled Mrs. Ford as she was dragged away.

"Urrrrrrahrrrurrrrrrrrrrrrrrrrr!" replied what was left of her husband.

"How can she not see the obvious?" Mary asked. The bifurcated neighbor sitting up in his coffin had made a strong impression, yes, yet she seemed almost more disgusted by Mrs. Ford.

"Don't judge too harshly, for once, my dear," Mr. Bennet told her. "Wishful thinking is a sin all England stands guilty of today, your fool of a father included. We told ourselves our long nightmare was over, that a new day had dawned. Alas, *that* was the real dream. But, goodness—just listen to me chattering away when there's work to be done!" He turned back to the casket and began tapping a finger against his upper lip. "How . . . to . . . kill it?"

Elizabeth gave a little start. She wasn't sure, though, what it was that really shocked her. Was it hearing her dear Papa talk about killing an "it," when "it" was a man she'd known all her young life? Or was it his cool, nonchalant tone as he did so?

"B-but, s-sir," Mr. Cummings said, "are you absolutely sh-sh-sure he's a . . . a . . . a . . . ?"

Mr. Bennet finished the vicar's thought for him.

"A dreadful? There can be no doubt. Our Dr. Long is no Hippocrates, to be certain, but even he's not so incompetent as to misdiagnose *death* when a man's been cut in half."

The vicar acknowledged the logic of it with a jittery nod. "I s-suppose you're right. All the same, must you . . . dispose of him here? P-p-practically on the altar? As you say, poor Mr. Ford has no legs . . . a-t-t-t-tached, I mean. Surely, he p-poses no danger in such a state."

"Mr. Cummings, I have seen nothing more than a head, a neck, and a pair of shoulders devour a highland warrior, kilt and all."

Elizabeth noticed her father's gaze flick, for just an instant, to her. If he was looking for any sign of surprise, he surely saw it, for Elizabeth was unaware that he'd ever laid eyes on an unmentionable at all.

"Yes," Mr. Bennet went on, eyes on the vicar again. "It's dangerous. Once it gets out of that box, it'll be slithering across your stone floors quick as a snake. It must be dealt with posthaste."

Mr. Ford chose that moment (and a fine one it was) to jerk toward Mr. Cummings simultaneously roaring and snapping his teeth. In doing so, he managed to bite off most of his own tongue. It fell, gray and flaccid as an old kipper, into his lap, where it remained until he noticed it, snatched it up, and greedily gobbled it down, moaning happily as he feasted upon his own rancid flesh.

Mr. Cummings cleared his throat. "All right, then. I shall b-b-b-bow to your superior experience in these matters. B-but," he dropped his voice and nodded at Elizabeth and Mary, "surely *they* needn't b-be present."

"On the contrary," Mr. Bennet said, "surely they should. Now, tell me, Sir: You have a shed around back, do you not? Where the groundskeepers and gravediggers keep their equipage?"

"Yes."

"Is it locked?"

"It shouldn't b-be. Not at the moment. Haines and Rainey are waiting just outside to b-b-b-bury Mr. Ford."

"Excellent. Mary—"

She didn't hear him, nor did Elizabeth. They were both totally absorbed by the sight of Mr. Ford gnawing uncertainly on his own left hand. The taste of death seemed to displease him, for he'd quickly spat up his half-masticated tongue, and his fingers went down with no more relish.

He looked up then, fixing upon Elizabeth's face with the dark, blank eyes of a mounted animal, and growled.

"*Mary*," Mr. Bennet said again.

"Yes, Papa?"

"Run out to the tool shed and fetch along the biggest pair of shears you can."

"Yes, Papa."

Mary started up the aisle.

"Oh, and daughter?" her father called after her, "I mean as big as *you* can handle. Do you understand?"

Mary was a rather pale, wan-looking thing, so one couldn't say she went white as a sheet: She'd already been so since birth. Now, however, she went nearly transparent. Yet she nodded and started off again at a smooth, steady pace.

Mr. Bennet smiled. "There's a good girl."

"Y-y-you mean to have her—? You would a-a-ask your own—? Sir! She's but a child!"

"Childhood is a luxury we can no longer afford," Mr. Bennet said. "But fear not, Mr. Cummings. I don't expect young Mary there to do what need be done." He turned to Elizabeth. "Not unless her sister fails."

Elizabeth gawked at her father. He was a man of keen wit, of jests and winks and sly asides. But he wasn't joking now. For some unfathomable reason, he wanted *her* to—

It was too awful even to contemplate.

"Papa . . . I can't."

"Tut tut, child. You *can*. This one is newly born to darkness. Still weak. Those to come won't be nearly so easy to deal with."

Mr. Ford swatted at the vicar hard enough to rock his coffin, sliding it a little closer to the edge of the bier. His rigor-stiffened muscles were relaxing, becoming more limber, gaining strength.

Elizabeth took a step back. "Why me?"

Her father's gaze, usually so full of impish affection when pointed her way, hardened till it bore into her like an augur. "Why not?"

She could think of a dozen reasons, of course, first and foremost being that she was a young lady. Yet something in her father's eyes gave his reply before she could even speak.

None of that matters. Not if the dreadfuls have returned.

At that moment, Mary came back inside carrying a huge pair of hedge clippers and, showing an initiative that put a smile on her father's face, a scythe.

"Capital! Well done, my child!" Mr. Bennet called to her. "Now, Mr. Cummings, don't faint just yet, if you please. I very much doubt you had the opportunity to administer last rites the first time Mr. Ford died." He leaned closer to the coffin and addressed himself to the moaning, slavering thing clawing at the empty air between them. "Looks like you're both in luck."

When Mary reached the bier, Mr. Bennet had her hand the clippers to her sister.

CHAPTER 3

A SHRIEK ECHOED OUT from the church, and Mrs. Bennet shrieked, too.

A moment later, there was a howl, and Mrs. Bennet howled.

Then there was a bellow and a squeal and a yelp and finally silence, and Mrs. Bennet bellowed and squealed and yelped but—a stranger to silence all her days—didn't stop there. Instead, she comforted herself (as was her way) with a caterwauled cataloging of the various and sundry misfortunes about to beset her and hers.

Jane and Kitty and Lydia huddled around their mother on the church steps, patting her and fanning her and cooing comfort. They were up to their twenty-third "Everything's going to be all right" when a grim-faced Mr. Bennet stalked from the church and swept right past the four of them.

"Where are you going, Mr. Bennet?" his wife called after him.

"Home!" he barked without looking back.

"Surely you're not walking!"

"We walked here, we can walk back!"

"But that was before—"

At last, Mr. Bennet stopped. "I will have no more of your buts! I have let them vex me too long!" He looked past Mrs. Bennet at his daughters, including Elizabeth and Mary, who were now trudging slump-shouldered from the chapel. "Fall in behind me, girls. We must quick-march to Longbourn. And if your mother can't keep up," he locked eyes with his wife, "we leave her."

He spun on his heel and stomped off again.

"Oh, Mr. Bennet, you can't, you *can't*!" Mrs. Bennet moaned, throwing the back of a hand to her forehead and going into a long, staggering swoon.

"He's not stopping, Mamma," Kitty told her.

"Well, come along, then, come along," Mrs. Bennet said, setting off after her husband.

Elizabeth, Mary, and Jane had already done so without pause.

It was a sunny, unseasonably warm April day—the reason they'd decided to walk to the church rather than take the carriage. Yet there was no birdsong to be heard as the Bennets began the mile-long trek home, nor were there foals, calves, or lambs to watch frolicking in the fields. All creatures great and small and in between, it seemed, had been put to flight by the horrible keening screeches cutting through the Hertfordshire woodlands.

And it wasn't even zombies making all the noise.

"They're back! They're back, after all these years!" Mrs. Bennet wailed. "The dreadfuls, right here in Meryton! And your father will be ripped to shreds and Longbourn will fall to that frightful cousin of his and he'll surely throw us out to starve in the gutter—if we should be so lucky before the unmentionables get us—and why oh why are we walking home when we could be set upon at any moment by a horde of sorry stricken and torn limb from limb? That must be what happened to that poor, dear, lovely what's-her-name who's been missing these past two weeks."

"Emily Ward," Jane said softly. Unlike her mother, she knew the name well: Emily Ward had been her friend.

"Why, if they can grab perfectly healthy young girls like her, a mature individual such as myself will be no match for them," Mrs. Bennet prattled on. "Look sharp, girls! They'll be coming for your beloved mother first!"

"You must try to remain calm, Mamma," said Mary. She herself did not look calm so much as addled: Her eyes were glassy, and she walked with the shuffling, stumbling steps of a clumsy somnambulist. "Remember: Mr. Ford hadn't been interred yet. If what I've read of the sorry stricken is correct, it will be days, perhaps even weeks, before more can dig their way from the grave to attack us."

"Days? Weeks?" Mrs. Bennet cried. "Do you hear that, Jane? You have mere days to marry a man of means and rescue us all! Or you, Elizabeth—you'll be out in two weeks' time. Catch a husband at the Goswicks' ball and spare us a fate worse than death! Oh! Oh, my! You don't suppose they'd cancel the ball, do you? They wouldn't! They can't!

I need both of you on the market if we're to head off utter disaster! Ohhh, by the time this business is done, we'll all be roaming about in our shrouds with fresh brain smeared around our mouths like so much marmalade, you mark my words!"

Mr. Bennet stayed well ahead of the rest of the party, either scouting for zombies or merely sparing his ears. Jane and Elizabeth, meanwhile, fell behind together, leaving it to their sisters to prop up their mother and, more importantly, so far as Mrs. Bennet was concerned, provide a captive audience for her babblings.

"Lizzy? Lizzy, what happened in the church? You and Mary look dreadf—I mean, horrible."

Without looking over or speaking a word, Elizabeth reached out and took her sister by the hand. They walked that way, together, until Elizabeth trusted herself to open her mouth without screaming.

"Father wanted us to kill him. It. The dreadful."

Jane gasped. "You and Mary?"

Elizabeth nodded.

"The clippers and scythe . . . those were for *you*?"

Elizabeth nodded again.

"Why on earth would Father wish you to do such a thing?"

"He didn't explain."

"Well, did you do as he asked?"

"No. Neither Mary nor I could do it. Papa kept telling us it wasn't Mr. Ford anymore. It wasn't a person. Yet it's one thing to accept the truth of that and quite another to lop off a man's head as easy as pruning a rose."

"So what did Father do?"

Elizabeth started to shrug, but it turned into a shiver. "He lopped off the man's head as easy as pruning a rose."

The girls walked in silence a moment before Jane spoke again.

"We've always wondered."

"Yes," Elizabeth said. "We've always wondered."

Their parents were fire married to ice, and the strain always showed. Yet Elizabeth and Jane had known since they were far younger than Lydia was now that some other wedge divided their mother and father. Something that had to do with them—and the strange plague that once threatened all England.

There was Mrs. Bennet's disgust for her husband's collection of exotic weapons. There was Mr. Bennet's air of chagrined resignation as Jane first, and now soon Elizabeth, came out into society. And there were the snatches of overheard arguments that seemingly made no sense— "warriors" countered with "ladies," "honor" parried with "propriety," "China" scoffed away with "England," and someone named "Mr. Lou" blunted by "every respectable bachelor in Hertfordshire."

"Soon," Elizabeth said, "we shall have our answers, I fear."

She squeezed Jane's hand, then let go, and the sisters walked on side by side but alone with their own thoughts. Up ahead, their father was still clomping wordlessly along the lane while their mother made up the difference by talking enough for two, if not two dozen.

"I just thank heaven Lord Lumpley wasn't there to see Mary running around with a scythe in her hands. The last thing we need is some sort of public spectacle with *gardening tools*."

"I rather think it was Mr. Ford creating the spectacle," Mary mumbled. And then, because she was too much in shock to stop herself: "Anyway, I don't care what Lord Lumpley thinks. The man is a libertine."

"Oh, he is, is he?" Mrs. Bennet hooted. "Well, it's not for the likes of you to sit in judgment on the likes of him. Some people might say the baron's a little too ... frisky. But such things are forgiven in our betters."

"Oh, Mamma—you just like him because he fancies Jane!" Lydia said. "I heard he danced with her *three times in a row* at her coming-out ball!"

"And he claimed every other dance at Haye-Park last October," Kitty chimed in, throwing a teasing glance back at Jane. "And at Stoke at Christmas and the Robinsons' hunt ball, too. Absolutely everyone's talking about it!"

Yet "absolutely everyone" did not include Jane, and she kept her opinion of Lord Lumpley to herself.

As did Elizabeth. There'd already been enough to inspire retching that morning without dragging *him* into it.

"Personally, I think our Jane's altogether too retiring for a man like Lord Lumpley," Lydia announced, and—perking up now that they'd abandoned looming doom for a subject more to her liking—she began skipping a gay circle around the others. "That's why he's going to marry *me* when I'm old enough!"

"That's the spirit, my darling," Mrs. Bennet said. "I'm glad at least one of you has the good sense to set her ambitions high."

Mr. Bennet finally slowed his pace and glanced back before shaking his head and carrying on even faster than before. Elizabeth caught only the quickest glimpse of his face, yet that was all she needed to recognize the expression upon it: deep, pained disappointment. It was one of the few expressions Mr. Bennet ever let crack his sardonic mask. Elizabeth always hated to see it—and hated it most when it was directed at his daughters.

She did not see it again for the next quarter hour, for Mr. Bennet did not look back. To the side, yes, to scan forest and meadow for movement, to eye the horizon for silhouetted human shapes, heads askew, limbs stiff. But otherwise he kept his gaze to the path. On what lay ahead.

When the Bennet caravan at last returned to Longbourn, they found the youngest girls' governess, Miss Chiselwood, taking the air around the grounds, a slim volume of romantic verse clasped in one bony hand.

"Oh," she said in her usual flat, listless way. She'd been a lively, cheerful young woman once, but Kitty and Lydia soon cured her of that, and she eyed the girls now like a bowl of old mold-encrusted porridge she was expected to eat with relish. "Back already?"

"And not a moment too soon," Mr. Bennet said, speeding past her bound not for the front door but, rather, around to the back of the house. "Oh." He skidded to a stop and turned toward the governess. "By the way, we will no longer be requiring your services, Miss Chiselwood. If you would be so good as to pack up your things, I'll have six months' wages and a letter of recommendation for you by the end of the day."

"No, Mr. Bennet, no!" Mrs. Bennet cried out.

"Yes, Mrs. Bennet, yes!" Mr. Bennet snapped back.

"Oh, thank you, God," Miss Chiselwood whispered, and she hurried off to her room, practically skipping. Mrs. Bennet scurried after her trying to explain that her husband was having "an attack" and didn't really mean anything he said, but the family's *former* governess was all too happy to ignore her.

Mr. Bennet started around the house again. "With me, girls! This way!"

And he led his daughters to Mrs. Bennet's "greenhouse"—really just a ramshackle hut rotting away beneath a great, green spider web of vines. A few seconds after he stalked in, a potted daffodil came flying out. Then a bluebell. Then a rhododendron, a primrose, an iris, and so on.

"Well, come along and help me," Mr. Bennet said as he added an armload of daisies to the mound of flowers and spilled soil and shards of clay heaped at his daughters' feet. "Your mother has just lost her potting shed." He smiled then, a grin of manic glee Elizabeth found too disquieting to share. "And I've finally got back my dojo!"

CHAPTER 4

"IS NOTHING SACRED to that woman?" Mr. Bennet grumbled, waving a hand at a musty corner of the greenhouse. "There are geraniums on my sword rack." He gathered up the offending flowers and carried them to the door. "Master Liu would flay the last strip of skin from my back."

It was his seventh reference to "the Master" since they had begun clearing out the jumbled bric-a-brac and half-dead plants, and with each new allusion Elizabeth had to work harder to suppress a shudder.

"My throwing daggers in with the trowels? Old Liu would dip me in honey and stake me to an anthill!"

"Are those ferns hanging from my bo staff? The Master would feed me my own fingernails!"

"Your mother's been using my hand claws as tillers! Master Liu would rip out my heart and chomp into it like an apple before my very eyes!"

Etcetera.

If this Liu person had anything to do with Mr. Bennet's plans for his daughters and his "dojo," Elizabeth was very uneasy indeed. Yet the girls kept to their sweeping and dusting. So far, all questions to their father had been turned aside with a shake of the head and a firm "In due time."

(Their mother, for her part, had made but one vain attempt to save her potting shed, but she'd retreated at the sight of her husband clutching a grime-covered spear. He'd found it staked to a currant bush and looked entirely inclined to use it for its intended purpose.)

"All right. That'll do for now," Mr. Bennet finally announced. He'd just tossed the geraniums onto the ever-growing heap of debris on the lawn and come back inside slapping the soil from his hands with obvious satisfaction. "Sit."

The girls all looked around the little hut, as if they might have simply overlooked the divans and settees their father had in mind for them.

"There are no chairs, Papa," Lydia said.

"There are no elephants, either. What is that to us?"

Mr. Bennet settled himself on the floor, legs crossed, back straight.

"We can't sit on the ground!" Kitty cried.

"On the contrary. It is quite easy," Mr. Bennet said. *"Sit!"*

Elizabeth caught Jane's eye and nodded quickly at the floor. Jane was the eldest of the Bennet sisters, the leader. It was upon her to set the proper example.

But what *was* proper? Elizabeth could see her sister wasn't sure.

She gave her head another downward jerk, and slowly, reluctantly Jane sank to the ground, her black skirt swirling in gray dust. Elizabeth followed suit, then Mary, then Kitty. Lydia remained upright, defiant, until Kitty yanked her to her knees with a sharp tug on the wrist.

"Good," Mr. Bennet said. "But not good enough. In future, whenever we are within these walls, I will expect instant obedience. If I do not get it, there will be grave consequences."

"Oh, really, Papa!" Lydia scoffed. "I can't picture you whipping us with a cat-o'-nine-tails like 'Old Liu'!"

Mr. Bennet glared at her. "Then you must change your picture of me. Whilst we are training, I am not your 'Papa.' I am your master, and you will mind me accordingly."

"'Training'?" Elizabeth said. "What sort of training?"

"Before I explain, we must have the first lesson. To attend me carefully, without the distraction of unnecessary comfort, you will learn to sit as warriors do." Mr. Bennet held out his hands, palms up, over his crossed legs. "Like me."

"Sit as *what* do?" Lydia said.

"We can't sit like that," Kitty protested.

Mr. Bennet shook his head in disgust. "You're all so quick to point out what you *can't* do. The time has come to learn what you *can*."

"Well, it's certainly not very ladylike," Lydia pointed out.

"Ladylike be damned!" her father thundered, and all his daughters gasped. Yet they all did as he said, too.

Or they tried to, at any rate. Layer upon layer of binding feminine underthings—shifts under corsets under petticoats—made even so simple a task as sitting on folded legs a challenge worthy of a Hindu contortionist. After ten minutes of not entirely successful sitting practice, Mr. Bennet declared that the girls were close enough, and he would begin.

"Years ago," he said, "when the threat from the dreadfuls was at its worst, certain Englishmen—and English*women*—turned to the East for guidance."

"You mean like Lady Catherine de Bourgh," Mary said.

"Hush, child! I've only just started!"

Mr. Bennet took a moment to compose himself, and began again.

"Years ago," he said, "when the threat from the dreadfuls was at its worst, certain Englishmen and Englishwomen—such as the famous Lady Catherine de Bourgh—turned to the East for guidance. In the Orient could be found specialized methods of individual combat that seemed perfectly suited to the problem at hand. This rankled our more fervent patriots, who would have preferred an English solution to an English problem. But those of a more pragmatic turn of mind—and the resources to follow its dictates—undertook the long trek to furthest Asia and apprenticed themselves to masters of the deadly arts. I was one such person."

Jane, Mary, Kitty, Lydia—all could contain themselves no longer.

"You have been to the Far East?"

"You fought in The Troubles?"

"Did you meet Lady Catherine?"

And, from Lydia: "My feet fell asleep. May I move my legs?"

Only Elizabeth remained silent, patiently waiting for more. Her father's words were a revelation, yet not entirely a surprise. It was more like the final piece in a puzzle: Even if it's missing, one can know its shape from the blank space it's meant to fill.

Elizabeth and her sisters had been living in that empty spot. It was their world.

Mr. Bennet held up his hands for silence. "Of my training in China, you will learn much. Of my experiences in The Troubles . . . you will learn what you must. And, yes, Lydia. You may move your legs."

With much grunting and panting and little half-muffled exclamations of annoyance, Lydia began uncrossing her legs, a process that took—what with all the snags on her stay and halfslip and crumpled muslin—not less than a minute.

"Tomorrow," Mr. Bennet said, eyelids wearily adroop, "you will wear simple sparring gowns. For now, however, it is the end of my tale that concerns us. After the Battle of Kent, when the dreadfuls were—supposedly—vanquished at last, I and my fellow initiates were expected to give up our warrior ways. Not to do so was to be seen as not entirely English anymore. Not entirely respectable. The pressure to acquiesce was quite intense, as you can imagine."

He paused for a quick eyeroll toward the house.

Yes, indeed. Elizabeth could easily imagine.

"I built this dojo—this temple of the deadly arts—not just for myself," Mr. Bennet continued. "I built it for you. My children. So that you, too, would be schooled in the Shaolin way. Now, far too belatedly, we begin your training. It will not be easy. You will be sorely tested. You will cry and bleed. You will face the derision, probably even the condemnation, of your community. Yet you will persevere on behalf of the very souls who now find you so ridiculous. For the dreadful scourge has returned, and once more *warriors must walk the green fields of England!*"

There was a long silence while the girls took all this in.

Eventually, Kitty cleared her throat.

"Ummm . . . what if we don't *want* to be warriors?"

"Then I will disown you, and you will, most likely, be torn apart and eaten by a pack of festering corpses." Mr. Bennet moved his gaze around the room, looking at each of the other girls in turn. "Any more questions?"

Elizabeth had several, of course. Yet, for some reason, one in particular came to her lips first.

"When do we begin?"

Mr. Bennet's expression remained grim even as his eyes seemed to flash her a secret smile.

"It has begun."

CHAPTER 5

FIRST, THE GIRLS had learned to sit. Next, they learned to stand.

The Natural Stance they mastered quickly, since it involved little more than keeping their feet together and their backs straight—exactly as they'd been taught by their mother and governesses all their lives. The Spread Eagle Stance took more getting used to. In fact, the first time their father said the words, "Now spread your legs wide like this," Mary gasped "Really, Papa!" and Kitty declared that she couldn't do it because it felt "naughty."

From standing, they moved on to yelling.

"A battle cry," Mr. Bennet said, "is a warrior's calling card. Only it does not say, 'Good afternoon. I have come for tea and crumpets.' It says, 'Death has come for you! Flee or be killed where you stand!' And it does so like this."

Mr. Bennet assumed the Spread Eagle Stance, scowled, and bellowed, "HAA-IEEEEEEEEEEEEEE!"

It was a very good battle cry indeed. So much so that Kitty instantly burst into tears. Once her father had her calmed, he asked Jane to try a cry of her own.

"Haiee," she said.

"Did you hear that, girls?" Mr. Bennet cupped a hand to his right ear. "I do believe a mouse just coughed."

Jane tried again.

"Haiee!"

"A consumptive mouse," Mr. Bennet said.

"Haa–ieeeee!"

"Which has stubbed its toe."

Mr. Bennet held up a hand and shook his head before Jane could unleash another of her half-hearted squeals.

"Your battle cry does more than announce your presence," he said. "It prepares you for combat by shattering the shackles of good manners and gentility. It is not a sound a gentleman or lady would choose to make. It is an animal sound—the roar of a killer stalking the jungle. As Master Liu used to say, a good battle cry 'unchains the tiger within.'"

"Perhaps I don't have a tiger inside me," Jane said.

"Everyone does, daughter. Everyone." Mr. Bennet turned to Lizzy. "You try it."

Elizabeth spread her legs, turned her feet outward, bent her knees, took a deep breath, closed her eyes—and split the world in two.

"HAAAAAAAAAAAAAAAAAAAA-IIIIIIIIIIIIIIIIII-EEEEEEEEEEEEEEEEEEEEEEEEEE!"

When she opened her eyes again, Elizabeth found her four sisters gawping at her, slack jawed.

"*She* certainly has a tiger," Lydia muttered, "and it's rabid."

"No," Mr. Bennet said. "It is hungry." He turned and headed for the door. "I must send word of what we saw in the church. Hopefully, we will not have to face what approaches alone. Keep practicing until I return, all of you."

"You want us to just stand around yelling?" Lydia asked.

"Only until you get it right," her father said, and then he was gone, striding across the lawn toward the back of the house.

"Haaiieee!" said Jane.

"Hiiyaaaa!" said Mary.

"Hooyaaah!" said Kitty.

"La!" said Lydia. "You have no idea how silly you all look!"

"Unfortunately, I think I do," Jane sighed. "Yet we must trust our father's wisdom."

"What if our father's a loony?" Kitty asked.

"You didn't see him with Mr. Ford," Elizabeth said. "What he did. It was not the work of a 'loony.' He *is* a warrior."

"And so are we to be," Jane said. Yet her words lacked the whip crack of conviction, and to Elizabeth she sounded resigned, not resolute.

"Outcasts, that's what all this will make us!" Kitty said, putting on a prodigious pout she'd learned from her mother. "Social papayas."

"Pariahs," Mary corrected. "And there's nothing wrong with standing apart. Fruitful, truthful observation requires a certain distance, I find, and our neighbors are entirely too—"

"Well, I don't think it's fair," Lydia cut in with a petulant stamp of one of her not-insubstantial feet. (Though only eleven, she was by far the stoutest of the Bennet girls.) "Jane's already out, and Lizzy will be within a fortnight, provided the Goswicks don't cancel the spring dance. But what of Lydia and Mary and me? No one's going to throw a ball for girls who run around screaming 'Haaiiieee!' like a bunch of savages."

"Lydia," Elizabeth said, shaking her head, "your coming out is still years off. You'd worry about a ball that far in the future when you saw an unmentionable in your church this very morning?"

Lydia shrugged. "Mr. Ford didn't look like much of a threat to me."

"Then imagine a thousand of him . . . with legs," Mary said. "From what I've read, there were more than that many at the Battle of Kent."

"So?" Kitty threw in. "That was Kent, and the battle put an end to them. Why, no one's even seen one of the things in years."

"Until today," Mary said. "For all we know, there are a hundred of them out in the woods this very moment, and they ate Emily Ward just like Mamma said."

Only Elizabeth noticed Jane wince.

"Well, Mamma also says there were never more than a dozen dreadfuls in Hertfordshire, even during the worst of it," Kitty sniffed. "So there."

"Mamma is not always right," Jane pointed out, understatement incarnate.

"All the same," Lydia said, "I'd still rather be an unmentionable than a *spinster*. If Father has his way, we'll all end up like Miss Chiselwood."

"Would that really be so bad?" Mary asked. "I'd hardly call becoming a governess a fate worse than death."

Lydia put her fists to her hips. "*I* would! If I'm not married by the time I'm seventeen, I'm running away to Dover and throwing myself into the sea."

As they had so many times over the years, Jane and Elizabeth shared a knowing glance and a mutual rolling of the eyes. It was actually a relief to set aside dreadfuls and battle cries and their father's possible insanity and commiserate again, for just a moment, over something as harmless as Kitty and Lydia's *amour*-mad ways.

"You may keep your date with the Channel when the time comes, if you so chose," Elizabeth told Lydia. "For now, however, we must follow the path our father has chosen for us . . . no matter how outlandish it might seem."

"Elizabeth is right. This is hardly the time to think of romance and matrimony," Mary said. "We must set aside such frivolousness."

"La!" Lydia snorted. "It set you aside a long time ago!"

"It's easy enough to *say* we should forget about love," Kitty added. "But I'd like to see any of you stick to it if some Sir Comely were to come along and woo you. Why, real passion can no more be 'set aside' than a dreadful will stay buried!"

Jane sighed.

"Sir Comely?" Elizabeth laughed.

"Mamma lets you read far too many novels," Mary said.

Yet their young sister had said something wise, quite without knowing it. Which was the only way she was likely to do it.

"Please, everyone," Jane said. "Let us return to our studies."

"Hiiyaaaa!"

"Haaiieee!"

"Hooyaaah!"

"La!"

"*HAAAAAAAAAAAAAAAAAAAAAAAAAA-IIIIIIIIIII-IEEEEEEEEEEEEEEEEEEEEEEEEE!*"

CHAPTER 6

THE SECOND DAY OF TRAINING began before dawn, with Mr. Bennet rousing everyone in the house by roaring "Novitiates, assemble!" over and over until everyone had hopped (or fallen) out of bed. The girls scrambled into their new sparring gowns and marched out to the dojo while their mother wailed about cracked windows and shattered nerves.

After warming up his pupils with some standing and yelling practice, Mr. Bennet moved on to actual hitting and kicking, although the girls had yet to hit or kick anything more solid than air. Then came the weapons. And the accidents.

Mary bloodied her nose with a quarterstaff. Kitty blackened her own eye with a pair of nunchucks and was inconsolable for a quarter hour. Lydia rebloodied Mary's nose with a wooden practice sword.

Only Elizabeth and Jane managed not to injure themselves (or Mary), yet their father was obviously unhappy with their limp grips and hesitant movements.

"A warrior *thrusts* with the sword," he barked at Jane. "You hold it out as if offering a guest a scone!"

"But I'm afraid I'll hurt someone."

"You *want* to hurt someone, child! Hurting someone is the whole point!"

Jane looked dubious.

Her father looked very, very troubled.

When the time for scones actually arrived, Mr. Bennet had no appetite for them or anything else on the breakfast table. Indeed, it was hard to see how anyone could eat with Mrs. Bennet fussing and flitting about as she was, clucking over this daughter's bruise or that daughter's scrape while continually haranguing her husband about his barbaric ways.

"I no longer need worry that our children will end up starving in the poorhouse. Obviously, their own father will see to it they're *beaten to death* long before that could happen!"

Mr. Bennet toyed disconsolately with his toast, saying nothing.

"Just look at them! Two days ago, they were proper young ladies. Now they look like escaped bedlamites!"

"Mamma, please," Elizabeth said.

Mr. Bennet sighed and stirred his tea, though his teacup was empty.

"You would throw away our respectability, our station, our prospects, because of a single unmentionable? I thank Heaven, then, that we only saw one. Two, and you'd have no doubt hurried home and burned Longbourn to the ground without waiting for ruin to overtake us!"

Mr. Bennet hid himself behind a letter the footman had just brought in.

"We may as well go lie down in the nearest cemetery and simply await our fate," Mrs. Bennet went on. "With the estate entailed and no male heir, there is no hope for us. Oh, if only you were a boy, Mary, as you were once so often thought. But, alas, you are all quite irreversibly—"

"Lord Lumpley is coming."

Mrs. Bennet whipped around to face her husband.

"The baron?" she asked.

"The baron."

"Is coming to Longbourn?"

"Is coming to Longbourn."

"To pay a call?"

"To pay a call."

"On us?"

"On *me*. I sent a letter yesterday requesting an audience to discuss the incident with Mr. Ford, and Lord Lumpley has agreed, though he chose to pay a call here instead of summoning me to him."

"I wonder why he'd do that?" Lydia asked, and just in case anyone couldn't tell the question was rhetorical, she winked and nodded at Jane and burst out laughing.

"Oh, thank you, Mr. Bennet!" Mrs. Bennet cried, and she swooped down on her husband and delivered one kiss after another to his forehead and cheeks. "Sweet, patient Mr. Bennet! Wily, crafty Mr. Bennet! Luring the baron here when you know how smitten he is with Jane! Oh, sly, shrewd Mr.—!"

"Enough!" cried flushed, flustered Mr. Bennet. "Lord Lumpley and I will be discussing unmentionables, not marriage!"

But Mrs. Bennet wasn't listening.

"Hill! Hill? *MRS. HILL!*" she blared. "Where is that wretched woman when you really need—ah, there you are! We have so much to do to get ready! You must cut fresh flowers, polish the silver, launder the table linens, set out the girls' best morning dresses . . . ooh, and run to the village for cakes! What? Which one first? Why, all of them, of course! The Baron of Lumpley is coming!"

Through it all, Lydia and Kitty whispered and tittered and snorted, ignoring Mary's disapproving glowers (it falling to their sister to sit around looking dour and long-suffering now that Miss Chiselwood was gone).

Elizabeth and Jane, meanwhile, were exchanging significant looks of their own. Elizabeth's was simultaneously concerned and fierce; Jane's, discomfited and mildly reproachful. The two girls disagreed on few things, and one of them was about to pay them a call.

"You don't seem as excited as your mother," Mr. Bennet said dryly, eyeing first Elizabeth, then Jane.

"My excitement is merely of a different sort," Elizabeth said.

"And I think it is premature for overexcitement of any sort," said Jane.

"I see." Mr. Bennet nodded sagely, then looked at Elizabeth again,

THEIR FATHER WAS OBVIOUSLY UNHAPPY WITH THEIR LIMP GRIPS
AND HESITANT MOVEMENTS.

eyebrow cocked. "You know, I'm suddenly put in mind of the next move I should like to teach you all. It is called the Fulcrum of Doom. We shall take it up directly when we return to the dojo."

The Fulcrum of Doom turned out to be a remarkably simple move involving no more than a quickly lifted leg and a strategically placed knee. (It was presumed the Doomee would be male. *Why* had to be explained with some delicacy.) After running his daughters through it to his satisfaction—and nearly being Fulcrumed himself more than once—Mr. Bennet chose to focus on sword work.

It was a bit frightening, picking up one of the long-bladed, foreign-looking *katanas* for the first time, and when Elizabeth and her sisters began taking slow practice swings, her hands were soon slick with sweat. No matter how tightly she tried to clamp down, the hilt felt lubricious, loose. As with everything her father had been trying to teach them the past day, Elizabeth found it difficult to get a grip.

Yet Mr. Bennet seemed pleased with the way she and Jane handled their swords, and he steadily increased the speed of the girls' swings and thrusts—right up to the moment Kitty's katana spun from her hands and speared a post mere inches from Mary's head.

"Smooth, controlled movements," Mr. Bennet growled. "Where's the poise? Where's the presence of mind?"

"Over there," Lydia said, pointing at Elizabeth and Jane.

Mr. Bennet glowered at her. "Prepare yourself for the punishment you have long deserved. The first and last time I made a joke while training under Master Liu, he took blow dart practice on my . . ."

He blanched and, for a moment, could go no further.

"Ten laps around the grounds, child," he finally said.

"Ohhh!"

"Ten laps! Go!"

Lydia shuffled off in a half-hearted jog, her arms hanging slack at her sides.

They practiced some more after that, but before long Mr. Bennet gave the girls the rest of the day off to prepare for Lord Lumpley's visit.

"I will remain in the dojo and am not to be disturbed," he told them glumly. "I find I have much to meditate on."

The girls marched off toward the house sluggishly, soaked with a perspiration that would be, for a proper young lady, an entirely alien and repulsive thing to experience. Yet, to her surprise, Elizabeth found that she didn't much mind. It was what was to come that bothered her.

"Up we go," she said to Jane as they trudged upstairs to change out of their soiled sparring gowns. "Onto the auction block."

"You're being ridiculous, Lizzy," Jane admonished her gently. "A man like Lord Lumpley could never take a serious interest in any of us."

It was true, Elizabeth knew. Yet it wasn't a serious or, more to the point, *honorable* interest that concerned her, and as she dressed for the baron's call, she paused from time to time to practice the Fulcrum of Doom.

CHAPTER 7

ONCE THE BENNET GIRLS were ready, they lined up in the drawing room for review. Mrs. Bennet gave each a thorough going-over, adjusting ribbons and straps, fussing over nonexistent stains and wrinkles, plucking out stray strands of hair, clucking over all the bruises and abrasions, etcetera. When she was satisfied (or as close to satisfied as she could ever come), she arranged her daughters artfully around the room: Elizabeth at the pianoforte, Jane and Mary doing needlework on a divan, Kitty and Lydia bent over a book of Latin conjugations Miss Chiselwood had left behind when fleeing from the house.

Then, the panorama prepared, they waited.

And waited.

And waited.

Lord Lumpley's note said he'd arrive at three, rather late in the day for a call, but allowances were made for an aristocrat. Or would be if one ever showed up.

By four, Jane was more tranquil even than usual, for, wearied by the day's training, she'd fallen fast asleep.

By four thirty, Kitty and Lydia's constant sniggering and sauciness had frayed Mary's nerves to the breaking point, and she threatened to use her knitting needles in a most unsisterly fashion.

By five, Mrs. Bennet was ranting that Lord Lumpley probably wasn't coming at all, having heard (she conjectured—*loudly*) that the girls had taken to beating each other with sticks under the direction of their deranged father.

And at precisely five fourteen, Mr. Bennet came in and told his wife to hold her tongue, if that were possible without causing herself grievous injury. The baron's carriage was pulling up out front.

"Well, don't just sit there!" Mrs. Bennet cried, shooing her daughters from the spots that she herself had cemented them in nearly two hours before. "Come and greet His Lordship!"

Mr. Bennet blocked the door. "For Heaven's sake, he's a baron, not the king. Keep your seats, all of you. I'll bring him in once we've had our talk."

Lord Lumpley's proximity actually made Mrs. Bennet *worse*, and she spent the next half hour telling her daughters not to fidget while doing that very thing to such an extent she appeared to be having some sort of seizure. She blinked, she tapped her feet, she jumped at every step in the hall, she squirmed, she coughed. The only symptom absent was frothing at the mouth.

Kitty and Lydia found it endlessly comical, Mary asked if she should run upstairs and fetch the laudanum, and Jane simply weathered it with quiet, forlorn fortitude.

Elizabeth, meanwhile, attempted to preserve her peace of mind with a concentration aid her father had spoken of that afternoon: a mantra, he'd called it.

Smooth stone beneath still water, Elizabeth said to herself. *Smooth stone, still water, smooth stone, still water, smooth EGAD HOW I WANT TO THROTTLE THAT WOMAN!*

At long last, her mother could take the suspense no longer, and she sprang from the chaise longue she'd been in danger of fainting upon and blurted out, "I swear, if His Lordship isn't in here in the next ten seconds, I'm going to drag him in by the ear like the naughty little boy he is!"

It was at this precise moment, of course, that the door to the drawing room opened and a half-amused, half-mortified Mr. Bennet stepped in to announce their guest, the Baron of Lumpley.

"Oh, My Lord!" Mrs. Bennet said, and it was unclear to all whether she was blaspheming or offering a greeting.

"Oh, My Lady," Lord Lumpley said with an elegantly arched eyebrow, and he slid smoothly across the room to press his lips to her trembling fingers. He was long accustomed to the awe he could inspire, no doubt, and he seemed to relish a fresh opportunity to be magnanimous about it.

Elizabeth fancied the man brought a whiff of sulphur in with him, though more likely his dressers had simply gone a little heavy on the eau de cologne. Certainly, they had labored long over him, for his girth—and he had plenty of it—had been packed into a black suit that, though beautifully cut, appeared to be on the verge of bursting at the seams any second. Around his neck, tied high enough to hide some if not all of his jowls, was an extravagant cravat such as to make Beau Brummell blush.

"My daughters," Mr. Bennet said, preparing to make introductions.

"Oh, I remember them well, Sir. The beautiful Jane and Elizabeth and . . . " The baron flicked his gaze quickly over the younger girls. "Myrtle and the rest." He resettled his stare on Jane. Jane alone. "It is a pleasure to be in your company again. I have so longed to see more of you."

Jane attempted to deflect his attentions with averted eyes and a small, demure smile, as it was not in her nature to be so flirtatious or brazen.

Elizabeth, on the other hand, was of a very different inclination: one the day's training had, somehow, tilted her toward all the more. She was readying what she considered a suitable reply, but only got as far as a sardonically cocked eyebrow when her mother spoke first.

"But His Lordship needs a place to sit! Lizzy, why don't you come over here next to me?"

"Oh, I would not dream of evicting a young lady from her seat," Lord Lumpley said.

He and Mrs. Bennet then waited for Elizabeth to make the appropriate reply: "It is no inconvenience, Sir. Pray, do sit."

"Thank you," she said instead, making no move to leave her place by Jane's side.

Mrs. Bennet scowled at her behind the baron's back, then turned and shooed "Myrtle" from her plush wing chair.

"But he said—," Mary began.

"Come and sit with your beloved mother!" Mrs. Bennet snapped.

Mary slouched over and slumped down beside Mrs. Bennet, while Lord Lumpley, with no more thanks to her than a silent nod, settled himself in her spot. He was only a few feet from Kitty and Lydia now, and when he noticed them admiring him, wide eyed, he flashed them a devilish grin that had both hiding behind their hands, giggling madly.

Mrs. Bennet cleared her throat and began conversation in the approved manner: with the most boring topic imaginable.

"It is quite an uncommonly warm spring we're having, is it not?"

Lord Lumpley acknowledged the comment with a benevolent nod. "It is indeed."

"Do you think that's why the unmentionables are back?" Mary asked.

Mrs. Bennet started as if she'd been pinched. Then Mary did the same—because she *had* been pinched.

"They're called *unmentionables* for a reason, my dear," Mrs. Bennet said.

"But it's what he came here to talk about, isn't it?"

"Not . . . to . . . us."

"It's quite all right, Mrs. Bennet," Lord Lumpley said. "I don't mind addressing the subject, now that it's been broached. It's quite natural, I suppose, that it should be foremost on everyone's minds."

He looked over at Mary, opened his mouth to speak—then abruptly lost interest in her and turned to Jane, instead.

As far as Elizabeth was concerned, there could be no question what was foremost on *his* mind.

"Your father and I have had the most productive conversation on the matter, and tomorrow steps will be taken to ensure the safety of all. As for why Mr. Ford should have succumbed to the plague now, when it hasn't been seen in these parts for so long, I cannot say. I will venture, however, that one unmentionable does not a plague make. There have been isolated incidents in the past. I see no reason why this wouldn't merely be another."

"Isolated incidents?" Elizabeth asked. She looked over at her father, who was still standing just inside the doorway.

He gave his head the smallest of shakes.

"But we do not *know* there are not others," Jane said softly. "There is, for instance, a girl who disappeared from Meryton but two weeks ago. Emily Ward. Would that not suggest that the menace wasn't limited to Mr. Ford?"

The baron put on a condescending smile. "I hope you'll forgive me for being frank, but the young lady's 'disappearance' is nothing new. It rather happens on a regular basis, and has more to do with coxcombs bound for Scotland than the supernatural. And even if unmentionables were to blame, perish the thought, remember we are speaking of a lone girl . . . and next the filthy rotters will be facing men. Trust me, dear lady: If—and I say again *if!*—there are more dreadfuls in Hertfordshire, they will be dealt with handily."

As the nobleman blathered away, Elizabeth kept her eyes on her father, gauging his reaction. Though Mr. Bennet was usually a master of droll dispassion, Elizabeth detected a seething uneasiness beneath his cultivated blankness. Before she could stop herself, she found herself giving voice to the words she guessed he was thinking.

"So you had dealings with zombies during The Troubles, then?"

Lord Lumpley, Mrs. Bennet, and even Jane flinched. The Zed Word wasn't supposed to be spoken in polite company.

The baron took a moment to compose himself before making his reply.

"I am but six-and-twenty years of age, so obviously I took part in no battle lo those many years ago. Yet I have faced the creatures. Before they became extinct—if something already dead can be said to do so!—my father used to import some from the north for the shooting season. Pathetic, shambling things, they were. It didn't even make for good sport."

"I would guess it is a bit more sporting, My Lord, if they outnumber you and there are no shotguns at hand," Elizabeth said. "Would you not agree, Father?"

"I might choose a word other than *sporting*," Mr. Bennet replied.

"Papa saw a zombie eat a Scotsman once!" Lydia threw in, oblivious, as always, to subtext and nuance in conversation or anything else. "Mary told me he said . . . what?"

She glared over at Kitty, who, ever her mother's daughter, was delivering a vicious pinch under the table.

"I'm sure His Lordship doesn't want to hear about that," Kitty said. "Particularly from you."

Then she turned back to the baron, hacked out what she took to be a decorous little cough, and didn't so much steer the conversation back to safer territory as pick it up and hurl it there.

"My, but the sun *was* strong today. Can you believe it's only April?"

For the next eternity or so, by Elizabeth's reckoning, the conversation limped along this line of thought very much like a zombie: lifeless and mindless and making a jelly of whatever healthy brains were within its reach. So oppressive did talk of the weather eventually become, Elizabeth very nearly offered to fetch a barometer and an almanac so the amateur meteorologists in the room could make a real study of it.

Her father finally put the conversation out of its (and Elizabeth's) misery.

"I do not wish to be rude, Sir, but I feel it my duty to point out the time. Soon enough, the roads of Hertfordshire might not be safe even in the daytime. At night, I fear, you already risk disaster."

Lord Lumpley's fleshy face went grave as he tore his gaze away from Jane (whom he'd been staring at without stop even though she, like Elizabeth, had been weathering the weather talk without adding a word to it).

"Your concern does you credit, Mr. Bennet. If only other responsibilities had not delayed me so long in reaching your door this evening." The baron turned toward the nearest window, and his lip curled ever so slightly—either a show of dread as day turned to dusk outside or distaste for the iron bars Mr. Bennet had insisted the servants put up the day before. "Yes, perhaps I should go . . . though if it's as dangerous as you say, I wonder if I should risk the trip at all."

And immediately, Elizabeth knew. The young nobleman had arrived late intentionally. He'd been fishing for an invitation to stay all along. He meant to sleep in their home! Or claim a bed in it, at any rate.

The young nobleman had a reputation for taking liberties, one Jane refused to give credence to, so without guile or distrust was she. But it was plain to Elizabeth he'd earned his reputation. And sought to do so again.

Mrs. Bennet seemed to see it all, as well—or at least that part of the picture that suited her. She perked up and leaned forward, eyes wide with delight.

Mr. Bennet was just the opposite: still, stone faced, inscrutable. It was a race to see who would speak first.

For once (and to Elizabeth's infinite relief), Mr. Bennet won.

"I think you need not worry, My Lord, assuming you don't allow us to detain you any further. After all, it is well established that you have the fastest carriage in the county. No doubt you could easily outpace any stiff-legged unfortunates we might have lumbering about—so long as you still have a few rays of light to steer by. And I'm sure you're anxious to begin the preparations we spoke of earlier, as well. You have many messages to dispatch, come morning—for which I again thank you. How lucky we are to have a young man as energetic and *fearless* as you to spearhead these vital efforts for us."

The baron's already ruddy face went a shade rosier. Mr. Bennet had assigned him a role—the courageous man of action—and he had no choice but to play it.

He cleared his throat and got to his feet. "Yes, well . . . a man does what he must. Even more so when he has rank and responsibility."

Mr. Bennet nodded solemnly.

Mrs. Bennet looked like she'd have used the Fulcrum of Doom on him, if only she knew how.

Before leaving, Lord Lumpley recovered enough to step to the divan and take Jane's hand in his. He lingered over it at such length and with such obvious longing Elizabeth began to wonder whether he was going to kiss it or eat it.

"I will see you at the ball at Pulvis Lodge, I presume?"

Jane nodded. "I will be there."

"Excellent. I ask now for the first dance. And the last. And as many in between as you might spare."

Though it was Jane's fingers he finally kissed, it was Mrs. Bennet who was on the brink of swooning.

"The least you could've done was invite him to stay to supper," she snipped at her husband when he returned to the drawing room a short while later, having seen the baron on his way. "Didn't you notice how he fawns over Jane?"

"A syphilitic bat could've seen it."

"Oh! Mr. Bennet! Really!"

"I'm sorry, Mrs. Bennet. I misspoke." Mr. Bennet dropped wearily into the very chair their guest had warmed with his well-padded hindquarters. "I meant to say, 'Yes. I noticed.'"

"Well, didn't it occur to you to capitalize on that?"

Mr. Bennet didn't speak to her or look at her. Instead, he turned a wistful, almost remorseful gaze on Jane.

Somehow, Elizabeth got the feeling he already *was* capitalizing on the baron's infatuation—and already regretting it, as well.

CHAPTER 8

WHEN RICHARD George Saunders-Castleton Harper-Milford Norman-Stilton-Harrowby Lumpley II, sixth Baron of Lumpley, knight of the Bath, and defender of the realm, awoke the next morning, the first thing he did was kick the empty gin bottles from his bed. Then he kicked off the dogs. And last (and with some regret) he kicked out the chambermaids.

He had things to do this day. Important matters that demanded his attention.

He needed a new truss, and only the best would do.

He stood and admired himself in the full-length mirror strategically placed near the bed. True, his manly pear-shaped form had been swelling of late—it was now more like a gourd mounted on the twin stickpins of his legs. But, oh, his regal brow! His piercing eyes! His lordly chins! His soft, pale, pillowy arms unsullied by sinew or muscle! It was, in all respects, not just his mirror image he beheld, but that of his friend and fellow master of the bacchanal arts, the Prince Regent.

What woman could resist such a man? What female—be she girl, matron, or crone—would not fling aside her dignity and self-respect like so many hastily discarded underthings at his first wink? What delicate beauty could he not gently coax into his tender embrace ... and then give the old how's your father?

Well, there might be one: fair Jane of the golden hair and the milk-white skin and the inviting décolletage and the horrid, horrid family. But he had reason to hope her virtue wasn't long for this earth.

And then the Baron of Lumpley groaned, for he remembered at last that he had work to do. Actual work! Damn the incessant burdens of noblesse oblige.

Without dressing (how could he without the usual retinue of six to help him?) he walked to the study and wrote the following note:

> *Hunt today—3 o'clock—come!*
> *L.*

Then he rang the bell and sat back, wrist aching from the strain of unaccustomed toil, and waited for his man Belgrave.

"My Lord?" Belgrave said blandly when he walked in a moment later. He was a studiously stoic little fellow of forty-and-some years with gray at his temples and a pale gray complexion and a gray, *gray* soul. If he noticed that his employer was lolling about without a stitch on, he didn't show it. He never seemed to notice anything, which was one of the reasons Lord Lumpley depended on him so. As a test, the baron had once strutted around an entire morning with half an apple clinched between his naked cheeks, and when at last Belgrave commented upon it, it was only to say, "Pardon me, My Lord, but you seem to have bruised your fruit. Shall I fetch something fresh?"

"Take this." Lord Lumpley held out the note. "Make copies, stamp them with my seal, and have them dispatched immediately to . . . oh . . . everyone."

"Everyone, My Lord?"

"Everyone within a twenty-mile radius."

"*Everyone* within a twenty-mile radius, My Lord?"

The baron heaved a sigh. Work, work, work!

"Everyone who matters."

"Ahhhh." Belgrave nodded. "The gentlemen of the area."

"Yes, yes. The usual bunch, you know who. Oh, and alert the Master of the Quorn. I'll be needing all his dogs this afternoon. We're to have one more hunt before The Season!"

"Very good, My Lord."

Belgrave began backing toward the door.

Lord Lumley cleared his throat.

"Tell me, Belgrave . . . what do you think of my riding attire?"

Belgrave regarded the baron with cool, pale blue eyes that never blinked. Ever.

"His Lordship is, as always, the very picture of virile English manhood. Though I might point out that the traditional color for the hunt is red."

"Ahhh, right you are, Belgrave. Make it so."

A few minutes later, the baron's dressing team arrived to begin stuffing him into his clothes. As the sockman worked on his left foot and the drawersman fussed over the fit of his trousers and the trussmen strained to stitch him up from behind in his fraying, crack-ribbed girdle, Lord Lumpley set his mind to the hunt.

How to snare Miss Jane Bennet?

Young ladies were always the most difficult quarry to corner, for they were ever surrounded by protectors: parents, patrons, governesses, guardians, chaperones. That's why he loved orphans and working girls so—and so often! Like that milliner's daughter, Emily What-Have-You. One day she was delivering him some new hats; practically the next, unfortunately, she was threatening to deliver a lot more than that. Such naïfs were his bread and butter.

Yet a gentleman cannot survive on bread alone, even buttered. He must have fine caviar. Champagne. Fresh meat. Like Jane Bennet.

He even thought he might make a full meal of her instead of the usual snack. She was so very, very proper—and so wonderfully *passive*. Just what he needed in a wife. An impenetrable veneer of propriety, and not a lot of questions.

Of course, she was miles beneath him, but who above would have him? He was, after all, only a baron—enough to impress the rustics thereabouts, but barely a step above a peasant so far as dukes and earls were concerned. Even a viscount outranked him. A bloody viscount!

It would have been possible, once, to marry an equal. But that had its disadvantages, seeing as he was related to most of them. His family used to push cousins on him all the time: *Keep it in the family, Dickie. Why marry an outsider?* He'd seen where that lead, though. It had been the Lumpley way for generations, and now his relations were as inbred as a pack of shipwrecked poodles. It was a miracle he'd turned out as well as he had.

Of course, that hadn't kept him from flirting with the idea—and doing much more than flirting with a few of his cousins. Which was why the rest of the family liked to pretend he was dead, and now he had this big old house all to himself.

"*Fini*, My Lord," his topsman said upon setting the hat just-so upon his head.

The baron's dressing team waited with bated breath as he took his time inspecting himself in the mirror. At long last, he nodded with satisfaction, and the dressers tried to hide their sighs of relief. As one, they bowed and began backing toward the door.

"Not just yet," the baron said, and he tapped a finger against his lower lip in a way his servants had all learned to dread. "It shall be quite some time before my guests arrive. I think I shall have a bath in the meantime."

He held his arms out straight to the sides and waited for his dressers to begin his *un*dressing. He didn't have to wait long. Thirty minutes later, he was naked again.

The rest of the day was a whirlwind of activity. Bath, dressers, meal, chambermaid, bath, dressers, meal, chambermaid (a different one), bath, dressers. And then at last it was time to head back downstairs and greet his guests.

He found his favorites—the young bounders, rakes, and scoundrels—red-coated and, having already polished off enough of the baron's port to float a small boat, rosy-cheeked. An assortment of stick-in-the-muds, some dressed for the hunt, some not, stood around trying to hide their disapproval with varying degrees of success. In their midst, Lord Lumpley noted with an annoyance *he* certainly didn't try to hide, was the stickiest stick from the muckiest mud: the local vicar, the Reverend Mr. Cummings. And—damnation!—the vicar noted him noting and headed his way.

The baron might have beat a quick retreat, but a thought hobbled him. He had agreed to speak to Cummings about a supposedly urgent matter—something that smug little nobody Bennet was insisting upon. The man actually wanted the vicar's permission to . . . oh, it was simply too ghastly.

And even ghastlier—Mr. Cummings was now upon him, and there was no escaping conversation.

"If I might have a word, My Lord."

"By all means, especially if it is *good-bye*."

Mr. Cummings scowled.

The baron laughed as if he'd been joking. "You must forgive me my attempt at wit. Simply whistling in the dark. This matter with the dreadful . . . most disturbing, is it not?"

"It certainly is." The vicar threw a pointed look over at the youngest, drunkest members of the hunting party, who were now badgering Belgrave to break into the brandies. "And hardly a fit subject for levity."

Lord Lumpley shrugged. "Men keep their courage up however they must."

Mr. Cummings tried to look shrewd. He had a round, bland face, best suited for displaying piety, mild reproach, and a hint of intestinal distress, and the expression didn't suit him.

"They do not look much afraid to me, Sir. And what could they possibly have to fear from foxes, at any rate?"

The baron sighed, weighed his options, then simply walked away, heading across the foyer for the front doors. Unfortunately, the vicar assumed he was meant to accompany him, and did so.

"I said—"

"It is bigger game we are after today," Lord Lumpley grated out, resenting each word. He hated justifying himself to anyone, but a clergyman! If he'd had his way, there would be a season for hunting them, just as with the foxes.

"So it is as I suspected," the vicar said. "Well, it's a good thing I came, then. Someone must endeavor to bring dignity to these proceedings."

The two had stepped outside now, and the baron found himself smiling despite the nasty little carbuncle he could not seem to excise from his side. On the lawn of his estate were more men dressed in red, some already atop their black or brown mounts. Grooms were bringing up more riderless horses from the stables, and the Master of the Quorn was surrounded by a pack of prancing, baying hounds.

The circumstances might have been a bit grotesque, but it was a hunt, and that was reason for cheer. A good belt of brandy and some fresh-spilled blood, and the day would turn out fine indeed.

"Mr. Cummings," Lord Lumpley said, "I resent your implication that any endeavor of mine would lack dignity. I consider myself a paragon of—ooh la la!"

The baron's eyes went so wide it was a wonder they stayed in his head, and though they didn't pop out, the lowest knots in his truss *did*.

Riding toward him on a blinding white stallion was Jane Bennet. Her appearance was shocking, scandalous, sensational in every sense of the word—and Lord Lumpley loved it.

She was wearing a plain gray frock barely a notch above a shift, and at her side was what appeared to be the scabbard for a long sword graced with neither guard nor knucklebow. She was seated sidesaddle, as convention dictated, yet she'd pushed her steed up to a most improper gallop, and the sight of her bouncing up and down on its broad back left the baron woozy with desire.

The girl's father and sister Elizabeth were riding alongside her, but Lord Lumpley paid them no heed until all three were reining up before him.

"My Lord," Mr. Bennet said with a bow of the head that struck the baron as a tad perfunctory. "Mr. Cummings."

"Mr. Bennet. So good to see you again." Lord Lumpley turned to Jane. "And what a lovely surprise to see you—and on horseback, no less! If I may say so, Miss Bennet, you have an excellent seat."

Jane smiled demurely and averted her eyes.

"I can't believe this is the first time you've noticed it, My Lord," her sister said. She, too, was wearing a scabbarded sword, though the baron hardly thought she needed it. Her tongue was sharper than any blade.

"I've never seen the young lady ride," Lord Lumpley replied. "At any rate, you'll both want to keep back after the hounds are loosed. There will be a great excitement amongst the horses, and even the most skillful rider might find his mount bolting. Once the hunting party is a safe distance ahead, you can follow along the lanes until—"

"My daughters will not be following the hunting party," Mr. Bennet said. "They will be in it."

The baron was too astounded to even take umbrage at the interruption, and it was Mr. Cummings who gasped and said, "You can't be serious."

"I am. Deadly serious. Unlike some, it would seem."

Mr. Bennet threw a look toward the front steps, which was now clotted with guffawing men stumbling from the manor house with half-filled glasses in their hands. Several stopped to gawk as they caught sight of the Bennet girls with their austere gowns and sheathed swords.

Mr. Bennet turned back to Lord Lumpley. "Do they even know why they're really here?"

The baron puffed himself up, breaking two more truss strings while he was at it. First the vicar dares question him, and now this two thousand per annum "gentleman"? If not for his designs on Jane, he would've put the upstart in his place right then and there.

"I'm sure many have guessed our true intentions, Bennet. I suppose it's time we told the rest."

Lord Lumpley stalked away before he could lose his temper and insult the father of the woman he loved. Well, lusted after.

"Belgrave!" he barked, and his manservant instantly appeared as if he'd hopped from his master's pocket. "Escort the rest of our guests outside, if you please."

"I'm afraid a few have already passed out, My Lord."

"Fine—the ones who can walk, then."

"Very good, My Lord."

Belgrave bowed and went back into the house. While he was gone, the baron positioned himself on the front steps, experimenting with various poses until he found one that struck the right balance of lordliness and sport.

"My friends," he said, once the last would-be huntsman had joined the crowd on the lawn, "welcome to Netherfield Park! Are you ready to slay your first dreadful?"

CHAPTER 9

ELIZABETH, FOR ONE, was *not* ready to slay her first dreadful. Yet at least she knew it. Looking at the men gathered before the baron's manor house, it was obvious most thought otherwise of themselves. They were laughing, cocksure, anything but scared.

Perhaps it was the drink Lord Lumpley had obviously been so generous with that afternoon. Perhaps it was simply the confidence of youth, for the loudest merrymakers were invariably the youngest.

But most likely it was plain ignorance. The great, undead herds of The Troubles had never made it as far as Meryton. Here and there in the crowd, however, you could pick out the men who'd seen them. They were the ones with grim, pinched faces and haunted eyes. The men like Elizabeth's father.

"We talked about quietly raising a militia," he spat as the baron brayed on with his welcome speech, "and the bloated dolt throws a *party*."

He got a few stares for that. It provided a moment of respite for Elizabeth and Jane, actually, for up to then the stares had been reserved for them. There had been a wave of whispers, too, and though Elizabeth did not catch any of the words, she knew exactly what was being said.

What are they wearing?

Are those swords?

The Bennets have always been eccentric, but now they've gone quite mad!

Holy Father, what hast Thou loosed on fair England?

This last wasn't being said but silently prayed, to judge by the expression on Mr. Cummings's face. He'd looked only slightly more appalled when Mr. Bennet had splattered his pulpit with zombie gore.

Elizabeth did her best to block it all out with her mantra (*smooth stone beneath still water, smooth stone beneath still water . . .*), but nothing could blunt the piercing sting of shame. After Papa had announced that she and Jane were to accompany him that afternoon—were, in fact, to have their coming out as warriors-in-training—she'd felt queasy and faint, as if Kitty had accidentally thwacked her upside the head with her fighting staff. Which, in a very few minutes, she did. Now, however, the pain was far sharper, stabbing deep into her heart.

Her mother had told her more than once she was a headstrong girl, insufficiently concerned with the good opinion of her neighbors. And it might have even been true, back when her gravest offense was rolling her eyes at someone else's foolishness or speaking with a tad more honesty than polite society permits. Yet that hardly mattered now, for no young lady's good name could survive the spectacle they were making of themselves.

The proof of that was beside her. Her sister Jane was perfection, with a reputation as unblemished as any could hope for with the Bennets for a family. Yet that hadn't turned aside any of the stares or stifled any of the snickers, and the demure, gentle-spirited girl listened in slump-shouldered silence atop her steed as Lord Lumpley did his best to rouse the crowd that found her so absurd.

"I'm sure you've all heard of the shocking incident in our very own St. Chad's Church a few days ago. Well, we'll have no more of that around here! We shall sweep the countryside clean of any such rubbish . . . then sleep sound in our beds tonight knowing the peril is safely behind us once again!"

"*Imbecile*," Mr. Bennet hissed so loudly his horse whinnied and pranced nervously beneath him.

"Are you ready to ride with me?" the baron cried.

"Ready!" called back a chorus of brandy-soaked voices.

"To your horses, then!"

There was a great commotion as drunken huntsmen staggered to steeds, tried to mount them, in many cases fell off, and then either lay on the ground laughing or berated some unlucky groom for his supposed incompetence in keeping the horse steady.

"Be ready with your steel, girls," Mr. Bennet said. "I don't know if these fools are going to kill any zombies today, but it's quite likely they're about to create a few."

"Yes, Father," Elizabeth and Jane said together.

Lord Lumpley had better luck getting himself mounted than most of his friends, and soon he came trotting toward the Bennets on a sleek, brown mare.

"I would suggest that the ladies stay to the rear. I would hate to see either of them unhorsed in all the commotion of the hunt."

"You need not worry about my Jane," Mr. Bennet said. "A finer horsewoman you will never see."

He peeped over at Elizabeth, offering wordless apologies with a doleful look. A more *awkward* horsewoman than she one would never see, for anyone else with as little horse sense wouldn't dare sit in the saddle. If her father had known of the baron's plans, it very likely would have been Jane and *Mary* he'd brought with him to Netherfield.

"As for this idea of a hunt," Mr. Bennet said, looking at Lord Lumpley again, "we spoke of using the hounds, yes, but only after we'd organized a proper—"

The baron stopped him with a raised hand. "We can discuss that later, Bennet. Now is the time for action." He swiveled around, puffed out his chest (so much so that Elizabeth thought she heard a faint popping noise coming from the vicinity of his stomach), and boomed: "Produce the object!"

With a sigh of weary irritation, Mr. Bennet pulled a swaddle-wrapped handkerchief from one of the pockets of his greatcoat. This he gave to Lord Lumpley.

"Master of the Quorn!" the baron bellowed.

A small, lean man hustled over, and Lord Lumpley handed him the handkerchief. The man then sprinted away toward the milling, whimpering foxhounds clustered nearby. With each step he took, the dogs grew louder, wilder, until they were practically dancing on each other's backs, barking madly.

The Master of the Quorn knelt before them, unwrapped the handkerchief, and let the dogs crowd in for a good sniff.

"Is that what I think it is?" Elizabeth asked.

Her father nodded.

In the church, after dispatching Mr. Ford, Mr. Bennet had collected a peculiar memento mori: the dead man's ears.

The hounds, it seemed, didn't like the smell of them. Their yips turned to whines, their tails curled between their legs, their ears flattened back on their heads, they cringed and wet the ground. One by one, however, they stuck their noses in the air, nostrils flaring.

When the Master of the Quorn stood up, they circled each other uncertainly for a moment, then slowly set off across the lawn. Once they were under way, they seemed to forget their fear. The barking began again, and their hesitant lope became a dash.

"They've got the scent!" someone called out.

"Tallyho!" Lord Lumpley shouted, and he gave his horse a hard slap of the crop to set her off. Within seconds, two dozen huntsmen were thundering away after him—and two of the more besotted ones quickly rolled backward off their charging mounts. Mr. Bennet and his daughters trotted over to make sure they were still alive.

They were . . . though to judge by their groans, they weren't especially happy about it.

"So," Elizabeth said, "tallyho, then?"

Mr. Bennet nodded. "Jane, if you would please catch up with Lord Lumpley and see to it he doesn't do anything *too* spectacularly stupid. Elizabeth . . . " Mr. Bennet reached over and patted her white-knuckled hands, which were wrapped so tightly around the reins that her fingernails bit into her palms. "Good luck."

They set off after the hunting party, but they didn't remain together long. Within a minute, Jane had not just caught up with the other riders but was passing most of them. Elizabeth, meanwhile, had to use all the skill and will at her disposal both to stay on her horse and to keep from screaming while doing so.

It didn't help, of course, that she had to ride sidesaddle, an experience akin to sitting on a rocking chair with no back set adrift in a rowboat in stormy seas. She'd never had the best "seat" to begin with, and that had been when riding at a leisurely amble along smooth country lanes. Going at a gallop through field and brush—as the party was doing now—convinced her she soon would have no seat at all.

Elizabeth's only consolation was the fact that she was doing better than many of the men. When she sent her horse flying over a narrow stream, she flashed past a red-coated fellow sitting in it shaking his head. When she took another leap over a low hedge, she noticed two huntsmen on the other side stumbling after the horses that had just thrown them. And when she rounded a stand of trees and barely avoided a gamekeeper's cottage half hidden in the shadow, she saw a horse standing stock still before it—and its former rider hanging half on, half off the roof.

Nerve-racking as the chase was, Elizabeth would've realized she was grateful for the pure, thought-obliterating terror of it if she could've slowed down long enough to think at all. Better to worry about falling off a horse than ponder the unsettling question the ride itself presented.

What exactly were they chasing?

Eventually, however, Elizabeth could avoid the question no longer. From up ahead, she heard a strangled blast of the hunting horn and the sharp, yelping screams of injured dogs.

A moment later, she reined up her horse beside a small lake. The rest of the hunting party was already there, on foot now—except for the few who'd wheeled their mounts around and gone galloping in the opposite direction as soon as they saw what the hounds had found.

A dripping, bedraggled figure was struggling to pull itself out of the water. From its waterlogged dress and long, brown hair it was easy to see it had once been a woman. The rest of it, though, hardly even seemed *human*. The flesh was bloated and green, and a swollen tongue protruded obscenely from its mouth, giving the creature the look of a giant frog. It was trying to walk to the shore with outstretched arms, yet it seemed to make no progress, and Elizabeth didn't understand why until she dismounted and forced herself to move closer.

A rope had been tied to the woman's waist, and the other end was wound around a gray lump in the water just behind her: a stone the size of a Christmas goose.

"Oh, no," Jane whispered, voice choked with pity and despair.

"Not her."

Bile burned the back of Elizabeth's throat.

She was looking at her sister's missing friend, Emily Ward. The girl had drowned herself. And now she was back.

Growling hounds ringed the shoreline before the dreadful. A few had apparently braved the shallows to attack it, for the creature's right sleeve was torn off, the green flesh beneath hanging ragged where it had been chewed and torn. In the brush some distance away were two dogs whimpering as they limped away from the trees the unmentionable had hurled them against.

"Good God," Lord Lumpley muttered, looking almost as green as the zombie. "Good God . . . "

"Not as sporting as you remember it, My Lord?" Mr. Bennet asked.

The baron simply shook his head. Most of his fellow huntsmen had stumbled off into the bracken to throw up, though a few—the older, sober ones, mostly—stood their ground.

The Reverend Mr. Cummings came rolling up in his little dogcart just as Lord Lumpley spun on his heel and streaked for the trees to join his retching friends. The vicar hopped from his carriage—then found his knees not entirely up to the task at hand. As he started toward the lake, his legs were wobbling so badly it looked like he'd slipped a pair of snakes down his trousers.

"B-but surely that's not Miss W-w-w-w-ard? G-G-God save us!"

"I wouldn't count on it," Mr. Bennet mumbled under his breath.

One of the more frenzied hounds made a running lunge for the dreadful, sinking its fangs deep into the thing's throat. The zombie screamed, though more in rage than pain, it seemed to Elizabeth, and then knocked the dog aside into the shallows.

The dreadful's shrieking suddenly stopped—because the hound had torn out all the flesh between the collarbone and jaw. There was no windpipe left to scream with.

And still Emily Ward struggled to reach land, the stone behind her moving but a fraction of an inch with each lurching step. Her mouth remained open wide, her arms out straight before her, as if she were beseeching, pleading for help.

"Well," Mr. Bennet said, "I don't suppose we'll have a better opportunity for practice than this. It's not often you find an unmentionable staked down for you."

Elizabeth moved a hand toward her sword. Not that she was so anxious to draw it. Gripping the hilt, she found, helped keep her hand from shaking.

"You . . . you want me to . . . ?"

"No." Her father's eyes slowly slid from hers, locking onto the silent figure standing at her side. "It is Jane's turn."

"Sir!" the vicar said. "Why do you insi-si-sist on subjecting your own d-daughters to all this—"

"Last rites again, if you please!" Mr. Bennet snapped without taking his gaze from Jane.

The vicar started to reply, but whatever he meant to say died, strangled by stutters, on his spluttering tongue. He stumbled away from the Bennets and faced the lake.

"Depart, O Christian soul, out of this world," he mumbled. "In the name of God the Father Almighty who c-c-created you . . . "

"I can't do it," Jane whispered.

"You must."

Tears streaked Jane's face, and she shook her head. "I won't."

Her father took an angry step toward her, scowling so fiercely he looked like another man entirely—a man Elizabeth might have fled from not so very long ago, before her training began. A man she still might flee from.

"You *must!*"

Jane's tears flowed faster, then turned to sobs.

"Crying will not save us!" her father raged. "Mercy will not save us! Only the sword will save us! Draw yours and use it, girl! Do it now!"

Yet Jane just buried her head in her hands and sobbed all the harder.

Mr. Bennet stepped up so close he was practically shouting in her ear. "Prove you are not weak! Prove you are not worthless! Prove . . . oh, hang it all."

And he wrapped his arms around his daughter and whispered "There, there." When he peeped Elizabeth's way a moment later, she saw her father once more, only more sad-eyed now. Defeated.

If they were to survive the coming days, this fragile, beautiful thing he cherished—her sister's compassion and gentleness, her spirit, her very soul—had to be destroyed. Or so he'd believed. Yet still, he couldn't bring himself to do it.

He'd failed. His daughters would never be warriors. Elizabeth looked around at the men watching them from beside the lake and peeping out from behind trees and bushes. Many of their faces were slack with dismay; just as many were curdled with disgust.

Her life would be in their hands, now—the hands of those who either lacked the fortitude to fight or judged her improper, mad, unworthy for daring to think a young lady might possess it. All she and Jane could do was slink home with their father, their reputations ruined, and pack away their weapons, and wait for the dreadfuls to come.

Or not.

Elizabeth heard the *shing* of a blade leaving its scabbard, saw a glint of sharp-edged steel, and realized only when she took her first step toward the water that it was she who'd drawn her sword. She went striding through the dogs, out into the lake, and aimed a swing of her katana at what was left of the dreadful's neck.

She missed, instead slicing off a raised arm that promptly plopped into the water and sank. As Elizabeth brought back the sword to try again, the zombie reached out and grabbed it—actually snatched the blade out of the air with its remaining hand and held tight to it, all the while straining against the rope around its waist, pushing its black, protruding tongue toward Elizabeth's face.

AS ELIZABETH BROUGHT BACK THE SWORD TO TRY AGAIN,
THE ZOMBIE REACHED OUT AND GRABBED IT.

The stench hit Elizabeth, then, the odor of rotting flesh so close, so overpowering, her vision blurred. The katana was ripped from her grip. Her knees began to buckle.

And then another blade flashed out, and Emily Ward's head toppled off its severed neck bone. As the rest of the body splashed backward after it, Elizabeth turned to find Jane at her side, still weeping. The sisters started to fall into each other's arms.

"Not bad!" an unfamiliar voice boomed out. "But not good! Now dry those tears! Your father is correct—warriors weep not!"

Elizabeth and Jane looked up, past their shocked father, past the pale, trembling Mr. Cummings, past the assorted huntsmen cowering in the woods, and beheld a large, raven-haired man standing, legs spread and arms akimbo, near the vicar's dogcart.

Lord Lumpley leaned out from behind a vine-choked oak. "Who are you?"

The man ignored him so utterly that one somehow understood he would've done the same even if he'd known he was a nobleman.

"You are Oscar Bennet?" he asked Elizabeth's father.

"I am."

The man started toward him through the brush with quick, confident steps. As he drew closer, Elizabeth noticed that he was extraordinarily young for one with such commanding ways. He was about Jane's age, she would have guessed—eighteen years old.

He was also extraordinarily handsome, though Elizabeth was still too stunned and distraught to register that fact fully.

The sword at his side, though—that she couldn't miss.

It was a katana.

"The Order sent you?" Mr. Bennet asked.

The young man gave his head a sharp, downward jerk. "Your message was received. I am the response." He looked at the girls with such stony coldness he seemed more statue than man. "I am to be your daughters' new master . . . and yours, as well, Oscar Bennet."

CHAPTER 10

THE STRANGER'S AIR of chilly calm seemed to help everyone recover their nerve—at least enough to stop throwing up or hiding in the shrubbery. Even the dogs settled down, though this was more because the dreadful had been dispensed with and an attempt to catch another scent (with Emily Ward's fresh-severed arm) had come to naught.

There were no more unmentionables near Netherfield Park—at least not any that smelled like Mr. Ford or Miss Ward.

"Oakham Mount might be a good spot to try for the scent again," Mr. Bennet suggested. "Perhaps it would be wise to carry on the search from there . . . this time with a little less pomp and a little more firepower."

Lord Lumpley kept sneaking nervous peeks both at the body lying in the shallows of the lake and at Jane on the shore, splattered with its blood. Elizabeth supposed he was trying to decide which sight he found more monstrous.

"Yes . . . yes, I see your point," he said. "We should proceed more in the manner of . . . a grouse hunt. I shall return to the house and see that the gun room is opened . . . for those who wish to continue."

He shuffled away listlessly, and before long he and his dogs (both of the hound and lap variety) were gone, with the Reverend Mr. Cummings trailing after them in the interests of "ministering to the sorry stricken." Mr. Bennet and the stranger had volunteered to attend to Emily Ward "in the necessary way," and no one seemed anxious to stay and see just what that meant.

After cutting the dead girl free from her drowning stone, the men carried her body a short distance into the woods. As they settled it down in a small, rocky clearing, Elizabeth steeled herself, walked back to the water, and collected Emily's head. She grasped it by the hair as she brought it to her father, holding it far out before her, like Diogenes with his lantern.

Jane turned her back as she went by.

"So . . . ," Elizabeth said once head and body were reunited. She had to lick her lips and swallow hard before she could go on. "What happens next?"

The stranger narrowed his dark eyes, squinting at her as if she were a pane of frosted glass he was trying to peer through.

Her father spoke up before the other man could.

"If you will permit it, sir, I would like to spare my daughter this one, last thing."

It disturbed Elizabeth to hear her father deferring to such a far younger man, yet it bothered her even more that she might be dismissed—as indeed she was.

"You have spared your daughters too much already, Oscar Bennet," the stranger said. "A final indulgence would be but a pebble atop Mount Fuji." He looked at Elizabeth and gave a brusque wave toward the lake. "Go. Wait."

Elizabeth held his gaze a moment, not moving, before choosing to do as he said.

"What will become of Emily's body?" Jane asked as her sister rejoined her by the water.

"I don't know. Something Papa did not want me to see."

Together, they watched their father and the stranger. But the men were shrouded in the shadows of the forest, and all they could discern was a flurry of movement, a ray of stray sunlight flashing off a raised blade, and then, a moment later, flames and smoke that rose high like a pyre before dying out with surprising speed.

When Mr. Bennet came to collect the girls, he looked as grim as Elizabeth had ever seen him.

"Come," he said. "We return to Longbourn."

"All of us?" Elizabeth asked.

The stranger was striding in the opposite direction, toward a large, black horse—practically a Clydesdale, it was so big. It stamped a huge hoof with impatience as it waited for its master, its reins wrapped around a low-hanging branch.

"Yes," Mr. Bennet said. "All of us."

During the ride back, Elizabeth had her best chance yet to make a thorough study of the mysterious young man from "the Order" (whatever that was). She and Jane were riding behind him and their father, yet she didn't need to look the stranger in the face to read his character. The stiffness of his bearing, the long straight line of his broad shoulders, the stern snap of his tone when speaking to Mr. Bennet, even the peculiar way he wore his long, thick, shiny-black hair, pulled up in a queue that sprouted from just below his crown—all spoke of discipline and strength of will. And haughtiness and pride, as well.

Elizabeth knew she should resent his arrogance, especially his condescension to her father, yet she found she couldn't. It was because he represented hope, she told herself. If, as Mr. Bennet insisted, she and her sisters needed to be molded into warriors, here might be the man to do it. After all, one doesn't forge a sword on a blancmange. It takes an anvil of iron. And this young man certainly seemed hard and cold enough to pass for one.

Upon reaching Longbourn, they found the rest of the girls engaged in proper-ish ladylike pursuits under the unenthused tutelage of Mrs. Hill the housekeeper, who'd been temporarily drafted into service as a reluctant replacement for Miss Chiselwood. Mary was hunched over a book (her history of The Troubles, Elizabeth was pleased to see); Kitty was working on her poise by toying with nunchucks while the etiquette guide she was supposed to be reading sat balanced atop her head. Lydia, meanwhile, was honing her embroidery skills with a needlepoint portrait of Mary, complete with halo, pimples, fangs, and the words OUR LITTLE

ANGEL—MAY GOD TAKE HER BACK SOON floating over her wispy hair. All were shocked into silence when the stranger marched in, boomed "To the dojo—*now!*" and immediately marched back out.

"Come along, girls, come along," Mr. Bennet said, waving them toward the door.

"Who was that?" Lydia asked.

"Our new master of the deadly arts, apparently," Elizabeth said.

"Our new—?" Kitty began. She looked over at Lydia, broke into giggles, and then both girls raced for the dojo with idiotic grins on their faces.

Even Mrs. Bennet was charmed by the stranger despite his best efforts to the contrary, asking "Who is that rude, handsome man?" after he brushed past her in the foyer.

He lost some of his comeliness, if not his rudeness, once he was in the dojo, for the state of the place puckered his perfect features into a prodigious grimace.

"Are those *daffodils*?"

Mr. Bennet peeped over at Elizabeth and jerked his head at the flower pots crammed into the corner.

"I wasn't expecting anyone from the Order quite so soon," he said as his daughter hustled the flowers out and tossed them over the nearest hedge.

The stranger let his scowl reply for him. When Elizabeth was back inside, he nodded at the floor and said, "Sit."

Mr. Bennet and the girls seated themselves in the warrior way—legs crossed, spines straight—and though the stranger didn't compliment them on it, he did allow his glower to fade.

"My name," he said, "is Geoffrey Hawksworth. You will call me '*Master* Hawksworth' or simply 'Master.' I have been sent by a party whose name your ears are, as yet, unfit to hear. Suffice it to say, I represent a fellowship to which your father, Oscar Bennet, once belonged—a secret league of warriors sworn to eternal vigilance and readiness. As part of his oath of fealty to the Order, he swore to raise all his progeny in the warrior way. But he broke that vow. He chose to live as a gentleman and bring you up to be ladies . . . and now you find yourselves helpless at the very hour The Enemy returns."

The young man pointed a redoubled frown at Mr. Bennet.

It pained Elizabeth to see her father bow his head, looking cowed.

"I have been tasked with setting right your father's failing," Master Hawksworth went on. "You *will* become warriors. I will make you so through exacting instruction, unremitting discipline, and a complete and utter absence of mercy. Do not mistake any of this for cruelty. It is a mercy to you, one for which you should be thankful, for it *might* save your lives. You will show your gratitude—and your devotion to your training— through absolute obedience. Anything I say, you must do without question. This is the first step on the path to preparedness, and you must take it with me now."

The young man paused then, and when he spoke again his voice was so soft it sounded almost tender.

"Do you understand?"

"Yes," the girls said.

"Yes, *what?*" Hawksworth prompted them gently.

"Yes, Master," Elizabeth said.

The Master nodded and almost—*almost*—smiled.

"Good," he said. And then suddenly he was spinning on his heel and stabbing at Kitty with an outstretched arm and a pointing finger, and everything mild or kindly or *human* about him was lost behind a mask of raw contempt. "*YOU!* Jump through the ceiling and catch me a swallow!"

Kitty blinked at him. "Ummm . . . Papa hasn't taught us how to do that yet . . . Master."

"I did not ask what *Papa* has taught you," Master Hawksworth snapped back. "I told you to jump—and you did not." He pointed at the floor now. "Fifty *dand-baithaks.*"

"Dandy-whats? Uhhh . . . Father hasn't taught us about those, either."

Master Hawksworth threw a quick, cold glare at Mr. Bennet, then shrugged off his coat and began unbuttoning his vest.

"Then I must demonstrate."

His vest joined his coat on the floor. When he began untying his cravat, Elizabeth could actually feel the burn of the blush on her cheeks. For a moment, it looked as though he meant to take off his shirt, as well. He was merely loosening it, though, giving his broad chest room to do its work.

When he was ready, he threw himself facedown. Then he pushed up with his arms, and his body lifted, all his weight suspended on his palms and toes.

"One," he said.

He lowered himself until his nose touched the floor, then pushed up again.

"Two."

And so it went, all the way to fifty. It took him no more than half a minute.

He stood up again and looked at Kitty.

"Now you."

Slowly, reluctantly, Kitty stretched out on the floor and attempted her first *dand-baithak*. Her arms shook under the strain of her weight, and by the time she could say "One" her face was as red as a beet.

"YOU!" Master Hawksworth barked, pointing at Mary this time. "Jump through the ceiling and catch me a swallow."

It had always been one of Mary's pleasures to learn from the mistakes of others, and this she tried to do again. She promptly got to her feet, stretched her arms out toward the ceiling, and hopped straight up with all her might.

Her feet made it all of four inches off the ground.

"I'm sorry, Master Hawksworth," she said. "I missed."

Master Hawksworth nodded. "But you did as I said without question."

Mary smiled primly and began to sit down.

"And you failed!" Master Hawksworth snapped. "Fifty *dand-baithaks*."

"But—"

"Sixty!"

"But—"

"Seventy!"

"But—"

"Eighty!"

Mary finally learned from her own mistake and got down on the floor.

"Master Hawksworth," Lydia said, "before you ask, I can't jump through the ceiling and catch you a swallow, either."

"So I would assume."

The Master stalked over to one of the weapons racks, pulled down a dagger, and held it out toward Lydia.

"You will kill *that*," he jerked his head at a fly buzzing around where the daffodils used to be, "then skin it before it hits the ground."

"You want me to skin a *fly*?"

"A novitiate never questions the master's orders! Fifty *dand-baithaks*!"

Lydia stretched out beside her huffing, puffing sisters.

Elizabeth saw where all this was heading: Within a minute, Jane was doing *dand-baithaks*, too, for though she attacked the fly without question, she missed it with every slice of the knife.

Then it was Elizabeth's turn.

"*HAAAAAAAAAAAAAAAAAAAAAAAAAA-IIIIIIIIIII-IEEEEEEEEEEEEEEEEEEEEEEEEEE!*" she cried, lunging at the fly.

It weaved under her first swipe. It danced around her second.

The third—to Elizabeth's own amazement—sent it dropping to the floor. Dead.

"Not bad, Elizabeth Bennet," the Master said. Yet his eyes said something more: When Elizabeth looked his way, she found him peering at her with what looked like naked—almost awestruck—fascination.

Master Hawksworth knelt down to inspect the fly lying before her.

"As at the lake, your zeal does you credit," he said, his tone warming for a moment before freezing back into brittle ice. "A pity your skills do not. This fly has not been skinned—it has merely lost a wing." He stood up with one hand held out. "Fifty *dand-baithaks*."

Elizabeth gave him back the dagger and went to the floor at his feet.

"You look displeased, Oscar Bennet," she heard Master Hawksworth say over her own panting and the roar of blood rushing in her ears. (The *dand-baithaks* were even more difficult than they looked.) "Do you wish to complain? If so, go ahead. I grant you dispensation this once."

"Yes, I am displeased," Mr. Bennet said. "It pains me to see my daughters so roughly treated." Elizabeth caught the faint, familiar sound of one of her father's sighs. "But no . . . I will not complain. We have been weak. *I* have been weak. I pray you will help us find our strength before it is too late."

"I do, as well, Oscar Bennet. I do, as well. Now—there is a beetle in that corner. Behead it!"

Elizabeth heard the *ka-chunk* of a blade striking wood and holding fast. Then Master Hawksworth grunted.

"Not bad. You haven't lost your old skills entirely, I see. But I told you to behead the beetle, not cut it in two."

"Fifty *dand-baithaks*, Master?"

"For you, Oscar Bennet?" the young man said. "One hundred."

CHAPTER 11

OVER THE NEXT TWO DAYS, the Bennet girls learned many new stances and moves and, along with their father, sparred with many new weapons.

There were, as a consequence, many, many mistakes and accidents—and many, many, *many dand-baithaks*.

Lydia titters when the Master squats, legs bent into a *U*, for "the Sumo Position"? Fifty *dand-baithaks*.

Mary accidentally knocks Kitty silly with her nunchucks? Fifty *dand-baithaks*.

Kitty un–accidentally knocks Mary silly with *her* nunchucks? Fifty *dand-baithaks*. For Mary again. For not dodging fast enough.

Mr. Bennet raises an eyebrow at Mary's punishment? One hundred *dand-baithaks* and five laps around the grounds.

Jane quickly proved the most graceful disciple, and Mr. Bennet, of course, the most accomplished—so much so that Master Hawksworth frequently had him run his daughters through their drills while he stood back nodding gravely. Yet Elizabeth, with her piercing warrior's cry and eagerness to try any maneuver or weapon, no matter the difficulty or danger, was without doubt the most ardent student in the dojo. Though why that should be even she couldn't say.

Certainly, the Master never spoke of it. He rarely spoke of anything except how this is done right or this was done wrong or how many *dand-baithaks* were needed to make amends for one's unworthiness. All the Bennets truly knew of him had to be sucked out as a leech draws blood—and there was, of course, but one leech for the job.

"A lovely English spring we're having, is it not?" Mrs. Bennet said over dinner the day after Master Hawksworth's arrival.

The Master didn't even look up from his food, which he'd insisted on preparing himself. Not that it required much in the way of preparation: It was simply white rice and (to the obvious disgust of all, save Mr. Bennet) raw fish.

Up to then, Master Hawksworth had declared English cooking to be "bricks in a warrior's stomach where fire out to be," and at mealtimes he'd remained in the dojo to eat alone. Eventually, however, he'd been coaxed inside easily enough. All Elizabeth had to say was, "It would be an honor if you joined us this evening, Master," and in he came.

"It's probably been twenty years since we had so balmy an April," Mrs. Bennet forged on.

Still Master Hawksworth said nothing.

"It was an unseasonably warm spring when The Troubles first began, as well," Mary said. "It is my conjecture that the heat in some way accounts for the return of the dreadf*OW!*"

"What of the temperatures where you come from, Mr. Hawksworth?" Mrs. Bennet said, lifting the shoe heel from her daughter's toes. "Do they range as unseasonably high?"

"Yes," the Master said.

He reached out with the two smooth sticks he used in lieu of a proper fork or spoon, grabbed hold of a mound of rice, and stuffed it into his mouth. Mrs. Bennet waited patiently while he finished chewing so he could finish his thought, but he simply speared a floppy pink wad of fish and stuffed it in after the rice.

Mrs. Bennet grimaced and looked away, and when she again found her voice (which, alas, was never lost for long) she abandoned warmth as both a topic of conversation and a model for her deportment.

"Well. I'm glad to see you're enjoying your food . . . if you can call it that. You'll find the streams of Hertfordshire overflowing with fat, juicy trout you may pluck out and tuck into at your leisure. If I may ask, where is it that you acquired a taste for such awfully *fresh* fare?"

"Japan."

Hawksworth shoveled in more rice.

"Japan?" Mrs. Bennet said. "That's the little island nation down around New South Wales, is it not? Full of Orientals?"

Hawksworth finally looked up from his plate—so he could scowl at Mrs. Bennet.

"Yes, yes," Mr. Bennet mumbled, wincing. "That is the place."

Elizabeth and Jane shared a wide-eyed glance. Master Hawksworth—a young man scarcely older than they—had actually traveled to Japan! If only he weren't so stern and taciturn. There were so many questions to ask!

For Mrs. Bennet, however, there was only one.

"Such a long journey would surely cost a fortune. Your family could afford such a venture?"

"No," Master Hawksworth said.

Mrs. Bennet frowned.

"But I have a patron for whom money is no object," the Master added.

Mrs. Bennet smiled.

Master Hawksworth was looking at Mr. Bennet.

"I shan't name names, yet I will say this: My benefactor has held true to the code others found it so easy to abandon once The Troubles were over. I was sent to Japan to learn and live by that code. Soon, your daughters will be living by it, as well. And perhaps dying by it . . . if they can earn such an honor."

Mr. Bennet listened intently, solemnly, and when Hawksworth was finished, he replied with a single nod.

Mrs. Bennet, on the other hand, had stopped paying any attention whatsoever after the words "money is no object."

"Tell me, Mr. Hawksworth," she chirped, "do you like to dance?"

The Master froze with a glistening glob of raw flesh halfway to his face. "Pardon me?"

"In a little more than a week, there is to be a ball," Mrs. Bennet said. "Some of our best local girls will be having their coming out—including our own Elizabeth. I'm sure you, as our guest, would be welcome."

Master Hawksworth stared at Mrs. Bennet the same way she'd have stared at him had he stuck his eating sticks in his ears and mooed like a cow. After a moment, however, he overcame his dismay and reverted to his standard expression—which was, actually, an almost total lack of expression at all.

"I have no time for such frivolity, and neither do my students."

"Your students?" Mrs. Bennet scoffed. And then, her voice edging toward panic as his meaning dawned on her: "Elizabeth? And Jane? But of course they *must* be at the ball."

"When there is so much for them to learn and so little time to learn it?" Hawksworth shook his head. "I cannot allow it."

"Who are you to allow or not allow anything here?"

"I am the Master."

"Not of me, you're not! And if I say Jane and Elizabeth are going to the ball, they're . . . oh, you tell him, Mr. Bennet!"

"We will discuss this after dinner," Mr. Bennet said softly. He seemed to be anticipating the conversation with all the enthusiasm of a condemned man looking ahead to his own hanging.

"Mr. Bennet!" his wife gasped. "You aren't actually siding with this . . . this . . . whatever he is?"

"*After dinner*, woman."

Which was answer enough for Mrs. Bennet.

"Ohhhhhhhhhh!" she cried, rolling her head and grabbing Mary with one hand, Kitty with the other. "My last hope, gone! Instead of throwing my eldest in the path of eligible bachelors, they're to be thrown to the unmentionables! And so go the rest of us, girls—to a potter's field or down a dreadful's gullet, one or the other! And all because your father started taking orders from some ponytailed stripling who doesn't even have the sense to cook his fish!"

Lydia and Kitty joined in with weeping of their own, and even Mary's eyes took to watering behind her spectacles (though Elizabeth suspected this had more to do with the way her mother was crushing her hand).

When Elizabeth glanced at Hawksworth to gauge his reaction to this spectacle, she was surprised to find him intently gauging *hers*. He seemed both puzzled and approving at the same time, as if he were asking himself a question Elizabeth herself had considered often over the years: How did she come to be in the same family as her younger sisters and mother?

As Elizabeth watched, a placid blankness fell over the Master's face, like a curtain being brought down on a play, and he looked away and rose from his seat.

"From now on," he said calmly, picking up his plate, "I shall take all my meals in the dojo."

Mr. Bennet watched him walk out with a look that was equal parts humiliation and jealousy. He then turned to his wife and undertook the fruitless task of calming her without outright giving in to her.

"I will speak to him in private, Mrs. Bennet. Our young friend doesn't understand the full importance of the ball, that's all."

"Explain it to him, then! Tell him the estate is entailed away, and helping two of our daughters land husbands is the least he can do if he's going to lead the other three to their doom!"

"Yes, well, there is more to the ball than the Master could guess, and I think he might change his mind once all the facts are laid out before him."

"What do you—?" Elizabeth began.

Her mother talked right over her question, though—and kept on talking until the opportunity to ask it was gone.

"The *Master!* Oh, how it rankles to hear you speak of the pup thus. So rude, he is! So aloof! To think that our very survival should require you to grovel before a guest in our own home—and such an ungracious one, at that!"

And so on.

As it turned out, a guest in their home Hawksworth was not, for he not only finished his dinner in the dojo, from then on he did his sleeping there, as well. Mrs. Bennet regarded his retreat from the dining table and guest room as a victory over the man, and the next morning she had another: Her husband informed her that the Master had relented. Jane and Elizabeth could attend the ball after all. Unfortunately, Mrs. Bennet had but a few hours to savor her triumph.

Mr. Bennet and the girls were practicing new stances with their Master—and, consequently, working on the speed of their laps and the crispness of their *dand-baithaks*—when the scream rang out from the house. It was a shriek of pure horror, high and piercing, and it didn't fade away but instead simply cut off, as if suddenly stifled.

Within seconds, Elizabeth and her father and sisters were charging inside, and they found Mrs. Bennet splayed out on the foyer floor. Her eyes were closed, and a kneeling Mrs. Hill was frantically fanning her with a piece of paper.

"My word!" the housekeeper cried. "I think she went and fainted for real, this time!"

"What happened?" Elizabeth asked.

"I don't know! Mrs. Goswick's man Bridges showed up with a letter, and she'd barely opened it before she was flat on her back!"

Mr. Bennet reached down and took the paper Mrs. Hill was using as a fan. She kept flapping her hand over Mrs. Bennet as he read the letter for all.

> Mrs. Bennet,
> It has come to our attention that your daughters, Miss Jane Bennet and Miss Elizabeth Bennet, have, of late, and at the behest of your husband, Mr. Bennet, become engaged in

most remarkable, and one could even say shocking, activities (of a martial nature—I trust you will know what I mean). As the girls have, apparently, committed themselves to these brutal pursuits, we would not, of course, and with regrets for the invitation previously extended, expect to see them at so genteel an occasion as the ball we will be hosting, Thursday next, at Pulvis Lodge.

Yours etcetera, etcetera, Mrs. J. Goswick.

"By gad," Mr. Bennet sighed when he reached the end. "The wretched woman does love her commas."

"Well, I think it was very kind of her to write as she did," Mary said. "To be thinking of Jane and Elizabeth's training when—"

"Oh, you stupid cow!" Lydia howled at her. "Don't you see what this means? Jane and Elizabeth aren't welcome at the spring ball. They've been told not to come! We're ruined!"

"Now I'll never get to go to a dance!" Kitty wailed. "Not even one!"

As Lydia and Kitty fell into each other's arms weeping, Elizabeth simply waited for whatever her own reaction might be. Tears, anger, bitter laughter . . . what was it to be? And why didn't it come more quickly?

Before she had her answer, Jane whirled around and ran up the stairs, her face in her hands. Elizabeth turned to go after her and found herself facing Master Hawksworth. He was about forty feet off, on the lawn, watching through the open front door. Yet the intensity of his gaze made her feel they were face to face, uncomfortably close.

Elizabeth stood there frozen, staring at the brawny, dark-haired man framed in the doorway, and the answer she'd been awaiting—the certainty she longed for—seemed to come nearer in that moment.

Then she heard the first of Jane's sobs upstairs, and she had, if not an answer, at least a purpose, and one she couldn't ignore.

She turned her back to the door and went after Jane. Yet even when she was on the stairs, well out of the Master's line of sight, she could feel

him watching her. It was as if he were searching for his own answer—
one that lay buried somewhere, somehow, within *her*.

CHAPTER 12

EACH NIGHT, as had long been their custom, Jane and Elizabeth ended
the day before the mirror in Jane's room, talking and brushing each other's
hair. The only difference after nearly a week of training in the deadly arts
was that now they were dressing each other's wounds, as well.

That morning, their instruction under Master Hawksworth had
reached a new stage. The girls weren't merely practicing anymore. They
were fighting—not just each other, but their father, too. Which meant
they'd done a lot of losing, and losing a sparring match with a mace or a
practice sword or even bare hands is bruising work.

Elizabeth winced as Jane ran the comb over a spot where her father
had rapped her with his bo staff. "A little tap," he'd called it at the time,
"to remind you to keep your guard up." When she'd wobbled and
feigned light-headedness, luring Mr. Bennet in for a (missed) lunge, she
didn't just get the usual "Not bad" from the Master, who watched the
matches, arms crossed, in a corner. She actually saw a hint of satisfaction
crack the granite hardness of the young man's face.

"Ow!"

Jane's comb had caught on the dressings wrapped round her head.

"I'm sorry, Lizzy. Why don't we stop?" Jane moaned, settling onto
her bed. "I feel as though my arms are about to fall off, anyhow."

"It's all right. It hardly matters if I have a tangle or two, does it? It's
not as though Mrs. Goswick will be dropping by." Elizabeth smiled at her
sister in the mirror. "Though I almost wish she would. I might not be
able to beat you or Father, but I'd love the chance to spar with *her*. She'd

come out of it with more than one 'little tap' to bandage, I'd wager."

"Lizzy, you must learn to be more forgiving," Jane said gravely. Yet she seemed to savor the image, and a moment later she returned her sister's smile—to Elizabeth's relief.

Master Hawksworth's resistance to the ball had been a disappointment, but it lacked the sting of a slight. So Mrs. Goswick's *un*vitation (as Elizabeth had dubbed it) had hurt Jane far more deeply. It had been four days since they'd received the lady's letter, and with each Elizabeth had tried a new tack with her brooding, wounded sister.

The first: enfolding arms and soft, soothing words.

The second: bitter recriminations and seething.

The third: refusing to speak of it.

The fourth: laughing about it.

This last had proved by far the most effective. She might have tried it first, only it had taken her all those days to be able to laugh again. She'd been in no hurry to marry, despite her mother's shoves toward the altar, yet to know that now a respectable marriage was forever denied her—that she and her sisters were, thanks to their father, outcasts—seemed to dry up every smile inside her. She'd been shocked to awaken that morning ready to make light of it all.

"It's not true, though," Jane said, and her smile turned sly in a way that was rare for her. "That it doesn't matter what you look like anymore, I mean. *Someone* notices."

"*Et tu*, Jane?" Elizabeth gasped in mock exasperation. "For Lydia and Kitty to indulge in such fantasies hardly surprises me: They need some outlet now that they have no coming-out balls or suitors to look forward to. But you—?"

Jane shook her head. "It is no fantasy. Master Hawksworth looks at you in a way he doesn't look at the rest of us."

"If he does, it is merely because he thinks me a promising student."

"I agree." Jane cocked a delicate eyebrow. "But promising *what*, I think, would be a fair question."

"Oh, don't look at me like that," Elizabeth laughed. "Salaciousness doesn't suit you."

"You're right," Jane sighed, collapsing onto her back. "And at any rate, I'm too tired for it."

Yet Elizabeth, despite her protestations, was not. She retrieved another brush from the bureau and continued working on her dark, gently curling hair, brushing out knots as she sought to unsnarl her own thoughts.

Yes—she *had* noticed how the Master looked at her. Not with the dewy eyes of the pitifully smitten. His gaze was sharper than that, piercing, as if he were straining to see something hidden behind her eyes.

And he wasn't the only one to lapse into the occasional stare. More than once, Elizabeth had found herself gazing upon him with what was, for her, an unfamiliar muddling of her thoughts. As a teacher, he was demanding, condescending, aloof. Yet he was also, without doubt, the most fascinating man she'd ever met.

It was more than his strapping handsomeness (though she had to admit, that counted for something). He was just so . . . different. And so unashamed about it. Elizabeth admired his confidence, even if it edged toward vanity. How he seemed to relish every opportunity to strip off coat and vest so as to demonstrate some new move. But perhaps such pride was simply the armor one needed to withstand the scorn of the Mrs. Goswicks (and, alas, the Mrs. Bennets) of this world.

If only there were some way she could strip away that armor and reach the man trapped within. He might be very different, underneath it all. Perhaps even as pleasing as his looks.

And his looks—they were pleasing indeed. So very, *very* pleasing . . .

"Lizzy, did you hear that?" Jane said.

Elizabeth blinked her eyes, and again she was seeing herself in the mirror instead of Master Hawksworth.

"Hmm, what, hear something?"

Jane was sitting up stiffly on her bed, and she turned toward the door and pointed. "Out there. In the hall."

Elizabeth listened. Then listened some more. And just when she was about to say "I don't hear anything," she did.

A soft, clacking sort of sound it was, like fingernails rapping lightly against glass or a fork tapped against a tabletop.

"You hear it?" Jane asked, voice low.

Elizabeth nodded.

"What do you think it is?"

"I . . . I don't know. I thought everyone else was asleep." Elizabeth attempted a nonchalant shrug, yet when she went on talking she did it at a whisper. "Perhaps it's a branch brushing against one of the windows."

"I don't think so."

Jane nodded at her own window. Outside, dark shapes loomed in the dim moonlight—the silhouettes of the nearest trees.

They were perfectly still. There was no wind that night.

The quiet clicking continued.

Then a floorboard creaked.

Elizabeth turned to the bureau, put the hairbrush upon it, and slid off the stiletto knife she'd left there earlier.

Jane reached under her pillow and pulled out her nunchucks.

Master Hawksworth had insisted that the girls begin sleeping with their weapons. "So that even in your dreams, you will remember you are warriors," he'd said. None of them had appreciated this much at first— particularly Lydia, who almost strangled herself with her own garrote one night as she dreamed she was putting on a new diamond choker. But Elizabeth was grateful for the edict now.

Slowly, she rose and crept toward the doorway. Moving silently was something they'd spent hours practicing that very day, walking again and again over a bed of twigs, dried leaves, and shards of shattered glass, doing laps and *dand-baithaks* by the score until they could all get across without making a sound. So there was no squeaking of old wood beneath their feet as they gathered together by the door.

The creaking outside, however, continued, as did the muffled rattle. "I will go first."

Whisper soft as Jane's words were, Elizabeth could still hear the tremble in them.

"We will go together," she said, and without waiting another moment—for what could waiting do but give fear more time to take root?—she opened the door.

Side by side, Jane and Elizabeth stepped forward, weapons at the ready. They found themselves in a soft, low light flickering along the hall—the glow of a single candle resting on the floor at the end of the corridor. Beside it in the dim light was a hunched form in a shroud-like gown, its back to the girls.

There was another rattle, and the thing at the end of the hall shifted its weight and moaned softly.

"It's trying to get into Father's room," Jane whispered.

Elizabeth started down the hall. "The stiletto would be best."

"No." Jane caught Elizabeth by the arm. "The nunchucks."

"Don't be a fool. This is work for a blade."

"That little thing? It has no range. With these, at least, I can stun it before—"

"You can't stun a zombie."

"Of course you can."

"No, you can't."

"We must ask Papa."

"Well, I hardly think now is the time."

"I didn't mean *now*."

Both girls raised their weapons and readied themselves for a charge. They froze, however, when the creature pressed itself to Mr. Bennet's door and *spoke*.

"Mr. Bennnn-nnnnnet . . . Mr. Bennnnn-nnnnnnet . . . open uuu-uuu-uuuuuup."

"I'm exhausted, woman," Elizabeth heard her father say. "Let me rest."

SIDE BY SIDE, JANE AND ELIZABETH STEPPED FORWARD,
WEAPONS AT THE READY.

"Oh, I won't disturb you. I just want a little company."

"You just want a male heir, you mean. And I'm too tired to give you one."

Jane gasped.

"Oh, my," said Elizabeth.

This was *worse* than finding a zombie in the house.

Mrs. Bennet finally heard the girls behind her and turned and screamed.

"What's going on?" cried Mary, bursting from her room clutching a trident.

Kitty and Lydia stumbled into the hall next, the former holding a battle-ax, the latter brandishing a chamber pot (for she'd ignored the Master's order and had left her cutlass out in the dojo).

"Who screamed? Who screamed?" Kitty panted.

Elizabeth nodded toward the far end of the hall.

"Oh, ummmm . . . I'm afraid that was me, dearest," said Mrs. Bennet, and she straightened up and started smoothing out the wrinkles in her nightgown. "Your sisters startled me, that's all."

"What were you doing out here, Mamma?" Lydia asked blearily, eyes half lidded.

Many's the time Elizabeth had thought her mother impervious to shame, but now, at last, she saw a blush on the lady's face.

"Just saying good night to your father."

"But you said good night to us all hours ago," Mary pointed out.

"Oh, hang it all! We're doomed! *Doomed!*" Mrs. Bennet blubbered, and she dashed down the hallway to her bedchamber, knocking her daughters aside like so many skittle pins.

"Good night, Mrs. Bennet!" Mr. Bennet called after her from behind his firmly locked door.

Mary, Kitty, and Lydia lowered their weapons and began shuffling wearily back to their beds.

"If these are the fruits of matrimony," Jane said softly, "we owe Mrs.

Goswick a letter of thanks."

Elizabeth trudged down the hall to retrieve the candle her mother had thoughtlessly left behind on the floor.

"Indeed," she sighed. "'Wedded bliss' would seem to be entirely overrated."

Countless times, she and Jane had exchanged similar sentiments after witnessing some unseemly scene between their parents. Yet, for the first time, the words felt strangely hollow to her.

She raised the candlestick to her face and puffed on the wick, but the little flame didn't go out.

CHAPTER 13

THE NEXT MORNING'S training began with the usual laps and *dand-baithaks* for everyone: for mustering on time instead of showing their devotion by arriving early; for breathing too loudly during morning meditation; for having their sparring gowns laced too tight; for having their sparring gowns laced too *loose*; for, in short, whatever Master Hawksworth could think up. The flimsiest of all the infractions was assigned to Mr. Bennet, who was sent outside to run a hundred sprints across the grounds—backward—for supposedly blinking too frequently.

"Remember: Even one wink of the eye gives The Enemy time to strike," the Master said. "Now, go!"

Mr. Bennet had lingered a moment, expressionless, before bowing and heading for the door.

It seemed to Elizabeth that Master Hawksworth relaxed a bit whenever her father wasn't around. He was less likely to dole out punishments from a corner of the dojo, leaving most of the actual demonstrations to Mr. Bennet, and more likely to take off his coat and vest and *move*. Sometimes, he merely demonstrated new stances. But other times—the times Elizabeth and her sisters loved most—he flew around the room showing off "ninja fighting styles" with names like the Striking Viper and the Tiger's Claw.

So it was to be this day.

"The time has come for the Way of the Panther," the Master said, stripping down to his shirt sleeves. "The panther is powerful, but supple. Quick, but controlled. Fierce, but poised. You, too, must be all these things. Like so."

He bounced off the walls demonstrating the Panther's Pounce. He sprang up into the rafters demonstrating the Panther's Bound. He whirled in blurred circles demonstrating the Panther's Swipe. And the girls watched in awe. His movements were so graceful, so beautiful, Elizabeth could imagine them more on the stage of a French ballet than in the middle of any battlefield.

And then the Master stopped dead in the middle of the dojo, suddenly still and stiff, not even breathing hard, and announced that it was time for the death move: the Panther's Kiss.

He looked into each of the girls' faces, lingering longest on Elizabeth before moving on to Jane.

"You," he said, and his eyes went sliding back to Elizabeth even before his head turned toward her, as well. It was as if the two parts of him weren't quite in alignment—clockwork gears no longer in mesh. "Up."

"Yes, Master."

Elizabeth stood, stepped forward, and let Hawksworth take her by the arm and spin her around so she was facing her sisters. Then he let go and slipped back behind her.

"The Kiss begins like this," Elizabeth heard him say. "Notice how I move slowly, smoothly. Not lunging but *sliding*—gliding in, so as not to startle my prey."

Something squeezed Elizabeth's waist, hard, like a corset being over-tightened. By the time she realized it was one of the Master's muscular arms wrapping around her, pinning her own arms to her sides, she felt his chest—his whole torso—brush up against her back.

"The left arm first, here, to prevent escape," Master Hawksworth said, pulling Elizabeth tightly against his body.

Elizabeth saw Mary stiffen and lean forward, taking in the demonstration with a peculiar intensity. Lydia and Kitty, meanwhile, were stifling grins, and even sweet Jane had a wicked gleam in her eye. It had been a hard time for them all, with many a tear, and Elizabeth would've been glad for the chance to give them some amusement if she hadn't been so mortified.

"Then the right arm," Hawksworth said. "Like this."

He stretched his other arm out straight over Elizabeth's shoulder, then bent it back, back, back until it was wrapped around her neck. Her whole body was pressing into his now, from her head to her heels. It almost felt as though he were a heavy cloak draped over her, or a bed upon which she was lying.

"Then," he said, "you squeeze."

The pressure on Elizabeth's waist and throat grew, escalating from (she had to admit) pleasant but discomfiting to simply uncomfortable. Instinctively, she tried to squirm, to loosen the grip ever tightening around her, but Master Hawksworth was too strong.

"The quarry cannot move . . . not even to draw air," Hawksworth said. His head was so close to Elizabeth's she could feel his breath blow over her ear as he spoke. "You can see why in some traditions this method goes by another name: the Python's Embrace."

He went on talking, but Elizabeth could catch only the occasional word—" . . . hold . . . minute . . . black . . . "—over the buzz growing ever louder in her ears and the pounding of her own heart. She could see the expressions on the other girls' faces begin to change, their lascivious glee dying, eyes growing wide. The whole room began to go gray around the edges, a dark circle on the periphery of her vision tightening until Elizabeth seemed to be looking down a long tunnel with her sisters at the end. And then even they faded away, and all she could see was a distant smear of gauzy light.

" . . . sleep . . . ," she heard Hawksworth say. " . . . death . . . "

The light began to go out.

Elizabeth wouldn't let it.

She brought her right knee forward, then kicked her foot back and up with all the strength she had left. It was a variation on the Fulcrum of Doom her father had taught her. The Axis of Calamity.

It found its intended target.

"Oooo!" Elizabeth heard Hawksworth say very, very clearly indeed, and the Python or the Panther, whichever, let her go, and she stumbled forward gasping for breath.

Jane was instantly at her side.

"Lizzy! Are you all right?"

"Yes . . . yes, I think so."

With each lungful of air, Elizabeth's world widened and brightened, until at last all the grayness was gone. And this is what she saw: Hawksworth bent over, head hanging low, hands in a most undignified arrangement. Mary was beside him, bending over to try to look him in the face.

"Master? Do you require aid?"

His first reply came out as a squeaky wheeze. Then he squeezed his eyes shut, took in a deep breath, and tried again.

"I am in no more pain than I deserve. Go. Find your father. He can take over your training while I . . . meditate on this."

"Master," Elizabeth said.

She started to ask what had just happened, if something had gone wrong, but she stopped herself. The student was not to question the master's actions. She started, then, to say she was sorry for panicking, but she stopped herself again. A warrior doesn't apologize.

Oh, how was she ever to truly *talk* to this man?

There was only one thing she could say, so she said it.

"How many *dand-baithaks?*"

"For you, Elizabeth Bennet?" Hawksworth said. "None. The fault was not yours. I let myself become . . . careless." He turned away and began hobbling, hunchbacked, toward the darkest corner of the dojo. "We will resume the Way of the Panther in one hour. Until then, leave me."

The girls bowed and began to file outside. Elizabeth left last, lingering in the doorway, unsure if there was more she still might try to say or more she longed to hear. Hawksworth settled himself, ever so slowly, into a stooped, cross-legged squat on the floor, his back still to her, and after a long, silent moment she moved on.

She found her sisters already gathered around Mr. Bennet.

"—and then she kicked Master Hawksworth in the . . . ," Mary was saying. Her cheeks flushed pink, and she leaned toward her father, hand cupped to mouth, and whispered in his ear.

Mr. Bennet frowned . . . yet it seemed to Elizabeth his eyes were smiling.

"Why did you do it, Lizzy?" Lydia asked as she joined them.

"Yes, tell us, Lizzy!" Kitty said. "Were you cross or simply frightened?"

"I was being strangled. Need I really explain beyond that?"

"Didn't you hear the Master say the Panther's Kiss can be used as a 'sleeper hold'?" Mary asked. "That he could bring you to the brink of unconsciousness without doing you any harm?"

"It is rather difficult to hear properly when being throttled," Elizabeth replied. "Shall I demonstrate?"

She brought her hands up toward Mary's throat, and her sister actually blanched and hopped back behind their father.

"No, that's quite all right, thank you."

Elizabeth dropped her arms to her sides, ashamed. She knew it wasn't her younger sisters she was angry at, thoughtless though they were.

"The Axis of Calamity, eh?" her father said. "I'm sure that made quite an impression on the Master . . . and perhaps, I'm beginning to think, just where he needed one most."

"What do you mean, Papa?" Mary asked.

Mr. Bennet ignored her.

"Now, seeing as you're back in my hands for the next hour, I'd say it's time for something your training has, so far, entirely overlooked. Something I feel I owe you all, given the sacrifices I've asked you to make."

He paused until Jane finally asked the inevitable question.

"Which is what, Father?"

Mr. Bennet smiled. "Fun. There is, you will observe, a stag striking a most majestic pose upon that hilltop."

The girls followed his gaze to the east, and saw, not a quarter mile away, the great, antlered buck their father spoke of.

"Kiss it."

"Kiss it?" Mary said.

"Yes. Catch it and kiss it."

Lydia grimaced. "On the lips?"

Mr. Bennet shrugged. "Or the nose or the cheek or whatever else you might prefer."

"You expect us," Jane said slowly, "to catch a deer and hold it long enough to kiss it?"

"Oh, goodness me, no!" Mr. Bennet chuckled. "Not all of you. But your training has, I suspect, brought you further, faster than you think, and one of you might manage it—and whichever of you it is will get the rest of the hour off to do whatever she pleases."

Jane was already halfway to the stag before anyone else was even running.

Elizabeth took off after the deer with no hope of actually catching it. The big buck quickly saw the girls coming, wheeled about, and bolted. How were such as they to catch one of the fleetest creatures in the forest?

Yet the distance between her and the hill disappeared with surprising speed, and even when she charged up the bluff and into the trees, she found herself hardly slowed at all. The deer kept to no path, of course, simply crashing through the bramble, and Elizabeth was soon doing the same—bursting through bushes, hurdling over streams and rocks, dodging tree trunks that flew past her in a smear of brown.

All those *dand-baithaks*, all those laps, all those hours meditating and sparring and wielding the weight of swords and axes and heavy wooden staffs—it was working!

All around, Elizabeth could hear her sisters laughing as they, too, discovered what they could now do. And she joined in.

The stag began to zigzag, cutting left, then right as the girls closed in. Though Elizabeth was now closer to him than ever, he grew harder to see: The chase had led them into the darkest, thickest of thickets. Soon, all she had to guide her was the sound of the buck's flight up ahead, but then even that began to fade. Elizabeth pushed herself harder, trying to squeeze out even more speed, and when she came to a tangle of thick vines, she sought to vault herself over it with one of the Master's moves, the Leaping Leopard, instead of sparing the extra second to go around. She sprung up high enough to catch sight of the deer again, ghostly white shapes—her sisters in their sparring gowns—converging on it from all sides.

Then her left foot caught on a vine, and she spun end over end to the earth.

She landed on her left knee, rolled, landed on her back, rolled, and kept landing and rolling and landing and rolling until she finally came to a stop against the broad base of an old oak tree. She lay there for a moment, panting, and allowed herself a small indulgence she would not have otherwise engaged in even if only Jane had been there to hear it.

"*Damn.*"

When she finally dared sit up and catalogue her wounds, she found, to her infinite relief, no twigs sticking from her side, no shattered femurs jutting from her thighs, no digits missing, no long strips of skin flapping loose and bloody. She could even stand up and limp around. So it only *felt like* she'd crushed every bone and organ in her body.

She'd raced into the forest faster than a fleeing stag. Now she began hobbling out again with all the speed of a three-legged tortoise.

Her sisters were nowhere in sight, and Elizabeth could only assume they were far off now, smothering the buck with kisses. Yet after she'd taken but a few steps back toward Longbourn, she noticed something moving off to her left—a dark shape blotting out rays of dappled sun. Perhaps she wasn't the only one who'd fallen behind.

She turned and started toward the shifting shadows. They were being cast by movement in a small glade, she saw as she drew closer. And there were *two* shapes.

It was Kitty and Lydia, surely, the two of them taking advantage of their father's indulgence to pause and pick wildflowers—or gossip about her and Master Hawksworth.

But hadn't she seen them heading the other way, mere strides behind the stag?

The thought came to her too late. The "Lydia?" was already halfway off her lips as she stepped into the dell.

Two dreadfuls looked her way.

They were on the other side of the clearing, turned toward each other, as though they'd been chatting away like two friendly neighbors. One must have been weeks if not months dead, for its clothes and flesh had rotted clear through in spots, and what remained was tattered and gray. Not much was left of its face—just clumps stuck to skull, some still heavy with thick, black hair. It had sported a beard, back when it wasn't an "it."

The other unmentionable was male, as well, yet it was far, far fresher. Though its skin was tinted green, it had yet to rot enough to begin falling off, and the clothes were dirty and frayed but hardly worm eaten. The mouth was set in a large O, the eyebrows arched high on its forehead. Whatever had killed it seemed to have been a considerable surprise.

Elizabeth knew the feeling. She started to let another "Damn" slip, but caught it just in time. It seemed unwise to have a curse on her lips with Judgment so close at hand.

The more decayed of the dreadfuls gurgled a sound at her, part growl, part groan, then began staggering toward her with startling speed.

Fast as the zombie was, and bruised and battered as Elizabeth was, she might have outrun it had she tried. Yet something—shock, training, or mere foolishness, she had no time to decide which—kept her from turning away.

She reached down, unsheathed the ankle dagger she'd worn to the dojo that morning, and assumed the Natural Stance. When the unmentionable was twenty feet off, she let the blade fly, and—to Elizabeth's relieved surprise—it buried itself between the creature's red, rheumy eyes.

She quickly decided on her next step: retrieve the dagger from the dead dreadful's head so she could turn on the other zombie and throw it again. Unfortunately, there was a snag to her plan.

The dreadful didn't die. It just kept coming toward her, arms out, mouth open wide, dagger handle jutting from its face.

Elizabeth didn't even get through her mantra once—"Smooth stone beneath still AHHH!"—and the unmentionable was on her, grabbing for her shoulders and snapping at her neck. She hopped back and, for the second time that morning, set a foot streaking into someone's nether regions.

Or some*thing's* nether regions, this time. Which made all the difference.

The unmentionable's unmentionables might have just been squashed flat, but the creature showed no sign of noticing. Instead, it merely took hold of the foot that had been planted in its mushy-rotten groin, pulled it up toward its mouth, and leaned in for a bite. Elizabeth toppled backward to the ground, unable to do anything but watch in horror as her toes approached the dreadful's gaping maw.

Just before the zombie could launch into its first chomp, there was a loud *pop*, and a spray of black pulp shot from the side of the creature's head. As slowly as a felled tree, the unmentionable tilted, teetered, and then toppled forward onto Elizabeth.

By the time she managed to struggle out from under it, she found the other zombie crouching down beside her . . . with a smoking flint-lock in its hand.

"I do apologize," the dreadful said. "It took me ever so long to get a clear shot."

CHAPTER 14

BY THE TIME THE UNMENTIONABLE had helped Elizabeth to her feet, it was obvious he wasn't an unmentionable at all. He was a man—albeit one with tousled hair, filthy clothes, and face and hands smeared with either thick green greasepaint or pea soup.

"What are you doing out here dressed like that?" Elizabeth asked, far, far too unnerved for a simple "Thank you" or "How do you do?"

The man grinned, flashing big, pearly white teeth.

"Testing a theory!" he enthused (and it was a disconcerting thing, seeing what looked like a dreadful enthuse). "I thought it might be possible to mingle with the zombies. Disguise life. They are frightfully dim, you know. That's one of the few advantages we have over them. We're easy to kill, and they're thick as bricks. I've often wondered, if people didn't make a habit of screaming and running around and such every time they saw a zombie, would the poor things even know whom to eat? Simply remaining calm might be the best defense we have, it seemed to me. Muss your hair, cock your head, and groan out a few oooohs and ahhhhs, and the undead might well shuffle right past!"

Despite everything—her stinging scrapes and throbbing bruises, the stench of rotting flesh on the air, the lingering jolt of terror she could still feel tingling over her goosepimpled skin—Elizabeth found herself smil-

BY THE TIME THE UNMENTIONABLE HAD HELPED ELIZABETH TO HER
FEET, IT WAS OBVIOUS HE WASN'T AN UNMENTIONABLE AT ALL.

ing back at the man.

"Was it working?" she asked.

"Well, no," the man said, still grinning. "When you arrived, I do believe our friend here was about to eat me. Then perhaps *you* would've had the chance to save *me*. That throw you made with your knife was absolutely smashing, by the by! Had the blade been but a little larger, it would have done the job admirably. As it is, I don't think it penetrated the medulla oblongata. That's the trick, you know—severing the connection between the cerebellum and the spinal cord. Or, barring that, making sure there's nothing left for the spinal cord to connect *to*. It's one of the great puzzles about the zombies, if you ask me: Why would the undead need their brains? If they're animated by, oh, *evil* or whatever you want to call it, how could anything purely physiological have any effect on . . . oh, dear. There's something hanging from one of my nostrils, isn't there?"

"No, no . . . it's just . . . "

Elizabeth kept gaping at the man as he rubbed his rather prodigious nose. When he was done, there was a bare spot on the tip where he'd wiped away the paint, a little dot of pink shining out from the chalky green.

"You're not from around here, are you?" Elizabeth said.

"No, indeed. I've just arrived from London with a company of His Majesty's finest. Well, I *hope* they're his finest. His Majesty's youngest and most ill trained, they seem to me. Not that I know anything about military discipline. And they're in fine, new, spotless red coats, at least, so I suppose that counts for something. They're all off that way." He flapped a long arm toward the west, then reconsidered and squinted to the east. "Or was it that way? I've managed to get myself more than a little lost, I must admit. At any rate, the soldiers are setting up camp outside that little village close by here . . . somewhere."

"You mean Meryton?"

"Yes, that's the one. Charming hamlet, that. A shame about the zombies."

"Yes. It is."

Elizabeth looked the man up and down again. Though he was tall and lean—clearly full grown, if nowhere near aged—there remained something childlike about him. Perhaps it was his natural exuberance, perhaps the wide, brown eyes so full of wonder. Perhaps it was the leaves and twigs in his dark hair, and the fact that he didn't appear to mind them in the slightest. Whatever it was, it made him seem both irrepressibly curious and achingly vulnerable, and Elizabeth felt the strange urge to take him by the hand and ask if he'd like a piece of candy.

"Did you bring more shot and powder for your pistol?" she asked.

"What? Oh. Powder?" The man stared at his flintlock as if he'd forgotten he was holding it. "No. If I did need this, I assumed, there'd hardly be time to reload for a second shot."

Elizabeth turned back to the dead dreadful stretched out on the ground and took hold of the dagger jutting from its forehead. After a little tugging, the blade popped free with a sickening slurp.

"I think it might be best if I were to escort you back to Meryton." She wiped the knife on the ground, then slid it back into its ankle scabbard, careful to keep any exposed leg hidden from the gentleman. "We can't have you wandering lost alone in these woods."

Elizabeth waited for those big, brown eyes to blink, for the ebullience to be replaced by indignation.

"You . . . escort *me*?" she expected to hear.

"Splendid!" the man said instead. "That'll give me a chance to ask about the zombies hereabouts. Was this the first one you've seen yourself?"

Elizabeth answered as she led the stranger out of the woods to the nearest lane, telling him about Mr. Ford's funeral and Lord Lumpley's dreadful (in every sense) hunting party. He showed no sign of surprise when she mentioned her own role in both events, merely asking when she was done, "Are all Hertfordshire girls so intrepid?"

"Only my sisters and myself, so far as I know."

"Ah. More's the pity . . . " The stranger had been wiping his face as they walked, and now he waved his green-smeared handkerchief the way they'd just come. "And what of that poor soul back there? Did you recognize him?"

Elizabeth shook her head. "There wasn't much left one *could* recognize."

"True. Yet from his clothes and what was left of his hair, I fancy we could whip up a hypothesis, or make a decent guess, at least. Now . . . "

The young man—for such he turned out to be when the paint came off his face—tapped a long finger against his chin.

"When I came across him in that clearing, he was crawling around stuffing voles in his mouth. I saw no sign of fresh soil upon him, nor was that a shroud he wore—it was shabby, worn clothing. A wild-haired, bearded fellow, he seemed to be, as well. So. Supposition: He was a nomadic peddler or vagabond who died in the woods some time ago, perhaps at the hands of a gentleman of the road, perhaps lost in foul weather, perhaps . . . oh, I don't know. Perhaps he was eaten by voles. It would explain his lust for revenge upon them. At any rate, he was never buried—which would be in keeping with the other zombies seen in the vicinity of late, as none so far have dug their way from an actual grave."

The man looked over at Elizabeth, obviously eager for her thoughts on his theory. He quickly furrowed his brow and brushed at his beak of a nose.

Without meaning to, she'd been giving him that look again.

"May I ask *you* a few questions?" she said.

"Certainly . . . so long as 'Were you dropped on your head as a child?' isn't among them. I've grown rather tired of that one."

"It's actually The Zed Word I'm wondering about."

"*Zombie*? What of it?"

"Well, there it is again. You *use* it. Quite liberally."

"Why shouldn't I?"

"It's not polite."

The young man threw his arms out and railed up at the heavens.

"Oh, we can't have that, can we? We can't go around being *impolite* when we're about to be overrun by reanimated cadavers! Egad—the English! How can we face a problem squarely when we can't even bring ourselves to name it?"

And just as suddenly as it had begun, the tirade ended, and the man looked into Elizabeth's eyes and smiled.

"What else were you wondering about?"

"Who *are* you?"

The question popped out with far less subtlety than Elizabeth would have preferred, and the man opened his eyes wide again, clapping a hand to his cheek as if he'd just been slapped.

"Oh, dear me! I've done it again! I am forever forgetting the importance of proper introductions. As there is no one here to do the honors for us . . . " He cleared his throat and, without missing a step, offered Elizabeth a bow. "Dr. Bertram Keckilpenny, at your service."

Elizabeth hoped her eyebrows didn't fly up *too* high at that "Doctor." Keckilpenny's intelligence was obvious, but he hardly seemed old enough to be anything but a particularly gifted (and eccentric) second-year at Cambridge.

"I am pleased to make your acquaintance. My name is Elizabeth Bennet."

It seemed horribly forward, introducing herself like that, and she felt all the more self-conscious when Keckilpenny goggled his eyes at her yet again.

"*Bennet*, you say? Bennet, Bennet, Bennet. Hmm. It seems to me that name's ever so important, somehow. You're not famous are you, Miss Bennet?"

"Me?" Elizabeth laughed. "No, I should think not."

The laughter died on her lips when she saw what stood in their path.

Up the lane a way was one of her neighbors—a gossip-prone crone by the name of Mrs. Adams. The old woman was watching their approach with a mix of horror and exhilaration on her face. She obviously couldn't wait to tell someone, anyone, of what she'd seen, and she wouldn't have far to go to do it, either: Meryton was just around the next bend.

"Good morning, Mrs. Adams!" Elizabeth called to her.

The woman managed a brusque nod, then turned and scurried toward town.

"Your question has proved prophetic, Doctor," Elizabeth said. "I believe I soon *will* be famous in these parts. Notorious, even . . . if I'm not already."

It took Keckilpenny a moment to grasp her meaning, so far removed were his thoughts from propriety and the need to keep up appearances.

"Ahhhhh." He looked over at Elizabeth's dirty, blood-speckled sparring gown, then down at his own shabby attempt to dress like a moldy old dreadful. "Well, I should think any young lady able to face a zombie without flinching wouldn't have any trouble facing her neighbors."

And he offered Elizabeth his arm.

She smiled gratefully and accepted, and the two of them strolled into Meryton with the stately grace of a lord and his lady about to be announced at a court ball. Elizabeth kept up conversation with Dr. Keckilpenny all through town, singling out points of particular interest to him (St. Chad's Church, the adjacent graveyard, the haberdashery where Emily Ward had once worked), the better to blot out the titters and whispers from all around. The shock and shame of being uninvited to the ball had nearly killed her mother, and now this scene—when, inevitably, relayed back to Longbourn by her Aunt Philips—might well finish the job.

Elizabeth silently castigated herself for thinking of this, even ever so briefly, as a possible silver lining to her humiliation.

She finally found refuge from her neighbors' reproachful stares when they reached the village green, for here it was soldiers doing all the staring. Some were putting up white-peaked tents, others were in the midst of marching drills complete with fife and drum, yet all (it seemed to Elizabeth) had their eyes on her.

"Porter!" Dr. Keckilpenny called to one of them. "I say, Private Porter!"

The soldier peered at him in confusion, then said, "It's Corporal Parker, Sir."

"Yes, yes, Parker, Parker. Do be a good fellow and fetch the colonel, would you? There's someone here I think he should meet."

"Very good, Sir. I'll go get the *captain*."

Cpl. Parker favored Elizabeth with a smirk before hustling away.

"I'm afraid I must bid you *au revoir*, Miss Bennet," Dr. Keckilpenny said, and he tapped the side of his head with a crooked finger. "There is fresh data here, much of it, and I must set it all down in my journals before it degrades. Friend Parker's name I can get wrong—as I get almost all names wrong until I've known someone at least a decade—but science demands precision. Before we part, however, I must thank you for taking the time and care to guide me here safely. You have my deepest gratitude," the young man put his hands over his heart, "and admiration. Ah! Capt. Cannon!"

The doctor looked off to the left, and before Elizabeth turned that way, too, she might have guessed from the sound of squeaking axles and grass being flattened that someone was pushing a wheelbarrow their way. As indeed someone was, though it wasn't so much a wheelbarrow as a wheeled *man*.

Strapped to a seatback mounted on a small cart was a big, bluff officer with bushy white eyebrows and mustache and mutton chops . . . and no arms or legs.

"Limbs, halt!" he barked.

The soldiers pushing him—one for each wooden shaft of the wheelbarrow—came to a sudden stop.

"Dr. Keckilpenny," the torso-man growled, "I've had two squads out combing the countryside for you when I can't spare so much as—"

"Oh, I know, I know, apologies, apologies!" Dr. Keckilpenny said cheerfully, and he began hurrying off into the camp. "But I'm back now, thanks to the young lady here. Allow me to introduce Miss Elizabeth Bennet. Miss Bennet—Capt. Cannon. Good-bye now. Must dash!"

He darted around a tent and was gone.

It seemed a decidedly unchivalrous exit, abandoning her to the fuming glower of a stranger, and such a truly strange one, at that.

Capt. Cannon took a moment to look Elizabeth up and down—then surprised her with a warm smile.

"You wouldn't be a relation of Mr. Oscar Bennet, would you?"

"Indeed, I would. He is my father."

"Capital!" the captain boomed. "Then once you're rested and refreshed, you may lead me straight to him. He's just the man we've come here to see!"

CHAPTER 15

CAPT. CANNON'S GOOD CHEER didn't last long: He turned grim again when Elizabeth told him, in answer to his question about her scrapes and bruises, that some she'd acquired courtesy of an unmentionable not half an hour before.

"Limbs! Lean!"

The soldiers behind him tilted his little cart up on its front wheel, lifting the armless, legless man closer to Elizabeth's ear.

"The dreadful," Capt. Cannon whispered. "He didn't *nip* you, did he?"

"No."

The captain sighed with relief. He obviously knew firsthand what had to be done after a nip from an unmentionable.

"Limbs! Pace!" he commanded, and his attendants lowered him again and began wheeling him first this way, then that. "So. Another rotter already. Blast!"

"We've encountered one other unmentionable, as well," Elizabeth said. "Aside from Mr. Ford, I mean. He was the first, from the church. I assume it was news of his . . . awakening that brought you to Meryton?"

"Precisely. Your father has friends in London who . . . ah! Lieutenant Tindall! What splendid timing. Limbs! Halt!"

The captain's "pacing" stopped just as a handsome, flaxen-haired young officer came striding up to offer a crisp salute.

"Sir," Lt. Tindall said, "we never found him."

"That's because he's back in his tent scribbling in his journals. Miss Bennet here was kind enough to return him to us."

"Miss *Bennet*?"

The young man turned a curious stare on Elizabeth. She thought she caught a slight wrinkling of his nose when he noticed her contusions and dirt-smeared sparring dress.

"That's right," Capt. Cannon said. "She'll be taking me to her father forthwith. And, Lieutenant, the game's afoot. I will require an escort. Re-group your search party and report back here."

"Right away, Sir."

Lt. Tindall saluted again and hurried off.

"He's been out looking for Dr. Keckilpenny?" Elizabeth asked the captain.

"Yes. Our 'necrosis consultant'—whatever that is—managed to get himself lost all of thirty minutes after we reached Meryton. And the doc-tor might be young . . . and inexperienced . . . and rather an odd duck, truth be told . . . "

Capt. Cannon seemed to lose his train of thought, and Elizabeth prodded him with what she guessed his next word was meant to be. "But . . . ?"

"But the War Office wanted him with us, so I couldn't let him stay lost. I see the lieutenant's ready for us. Shall we, Miss Bennet?"

And so began the march to Longbourn. The soldiers did most of the marching, actually. Elizabeth simply walked, though she kept finding herself stepping in time to the *tromp-tromp-tromp* of the infantrymen's heavy footfalls. Lt. Tindall was to one side of her, Capt. Cannon and his

Limbs to the other, while behind were a dozen troops, each with a Brown Bess on his shoulder.

As if Elizabeth's entry into Meryton hadn't attracted notice enough, now she was leaving at the head of a parade. At least this time no one laughed.

It would have been impossible to carry on a quiet conversation with the captain now that the under-greased wheels of his cart were squeaking and rumbling along the road, so Elizabeth turned to Lt. Tindall instead. He presented quite a pleasing profile, yet with his ramrod bearing and unwavering gaze—never blinking, always straight ahead—he hardly seemed amenable to banter, and she said nothing. Of course, it wouldn't do for her to make conversation with the foot soldiers, either (though they were all around Elizabeth's own age and seemed much more prone to friendly smiles than she would've imagined battle-hardened warriors to be). So it was a long, silent, awkward journey back to Longbourn.

As they neared her family's small estate, Elizabeth became aware of a very different sort of discomfort than mere embarrassment. A strange chill was running up and down her arms and over the back of her neck, and it seemed to grow stronger with each step. It wasn't a cool breeze; the air was dead still and unseasonably warm. It was more like her skin was feeling some other swirl in the ether, not a wind but a shift. A change.

A presence.

They were just passing the spot on the road she'd led Dr. Keckilpenny to from the forest sometime before. The dreadful the young doctor had killed would be but sixty or seventy yards off, hidden behind hillocks and bramble. Elizabeth dredged up the memory of it, trying to recall every detail, each dollop of gore upon the ground.

Was it possible to stun a dreadful? Could one of the sorry stricken be knocked unconscious but not killed?

Did a zombie still prowl the woods around Longbourn?

Instinctively, Elizabeth looked over at Capt. Cannon, as she would have turned to her father had he been there. Or Master Hawksworth.

"It's the stench," the captain said, and Elizabeth knew he was speaking to her though he was peering off into the woods. "Even when you don't know you're smelling it, you are."

"Sir?" Lt. Tindall said. He hadn't noticed a thing.

"On your guard, men," the captain rumbled.

The soldiers slowed their march to a scuffling stumble, and Lt. Tindall put his hand to the hilt of his sword.

Elizabeth suddenly missed her katana.

"There's the bugger!" one of the soldiers cried out, pointing at a huge, knot-rippled tree up ahead.

Standing beside it was a shadowy figure cloaked in black.

"It's a flippin' road agent!" another soldier laughed, sounding relieved.

Indeed, Elizabeth could see as they drew slowly closer, the man was wearing a mask and tricornered hat, and he had a flintlock pistol clutched in his right hand.

"Why, it must be the Black Thistle!"

"The *what*?" Lt. Tindall said.

"A highwayman," Elizabeth explained. "Hertfordshire's most infamous. But he hasn't been heard from in months."

"The knife in his belly accounts for that, I'll wager," Capt. Cannon said.

The soldiers all stopped, even the Limbs, though the captain hadn't told them to halt.

Capt. Cannon was right. Jutting from the bandit's side, pinning his cloak tight to his body, was the rough-hewn wooden handle of a large knife.

"Eep," a soldier said.

"Bloody 'ell," muttered another.

The Black Thistle unleashed a blood-freezing shriek and came charging toward them at a lurching lope.

"Fire at will," Capt. Cannon said coolly.

Unfortunately, no one had the will to fire. Half the captain's soldiers tossed down their muskets. All of them turned and ran.

"Blast," Capt. Cannon groaned, sounding more resigned than surprised or angry. His Limbs had turned and run off, too, so all he could do was watch the unmentionable come straight at him, its black cloak flapping as it ran.

Elizabeth drew her ankle dagger and stepped in front of the captain's cart, praying her second throw of the day would prove deadlier than the first.

She never even got a chance to try it. Lt. Tindall immediately stepped in front of *her*, pushing her aside with a sweep of the arm that sent her stumbling back into what would have been the captain's lap, if he'd had one.

"Run!" the lieutenant yelled, bringing up his sword as the dreadful closed in. "You might yet escape!"

"I don't *want* to!" Elizabeth started to say.

The unmentionable leapt at them with another deafening shriek.

Lt. Tindall impaled it on his sword.

The zombie grabbed the soldier's head and stuffed it into its mouth.

Fortunately for the lieutenant, there were two things in the way of a clean bite: the dreadful's black mask and his own high-peaked shako hat. Bits of both were disappearing down the creature's gullet as Lt. Tindall frantically jerked his sword this way and that in its belly, dislodging chunks of ragged, desiccated flesh it seemed to miss not at all. The zombie just kept chomping away, oblivious in its rapacity, holding Lt. Tindall in place with gray, scaly hands . . . in one of which, Elizabeth noticed, it still clutched its flintlock pistol.

The hammer was cocked.

Elizabeth dropped her dagger, sprang toward the unmentionable, and tried to pry the flintlock from its grip. She quickly got the gun—and the hand wrapped around it, as well. It snapped off at the wrist with a dry crackle.

The zombie threw Lt. Tindall aside and turned toward Elizabeth.

"Give my regards to Satan," she said, and she brought up the flint-lock and pulled back on the finger still wrapped around the trigger.

The hammer came down with a dull click . . . and that was it. Even if there were any powder left in the pistol, it had long since been turned to useless grit by rain and frost.

"Drat," said Elizabeth, though even to her own ears this sounded woefully inadequate, considering the calamity at hand.

The dreadful took two steps toward her. Somewhere between the first and the second, its head was sliced off by two different swords that met in the middle of its neck. It took the rest of its body a moment to notice, though, and it pitched forward into the dirt with its legs still trying to walk.

"Ewwww," said Kitty as the Black Thistle convulsed and finally died.

"La!" said Lydia, her katana, like her sister's, smeared with black slime. "Oh, Lizzy, if you could only see the look on your face!"

CHAPTER 16

ONCE HE'D PICKED HIMSELF UP and carefully dusted himself off, Lt. Tindall deigned to thank Elizabeth's sisters. But there was an icy edge to his tone, Elizabeth thought, especially when compared to Capt. Cannon's warm compliments on the girls' courage and prowess. Lydia and Kitty seemed not to notice the younger man's frostiness, however. In fact, they barely glanced at the captain, as the lieutenant's fair-haired, square-jawed comeliness proved so mesmerizing it trumped even the sight of an armless, legless man riding in a wheelbarrow.

The headless, lifeless man lying in the road they ignored, too, though it was easier to see the effort that required. As soon as they could, both girls put their backs to the body, and when Lt. Tindall trundled his commander away so that they might "regroup the column," their inevitable titters sounded, at first, forced and joyless.

"Ooh, he looks good in red," Lydia said.

"He'd look good in anything," said Kitty.

"Wherever did you find him, Lizzy?"

"Yes, Lizzy—where have you been?"

"We've been looking for you everywhere."

"Even Master Hawksworth was worried."

"'Even'?"

"You're right. *Especially* him!"

"Oh, I almost kissed the deer!"

"Me, too!"

"Jane came the closest, of course."

"Mary was nowhere near it."

"It's a shame, really. For what other kisses can the poor girl look forward to?"

"I can guess which ones she *wishes* were—"

"Come," Elizabeth cut in, setting off down the road. If someone didn't interrupt her sisters, they'd still be standing there chattering come nightfall. "There are soldiers scattered throughout these woods like so many acorns. Let us help gather them up."

It took but a few minutes of searching to bring everyone together again. The soldiers that didn't come creeping sheepishly out from behind trees and rocks were herded up the road by Lt. Tindall and Capt. Cannon. While they collected their discarded muskets and cleared the zombie carcass from the road, Lydia and Kitty stood to the side, attempting to engage the lieutenant in idle conversation. (Lydia: "What a shame your darling hat was eaten. We can recommend a haberdasher in town, if you like." Kitty: "He does all our bonnets!") Through it all, however, Lt. Tindall remained as stiff as a tin soldier, and once the party was moving on to Longbourn again, he ignored the girls altogether.

Unfazed, they simply went back to peppering their sister with questions about where she'd been and what she'd been doing. They found Dr. Keckilpenny particularly fascinating, of course—especially when they learned (after much wheedling) that he was young and rather handsome, in his gangly, gawky way.

"I wonder what Master Hawksworth would make of that," said Lydia.

"He'd probably do a Panther's Pounce right on this doctor fellow's head!" Kitty laughed.

"Ooooo! Let us see!"

Lydia grabbed Kitty by the arm and practically dragged her toward the forest, where Master Hawksworth and the others were still searching for Elizabeth.

"Surely that can wait until we reach Longbourn," Elizabeth said. "We still need to show the captain and his men the way to the house."

"One can do that as easily as three!" Lydia called back over her shoulder.

"But there might be more dreadfuls about!"

"Oh, I don't think so. And anyway, we've still got our swords!"

And Lydia tugged her rather alarmed-looking sister into the shadowy murk of the woods.

"I hope you will excuse my sisters' impetuousness," Elizabeth said to Capt. Cannon and Lt. Tindall. "They are so young. . . . "

"Yes. Quite," the lieutenant sniffed, clearly wondering—if not asking—about the kind of young lady who could run around the countryside alternately gossiping and decapitating the living dead.

The captain, for his part, blew out a snort not unlike the whinnying of a horse. "There is nothing to excuse, Miss Bennet. I can but wish my own troops had half your sisters' boldness!"

To a man, the foot soldiers cringed and drooped their shoulders, and as Elizabeth led them up the lane, they marched with such shambling, shuffling steps they seemed no livelier than a platoon of dreadfuls.

When they at last reached Longbourn, they found Mrs. Bennet

wearing a groove into the lawn with her pacing, weeping and wailing as Mrs. Hill toddled along behind to keep her supplied with fresh hankies.

"Oh, I knew this day would come! Off they trot into the wilds without a care in the world what should happen to their poor mother, and now the unmentionables shall have their luncheon! Oh, my sweet girls! My sweet, tender, juicy girls! How could Mr. Bennet—*Lizzy!*"

Mrs. Bennet raced to her daughter and threw her arms around her.

"Oh, Lizzy! At least *you* are still alive! Oh, my dearest, my beloved, my—"

She pushed Elizabeth aside and stepped toward Capt. Cannon with wide, moist eyes.

"Cuthbert?" she whimpered.

"Prudence?" he replied.

"Oh, Cuthbert! It *is* you! After all these years!"

"Limbs! Embrace the lady!"

The captain's attendants put down the wheelbarrow and stepped forward with obvious reluctance.

"Limbs! Halt!" Capt. Cannon choked out. "Pru, if I'd . . . The Troubles . . . I didn't think you'd . . . " He cleared his throat and straightened his back and started over again, as if addressing the woman before him for the first time. "You are the lady of the house?"

"I am," Mrs. Bennet said softly, eyes downcast, and for a moment, Elizabeth thought her mother actually looked diffident.

A very *brief* moment.

"I have come to see Mr. Bennet on a matter of great importance," Capt. Cannon said.

Mrs. Bennet reached back so Mrs. Hill could slap a dry handkerchief into her hand.

"He has abandoned me!" Mrs. Bennet cried, pressing the linen to her quivering lips. "Left me here all alone while he gallivants about the ghoul-plagued woodlands searching for our wayward daughter!"

"Mamma! I am not 'wayward'! It's just that—"

"OH, CUTHBERT! IT *IS* YOU! AFTER ALL THESE YEARS!"

Elizabeth clamped her lips together. The tale she had to tell—particularly injuring herself trying to kiss a deer and being set upon by dreadfuls not once but twice—would soothe her mother not a jot.

She opened her mouth again when she'd settled on the best possible distraction.

"Let us discuss all that later. Lydia and Kitty should be back shortly with Papa and the others. Until they return, we have guests to entertain, do we not?"

Mrs. Bennet shifted her gaze to Capt. Cannon and shoved her hankie back at Mrs. Hill, her tears instantly dried.

"So we do," she said. "For surely these fine officers would consent to keep us company until they can see to their business with Mr. Bennet?"

"It would be an honor," Capt. Cannon said. "Isn't that right, Lieutenant?"

Lt. Tindall had been watching the various reunions—Elizabeth and Mrs. Bennet, "Cuthbert" and "Prudence," Mrs. Hill and the handkerchief—with something exceedingly close to a sneer. He answered the captain with a noncommittal noise halfway between a "Yes" and a growl.

"Right Limb!" Capt. Cannon barked. "Escort Mrs. Bennet inside!"

One of the soldiers marched up to the lady and offered her a crooked arm, which she accepted with a smile not for him but for the captain.

"Left Limb! Return to post and follow! Drawing room, ho!"

As Capt. Cannon's wheelbarrow squeaked off toward the house, the lieutenant followed with all the enthusiasm of a puppy being dragged along on a leash. So out of sorts was he that he forgot to offer Elizabeth his own, very real arm. Or at least Elizabeth chose to believe he'd merely forgotten.

She herself was far more anxious to get inside. Not that entertaining guests with her mother was something she usually looked forward to. But when the caller was Cuthbert Cannon and the hostess his "Pru"— now that could prove interesting indeed.

CHAPTER 17

ONCE CAPT. CANNON had been wheeled into the drawing room, Left Limb was put at ease in the corner while Right Limb was kept busy sugaring tea and tilting the cup just so, to keep its contents from his commander's voluminous whiskers.

"Tell me, Captain," Elizabeth said before her mother could make the day's temperature the principal topic of conversation, "you have been to Hertfordshire before?"

Capt. Cannon's gaze darted to Mrs. Bennet, and he hacked out a jowl-quivering cough.

"Yes. I was stationed here briefly twenty-odd years ago. Of course, at the time I was but a reedy little ensign barely big enough to hold up my own epaulets."

"Oh, pish tosh," Mrs. Bennet chided. "You were the prettiest thing in Colonel Miller's regiment!"

The captain turned the same shade of red as his uniform.

Lt. Tindall, on the other hand, went pale green. Elizabeth guessed he would've preferred a lively discussion about their chances for rain that week.

"Oh, how it broke my heart to see you go," Mrs. Bennet went on, dreamy eyed. She awoke from her reverie with a little start and added, "All you fine young men, I mean. The regiment. As a whole. Altogether."

"Yes, well, duty called," Capt. Cannon said.

"You were sent away to fight the dreadfuls?" Elizabeth asked. Usually, she would've left it to Lydia or Mary to pose such a tactless question. But her sisters weren't there, and she couldn't resist.

The captain nodded. "Cornwallis's Folly. The Sack of Birmingham. Wellington's Last Stand. The Battle of Kent. I was at them all, though less of me made it to each in turn. A bite on the wrist, and my left arm had to go. A nasty scratch on the ankle, and the left leg went with it. A rotter ate my right hand before my very eyes. The company surgeon took the rest. And the right leg? That's the one that almost got me. A break in the skin no bigger than a pinprick where a dreadful swiped at my thigh—that's all it took. I didn't even notice it for half a day, and by then the blight nearly had me. Another hour, the surgeon said, and he would've been sawing off my head, not my leg. And still I kept on fighting! By the end, I'd looked into the putrid eyes of so many unmentionables, I could truthfully say I feared neither Death nor Hell, for I'd grappled hand-to-hand against the one and marched time and again into the other. Somehow, I survived it all. But after leaving Hertfordshire lo those many years ago, I daresay I never again *lived*."

As the man spoke, an air of gloom fell over the room as stifling as a London fog, and for a long while after he stopped, the only sound was that of Mrs. Hill's heavy footfalls in the hallway.

"It must be said, though," Lt. Tindall finally pronounced, "Hertfordshire certainly gets its measure of sunshine in the spring. I should think we had just made camp in the West Indies, to judge by the clime this day."

"Oh, my, yes. It has been most unusually warm of late," Mrs. Bennet said. Yet her voice was strained and quavery; she wasn't seizing upon the change of subject with the greedy, grateful grasp Elizabeth would have normally expected.

Before the room could slip back into silence, however, there was a great commotion out in the foyer, and presently Elizabeth's father burst in with all his other daughters.

"Lizzy, my dear, you had me worried sick!" Mr. Bennet exclaimed with uncharacteristic fervor. "I half-thought you'd joined the sorry stricken . . . and then I hear you've joined His Majesty's infantry, instead!"

Jane simply rushed to Elizabeth's side, threw her arms around her neck, and kissed her on the cheek, while Kitty and Lydia laughed and even dour Mary unleashed a grin.

"Oh, Jane, Papa, I'm so sorry to have caused you such distress, truly I am," Elizabeth said. "Everything happened so fast, I suppose I wasn't thinking very clearly."

"At least for you, unlike some others, that is a rare offense," her father replied. "And it's one I'm hoping you won't repeat. Now—" He turned toward the bulky, red-coated trunk propped up nearby. "Capt. Cannon, I presume? Allow me to welcome you to Longbourn. You and your regiment have arrived not a moment too soon."

The captain either squirmed uncomfortably or simply lost his balance, and Left Limb had to lean in to steady him.

"Yes, well, thank you, Mr. Bennet. I'm looking forward to discussing the matter before us in some depth . . . and in private."

"By all means. We may adjourn to my library."

"Perfect. Limbs! To your posts!"

As Right Limb and Left Limb lifted up the wheelbarrow, Lt. Tindall rose to go with the other men.

"Not you, Lieutenant," Capt. Cannon said. The words came out blunt and gruff—more so than the captain intended, apparently, for he tried to make amends with a smile so unconvincing it could have been drawn on with a child's pastels. "I'd hate to have the ladies see us in full retreat. You shall be my rearguard action—and I can't imagine a better man for the job. Keep our hostess and her lovely daughters entertained until my business with Mr. Bennet is done. That's an order—and a more pleasant one you're not likely to get anytime soon. Limbs! Bow to the ladies before we leave!"

The captain's attendants dipped him forward slightly, then began weaving the wheelbarrow around the furniture, headed for the door.

"Well . . . ," Lt. Tindall began. Then, obviously at a loss, he simply sat down again.

It did not bode well, Elizabeth thought, for the lieutenant's abilities as an entertainer of ladies.

The other girls, though still flushed from the afternoon's excitement, began seating themselves around the room, their scabbarded katanas clanking against furniture and nearly upending the tea service. Lt. Tindall took it in with the pinched expression of a grand dame who's just found a fly in her cucumber sandwich until Jane settled herself on a divan directly in his line of sight, giving him, for the first time, an unobstructed view of her face and figure.

Smoothly, gracefully she assumed her usual repose for such occasions: hands folded in lap, eyes turned decorously downward, small, prim smile on a face radiant with sedate beauty. And as he watched her, the lieutenant dutifully assumed the usual look of young men beholding her for the first time: spine straightening, eyes widening slightly, jaw dropping (or, in this case, unclenching, at least).

Usually, Mrs. Bennet watched for this effect on eligible gentlemen like a hawk watches a field for mice. Yet after seeing to the appropriate introductions, she lapsed back into—miracle of miracles!—a quiet, distant, contemplative state, and it was left to Elizabeth to do the hostessing. (Shy, delicate, gentle Jane, though the eldest, could no more initiate conversation with a newly met man than a rose petal could belch.)

"So, have you served under Captain Cannon long?"

"No." Lt. Tindall tore his gaze from Jane with such obvious effort that even Mary made note of it and looked, for a second, as though she might roll her eyes. "Our company is newly mustered. Even the captain I've known only a few days."

Mrs. Bennet suddenly came to life again. "You probably haven't met his family then, have you? His children? His wife?"

"There is no such family to meet. I do not believe the captain ever married."

"Ah," Mrs. Bennet said. "You know, Lieutenant, one of our local estates is hosting a spring ball in just four days' time, and I shall see to it that you're invited!"

Every other Bennet in the room sucked in her breath, but the lady simply went prattling on with her old unmindful garrulousness.

"I'm sure it can be arranged easily enough. It's something of a tradition here, actually, inviting officers from visiting regiments to our country dances. Shows our support for the crown, I like to think. And it builds ties to the community that I'm sure you and the captain will find rewarding. So many great, ah, friendships have blossomed from such opportunities to associate socially."

"You and your daughters will be attending?" Lt. Tindall asked, looking at Jane. He was so blinded by her beauty he didn't seem to notice the look of horror on her face.

"Oh, yes, certainly!" Mrs. Bennet proclaimed. "Not the youngest, of course—such things are still years away for them. But Jane will be there, and our Lizzy will be having her coming out!"

"*Mamma*," Elizabeth said. She couldn't contradict her mother in front of a guest, of course, but neither could she sit idly by and let her make promises she couldn't keep.

Though Mrs. Bennet had waged a campaign on Jane and Elizabeth's behalf—sending pleading letters to Mrs. Goswick and enlisting their Aunt Philips to do the same—it had so far come to naught. Mrs. Goswick hadn't even bothered to reply, and the one time Mrs. Bennet and Mrs. Philips had gone round to make a call, they'd been told the lady was out. All day. Every day. Indefinitely. Yet Mrs. Bennet kept insisting that the "misunderstanding" would soon be put right.

Elizabeth tried to warn her mother away from the subject with an angry flash of the eyes, but it had the same effect as any other attempt she'd ever made at keeping her mother from talking: none at all.

"How many officers are in your regiment, Lieutenant? I shall see to it they all get a chance to dance with one of my fair daughters!"

"Mamma, please."

It was Jane protesting this time, although she did it so quietly no one but Elizabeth seemed to hear.

"We are not a full regiment but just a company of one hundred," Lt. Tindall said. "The only officers are the captain, myself, and a young ensign barely old enough to attend balls himself."

"Oh. There are so few of you?" Mrs. Bennet marveled, sobered . . . for all of two seconds. "Well, that should make you very much in demand, Lieutenant. You'll never get a second's rest once the music starts!"

"Fortunately, I have just completed a month's leave on my family estate in Oxfordshire, and I find myself refreshed and ready for any challenge."

The lieutenant's lips twisted to the side, signaling (in case his words hadn't done so sufficiently) that he was being amusing. And, indeed, Mrs. Bennet seemed mightily amused. Or pleased, at any rate.

A huge grin had spread wide on her face the moment she heard the words "my family estate."

"Oh, my girls will put that to the test, Lieutenant!" she cried with glee. "They shall! They truly shall!"

Jane's gaze went so low it looked like she was searching for something that had fallen down her dress.

"I must admit," Lt. Tindall said, "it pleases me to learn that your daughters have time for more la—" the young officer coughed, "traditional pursuits."

Ladylike—clearly that was the word that had stuck in the man's throat. Elizabeth felt a sudden, near-overpowering urge to stick her foot there, too.

"Oh, pay no mind to those toys," Mrs. Bennet said, nodding at Jane's katana. "My girls are as genteel and well bred as am I! La!"

The lieutenant was casting a rather dubious glance at Lydia and Kitty—a decapitated dreadful was proof their swords were no toys—when Jane found the strength to speak to the young man at last.

"Can one not be genteel and well bred *and* do one's duty?" she said softly.

Lt. Tindall's eyes—both as blue and, till then, distant as the sky—went dewy. "I'm sure some could."

"How do *you* manage it, Lieutenant?" Jane asked.

From Elizabeth, the question would have sounded impudent. From her sister, however, it was the essence of sincerity.

"I endeavor to always remember who and what I do my duty *for*," Lt. Tindall answered solemnly.

Jane nodded. "It has been the same for me, Sir."

Lt. Tindall just gaped at her a moment, obviously overcome with admiration. Without trying to—she never did—St. Jane had converted another worshipper.

The spell was broken by the tromp of heavy footsteps in the hall, and Master Hawksworth came bursting in. He scanned the room with a single jerk of the head, not lingering for so much as a second on the stranger in red. When he saw Elizabeth, he sucked in a gulp of air, close to but not quite a gasp, and took a step toward her.

"You are well then, Elizabeth Bennet?"

"You weren't told?"

Elizabeth glanced at her sisters, confused.

Lydia shrugged. "We couldn't find him."

"I became separated from the others during the search," Master Hawksworth said. "Where were you? What happened?"

"I fell in the forest, Master."

Elizabeth wasn't looking at Lt. Tindall, so she couldn't see his eyebrows arch at her "Master." Though she fancied she could feel the little breeze they stirred as they flew up his forehead.

"While attempting a Leaping Leopard," she went on. "And there was a dreadful."

Master Hawksworth had been breathing hard, as if out of breath. Now he froze.

"You slew it?"

"I fought it, but . . . no. It got the better of me. Fortunately, there was someone else there. He was armed with a pistol, and—"

"*Him?*"

The Master jerked his head at Lt. Tindall without bothering to look his way.

"No, Master. Another man. A doctor by the name of Keckilpenny."

Master Hawksworth almost seemed to shrivel. His head hung a little lower, and his shoulders sagged. But then he quickly drew himself up to his full height and assumed what Elizabeth had come to think of as the Master Stance: chin up, arms crossed, legs spread wide.

"Fetch your katana and daggers and bring them to the dojo immediately, Elizabeth Bennet. You are obviously in need of special tutoring."

"Yes, Master."

"I killed a dreadful, Master!" Lydia crowed as Elizabeth rose to go.

"I helped!" Kitty protested.

"Oh, a little. But it was *my* idea."

"All you said was 'Let's behead it.' I'm the one who suggested 'Satan's Scissors'!"

"Oh, girls, girls, hush, please! I can't stand to hear another word!" Mrs. Bennet wailed, fanning herself with a fresh hankie.

Everyone else ignored them.

"Don't tell me you actually approve of all this?" Lt. Tindall said to Master Hawksworth. "Young ladies going about fighting with these strange, barbaric weapons?"

"I'll tell you what I don't approve of," the Master grated out. "Failure." He spun on his heel and started for the door, speaking over his shoulder to Elizabeth again. "Now come. After you've finished your *dandbaithaks*—a hundred should suffice—we will identify where you erred and ensure it never happens again."

Elizabeth followed wearily, still aching from her fall and the fights with the dreadfuls and the walk to Meryton and back again. Yet despite it all, it was such sweet relief to escape the drawing room—and her mother and Lt. Tindall—she almost pitied her sisters.

CHAPTER 18

MR. BENNET'S LIBRARY—his private sanctuary, his refuge from foolishness and chatter and, in short, Everyone Else—had never felt more crowded. The captain's Limbs were, by necessity, big, burly men, being beasts of a very peculiar burden (and one which weighed no less than fifteen stone). Standing at attention bracketing the captain, they blocked off an entire bookcase.

It was somewhat unsettling to find so many soldiers facing him across the top of his desk: It made Mr. Bennet feel a little like he was facing a firing squad. Yet the one thing that would have perturbed almost any other gentleman—the fact that the guest seated directly across from him had nary a (lowercase *l*) limb left—was, for Mr. Bennet, a much-welcome comfort. There was no need to ask the captain whether he'd served during The Troubles. Lydia and Kitty had described how the other soldiers broke ranks and ran from a single charging dreadful, but their commander was obviously a man of experience—hard, hellish experience. And that was precisely the kind all England needed to call on now.

Mr. Bennet told the captain all that had happened since he'd sent word of the dreadfuls' return to the War Office in London. Some of it, he learned, Elizabeth had already passed along. There was much his daughter didn't know, however, perceptive though she was. Much Mr. Bennet had been holding back for just this moment, when there would be no questions, no gasps. Just much-needed action.

"As I'm sure you noticed when you marched past St. Chad's," he said, "we haven't taken the necessary measures at the cemetery. Until now, I've lacked both the manpower and the standing for such a step. I thought

I might have an ally: a peer with an estate near here. Unfortunately—and unsurprisingly—he proved unreliable. In fact, I don't think he's so much as set foot outside his manor house since catching sight of his first unmentionable. And without his influence. . . ." Mr. Bennet shook his head and sighed. "People have forgotten what once was necessary. That's especially true in a quiet little hamlet like this that never saw the worst of it even when half the Midlands was feasting on the other half's brains. Of course, there are strategic advantages to such naiveté. I'm sure you remember well the danger posed by panic *en masse*. But now that you and the rest of your regiment are here, I think we can safely—"

"There is no regiment," Capt. Cannon said.

Mr. Bennet cocked an ear, as if he'd simply misheard what the man had said as opposed to disbelieving it.

"Pardon?"

"My company is attached to no regiment," the captain said. "We are here alone. One hundred men, all told."

"But . . . surely you must realize . . . if it's all beginning again . . . beginning here in Hertfordshire, this time. . . ."

Capt. Cannon simply stared back at his host with an air of imperturbable composure Mr. Bennet found both admirable and infuriating.

"Damn it, man, the Burial Act's been repealed five years now!" he snapped. "Five years we've been letting people bury their dead with their heads on their necks! Which means this very moment there's probably a pack of zombies tunneling around under St. Chad's cemetery like so many moles! Have you any idea how many men—well-trained, *disciplined* men—it will take to deal with that? And how many more will be needed to secure the roads and patrol the countryside?"

"The War Office felt a company of a hundred would be sufficient for the task at hand here," the captain said coolly.

"The only thing a company of a hundred will be sufficient for, Captain, is hors d'oeuvres! It's been weeks since the first unmentionable sat up in his coffin. You know what could be coming next. A thousand men would be hard pressed to do what needs done in time!"

"Nevertheless," Capt. Cannon said, "we have one hundred."

"Why, by God? No more could be spared?"

"No more are being made available," the captain said, and his expression finally changed. No longer was it simply impassive. Now it was a wall of cold stone.

This far and no further, the look said.

Mr. Bennet leaned back in his chair and blew out a long breath. First the Order let him down by sending such a young master—and one, he was discovering, who was prone to diversion. Now his old comrades in the War Office had disappointed him, as well. More than disappointed him. Thrown him and his family to the undead wolves.

"You know, Captain," he sighed, "the only reason I hadn't lost hope entirely was because the army was on its way. Now, however . . . "

"I would take it as a great favor, Mr. Bennet, if you didn't panic quite yet."

Mr. Bennet searched Capt. Cannon's face for any sign he was being insulted. Yet the other man's expression had softened, as had his voice, and it was quickly clear no slight was intended. He'd merely been reminding Mr. Bennet of something he'd lost sight of: that the soldiers were being thrown to the wolves, too, and the captain might need his help as much as vice versa.

"Agreed," he said with a slight, wry smile. "I won't panic . . . yet. There will be plenty of time for that later, I'll wager."

The captain nodded. "Indeed, there will."

The two old warriors meditated for a moment on what might be in store for them. Then Capt. Cannon broke the gloomy silence by lifting his chin and saying, "Right Limb. Nose. Itch."

"Well," Mr. Bennet said as the Limb leaned in to scratch at the captain's bulbous nose, "I had been counting on the sway a full regimental colonel would have. There will be resistance when we make our first move, and that will be more difficult to overcome now. Much more difficult, I'm afraid."

"Lower. Over. Harder. Not that hard!" The captain dismissed Right Limb with a jerk of the head. "Mr. Bennet, you are a man of great cleverness, I've been told. A man of courage and honor. Unfortunately, what we need is a man of rank. Someone whose name—or, preferably, *title*—could ease the way for us in the days ahead. This nobleman you spoke of, for instance. . . ."

Mr. Bennet nodded glumly.

"Yes, yes. I was just thinking the same thing," he said. "And believe me, you don't find it half so unfortunate as do I."

CHAPTER 19

MASTER HAWKSWORTH PACED slowly around Elizabeth as she did her *dand-baithaks*, and though he kept his observations to her technique—"Back straight, Elizabeth Bennet!" . . . "Nose to the floor, Elizabeth Bennet!" . . . "I can hear you breathing, Elizabeth Bennet!"—she couldn't help but wonder how much he was simply observing *her*. This was, after all, the first time the two of them had been alone in the dojo, and she, for one, was keenly aware that the flush to her cheeks and the tightness in her chest weren't entirely due to the exercise.

The Master had been worried about her, that much had been obvious back in the house. And despite all his bluster, it wasn't the cold, calculating, utilitarian worry of a warrior who needed every sword he could muster against The Enemy.

He *cared*. Elizabeth was sure of it.

What she wasn't so sure of was what—if anything—she should do about it.

When Master Hawksworth finally let her get up off the floor, he kept circling, looking her over. She knew she was supposed to keep her gaze straight ahead, "piercing infinity" as the Master called it when drilling the girls on their warrior scowls. Yet her self-consciousness grew so acute Elizabeth couldn't keep her eyes up, and soon her gaze was piercing nothing save her own toes.

Master Hawksworth stopped directly before her, his chest mere inches from hers.

"What's this? Staring at the floor? Have I mistakenly brought *Jane* Bennet to the dojo?"

Elizabeth forced herself to look up and meet the Master's stare.

He nodded once, brusquely. "There. Now I know I am looking at *Elizabeth* Bennet."

"And you are grateful to see her?"

Master Hawksworth's face took on the look of pained astonishment Elizabeth imagined he wore when he first felt the Fulcrum of Doom, and as he whirled away, putting his back to her, she cursed her own reckless presumption. It wasn't Jane anyone would mistake her for now; it was foolish, imprudent Lydia.

"A student doesn't—!" the Master began. "I am . . . I should . . . !"

Then he slumped and sighed and was silent. When he went on again a moment later, he sounded not outraged but resigned.

"Why should I be surprised that you would speak so boldly? You, who are the very model of . . . "

Whatever his last word was, it came out so softly Elizabeth couldn't even hear it.

He turned toward her again, straightening his back and setting his legs apart as if facing a foe. Yet his expression remained wounded, torn.

"Yes," he said, "I *am* grateful to see you. Grateful catastrophe did not befall you today. *Very* grateful to have you back in my dojo. Do you know why?"

Elizabeth fought to swallow a lump in her throat. It felt like it was the size of a baked potato, or perhaps even a smallish ham.

"No," she croaked.

"You *should* know. You should feel it. For it was obvious to me the first time I laid eyes on you. You are special, Elizabeth Bennet."

Master Hawksworth stepped up close to her again—so close, in fact, Elizabeth worried parts of their bodies she blushed to even think of would soon be rubbing up against each other.

The Master stopped just in time.

"At the lake. With the unmentionable. Your father ordered your sister to attack, yet it was *you* who took action. You, who are as much the lady as she, you could lay that aside and charge in and *fight*. Without much competence, perhaps, but with all the courage any warrior could hope for. The skills will come with time. That is why I push you so hard. The courage, though . . . at times I think it is something one must be born with. As you were."

Elizabeth wondered if she should say "Thank you," but found herself too flustered to speak at all. Before, the highest praise the Master had doled out to anyone was "Not bad," a phrase that implied no matter how well one had done, he could do better blindfolded. Yet now it almost sounded as though he *admired* her.

"Elizabeth Bennet," he said, voice barely above a whisper, "I need you to teach me—"

And somewhere in that moment, as he either searched for the right word or the nerve to say it, it ended. Elizabeth saw it in his eyes. They went distant again. Dead.

"—how to fillet a spider!" Master Hawksworth barked, and he leapt aside, arm stretched out toward a fresh-spun cobweb in the corner.

"HAAAAAAAA-IIIIIEEEEEEEEEEEEEEEE!" Elizabeth cried, grateful for the excuse to move, scream, give her heart something to thump over other than feelings she didn't understand.

She charged the web, unsheathed her blade and, with a few quick cuts, diced the spider. It was as close to "fillet" as she could get.

"Not bad . . . not bad," Master Hawksworth mused as he leaned in to inspect the spider. He was careful to keep his distance now, and his hands were clasped behind his back. "Tell me, how is it you failed in the forest?"

Elizabeth kept her eyes on his as she told him of her brief battle with the zombie that afternoon. She was looking for some hint of the vulnerability, the humanity he'd allowed her to see just a minute before. But his armor was firmly back in place now, and she could see nothing beyond it.

"So, this doctor. He is a good shot?" he said when she was done.

"I very much doubt it. He was simply too close to miss."

The Master shook his head. "An inelegant solution. A warrior prefers to deal death with his own hands."

"Dr. Keckilpenny is not a warrior. He puts his faith in the sciences rather than the deadly arts."

"Yes, I've heard of such men. They believe we can *think* our enemies away. Fools!"

"Is it not to a warrior's advantage to understand his enemy?"

Hawksworth gave Elizabeth a long, hard look, and for a moment she feared she'd let this new, disconcerting informality between them loosen her tongue overmuch yet again. She had caught a glimpse of the real Geoffrey Hawksworth, yes, but it wasn't to him she was speaking now. It was the Master.

She almost started shaking out her aching arms in preparation for the inevitable *dand-baithaks*.

"Do you truly think there is anything about the unmentionables one could understand?" Master Hawksworth finally said.

"That is what the 'fools' intend to discover," Elizabeth might have replied, but she felt weary and wary now, and she said nothing.

The Master stared at her for a painfully long time before shrugging his own question away.

"No. Understanding didn't stop the dreadfuls the last time. This—" He launched himself into the air, grabbed hold of a post, swung around it, then landed in a perfect Hour Glass Stance, fists up. "—is what stopped them."

A Leaping Leopard brought him across the room, and he set down with surprising lightness inches from Elizabeth again.

"Yes, you are special, Elizabeth Bennet. Yet clearly you are not ready to face what awaits unaided. So we must focus, for the moment, on moves you can use in tandem with a more skillful ally. Pas de deux, you might call them—though these are dances of death. Natural stance!"

Elizabeth assumed the position, and Master Hawksworth took a step back and did the same.

"These moves will require us to act in unison, in harmony, as one," he said. "So . . . no Fulcrum of Doom or Axis of Calamity from you. And I will not again allow myself to become careless or distracted. Do you understand?"

"Yes, Master," Elizabeth said, though it wasn't entirely true.

"Good. Then take my hands." Master Hawksworth reached out toward Elizabeth. "This move is called the Hawk and the Dove. It begins like this. . . ."

CHAPTER 20

THE BARON OF LUMPLEY awoke with his arms around one of his hounds and a pile of empty gin bottles nestled against his back. He felt blearily around the bed for the chambermaids, but the only naked rump to slap was his own.

Then he remembered.

He'd been wrestling around with Yvonne, Yvette, Y what-have-you, the French one, the night before. She was a slender little doe-eyed thing with dark curls and milky skin and, most appealing of all, an almost complete inability to speak English. Only the baron had rolled over her a little too roughly at one point, his lordly girth flattening her, forcing the air from her lungs, and she'd wheezed out a sound that needed no translation: "Ohhhh!" And when he'd glanced down at her, it hadn't been Ywhoever he'd seen beneath him.

It was Emily Ward.

How easily he'd forgotten that name just a few weeks before, as he'd let so many names flit from his memory when they (and their bearers) no longer served a purpose. Yet now he couldn't forget it no matter how hard he tried, and the same was true of the face that went with it. The faces, really—one pert and pretty, the other puffy, putrescent.

"Go! Get away from me! Leave me alone!" he'd howled, pressing his hands to his eyes, and the chambermaid had shrieked and snatched up her clothes and scurried from the room, leaving him to greedily glug down more gin until he collapsed into dreamless oblivion.

And now he was awake again—sort of. But why why *why*? Being awake meant being aware, and that was the exact thing he didn't want to be.

There was a soft knock on the door, and the baron lifted his head off his pillow—or was it another dog?—and spoke the first words of a new day.

"Hmf ibbit?"

"It's me, Milord. Lucy. Belgrave sent me up to see if there was anything you'd be needing right about now. Or wanting."

Ahhhhhhh, Lucy, she of the hips as wide and sturdy as the White Cliffs of Dover. She was an old favorite of his. Belgrave, God bless the man, was trying to cheer him up.

Yet for once the thought of her did nothing to rouse him, and he remained stretched across his bed like a beached whale.

"Guh awuh," he said.

"As you wish, Milord."

A while later—ten minutes, perhaps, or maybe two hours, Lord Lumpley neither knew nor cared—he pushed himself up and, resenting every second of his labors, pulled on a stained and wrinkled robe. Then he shuffled to a pair of double doors, threw them open, and stepped out onto a balcony overlooking Netherfield's long, lush front lawn.

It was another bright-sunny day in what seemed like an infinite succession of them, and the baron knew he should be out and about making the most of it. There was so much he could be doing! Racing over the roads in his cabriolet, whipping his horses, terrorizing the locals. Wasn't that just what he needed? Wouldn't that bring him roaring back to life?

Lord Lumpley was still squinting, watering eyes adjusting to the light, when a shimmering figure moved out of the trees lining the lawn. With his first blink, it took shape: a girl in white, ghostly pale except for the scarlet splotches around her mouth and hands.

With his second blink, she was gone.

The baron cursed. He couldn't even step outside without seeing things.

Blast those damned dreadfuls! They had him so unnerved he wasn't having any *fun*!

After the debacle with the hunt, he'd written his old friend and mentor the Prince Regent asking for guidance—perhaps even protection. Yet he'd received no response, and Belgrave had informed him that the posts had grown exceedingly spotty of late, with no word from outside Hertfordshire in some days. He was tempted to hop into the cabriolet and make for London and never look back.

Everyone agreed there was no cause for alarm yet, though. ("Everyone" was Belgrave, whose job it was to agree.) A few dreadfuls had popped up and been handily dealt with. What of it? For that he was supposed to quit his estate when he could only barely quit his own bed? He lacked the energy to so much as stretch out his arms for a dressing, let alone brave the long ride to town.

He needed something to rouse him from his languor, cleanse him of the darkness that had become stuck to him like pitch the moment he saw Emily Ward walking out of that lake. The old pleasures wouldn't do. New, fresh—that's what he needed. Something unspoiled. Something *alive*.

And then there it was again: movement down by the lawn. It was on the road this time, though, and there was no mistaking those straight lines and bright red coats for anything but British soldiers.

Huzzah! The Prince Regent hadn't abandoned him, after all! On your guard, trollops of London. The baron of rumpy-pumpy would soon be on your scent again!

But . . . what *was* that contraption those two soldiers were pushing? It appeared to be some kind of wheeled sedan chair, for riding upon it was a man: a stout, white-haired officer with his limbs contorted into such unnatural positions—arms tucked behind his back, legs disappearing into the straps and harnesses of his curious conveyance—it almost looked as though he didn't have any at all.

And then the baron noticed the man walking beside the officer, a gentleman dressed not in red but in black and gray, and in an instant all his reborn joie de vivre collapsed like a punctured soufflé.

Oscar Bennet. The mere sight of him conjured up so much. The crushing burden of responsibility. The evil lurking in the woods. Emily Ward staggering out of the lake. Jane Bennet drawing a sword and stepping toward her. Jane Bennet weeping in the shallows, her thin white gown soaked almost to the point of transparency. Jane Bennet bouncing up and down atop a charging stallion.

Jane Bennet bouncing up and down atop a charging stallion!

The soufflé reinflated.

Lord Lumpley walked back to his bed and reached for the bell cord, but before he could even give it a tug Belgrave came sidling into the room.

"A troop of soldiers approaches, My Lord."

"Yes, yes, so I have seen. And I suppose I can't very well greet them like this."

The baron swept a hand over his exposed pulchritude. He'd managed to put on a robe, but he refused to stoop so low as to tie his own sash.

"Shall I send up your dressers, My Lord?"

"Immediately! I find myself truly awake for the first time in days, Belgrave. I am refreshed! Rekindled! *Roused!*"

"I exult for you, My Lord."

Belgrave bowed and started backing out of the bedchamber.

Lord Lumpley walked again to the balcony, chuckling, as his steward left.

"Thank you, Mr. Bennet," he said to the small figure drawing nearer, the dark, straight line of a sheathed sword now visible at its side. "You give me fresh reason to live."

When the baron finally came downstairs (after taking half an hour to decide which trousers and vest best suited his mood), he found his guests installed in the library. He also found that said guests were both larger in number and, in one case, shockingly smaller in stature than he'd anticipated.

Two infantrymen were standing at attention when he walked in. He was on the verge of taking offense—common foot soldiers stamping their common feet across his Turkish rugs?—when the officer spoke up from his wheeled chair-barrow.

"Limbs! Bow to His Lordship."

The soldiers not only bowed, they reached over and tilted the officer toward the floor, as well.

"Egad!" Lord Lumpley blurted out. "You're got no arms or legs!"

The officer peeped up at him with the sort of look that said, quite plainly, that he was well aware of this state of affairs and required no reminders.

The baron mumbled out a lame, not to mention somewhat puzzling, "Ummm . . . good for you."

Introductions followed, facilitated by Mr. Bennet, who'd risen from a chair nearby to offer a (by Lord Lumpley's estimation) rather shallow bow.

Once the baron was settled on a loveseat, Mr. Bennet sat down again, as well, and Capt. Cannon's Limbs propped him up straight and went back to attention.

"So, Captain," Lord Lumpley said, "what brings you to Netherfield Park? Were it just you and your men, I might assume you'd been sent to see to my safe passage to London. Given Mr. Bennet's presence, however, I presume you expect *me* to serve *you* in some fashion."

Capt. Cannon's face—what was visible of it through his thick, white whiskers—flushed pink. "Your service would be to the crown, Sir."

"And the good people of Hertfordshire," Mr. Bennet added.

"Yes, of course," the baron said. "I've been sick with worry about them, every one. And on their behalf, you want me to do what, exactly?"

The captain and Mr. Bennet exchanged a glance, and the former forged on with an explanation, clearly by prearrangement.

Lord Lumpley had his own prearranged plan, mapped out as his dressers toiled over him upstairs. The first step: resistance to whatever Bennet and the soldiers might propose. To his simultaneous disgust and satisfaction, the baron found no feigning was necessary.

"Yes, enough, all right," he said before Capt. Cannon was even done speaking. "Mr. Bennet tried to persuade me to aid him in this endeavor once before. It is beyond appalling."

"That is as may be, yet it must be done," Mr. Bennet replied. "And quickly, My Lord. Our time runs short. I do not know if word has reached you, but yesterday another unmentionable was found on the prowl not two miles from here. It nearly did in one of my own daughters."

"Jane?"

"Elizabeth."

"Oh."

Even to Lord Lumpley's ears, his "Oh" sounded a little *too* relieved—not that Elizabeth had lived, but that it had been she and not her elder sister who'd been attacked.

"I'm so happy to hear the young lady managed to escape," he added quickly. And then he carried on just as fast, for he'd stumbled upon the path to take him where he all along intended to go. "I assume it was the training you've insisted on for your daughters that made the difference. That was quite a display they put on during the unpleasantness at the lake. Oh, I know some were scandalized by it. That tongues have been wagging from here to Wales. 'Unladylike,' 'uncivilized,' 'un-English,' they say. I've even heard that your Jane and Elizabeth have been asked not to attend the spring ball at Pulvis Lodge! But no such flighty flibbertigibbet am I. I've come to see the need for these special skills, barbarous though they are. During the hunt, you and your daughters spared me the need to wade in and do battle with that foul creature myself, as surely I would have done had you not been present. And imagine the tragic turmoil if a person of such far-ranging influence as I should fall victim to an un-mentionable. Why, a man of my importance owes it to his countrymen to protect himself any way he can, wouldn't you say?"

The baron pretended to muse a moment, tapping a finger against the uppermost of his chins.

"I say . . . I seem to have struck upon a notion there."

"Oh?" Mr. Bennet said, and like the baron's "Oh" of a moment before, it seemed to convey much for what's basically one step up from a grunt. It was a wry and weary "Oh," slightly sad and entirely unsurprised.

"Imagine, Mr. Bennet," Lord Lumpley said, "what a boon it would be for your daughters—and all who might emulate them—should a person of standing be seen to take them to his bosom not in *spite* of their unconventional ways but *because* of them. Socially, they could be redeemed, and it would be all the easier for you to accomplish whatever you think necessary."

Mr. Bennet sat stock still as he listened, and even when he spoke he somehow looked less like a flesh-and-blood man than a portrait of himself, the expression on his face painted after a particularly long day.

"And how would you propose to take them to your bosom, exactly?"

"Well, what if I were to accept the services of one of your daughters as a sort of . . ." The baron shook his head, laughing. "It sounds ridiculous saying it, but . . . as a bodyguard. It might add fuel to the flame of scandal, at first, yet with time it would be accepted. And, at any rate, perhaps a little tonguewagging's just what we need to demonstrate the seriousness of the situation. 'If even the baron of Lumpley is again embracing the old Orientalism that held such sway during The Troubles . . . !' That sort of thing."

"I see," Mr. Bennet said, inflectionless. "And which of my daughters did you have in mind?"

"I suppose the eldest would make the most sense. Jane. Despite all the hysterics at the lake, she did slay a dreadful. And she's already out, so it wouldn't be *that* shocking for her to spend her days in the company of a gentleman. Of course, we couldn't be alone together. That would never do! Fortunately, there is no lack of chaperones around Netherfield. Though I have no relations or guests with me, at the moment, there are always servants about . . . not to mention uninvited callers."

"You ask for one of Mr. Bennet's daughters as a bodyguard?" Capt. Cannon spluttered. "With your *servants* as chaperones?"

The man looked as though he'd never missed his arms more—for before him was a rascal in desperate need of thrashing, rank be damned.

Mr. Bennet grunted out a little cough and finally shifted in his seat. "Actually, Captain, I find the proposal rather appeals to me. Do I take it, My Lord, that—if I agree to the course you've put forth—you will do everything in your power to aid our friend here?"

He nodded at Capt. Cannon.

Lord Lumpley put on an expression suggesting mild indignation. "You make it sound like a quid pro quo, Mr. Bennet . . . although I certainly will feel safer remaining in Hertfordshire to assist the captain if some gesture is made toward ensuring my safety."

"Everything in your power," Mr. Bennet pressed. "Whatever the captain needs. On your word of honor."

Damnable nerve, the baron thought.

"Of course," he said.

Mr. Bennet nodded, then had the impudence—what reserves the man had!—to stand up first.

"Jane will be here tomorrow noon."

"Excellent! I'll have a room prepared for her in the south wing."

"Yes, do. And you might want to alert your steward and groundskeeper and stable boys and all the rest, too."

"Oh?" Lord Lumpley and Capt. Cannon said together, and this time the word's meaning was as simple as its sound. Pure surprise, nothing more.

"I assume it would be your first request," Mr. Bennet said to the captain, "that you be allowed to establish headquarters on good, defensible high ground, clear of any cover for an advancing enemy, close enough to town to defend it yet not so close as to draw unwanted attention, with plenty of ready shelter its master has, at present, no need for."

"Yes, I suppose. . . ." Capt. Cannon finally caught on, and a huge grin pushed his white side-whiskers heavenward. "Netherfield Park would make the *perfect* base of operations. Limbs! To your posts! By jingo, if we move fast, we can break camp and be back this very day! I thank you, My Lord! The king thanks you! You are the very model of munificence, Sir!"

"Just a minute, now," Lord Lumpley began limply, but in all the commotion of the Limbs quick-stepping in a pivot and wheeling the captain toward the library doors, nobody seemed to hear him.

"I daresay you were right about my daughter not wanting for chaperones," Mr. Bennet said as he and the soldiers took their leave with jerky, hurried bows. "Before she even arrives, there will be all of a hundred of them billeted on your estate!"

CHAPTER 21

THERE HAD BEEN NO MORE late-night prowlings through the Bennet house since the girls had mistaken their mother for an unmentionable more than a week before. Whatever Mrs. Bennet had been after in Mr. Bennet's room—and Elizabeth had worked very, very hard to convince herself she didn't know what that was—she'd apparently given up hope of procuring it. So when Elizabeth once again heard shuffling steps and the creak of a floorboard outside her bedroom door, she stuffed her hand under her pillow and wrapped it around the hilt of a dirk.

It was the dead of night, yet her sleep had been light. Exhausted as her body was from another day of training, her mind remained restless, returning again and again to the same troubling thoughts. And feelings.

There was a light rap on her door, and it began to swing slowly open.

"Don't shoot, Lizzy. It's me."

Elizabeth pushed herself up and smiled sleepily. "Oh, I wasn't going to shoot you, Jane. I was about to *stab* you."

Candlelight spread out into the room, and as Jane stepped in after it, Elizabeth could see her sister's eyes glistening moistly in the dim flicker.

"I need help packing for Netherfield," Jane said.

Elizabeth stood and started toward her. "But we finished that hours ago."

"I know. And I finished again at midnight." Jane's lips trembled, and a single tear trickled down her right cheek. "I just can't stop *un*packing."

"Dear, sweet Jane . . ."

Elizabeth wrapped her arms gingerly around her sister—careful not to brush against the candle—and held her for a moment. Then she hurried her across the hall to her room and quickly closed the door. (Lydia had grown altogether too fond of her throwing stars of late, and anyone or anything that startled or provoked her ran the risk of quick, painful perforation.)

"Oh, Lizzy," Jane said after another hug, "I feel as if I'm being sent to Lord Lumpley as some kind of . . . you know. . . . "

Elizabeth did know. The gist anyway, if not the exact word Jane couldn't bring herself to say. *Concubine* would have been her first guess.

The phrase Elizabeth had settled on in her own mind was *virgin sacrifice*.

She led Jane to the bed, sat her down, and kissed her on the forehead. Then she turned to a large (and empty) chest surrounded by stacks of neatly folded clothes.

"You must simply think of yourself as a special sort of governess." She picked up a riding habit and put it in the trunk. "And of Lord Lumpley as a particularly naughty child."

"Oh, it's not him that I worry about," Jane said. "You know I don't share your misgivings about the baron. He's always been a perfect gentleman with *me*. No . . . it's what people will say that pains me."

Elizabeth shrugged even as she kept loading the trunk. "Could it be any worse than what they're saying already? And if His Lordship is to be believed, they won't be saying it long—because he's going to change their minds about it all."

"Do you believe that, Lizzy?"

"Well . . . the baron *might* be right. But I beg you to be wary of anything else the man says. And I don't just say that because I dislike him. You know there have been rumors . . . about Lord Lumpley and certain girls. . . ."

Such a flush came to Jane's face, for a moment it seemed to glow as bright as the candle, and she reached out and snagged Elizabeth by the hand.

"Oh, please say you'll come to Netherfield tomorrow! I simply couldn't bear going there without you by my side to give me strength."

"Of course, I shall go with you. Though . . ." Elizabeth gave Jane's hand a squeeze and then, overcome by the sudden urge to turn away, went back to packing. "I suppose I shall have to ask the Master for permission, as well."

"Surely, he'd excuse even his favorite pupil for just this one morning," Jane said. She was obviously struggling to lighten her tone, brighten the mood, turn playful, yet Elizabeth found she couldn't play along, and instead she changed the subject.

"Well, I can think of one person, at least, who will be absolutely enchanted by the idea."

"Oh, goodness, yes. No doubt Mamma will want you to visit me at Netherfield often, so that you might secure for yourself whichever gentleman there I don't entrap. Why, she and Aunt Philips are probably already planning a double wedding!"

Elizabeth let loose a very unladylike snort, sparking in Jane a burst of barely stifled giggles.

Their mother had, at first, reacted to news of the arrangement with Lord Lumpley with shocked silence—silence from her being so shocking that no one else there could speak for a full half minute, and the whole family simply sat around the drawing room watching matriarch gawk at patriarch with her mouth hanging open.

"One of our daughters? A *bodyguard*?" she finally said. "It's outrageous. Disgraceful. Unheard of. We'll be the laughingstock of all Hertfordshire."

"As if we aren't now," Kitty grumbled.

"Actually, Mamma," Mary said, nodding down at the thick book spread open in her lap, "according to this, Lady Catherine de Bourgh herself served as personal guard to the Duke of York during the Black Country Campaign of 17—"

"*Sss sss sss*," Mrs. Bennet hissed, silencing Mary with waggling fingers. As always, she found facts antithetical to good conversation. "We're talking about Jane's reputation. And ours!"

"Lord Lumpley would tell you he's *rescuing* our reputation, gallant gentleman that he is," Mr. Bennet said. "At any rate, there can hardly be anything untoward about the arrangement if it's been endorsed by a captain of the king's army—and when he and his junior officers will ever be on hand. Why, I wager Jane will end up spending as much time with young Lt. Tindall as with the baron."

Mrs. Bennet pondered this for a long, long time—for her. Meaning all of two seconds passed before she turned to Jane and said, "Don't forget to take that lovely muslin gown Mrs. Gardiner bought for you in London. And we simply must do something different with your hair. Hill! *Hill?* Where is that infernal woman? She needs to run to town this instant if we're to have a new bonnet before Mr. Ward closes shop. HILL!"

Soon she was hustling upstairs to go through Jane's closet and dressers, with Kitty and Lydia skittering after her tittering. Jane remained behind, frozen in the armchair she'd been sitting in when she'd received the news.

Her father walked over to pat her on the back of the hand.

"I know, my dear. I am tossing you into the lion's den. Please believe me, I wouldn't do it if you weren't more than a match for any wanton tom who sought to add you to his pride."

"Papa!" Jane cried, horrified.

Mr. Bennet gave her another pat. "That's the way, child, that's the way. Just keep blushing like that—with your katana at the ready—and you'll be all right. Now, I suppose I must go to the dojo and inform Master Hawksworth."

"Are you sure he'll approve?" Elizabeth asked.

She certainly didn't, but there was little she could do about it. The Master, on the other hand . . .

"Our training has brought us so far so fast, but this?" she went on. "The Master might not think Jane's ready."

"I am beginning to wonder," Mr. Bennet replied, one eyebrow arching high, "if our young master is truly the best judge of what my daughters are and are not ready for."

It was Elizabeth's turn to blush. Her sisters' teasing she could tolerate, but from her father it was something else entirely. Though, really, how could he have missed Master Hawksworth's attentions? The Master was forever creating excuses for them to be alone to work on their pas de deux moves: At one point, every other Bennet in the dojo was accused of bad posture and sent off for a dozen laps around the estate. And he continued to give Elizabeth looks that lingered so long that Mary even asked him once if he were attempting some Oriental form of mesmerism. Yet it wasn't yearning that Elizabeth saw in his gaze; it seemed more like a perpetually unquenched curiosity. What he was so curious *about*, though, she didn't know, and even when they were together, just the two of them grappling and tussling and clasping hands, she couldn't bring herself to ask.

Mr. Bennet paused a moment, waiting to see what reply his daughter might make to his observation about the Master. Yet Elizabeth found herself, for once, at a loss for the right words, and her father simply grunted and left the room.

"Well, come along, Jane," she said brightly, trying to cover with false cheer as she grabbed her sister by the arm and tugged her toward the door. "Knowing Mamma, we will find her stuffing a trunk with evening dresses, slippers, and gloves—and not so much as a butter knife for you to guard a body with!"

And so it had been, of course. Eventually, Mrs. Bennet moved on to other matters: Jane's hair, the new bonnet, experimenting (over Kitty's howls of protest) on Jane's already perfect complexion with the French rouge Mrs. Hill had found hidden in the younger girl's dresser. Which was all well and good, from Elizabeth's perspective, for at last she could slip in and pack a few things that might actually be of some use.

And now, hours later, here she was doing it all over again.

"Do you really think there's need for that?" Jane asked as Elizabeth picked up her sparring gown. "I can't imagine I'll be doing many *dand-baithaks* while at Netherfield Park."

"Perhaps we might do some sword work together during one of my many visits," Elizabeth replied. "It would be wise, I think, to remind the baron what you're capable of with a katana . . . though I will admit, I would be happier packing a chastity belt."

"*Lizzy!*"

"For Lord Lumpley, of course," Elizabeth said. "I suspect the man already wears a truss. A chastity belt would require but the tiniest bit of extra—"

"Elizabeth Bennet, you should be ashamed of yourself," Jane said. But she was grinning as she said it. "You say the most awful things!"

Elizabeth smiled back, pleased to see she'd lifted her sister's spirits. Yet it would take a lot more than naughty quips, she knew, to actually keep Jane safe.

She put a pair of tekko brass knuckles in the trunk. Then an ivory-handled push dagger. Then her sister's nunchucks. Then her flintlock pistol and powder horn. Then a bag of shot. Then a retractable bo staff and ninja hand claws and a battle-axe and . . . and . . . and . . .

CHAPTER 22

EARLY THE NEXT MORNING, the Bennets lined up outside the house to bid Jane adieu.

"I'm sure you will acquit yourself well," said Mary.

"Just you with a baron and a hundred soldiers—I'm so jealous!" said Kitty.

"I should be so lucky when I'm your age!" said Lydia.

"Be careful, my dear," said Mrs. Bennet. "But not *too* careful." And she gave Jane a broad wink.

Master Hawksworth watched all the proceedings from the doorway of the dojo. The only farewell he offered to Jane was a solemn bow. Yet this, in its own way, seemed as heartfelt as anything the Bennets had to say.

As Jane returned the bow, the Master's eyes flicked, for just an instant, to Elizabeth and her father.

Mr. Bennet, Elizabeth noticed, was watching the younger man with a look of dry disdain. When the Master noticed it as well, he abruptly spun on his heel and stalked back into the dojo.

Something had shifted between her father and Master Hawksworth—something, Elizabeth feared, that had to do with her. Just that morning, when she'd asked if she might accompany Jane to Netherfield, Mr. Bennet had said, "That's a splendid idea. I'll tell Hawksworth you shall be gone for the day."

Not "ask the Master." "*Tell* Hawksworth."

Whatever it meant, she had no chance to ask about it, however slyly she might have gone about it, for when they left Longbourn, her father suddenly began acting like her mother. He'd decided that they should walk (an armed servant in a dogcart having been dispatched with Jane's trunk at first light), and all the way to Netherfield Park he kept up a stream of nervous chatter. Fortunately, it wasn't the need for an heir or rich sons-in-law or the certainty of his own encroaching doom that occupied him: He was reviewing fighting techniques, tossing out bits of zombie lore ("Have I mentioned their fondness for cabbage patches?"), and reminding Jane, not once but twice, of the efficaciousness of the Fulcrum of Doom and its sundry variations.

It was as if all their father had learned through months of study in the Orient and years battling the unmentionables might be imparted to his daughters in one fifty-minute walk, provided he talked quickly enough. He barely paused for so much as a breath until he spotted something by the side of the road that, for a moment, seemed to take it away entirely.

"Well, well, well . . . and I was just about to get to this, too," he muttered, and he slowly approached a small mound of what looked like mincemeat or the contents of a particularly lumpy haggis. "It appears Fate has taken an interest in your education."

"What is it?" Elizabeth asked.

"Zombie droppings."

"Zombie . . . *droppings*?"

"Oh, my," Jane said. "I didn't think unmentionables would need to, um, you know. . . . "

"They don't. Not the way the living do, at least." Mr. Bennet pulled out a dagger, knelt down beside the gloppy mess, and began sifting through it with the tip of the blade. "It moves through their bodies without being digested and then eventually just . . . falls out. That's how you can tell it's from a dreadful."

He stabbed something, brought it up to his nose, and gave it a sniff.

It was a finger. A wedding band was still attached just above the exposed knuckle bone.

"Fresh. We must be doubly wary," Mr. Bennet said. Then he flicked the finger into the brush, stood up, and started off again up the lane. "Now where was I? Oh, yes! Eyes! Always a nice, soft, vulnerable target in a human foe, but don't bother with them when you're up against a dreadful. They seem to see without the things, somehow. . . . "

He carried on along this line for only another minute or so, for soon the lane curved around to the baron's estate and a shrill voice squeaked out, "Who goes there?"

About fifty feet ahead, a young solider stood in the middle of the road, his wobbling Brown Bess pointed at the Bennets.

"Friends, lad!" Mr. Bennet called out. "Living, breathing friends, as you can tell from the fact that I'm answering you at all! I commend you on your caution—keep it up, by all means—but if you could stand down for now, it would be appreciated!"

The soldier lowered his musket.

"You may pass," he squawked.

He did his best to look stout and manly as Mr. Bennet and the girls passed him by, but with his splotchy skin and baggy uniform he appeared more boy than man.

"Are foot soldiers always so young?" Elizabeth asked.

"Not for long," her father replied.

Before Elizabeth could ask what *that* meant, he was waving at a stiff figure on the other side of the estate's lush front lawn.

"Lieutenant Tindall! Good morning! Where might the captain be?"

The lieutenant was watching a small squad of soldiers drill with muskets on their shoulders—watching and not approving, to judge by the scowl Elizabeth could see even from so far away.

When he turned to face the Bennets, the scowl deepened.

He started toward them with quick, crisp steps, his back still perfectly straight, as though he wished to demonstrate how a *real* English soldier marches.

"Mr. Bennet," he said as he drew near, and he gave the girls a brusque nod of greeting. "Ladies."

His gaze didn't linger on Jane, as it had back at Longbourn. Quite the opposite: It was clear he was taking pains not to look at her at all.

"Captain Cannon is awaiting your arrival with Lord Lumpley," he said to Mr. Bennet. "It is the captain's wish that His Lordship and his new . . . " It was hard to believe the man's upper lip could curl any further, yet he managed it. ". . . *escort* should set off for Meryton immediately. There is a vicar who needs talking to, I gather."

"Capital!" Mr. Bennet enthused. "I'm glad to find we're wasting no time this morning—enough has been squandered already. If you would show the way?"

Lt. Tindall bowed stiffly, then marched off again with a strained "Follow me."

Elizabeth peeped over at her sister as the Bennets followed. Jane looked pale and pinch-cheeked, and her wide eyes were pointed at the grass. Humility had always been her natural state, but this was *humiliation*.

Elizabeth took her by the arm.

"Don't be anxious, Jane. You do what you must for king and country, and you will do it with honor. Surely, anyone with even the slightest sense will appreciate that. As for those who disapprove, well, I would say let the unmentionables have them, but they're so narrow-minded there's probably not enough in their heads to tempt even the most peckish dreadful."

The lieutenant marred his perfect marching with a clumsy stumble step.

"Thank you, Elizabeth," Jane said, attempting (and not quite succeeding at) a smile. "I only wish I had your confidence."

"Pish tosh, you have nothing to worry about," Mr. Bennet said. "You will be marvelous, my dear, and no one will be able to deny it."

Yet though he reached over to give Jane a pat on the back, it seemed to Elizabeth he was as anxious as the lieutenant to avoid her eyes. His reassuring words, she suspected, were as much for himself as his daughter.

A moment later, they were joining Lord Lumpley and Capt. Cannon in front of the house. With them were the captain's Limbs, of course, as well as a groom behind the reins of a stylish phaeton.

"Ahhhh, my bodyguard! I feel safer already!" Lord Lumpley crowed as the Bennets walked up. He swept Lt. Tindall aside and bowed before Jane, then popped back up grinning. "I would have one of the maids show you to your room so you might get settled, but the captain is anxious to get his new plow horse—*me*—in harness. So it's off to Meryton to twist the vicar's arm, I'm afraid."

The baron slipped between Mr. Bennet and Jane, hooked the girl by the arm, and pulled her toward the waiting carriage.

"Captain!" Lt. Tindall blurted out. "Request permission to accompany the party to Meryton, Sir!"

Jane turned back to look at him, and the lieutenant met her gaze at last. The young man's handsome face went red, and he let his mouth hang slightly open, as if the words he was on the verge of speaking had some-how become stuck upon his tongue.

"That won't be necessary," Capt. Cannon said. "I'd like Mr. Bennet to go, the better to impress upon this Reverend Mr. Cummings the vital importance of what we propose to do. And he can bring Ensign Pratt and his men along to add further weight."

"Begging your pardon, Sir, but—" the lieutenant began.

The captain simply looked over at Mr. Bennet and went on talking.

"I've left a small garrison in Meryton, quartered at the Sow's Head Inn. You can collect them upon your arrival. I'm sending the proper equipment for them with the assumption that Mr. Cummings will see reason."

"A dangerous assumption to make of any man, particularly a vicar," Mr. Bennet said. "You're not coming along?"

"No. My first order of business is a thorough reconnoiter of the area. We don't want any unpleasant surprises, do we?"

"If you encounter dreadfuls, it shan't be pleasant, but it should come as no surprise," Mr. Bennet said softly, and he leaned in closely to tell the captain of the zombie scat they'd found by the road.

If he was trying not to panic Lord Lumpley, he needn't have both-ered. The baron was far too busy trying to interest Jane in the glories of his estate—and, by extension, the glories of *him*—to pay any attention to the men.

"And there was but one dropping?" Capt. Cannon said when he was done.

"There was but one *that I saw.*"

The captain nodded gravely.

"Well . . . off to Meryton." Mr. Bennet turned to Elizabeth. "I'm sorry to abandon you like this, but obviously plans have changed. I leave it to you to decide how best to use your time until we return. Perhaps the lieutenant might have one of his men instruct you in the use of a Brown Bess. We have entirely neglected the musket in our training, and I can't imagine a better opportunity to correct that."

"Yes, Papa."

"There's a good girl."

Mr. Bennet stepped up into the phaeton and inserted himself between Lord Lumpley and Jane. It looked to be an uncomfortably snug fit.

"Good-bye, Lizzy!" Jane called as the carriage rolled off. She had to lean around Mr. Bennet and Lord Lumpley to wave at her sister and, Lord Lumpley being Lord Lumpley, that called for quite a bit of leaning indeed. All Elizabeth could see of Jane's face were her eyes, as big and round as a pair of blue buttons.

The shyest, gentlest of the Bennet girls was on her way to a town filled with disapproving prudes, a lecherous nobleman on one side, a sword on the other.

Elizabeth found herself worrying far less about the unmentionables lurking along the road than the possibility that her sister might very soon die of embarrassment.

CHAPTER 23

"I MUST TAKE MY LEAVE as well, Miss Bennet," Capt. Cannon said as the baron's carriage rolled off up the drive. "But I find your father's suggestion an excellent one, and I leave it to the lieutenant here to arrange for musketry instruction, if you so choose. Limbs! Bow to the lady!"

The Limbs did as they were told, then whisked the captain away as he barked out "Hut two, hut two—on the double now!"

Elizabeth and Lt. Tindall stood silently for a moment in the shadow of the great house.

"Well," the lieutenant said.

"Well," said Elizabeth.

Another moment passed.

"Miss Bennet?"

"Lieutenant?"

"Would you be offended if I were to speak frankly?"

"That depends on what you might say."

"I see."

Another long pause followed.

Eventually, Lt. Tindall drew in a deep breath, as if gathering his strength for some powerful exertion. Which he was.

With an effort so apparent Elizabeth thought at first he was about to sneeze, the young soldier forced himself to speak.

"I apologize for my earlier coldness, which was not intended as a slight, only I find myself, in all honesty, distressed, having discovered your sister to be, in the brief time I had to become acquainted with her, a young lady of exceptional qualities, none of them having anything to do with fighting and killing, and it pains me quite deeply to see her forced into a role so alien not just to her whole sex but to her tender spirit in particular, and it is, in addition, galling to find that your father's obsession with the unmentionables and the savageries of the East should result in your sister's most intimate connection with a man of such patently low morals as the grotesque satyr who owns this estate, and furthermore . . . have I said something amusing?"

Elizabeth, to her own surprise, was smiling. For the first time, she found herself almost liking the man.

"No, nothing amusing," she said. "Gratifying. Perhaps you could show me the way to the gunnery or whatever you call it, and we might talk further."

The lieutenant nodded and stretched out an arm toward a row of tents lining one side of the lawn. "This way."

They walked away from the house side by side.

"I appreciate your candor, Lieutenant," Elizabeth said. "Actually, I find myself in accord with your sentiments in one or two respects. Yet I must trust in my father, as you must trust your captain. They lived through the worst of The Troubles. Whatever they think necessary, I am inclined to do, and I know Jane feels likewise."

"That would seem sensible," the lieutenant said, looking straight ahead.

He didn't sound convinced. There was altogether too much emphasis, Elizabeth though, on the word *seem*.

"And might I point out," she pressed on, "that what my sisters and I are doing is hardly unprecedented. No less a personage than Lady Catherine de Bourgh once took up the sword to meet the threat of the dreadfuls."

"Yes, Lady Catherine . . . our own Joan of Arc," Lt. Tindall said. If he didn't seem to be wishing a bonfire upon Lady Catherine, he clearly didn't mean the analogy as a compliment, either. "At least she had the good taste to go into seclusion after the Battle of Kent and leave the defense of the realm to the king's army."

"And you think Jane and I should do likewise? Simply stand aside while all we hold dear is imperiled?"

"*Yes*," the lieutenant said without hesitation.

A little high-pitched "hmf!" of irritation escaped Elizabeth's lips, and she had to clamp her teeth to keep from saying more.

Almost! *Almost* she'd allowed herself to think well of the man! She was growing as soft-hearted as Jane!

"You think me a prig," Lt. Tindall said rather ruefully. "But what I am is a soldier who loves his country. Its traditions. Its values. Everything it stands for. And if we destroy the unmentionables but allow them to destroy all that—including our ideal of genteel English womanhood—can we even say we've truly won?"

"*Yes*," Elizabeth said, pleased to throw the word back in the lieutenant's face with certitude equal to his own. "And if you preserve genteel English womanhood while serving up genteel English *women* as so much steak tartare, I would say that you have most definitely lost."

"You must keep faith in those things that have made England great, Miss Bennet."

"Those were General Cornwallis's sentiments, too, Lieutenant Tindall. And the last time he was seen, I believe, he was feasting upon one of his own dragoons."

In her pique, Elizabeth had sped up her pace considerably, so much so that the lieutenant had to scurry to keep up with her. But now she came to such a sudden stop the young man shot past her by several steps.

"Ah!" she said. "Muskets! Who's going to teach me to shoot, then? You, Lieutenant?"

Before them were a dozen soldiers, each with a Brown Bess in his hands. They looked tentative and bewildered to Elizabeth—not like fierce warriors at all. They were watching a tub-gutted sergeant as he held up his own musket with one hand and reached down to a black box at his side with the other.

"CarTOUCHE!" the sergeant boomed.

The soldiers groped at identical boxes hanging at their hips.

The sergeant pulled out a small, yellowish tube.

"Paper CHARGE!"

The soldiers pulled out their own charges with much fumbling and furrowing of brows. More than one dropped the little tube and had to bend down and pick it up off the lawn.

"Bite top off CHARGE! Keep ball in MOUTH!"

The sergeant put the tube up to his teeth, ripped off the top, and spat away a loose wad of paper.

The soldiers struggled to do the same, many of them grimacing. Apparently, paper charges didn't taste particularly good.

"Powder in PAN! Lock pa—SimmmmmmmMONS! What is the probLEM?"

One of the soldiers had gone pop-eyed.

"Cuuuuuuuuu cuuuuu cuuuuuuu," he wheezed.

"I think he swallowed his musket ball, Sergeant," the soldier next to him said.

Simmons nodded emphatically.

"Dammit!"

The sergeant stomped over and swatted Simmons on the back until a small gray ball exploded from the man's mouth with such force he could have almost served as a musket himself.

"All RIGHT! Begin aGAIN!"

"With all due respect, Lieutenant," Elizabeth said, "after seeing this, not to mention the incident upon the road the other day, I'm not especially inclined to return to my needlework and let the king's army attend to anything."

Lt. Tindall snapped up to his full height as if something very sharp had just been poked into something very tender.

"These are new recruits, conscripted in London little more than a week ago. They still need much in the way of training. And, I might add, it doesn't help matters much when that training is disrupted by the presence of a young lady. To allow you to actually join in . . . it's madness."

Elizabeth straightened up as tall as she could, too, lifting her chin high. "So you refuse to teach me to shoot?"

The lieutenant shook his head. "No. I have orders and I will follow them. If you insist on this frivolous exercise, I will find someone who might be spared to indulge you. I would ask, however, that you remove yourself to the back lawn so as not to create a spectacle and further distract the men."

Elizabeth found herself gripping the hilt of her katana. The sword might have even slid an inch or two from its scabbard by the time she noticed.

"Far be it for me to wreck the morale of the whole English army," she said. "You need not worry about further distractions on my account. Good day to you, Sir."

She whirled around and headed for the trees on the far side of the lawn.

"Miss Bennet! Wait! Where are you going?"

Elizabeth stopped and looked back just long enough to say, "Home. And no, I will not require an escort. This sword is all I need!"

Then she was off again. She didn't slow down until she was on the path that led to Longbourn—and she was certain she was out of sight.

"Yes, that's the way to prove you wouldn't be a distraction," she fumed. "That's how to prove your mettle. Throw a tantrum and stomp off like a child!"

She knew she should go back. To do as her father asked. To learn to use a musket. To apologize to the lieutenant for causing a scene. To avoid the unmentionable eager to refill its belly with fresh meat.

Yet though she slowed, she couldn't turn herself around. She was grateful to be heading back to Longbourn, she realized. Perhaps she was even excited. But why?

Could it be something as foolish as, as improper as, as hopeless as—?

A tall, thin figure came bounding out of the brush by the road, and Elizabeth whirled on it, blade already flashing brightly in the sun.

"Ahhhh, Miss Bennet!" Dr. Keckilpenny said, his toothy grin undimmed by the katana poised to slice through his scrawny neck. "I'm so glad I caught up to you! Good morning! Sorry to startle you! My, what an exquisite piece of cutlery!"

Elizabeth resheathed her sword and heaved a sigh heavy with both embarrassment and thwarted bloodlust. "Good morning, Doctor. I'm honored to find that you remember me. When we first met, you said you had to know someone at least ten years before you could recall their name."

Dr. Keckilpenny furrowed his brow and frowned. "Did I? I have no memory of that, of course, but it's certainly true enough. Only . . . yes. *Elizabeth Bennet*."

The doctor was in proper (if wrinkled and rumpled) clothes this day, and his dark hair, though free of the leaves and twigs he'd sported in his zombie disguise, was as wild as the thicket he'd just crashed through.

In his hands was something that looked very much like a butterfly net.

"Well," he said with a shrug of his bony shoulders, "how could I forget after our first meeting proved so memorable?"

He planted the long pole he was carrying in the ground and leaned against it. Straps and buckles ringed the inside of the netting, Elizabeth now saw, and it didn't hang limp but rather jutted out stiffly, as if the mesh had been woven from copper wire. If this were a butterfly net, it had been designed for butterflies the size and strength of eagles.

"I say, Miss Bennet," Dr. Keckilpenny said, "are you engaged?"

Elizabeth blinked. "Excuse me?"

"Are you engaged, at the moment? Occupied? Busy? Unavailable? Spoken for? I was just about to head off into the woods again when I spied you up this way, and I thought to myself, 'Ooooo, I'd really rather not be eaten. I wonder if the young lady would care to join me. I'm no duke or earl or what have you, but if I'm lucky, perhaps I'll rate my own Bennet as a bodyguard!'"

"Oh. Of course. So you've heard about that. Well . . . "

Elizabeth looked away, facing again the winding lane to Longbourn, feeling again the tug that drew her on—a pull that intrigued and confused and perhaps even frightened her.

She decided to test her strength against it.

"I would be delighted to accompany you."

Elizabeth turned toward Dr. Keckilpenny, putting the road behind her.

"Splendid! Come along, then! This way!" The doctor went striding back into the trees, then spun around before Elizabeth could follow and marched in the opposite direction. "Or was it this way?"

"Um . . . and what exactly are we doing?"

"Why, isn't it obvious?" Dr. Keckilpenny gave his net a shake as he shot past Elizabeth, bound for the other side of the lane and the murky woods beyond. "We're off to catch ourselves a zombie!"

CHAPTER 24

TO SAY THAT LORD LUMPLEY had beguiled more than one young lady under her father's nose would, by the baron's own reckoning, grossly underestimate his verve, nerve, and skill. Several of his seductions had been conducted in such plain sight they weren't so much under a parent's nose as dancing atop it, right between the eyes.

Wooing Jane Bennet in the presence of her father, however, presented challenges of a sort he'd never before encountered, and though he spent the entire ride to Meryton trying to work his charms on her, he ended the trip quite certain he'd have met with more success making love to an unmentionable.

There was, for one thing, Jane's demure-unto-nonexistent personality. If Lord Lumpley smiled at her, she blushed and looked away. If he tried to talk to her, she blushed and looked away. If he ignored her, she blushed and looked away. If the girl hadn't looked so incredibly fetching blushing and looking away, he would've tired of the whole enterprise and told her father to go stuff himself.

There was, in addition, the fact that both Bennets were armed with swords half again as long as the baron was tall. He'd endured many a slap to the cheek in his time and found every way possible to dodge a duel, but this was the first time he'd had to worry about disembowelment.

Yet instead of cooling his ardor, all this merely fanned it to a higher flame. The thrill of the hunt had taken on a very real hint of danger, and what's more . . . well, it was strange, but Lord Lumpley was finding the sight of a beautiful woman wielding a deadly weapon to be almost unbearably arousing.

If anyone in Meryton had the same reaction, they did a good job hiding it. Smirks, leers, sneers, glowers—that was all he saw as they rode into town. And though most everyone was careful to greet him with smiling civility after he and his party climbed down from the carriage, the Bennets were acknowledged with no more than stiff nods, when they were acknowledged at all.

Mr. Bennet, inscrutable old rogue that he was, bluffed indifference, but his daughter's response was predictable. She blushed. She looked away. At one point—after a gaggle of young girls broke into giggles upon spotting Jane's sword—Mr. Bennet lay a hand on her shoulder and whispered in her ear. Whatever he said seemed to give her strength, for she nodded and, for the moment at least, kept her gaze up, proud and straight. But Lord Lumpley could see the barely checked tears glistening in her eyes.

Which was all fine by the baron. A woman armed might have been exciting, but a woman wounded presented opportunity. Whatever respectability the Bennets had left flowed solely from their new connection to a nobleman—a connection he could sever at his leisure. So Jane and her father had reason to fear him, too: They could take off his head, yes, but he could cut the whole family off at the knees.

Lord Lumpley occupied himself with these thoughts (along with idle imaginings about Jane that need not be described) as Mr. Bennet led them here and there around the village. First they collected Ensign Pratt and his pitiful little "garrison" of seven rather shabby-looking soldiers, pausing to suffer through the innkeeper's complaints about bad business. The regular hackney runs from London had been mysteriously suspended, there were no other travelers upon the roads, deliveries of ale and cheese from neighboring towns were long overdue, etcetera. Naturally, the baron found it hard to keep his eyes open while a tradesman wound out his woes, but Mr. Bennet listened to the fellow's grumblings with grim attentiveness.

While the innkeeper prattled on, Ensign Pratt dispatched his troops to collect the cargo that had (at Capt. Cannon's insistence) been hauled to town in the back of Lord Lumpley's fine phaeton as though it were a common lorry. And if that hadn't been indignity enough, it was then on to see a blacksmith, of all things. The baron refused to set foot inside the establishment, of course, and actually managed a minute alone with Jane while Mr. Bennet and the ensign disappeared into the smithy's dark, smoky shop.

"I have not had a chance to tell you, Miss Bennet, how smart you look with a sword at your side. It is quite unconventional, I'll grant, yet also, in its own way, quite uncommonly fetching. I fancy it will be all the rage for the ladies at court come autumn!"

"Thank you, My Lord," Jane said, face reddening, gaze falling to a spot just to the left of the baron's boots. The girl was nothing if not consistent.

"I hope you'll offer a demonstration later of your skills with a blade. You see, I fancy myself a swordsman, of sorts, and I'd very much like to see how you handle yourself with one."

The girl looked up, fixing her sky-blue eyes on him at last, and the baron feared she might remind him that no such demonstration was necessary: He'd seen her wield a sword once already, when she'd dealt with poor Emily Ward back at the lake.

At just that moment, though, a studiously respectable couple came by—a Mr. and Mrs. Beechman, it seemed from Jane's greeting—and though they gave Lord Lumpley a smile and a nod, the girl they ignored, sweeping past her with their noses so high in the air it was a wonder they could see where they were going.

Jane reverted to her customary pose, head hanging even lower, blush even deeper.

"You mustn't let the snubs of the small-minded upset you, my dear," the baron said. "Live as I do. Follow your conscience. Your heart."

Your loins, he didn't add, though the thought of it put a grin on his face he didn't even bother to hide. For all her weapons and warrior posturing, this Jane was a simple, naive thing, sensitive and overdeferential. She would think it a comforting smile, not a leer. And she would think him a friend—if not now, then one day. Hopefully, soon.

He was on the verge of risking a reassuring pat on the hand when Mr. Bennet and Ensign Pratt came back, and the baron was so piqued by the swiftness of their return he barely even noticed that they were now lugging huge, black-headed hammers.

"Thank you for your patience, My Lord," Mr. Bennet said. "Our preparations are now complete. It's on to the vicarage, where I hope the Reverend Mr. Cummings will prove as susceptible to your powers of persuasion as so many before him."

The insufferable man offered up one of his little smirks, and it was for the baron now to guess what intent lay behind another's smile.

The vicar they found preparing his Easter sermon, and he was displeased to be called away for anything of lesser importance. He was a meek, mewling sort generally, his rectoral style leaning more toward unctuous sanctimony than hellfire and damnation. It was one of the few reasons the baron had been able to tolerate the man: Anyone who took all that good-and-evil claptrap too seriously would've proved a thorn in his side.

Upon hearing what Mr. Bennet and the ensign proposed to do, however, Mr. Cummings unleashed a self-righteous rage the likes of which he'd never even hinted at from the pulpit.

"It's abominable! Unspeakable! Sacrilege!"

"First and foremost, it is necessary," Mr. Bennet replied coolly. "And, secondly, it is overdue. As for all those other things, I can but agree. Your complaint, however, would best be lodged in the form of prayer, for is it not a higher authority than any of us who has, for His own mysterious reasons, loosed 'unspeakable abominations' upon us first?"

"YOU BLASPHEME!"

"I apologize if I do," Mr. Bennet said with a shrug. "I merely thought to observe."

He glanced at Ensign Pratt, then Lord Lumpley, signaling that it was up to them now to help the vicar see the light.

"I tell you, Sir, this is of the highest strategic importance," the ensign squeaked. (Though an officer, he was little more than a boy—and one so diminutive and baby faced he made the young troops he commanded look like a company of snowy-bearded Methuselahs.) "Captain Cannon absolutely insists that we proceed without delay."

"I do not answer to Captain Cannon! I answer to almighty God!"

"As must we all, Mr. Cummings," the baron said. "Yet I have no desire to stand before Him any earlier than I have to. If Captain Cannon and Mr. Bennet feel that this unpleasant necessity will delay that day for any of us, I think it prudent to see it through forthwith. And you can be assured that this is an attitude I will not keep to myself if any in the community raise objections."

"Have you not heard a word I've said? *I* object!" Mr. Cummings roared. "I cannot allow you to defile hallowed ground!"

Lord Lumpley jerked back as if struck. Hang his "powers of persuasion." This self-righteous upstart needed to be squashed like a bug!

"*You* cannot allow *me*?" he said. "Might I remind you, Mr. Cummings, that the Archbishop of Canterbury has been a guest in my home?" *And nearly emptied my damned wine cellar!* "That the Prince Regent is a close, personal friend?" *Why, I've seen the man naked!* "That I am the sixth baron of Lumpley and a knight of the Bath—which makes me the closest thing you grubby bumpkins have to *royalty* in this miserable backwater?"

Mr. Cummings, Mr. Bennet, and Ensign Pratt all popped their eyes wide in surprise.

Oh, the baron thought. *Perhaps I shouldn't have said that last part out loud.*

The vicar sucked in a deep breath, the scowl on his face making it plain how he intended to use it. It had been a long, long time since anyone had dared rebuke Lord Lumpley in public. Now his state of grace was about to end.

The baron steeled himself for thunder, but heard a soft, melodious whisper instead.

"Gentlemen, please," Jane said, "if I may offer a suggestion?"

The girl was sitting in a corner of the vicarage's cramped drawing room, so silent the men had, for a time, forgotten she was there at all. Though she'd asked for permission to address them, she didn't wait for anyone to give it.

"It seems to me," she said, her soft voice gaining strength without losing its gentle lilt, "that you are speaking of all or nothing when a compromise could easily be reached. The Reverend Mr. Cummings has his sacred duties to think of, and it does him credit that he takes them so seriously. Yet if he would consent to do as my father and Captain Cannon ask just once— simply in the way of a trial, without necessarily following through to the admittedly gruesome conclusion they seek—then we will know whether this course of action is truly warranted. If Papa and the captain are mistaken, we will quickly know, and the matter can be laid to rest permanently . . . so to speak. And it should be made clear to Mr. Cummings that arrangements have been made to ensure that, whatever we do, privacy and dignity will be maintained as much as possible and, of course, that the vicar himself isn't just welcome to observe these proceedings but is respectfully entreated to oversee them."

Her conciliatory tone, her well-chosen words, her obvious good sense, and, above all, her generous spirit—they worked a spell on Mr. Cummings that he couldn't resist. By the time she was through, not only was his frown gone, he was smiling upon her pleasantly, utterly pacified.

Mr. Bennet, meanwhile, beamed with a pride tinged with regret. For all his efforts to turn Jane into a warrior, peacemaking clearly suited her better. She'd certainly done a better job of it than the baron had with all his bluster, and even he paused to appreciate her sweetness and sagacity—before being distracted by her décolletage as she rose to go.

The party left the vicarage to see her suggestion through. Once outside, they collected Ensign Pratt's men, who were leaning against the stone wall that ran along the road, smoking pipes and grumbling amongst themselves.

"Pick up that gear and fall in!" the ensign roared. (Or tried to. It came out more like a mewl.) "Snap to it, now! Hut hut!"

The soldiers hopped up and grabbed the poles and rolled canvas and bags of tent pegs Lord Lumpley and the Bennets had brought from Netherfield Park. Yet one pile, the baron noticed, went untouched until all the other items had been claimed.

Only the slowest and unluckiest men ended up with the *shovels*.

"Come on!" the ensign yipped. "Look alive, look alive!"

Once Pratt had lined up his squad, the whole group—the soldiers, the Bennets, the vicar, and (because he'd been too slow thinking up a way to get out of it) the baron—turned and headed toward the cemetery.

CHAPTER 25

DR. KECKILPENNY did a few more spins—"This is the way, I'm sure of it. Then again . . . "—before Elizabeth could ask him where exactly he was trying to lead her.

"That little lake on the estate." He turned toward Lord Lumpley's manor house, then whirled round toward the forest, then back to the house, then back to the trees. "You know the one. Where the girl zombie came out of the water."

Elizabeth nodded somberly, unsure which memory disheartened her more: a stricken Emily Ward shuffling toward her, bloated and rank, or her own failure to end the girl's curse with a swift slice of the sword.

"I'm afraid you haven't been right yet," she said. "It's this way."

She led him up the lane that led to Longbourn, and Meryton beyond.

"Thank you. Once again, I find myself indebted to my native guide." Dr. Keckilpenny nodded at the katana at Elizabeth's side. "And it reassures me to see you've brought something a tad more formidable than that

wee stickpin you were using the other day—not that you didn't use it as
well as one might. I've managed to misplace my pistol, you see, and my
net here isn't going to do us much good if we happen upon a zombie *herd*.
So our lives could be very much in your dainty hands."

"It flatters me that you seem so sanguine about that, Doctor. And
surprises me. Not all are so liberal in their thinking when young ladies
take up the sword."

"For anyone who has made a serious study of The Troubles, it is not
liberality but simple good sense. Clinging to the old ways in times such
as these would be like . . . " Dr. Keckilpenny rolled his eyes heavenward
and chewed at his lower lip. "A drowning man clutching a brick? Does
that make sense? Metaphors are not my forte."

"I beg to differ. That one was rather good."

"Really? Thank you. I shall have to use it again sometime, provided
I can remember it."

They took their next few steps without speaking. But Dr. Keckilpenny, rather like Elizabeth's mother, seemed averse to silence, and soon
he looked over and said, "Well, aren't you going to ask me why anyone
should wish to capture a zombie?"

"I thought it obvious, given your interests. You want to examine it.
Observe it at close quarter. Learn from it."

"Precisely!" The young doctor flashed one of his toothy grins.
"Then you don't think me mad?"

Elizabeth shrugged. "Curiosity hardly makes one mad."

Dr. Keckilpenny's smile grew so broad Elizabeth almost wondered
how his lean, narrow face could contain it.

"What a splendid sentiment! And so, *so* rare. I should translate it into
Latin and declare it my motto. Now, how would that go? *Curiositas non
novo a vir rabidus*, perhaps? I'm not sure. I was always so much better with
Greek, but it doesn't look nearly so good carved into marble."

To her surprise, Elizabeth found herself laughing.

"Ahhhh," Dr. Keckilpenny said, "*now* you think me mad."

"Not at all. Though I suppose I could ask why you'd bother making a study of the unmentionables. We have a chronicle of The Troubles at home, and from what I've read—"

"Which one?"

"Pardon?"

"Which 'chronicle of The Troubles'?"

"Gibbon's *A Complete History of the Most Tragic and Awful Events Following the Rise of the Sorry Stricken from Their Graves and the Ensuing Horrors Which*—"

"Yes yes yes, I know it well." Dr. Keckilpenny waved a long hand before his face, as if dispelling an unpleasant odor. "Rubbish, every word. But do go on, please."

"Well, according to Mr. Gibbon, the greatest minds in England tried to study captive dreadfuls when the strange plague first appeared, the only result being that many of those great minds were very quickly ripped from their vessels and devoured."

"Assuming all that's true—and when it comes to the history of the plague, I've found that to be a foolish thing to do—" Dr. Keckilpenny paused just long enough to wink and put a finger beside his beaklike nose. "I would point out that we are now in the nineteenth century. Time has marched on, and knowledge with it. The menace may have returned, but there are modern men of science ready to confront it. And this time, science shall prevail."

"Perhaps. I think I know, however, how my mmm—"

The word Elizabeth had said so often, so freely of late—*master*—stuck in her throat.

Was it that she was beginning to see Geoffrey Hawksworth as something less than a master . . . or something more?

She brought a fist to her lips and coughed demurely until she could carry on.

"Ah, how my instructor in the deadly arts would respond to that. Science, he would say, has created no weapon more dependably lethal than a sharp blade wielded by strong hands."

Dr. Keckilpenny gave Elizabeth the same look of amused bemusement she'd seen a thousand times on her father's face.

"Oh?" he chuckled. "Well, I should very much like to see how your instructor would fare with his sharp blade and strong hands were he up against a single man armed with a—"

There was a sharp *crack*, and a little burst of dirt and gravel flew up a few inches from Elizabeth's right foot. Elizabeth and Dr. Keckilpenny stared down at the newly dug pockmark in the road, then stared at each other, then stared straight ahead.

A soldier was before them, perhaps forty feet off, a musket clutched in his hands and a puff of smoking floating off above his head. It was the same sentry who'd challenged Elizabeth and Jane and Mr. Bennet when they'd approached Netherfield Park that morning.

"Uhhhh . . . who goes there?" he said.

"I am not a military man, so you might want to take this with a grain of salt," Dr. Keckilpenny replied. "But in my experience, one asks that *before* one shoots."

"Yes, Sir. Sorry, Sir. It was an accident, Sir."

"Think nothing of it, Corporal Holmes. What's a little crossfire between friends?"

"It's Private Jones, Sir. And thank you, Sir. It won't happen again, Sir."

"Good, good. We'll just be on our way, then. Miss Bennet?"

The doctor bowed and swept an arm out toward the road ahead.

"Actually, this is where we leave the lane anyway," Elizabeth said. "We'll need to cross this meadow and go over that knoll to reach the lake."

Dr. Keckilpenny pivoted so his arm was now stretched out toward the hill beyond. "Lead on."

The close call with a musket ball squelched, for a time, anyone's taste for banter, and it wasn't until they were halfway across the field that Dr. Keckilpenny looked back over his shoulder and said, "I suggest we return by a different route."

Elizabeth glanced back, too. Three other soldiers had joined Pvt. Jones, drawn by the sound of gunfire, no doubt. The sentry was simultaneously gesturing at Elizabeth and the doctor and squinting down into the barrel of his Brown Bess as if he'd lost his ramrod in it.

"I agree," Elizabeth said. "Though I wouldn't worry overmuch about being shot by mistake, since most of the soldiers I've seen have neither the skill nor the inclination to fire their muskets at all. I know that you said you're not a military man, yet don't you find it queer that Captain Cannon should come to Hertfordshire with such poorly trained troops?"

"I do when I let myself notice it. Unfortunately—or, perhaps, fortunately—my mind is rather like a microscope or a spyglass: It can focus with great clarity upon one point, but all else is consequently blocked out. And for the past two months, my focus has been on zombies."

"*Two* months?" Elizabeth said. It hadn't been one since Mr. Ford crashed his own funeral. Apparently, Dr. Keckilpenny was as haphazard with dates as he was with names.

"Yes, and the most fascinating months of my life they've been!" the doctor enthused. "To think I once believed I'd never see a zombie. Their very existence flies in the face of science, and now we've been given a second chance to answer all the old questions. What could reanimate the flesh of the dead? What drives the resurrected to feed on the living? Why only people? Why only in Britain? Why are you taking out your sword?"

It took Elizabeth a moment to realize this last was not one of the "old questions" but a very new and immediate one: She'd drawn her katana without even thinking about it.

"I . . . ," she began, not knowing what words might come next. And then there it was, rising up from the level of instinct and pure sensation to tangible, relatable thought. "I smell something."

They'd stopped halfway up the wooded rise blocking the way to the lake, and Dr. Keckilpenny turned a wary gaze to the top of the hill.

"Or some *things*, I warrant," he whispered.

He looked at Elizabeth again, and the two of them simply stood there, gazing into each other's eyes, until, at a signal from neither, they both turned and started up the hill again at precisely the same moment. They moved slowly, choosing their steps with care, and when they reached the crest they crouched down, Elizabeth on one side of an old, rough-trunked elm, Dr. Keckilpenny on the other.

Below was the lake. Beside it, three figures.

One sat on the bank, back propped against a rotted-out log. The other two were stooped over it, scooping something glutinous and oozy from the top of its head.

"Excellent," Dr. Keckilpenny said under his breath.

Elizabeth shot him a horrified glower. Then she stood and started toward the water.

"Miss Bennet, wait . . . stop, please . . . *Elizabeth!*"

The doctor might as well have not spoken at all. The only sound Elizabeth heard was the awful moist smacking of the unmentionables' mastication. All she saw was the crimson-streaked pulp disappearing into their rotten maws. All she felt was her katana in her hands, and then the air streaking through her hair as she charged down the hill. And the only man she was thinking of was Lt. Tindall and the self-righteous sneer she longed to wipe from his face—and every other face that might sneer at her and her sisters.

"HAAAAAAAA-IEEEEEEEEEEEEEE!"

The nearest of the zombies sprang toward her, its mouth still oozing half-chewed goo. It had been a woman not so long ago. Now it fought to fully free its desiccated, purple-mottled arms from the tangles of its shroud, the better to get its clawlike fingerbones into Elizabeth's eyes.

Elizabeth took its arms off at the elbows with her first swing of the sword. The second took off its head.

And it felt good.

She had killed unassisted. She *was* a warrior, and a thousand times more worthy to call herself such than the lieutenant and his bumbling redcoats. She turned to face the other unmentionable's charge feeling indomitable, unfettered, free.

Which made it all the more of a shock when the net came down over her head and the leather straps cinched tight, pinning her arms to her sides. A jarring jerk tugged her off her feet, and she lost her grip on her sword as she crashed to the muddy bank on her backside. She could but watch, helpless, as the oncoming zombie—a male with gray, dirt-streaked skin that had yet to decay enough to fall away from the bone—lunged at her, its black tongue waggling obscenely.

Then the dreadful, too, was splashing down into the mud, its hands inches from Elizabeth's feet. The thing flailed at her, wailing, yet it could come no closer.

The straps around her loosened, the net lifted away, and Dr. Keckilpenny bent down and offered Elizabeth his hand.

"I'm terribly sorry about that," he said, "but if you'll recall, I wanted one of them alive . . . as it were."

Elizabeth pushed herself up without the doctor's help. When she was on her feet, she noticed at last the bear trap clamped around the dreadful's ankle and the short length of chain staked to the log beyond. She saw, too, that the body from which the unmentionables had been feeding wasn't a proper body at all: It was simply clothes stuffed with straw topped by a chamber pot "head."

In the pot were the bloody, mashed remnants of a human brain.

Despite all she'd seen the past few weeks, Elizabeth blanched and looked away. She tried to hide her revulsion by pretending she was merely retrieving her katana.

No more than a minute before, she'd felt invincible. Yet now that seemed so long ago she could barely believe it ever happened, and all she could feel was disgust—as much for the pride that had momentarily blinded her as for the grotesque lumps of flesh clotting the chamber pot.

"Your bait, Doctor," she said, careful to keep her voice from waver-

THE THING FLAILED AT HER, WAILING, YET IT COULD COME NO CLOSER

ing. "Is it what I think it is?"

Dr. Keckilpenny nodded. "Every zombie's favorite delicacy. Nothing but the real thing would do, so I brought along my own supply. Don't ask me where I got it. Suffice it to say, the first thing one learns in medical college is how to acquire one's own specimens."

"And now you have another." Elizabeth turned to the slavering dreadful writhing on the ground nearby, its arms stretched out to paw uselessly at the muck and leaves between them. "What do you propose to do with it?"

"I propose," Dr. Keckilpenny said, the old gleam firing up again in his eyes, "to turn 'it' back into a 'him.'"

CHAPTER 26

AFTER SOME QUICK (and, thanks again to Jane, courteous) debate, a subject was settled on for the experiment the Reverend Mr. Cummings had agreed to. Since it wouldn't do to unduly disturb a respectable member of the community, the party would remove itself to a far corner of the parish grounds and pay a call on a connectionless pauper woman who'd been planted there three months before. This had the added benefit of seclusion, the gravesite being further removed from the road.

All the same, before a single spade bit into the earth, Mr. Bennet insisted that the tent canvases the troops had brought be strung up around the grave.

"It wouldn't do to have our trial here observed," he explained while the soldiers argued over the best spots to pound in their tent pegs. "We have been spared panic in Meryton, thanks to complacency and ignorance. It is to our advantage to preserve that just a little longer, if we can."

"In my experience, complacency and ignorance usually do a fine job preserving themselves," Lord Lumpley yawned, idly eyeing Jane as he leaned against a mausoleum nearby. "But if you feel you must put up your little dressing screens . . . "

"Why, though, Father?" Jane asked. "What advantage could come from hiding the truth?"

"He wishes to avoid another Birmingham," Ensign Pratt chirped. The junior officer was doing his best to loom up over his men as they began hammering pegs into the ground, but given his size, looming over anything larger than a dachshund was an impossibility. "People fleeing in huge mobs, clogging the roads, falling prey to the dreadful swarms."

"Not just falling prey to them. Feeding them." Mr. Bennet gave Ensign Pratt an approving nod. "I'm glad to know you're old enough to have at least *read* of The Troubles."

"Might have a hard time putting up those tents, Sir," one of the soldiers reported. He waved his hammer at a peg he'd just pummeled into the turf with one blow. "Ground here's all marshy like."

"I'm sure they'll hold, Roper. Carry on." The ensign looked over at Mr. Bennet. "At least it will make for quick digging."

"That it will," Mr. Bennet said, poking a toe into the spongy sod. "For everyone."

He threw his daughter a somber glance that moved her hand to her sword.

Ensign Pratt frowned, but Mr. Cummings didn't even seem to notice anything was amiss, for he'd been busy leafing through his *Book of Common Prayer* in search of something appropriate for such an *un*common occasion.

Lord Lumpley, on the other hand, couldn't help but notice, given that his eyes rarely strayed from Jane. He straightened up and began backing away from the others.

"Well, now that we've got this under way, no doubt there are other matters I could be attending to around the village. Perhaps Miss Bennet and I might—"

glued to his book, "'which is presented to the reader that he may j-judge the manner in which our Reformers made use of the liturgical commmmmpositions of this gr-great mmmmm-man.'"

"I think you're reading footnotes now, Mr. Cummings," Jane said with remarkable gentleness, considering that she was, at the time, endeavoring to pry a hand off the hem of her dress with the point of a sword.

"Let the vicar read what he would," her father told her. "I doubt if anyone could find the perfect prayer for consecrating *this*."

He knelt down near the flailing stubs. They were wriggling their way farther from the earth while the little swelling between grew larger.

Any second now, the top of the dreadful's head was going to break the surface.

"Obviously, I have miscalculated," Mr. Bennet said. "Usually one can count on a steady rate of one-and-one-half feet per week, but our friend here is arriving ahead of schedule. Perhaps my mistake was in backdating from Mr. Ford's conversion, when the plague might have in fact arrived much sooner. Ahhh, well. It's not my first mistake, and I can only hope it won't be my last." He shrugged and turned to the soldiers clumped together nearby. "If someone would be so kind as to fetch one of the smithy's hammers, please. So that I might make a demonstration."

Half the soldiers whirled away to do as he asked, desperate for any excuse to put distance between themselves and the unmentionable about to sprout like some ghastly flower. The other half simply stared with their mouths agape.

"Papa, we are being watched." Jane nodded at the road. "By Mrs. Long and her nieces, I believe."

"Then it may as well be all Meryton, I'm afraid." Mr. Bennet waved to their far-off audience. "Hello, there! Just enjoying a lovely little morning picnic! Would you care to join us?"

The women scurried off down the lane.

One of Ensign Pratt's men returned with a heavy black hammer just as the ground split open to reveal a tuft of mud-clogged hair.

"Thank you." Mr. Bennet took the hammer but made no move to use it. "Tell me, My Lord—I find I've lost track of the social calendar. The spring ball at Pulvis Lodge is set for tomorrow night, is it not?"

A scaly forehead, alive with writhing worms, rose out of the moist loam, as did the sound of low, muffled moaning. Yet still Mr. Bennet remained crouched mere feet away, doing nothing.

"The ball, you say?" The baron looked back and forth from the unmentionable to Mr. Bennet, seemingly unsure which he found more alarming. "Yes, yes—tomorrow, it is. Do you wish it canceled?"

More soil crumbled aside, and eyebrows became visible. They were followed a moment later by the eyes themselves—bloodshot, bulging, and wild with hate or hunger or both.

"Quite the contrary," Mr. Bennet said. "I merely think it should be moved to a new venue. Someplace larger affording better protection for the guests."

"Aren't you going to do something about that?" Ensign Pratt yelped, pointing at the dreadful wriggling its way from the grave. The thing's nose (what was left of it) was now above ground, and the handless arms were visible up to the elbows.

"When the moment is right," Mr. Bennet said.

Mr. Cummings began reading aloud from what appeared to be the prayer book's introduction.

"It has been the awwww-bject of the editor in preparing for the public the present edition to increase the utility of our admirable l-l-liturgy by rendering it more generally and completely unnnnnnder-stood. . . . "

"Are you saying you want *me* to host the ball?" the baron said. "You press your luck, Bennet."

"Indeed, I do."

The head was now out far enough to reveal the chalky, desiccated face of an old woman. The unmentionable's contortions were growing wilder as the dirt loosened around it, and the ground began to swell up where its shoulders would, before long, pop up into the sunshine.

"Under normal circumstances," Mr. Bennet said, "I could deny a man such as yourself nothing, My Lord. Yet these are hardly normal circumstances, I think you'll agree, and I find instead that I must ask of you absolutely everything."

"I say!" Ensign Pratt cried, his voice cracking. He seemed to be working very, very hard to hold in a "Fire!" "Could you settle this matter another time, perhaps?"

The dreadful's moaning had turned to snuffling snarls as its mouth approached the surface. For reasons knowable only to itself, the creature seemed to find Mr. Cummings the most appetizing of all those present, and it locked its bugged-out eyes on the vicar and began jerking its head back and forth, chomping at mud in its eagerness to feast on flesh.

"All right. I suppose she's out far enough," Mr. Bennet said. "Jane, Ensign, men—observe."

He hefted the blacksmith's hammer and brought it down on the unmentionable's crown. The whole skull exploded in a spray of pulp and bone, and the zombie instantly stopped its struggling, half its head splattered on the ground, the other half on Mr. Bennet's breeches.

"Ahhh . . . note for next time," Mr. Bennet said. "I forgot to take us by the butcher's. You'll probably want to procure suitable aprons before you proceed. It would be a shame to sully such splendid, spotless new uniforms with . . . oh."

Ensign Pratt had sullied his splendid, spotless new uniform by fainting.

"'Next t-time'?" Mr. Cummings muttered as the soldiers propped up their fallen officer and fanned him with their hats. The clergyman's prayer book had slipped from his fingers and lay splayed on the ground, forgotten. "'Proceed'?"

"I'm sorry, Mr. Cummings, but surely you can see my father and the captain were correct," Jane said. "Everyone laid to rest in the old way the last few years will have to be dealt with."

HE HEFTED THE BLACKSMITH'S HAMMER AND BROUGHT IT DOWN
ON THE UNMENTIONABLE'S CROWN.

By "the old way," of course, she meant unbeheaded.

The vicar stumbled, rested a hand atop a headstone for support and then, when he saw what he was leaning on, jerked away.

"How many of those markers have you added here since the Burial Act was repealed?" Mr. Bennet asked him. "Twenty? Thirty? If you can't recall, you need not worry: Soon enough an exact count will be easy indeed. Fancy caskets might last a little longer in the ground, but they won't hold what lies within them forever."

"I suppose it's t-t-true. . . . God help us. . . . " Mr. Cummings dared a glance at the dark circle of gore around the now-motionless unmentionable. "This calls for suh-suh-sssssssswift action." He straightened his black frock coat with a trembly tug, then turned and tottered off toward the vicarage. "I shall write my bishop immediately."

"Excuse me?" Mr. Bennet said.

"I l-l-lack the authority to approve a m-m-mass disinterment," Mr. Cummings muttered as he shuffled away. "I must consult with the head of the d-d-diocese . . . perhaps even the archbishop himmmmself. But I will state the matter's urgency in no uncertain terms, you may rest assured."

"Get your head out of your cassock, you fool!" Lord Lumpley called after him. "There's no time for any of that!"

Jane slipped swiftly past the baron, catching up to Mr. Cummings in but a few, fleet-footed strides.

"You look weak." She wrapped an arm around the man's waist. "Allow me to help, Mr. Cummings."

In a blink, she was behind him, her other arm crooked around his neck.

She'd seen the Panther's Kiss performed only once, but she was a very attentive pupil.

The vicar squirmed weakly, sagged, then dropped to the ground.

"Oh, dear," Jane said. "It appears Mr. Cummings has fainted, just like Ensign Pratt."

"Well, I suppose the grass here is as soft as any bed. We'll just let him rest on"—Mr. Bennet peered at the headstone marking the plot Mr. Cummings was stretched out upon—"Mrs. Foreman until his nerves recover. She was buried during The Troubles, so I don't suppose the lady will be raising any objections. And while our friend the vicar is recuperating, we might as well carry on with our labors here. He did call for swift action before he went all woozy and incomprehensible." He turned one of his dry little smirks on Lord Lumpley. "Isn't that right?"

"Yes. Quite," the baron grated out. "Though it does make me curious. If I should refuse to host the ball at Netherfield—which I assume you wish me to do for some devious reason all your own—will I suddenly find myself becoming 'woozy and incomprehensible,' as well?"

"Oh, I can't imagine that, my Lord." Jane turned and started walking toward the baron. "Your constitution seems quite sound. If not for your rather strongly worded intervention when the dreadful took hold of me, I suspect I'd now be stretched out on the ground like Mr. Cummings and Ensign Pratt." She stopped directly before Lord Lumpley and held his gaze for a long moment with no hint of a blush to her cheeks. "No, the only thing you should suffer should you decline, I think, would be the loss of an opportunity to dance with me and my sister, for as you know we would not be welcome at Pulvis Lodge."

Behind her, Mr. Bennet shifted uneasily, jaw clenching. He might have assigned this role to his daughter, but he was troubled now to see how well she could play it.

Lord Lumpley noticed—and was pleased.

"Well, since you put it like that, the matter is settled," he said. "You and I must return to Netherfield at once, Miss Bennet. Balls don't throw themselves, you know, and I'm certain you will soon prove yourself ever so helpful with mine."

CHAPTER 27

IT WAS OBVIOUS to Mary that the Master was distracted. He'd run through half a dozen new stances with her and Kitty and Lydia that morning, yet his drills had been slow, sloppy. Usually, he moved with an especially animated grace, almost a delight, when Mr. Bennet wasn't around, as if (Mary conjectured) he didn't want to show the older man up. But not now. Why, he didn't even bother taking off his coat and vest (something Mary was able to note without acknowledging how disappointed this made her).

Things didn't improve when the Master switched to weapons practice. He started off trying to instruct the girls in the art of throwing bolas ("the ancient Patagonian balls of death," he called them), but he could hardly even get his swinging, and when they ended up in a bunch around the post in the center of the dojo, he gave up entirely with a grunt of disgust.

Mary could guess what Lydia and Kitty made of all this. They kept on whispering and tittering no matter how many laps around the grounds it earned them.

Master Hawksworth was pouting, they thought. Moping. Heartsick because Lizzy wasn't there to moon over.

Mary knew better (as she did with all things, of course). From the beginning, she'd admired the Master's stern resolve and seriousness of purpose. She fancied him, in fact, to be a kindred spirit in that way. It would be only natural that her frivolous sisters would fail to understand him, just as they failed to understand her.

Master Hawksworth wasn't pining for Elizabeth. It was battle he

yearned for. In the weeks since he'd come to Longbourn, almost everyone seemed to have slain a dreadful except the very man who was surely
most adept at it.

Oh, and her.

Elizabeth, Lydia, Kitty, even sweet, gentle Jane—all had changed
since the Master came. And they'd all proved it, one way or another. Yet
Mary hadn't had the chance. How she feared what would happen when
that moment arrived. And yet she longed for it, too, especially if the Master should be there to share it with her.

She could imagine them fighting back to back, shoulder to shoulder, even arm in arm (though it was harder to work out exactly what
that would look like). Her sisters kept joking about the Master's "star
pupil," Lizzy. Yet perhaps it would turn out to be *she* whom he truly—

"Pay attention, Mary Bennet!" Master Hawksworth snapped. "The
warrior who daydreams soon sleeps the dreamless slumber of the dead!"

"Yes, Master. I'm sorry, Master. It won't happen again, Master."

Kitty snickered. Lydia snorted.

Master Hawksworth simply ignored them this time.

"I shall begin again," he said. "The secret to the bullwhip is in the
wrist. Your arm moves, yes, but the snap comes from the hand. Like so."

He moved his arm up and then quickly down again, the wrist jerking. His whip remained flaccid, though, and there was no *crack*. When he
tried again, the result was the same: The leather cord hung limp and rather
sad from his hand.

Master Hawksworth tossed the bullwhip aside.

"These pathetic English whips—they have no sinew, no strength. Like
so many of the English themselves. Bah! I don't even know why I try."

"'Try,' Master?" Mary said. "Did you not tell us once that *try* is a
word the warrior does not know? That one either does, or does not?"

The girls were sitting cross-legged on the floor for the Master's
demonstration, and he whirled around on them so fast that not only did
they all cringe, Lydia actually toppled over onto her back.

"Mary Bennet," Master Hawksworth growled, "you—"

Something stopped him.

Mary thought it might be the sincerity that (she hoped) shone through the trepidation on her face. She hadn't meant to question him. She . . . well, she simply couldn't stop herself. She wanted to help, as she'd so often helped her family with her insightful observations and timely axioms.

"You," the Master said again, "are . . . correct."

"She's *what?*" Lydia blurted out. She looked keenly disappointed that her sister wouldn't be joining her on the floor for a round of *dand-baithaks*.

Master Hawksworth strode over to his sheathed katana, took it down from the peg from which it hung, and began strapping it on. "Prepare yourselves. We go on patrol."

"On patrol?" Kitty said. "You mean as in . . . looking for zombies?"

The Master closed his eyes tightly for a second. It wasn't quite a flinch, but it was more than a blink.

Ahhh, Mary thought, *a warrior* and *a gentleman*.

"'Unmentionables,' Kitty," she chided. "Don't forget: A young lady doesn't use the Zed Word."

"Yes, well . . . should we get our swords so we can lop off more *unmentionables'* heads?" Lydia asked.

Master Hawksworth blink-flinched again. "Your swords, your maces, your throwing stars, your pikes. Whatever you prefer." He turned to Mary. "Your father tells me you've taken an interest in his flintlocks of late."

"Yes, Master! It's true, Master! I have, Master!"

"Bring one."

"Thank you, Master! I will, Master! The finest we have is a French dueling pistol. It's in the house, in my room. I've been sleeping with it, as you instructed we should with our favorites. I always start out with it under my pillow, yet many's the time I've awakened to find myself stroking it in my—"

"Yes, yes, fine," Master Hawksworth said. "Collect it and let us depart."

"Right away, Master!"

Mary was already flying out of the dojo when she realized Master Hawksworth had contradicted himself again: He usually had little use for firearms, and more than once he'd grumbled about the "contemptible weakness" of the young doctor who could rescue Elizabeth only with the aid of a flintlock pistol.

Normally, she would have filed this away to be brought to the Master's attention later. (Again, she wouldn't be questioning him but merely pointing out where his teachings might be made more uniform.) Outside, however, she found awaiting her such a surprise, even her well-honed ability to retain a failing for future comment was, for once, overthrown.

A dozen soldiers were loitering under an alder on the lawn, some sitting, some laughing, some smoking pipes. When they caught sight of Mary heading for the house, they fell silent, watching her with expressions that seemed either slyly insinuating or strangely pitying.

Mary was tempted to shoo them off the property as one might chase away a stray cat trying to make rude use of one's flower beds. It was hard to imagine how she might do this while maintaining her own ladylike grace, however, and she instead resolved to tell Capt. Cannon of the incident the next time she saw him. He seemed like such a dignified man, despite his less-than-dignified means of locomotion, and she couldn't imagine he'd approve of his troops loafing on decent citizens' lawns when they should be out hunting dreadfuls.

When Mary stepped inside the house, she found another surprise awaiting her: The usually industrious Mrs. Hill was sulking in a chair in the foyer.

"Tell me, Hill," Mary said, "were you aware that a group of soldiers was—"

"I don't know anything about anything!" the housekeeper cried, and she hopped to her feet and trundled off down the hall. "Or anyone! Not anymore!"

As Mary watched her disappear into the kitchen, too stunned to do more than gawp, she became aware of a voice droning away in the drawing room—a low, gravelly, indisputably *male* voice that was most certainly not her father's.

"Oh! Mark you yon pair, in the sunshine of youth," she heard it say as she moved closer, gliding silently ninja-style without even realizing she was doing so. "Love twin'd round their childhood his flow'rs as they grew. They flourish awhile, in the season of truth, till chill'd by the winter of Love's last adieu!"

It made no sense whatsoever to Mary, and she could but conclude it was the ravings of a madman.

"Sweet lady!" the voice went on. "Why thus doth a tear steal its way down a cheek which outrivals thy bosom in hue?"

Mary shrieked out her battle cry and burst through the door, certain that her mother was being menaced by a slavering reprobate.

And Mrs. Bennet was indeed in the drawing room—though it was Mary who shocked and unnerved her, not the three men huddled around her chaise longue: Cuthbert Cannon in his wheelbarrow, Left Limb on bended knee with a single rose in his hands, and Right Limb holding up a copy of something called *Hours of Idleness* so the captain could orate from its pages.

"Mary! My heavens, you give me palpitations!" Mrs. Bennet exclaimed, fluttering her hands over her chest. "Why must you come stomping in here like an Indian elephant?"

"I . . . I . . . I thought something was amiss."

"Amiss? Whatever could be amiss, child? Our friend Captain Cannon was simply paying a perfectly respectable afternoon call on your father and, since Mr. Bennet is elsewhere, paid his compliments to me instead and, as sometimes will happen when two people engage in harmless conversation long enough, the talk turned to literary matters, the captain being an enthusiast, it turns out, of fine English verse, and, having as he did a particularly superior volume upon his person, it was proposed that he favor me with a reading from it, which he was doing, quite innocently, when you came barging in to startle your poor, long-suffering mother into convulsions."

"I'm sorry, Mamma. And I apologize to you for my most uncouth intrusion, Captain. If I'd but known—"

"Well, now you know, so why don't you run along and leave us genteel people in peace?" Mrs. Bennet said. "I'm sure your master must have some new bit of savagery to teach you out in his hojo."

"Dojo, Mother. I apologize again, Captain. Good day."

Mary backed out of the room and closed the door. It didn't occur to her to wonder why one of the captain's Limbs should be holding a rose until she was halfway up the stairs, and by then her thoughts were already racing on to something infinitely more important: the need to get outside with her flintlock before Master Hawksworth grew displeased by her delay.

She found the Master and her sisters waiting out by the road. Kitty had her sword at her side and nunchucks strapped to her back; Lydia carried a staff, and throwing stars hung from bandoliers criss-crossing her chest. Master Hawksworth, to Mary's surprise, was holding one of her father's old crossbows, bolt loaded and bow string pulled back.

"I'm ready, Master," Mary said. "Where shall we begin our patrol?"

Master Hawksworth turned to the west. "That way."

Kitty and Lydia leered at each other.

He was taking them toward Netherfield Park.

The Master had the girls fan out and move ahead of him. "So that I might observe how *you* observe," he said. Accordingly, Mary did her utmost to radiate alertness, keeping her back straight and her head moving from side to side as she scanned the shaded bramble on each side of the road. Kitty did the same, matching Mary's slow, steady pace.

Lydia, on the other hand, kept pushing out ahead of the others with a step so lively she was practically skipping.

"May I ask something, Master?" she said.

Mary heard Master Hawksworth blow out a long breath. She

would've thought it a sigh from anyone else, but from the Master such a show of weariness and human weakness was out of the question. So he was just . . . exhaling. Heavily.

"If your question is about *the deadly arts*," he grated out, "you may ask it."

"Oh, it is." Lydia spun around and began walking backward, facing the Master. "Why have you brought us out on patrol today?"

"Lydia Bennet," Master Hawksworth began.

"I only ask," Lydia plowed on, "because it makes me think we've reached some new level of *the deadly arts*. Am I correct? Or is there another reason we left the dojo today? Other than *the deadly arts*, I mean."

"Lydia," Mary chided, "you're being disrespectful."

"No, she's not!" Kitty said. "She's merely asking a question about our proficiency in *the deadly arts*." She looked over at Lydia, and the two of them smirked at each other again in a way they perhaps fancied furtive. "You're wondering, as am I, whether this means we're equal to Jane and Elizabeth. In *the deadly arts*. After all, they've been allowed to venture out now and make use of their new skills, while we've only had a break from training in the dojo *once*, and then for all of two hours."

"In which time, we slew an unmentionable," Lydia pointed out.

"Exactly! It's not fair, letting Jane and Elizabeth run around with Lord Lumpley and Lieutenant Tindall and Doctor Picklewilly or whatever his name is while we're still stuck at home."

"Training in *the deadly arts*," Lydia threw in.

Kitty nodded. "Yes, I should have said. Because that is what we're talking about, after all."

"Exactly. *The deadly arts*. And not whether or not the Master misses his special apprentice."

"Lydia Bennet!" Mary snapped. "You go too far!"

Lydia gave her the kind of look that, not so long before, would have preceded the sticking out of a tongue.

"What? I was merely clarifying what we *aren't* talking about. Lizzy.

And Master Hawksworth. And what they think of each other. None of that has nothing to do with *the deadly arts*, so why would I bring it up?"

"ENOUGH!"

The Master's roar was so loud it didn't just freeze all three girls in their tracks, it startled something out of hiding in the brush nearby. There was a sudden rustle of leaves, a snapping of twigs, a pounding as of heavy footfalls . . . and a doe and her fawn darted across the road.

"May we kiss them, Master?" Lydia asked, already taking a few bounding strides ahead.

"No! We stay together!"

As sharp as the Master's voice was, there was also a curious, distant quality to it that drew Mary around to look at him.

She found nothing to see. There was no sign of him on the road.

"Master?" Mary gasped. "He's gone!"

"Not far," Kitty said. "Look up, Mary."

Mary looked up.

Master Hawksworth was standing on a thick branch jutting out over the lane.

"If that had been an unmentionable," he said, "claiming the high ground could have been the first step on the path to victory. From here, a warrior might use throwing stars or daggers to harass his foe, returning to the ground for an honorable kill stroke at the moment of his choosing. Remember that the next time you find yourself taken by surprise, Mary Bennet."

"Yes, Master. I will."

Master Hawksworth dropped to the ground with a beautifully executed Leaping Leopard—then immediately Leopard Leapt right back up to the same branch again.

"Yes, yes . . . I see," Mary said. "I shan't forget when the opportunity presents itself, Master."

"Mary, you dolt!" Kitty cried. "The opportunity's here!"

Mary turned around to find her sisters gone.

"High ground, Mary!" Lydia called out. "High ground!"

Mary followed the sound of her sister's voice and spied Lydia clambering up a nearby tree. Kitty was already straddling a branch higher up, arms wrapped around the trunk.

"Don't look at us!" Kitty pointed frantically downward. "Look at him! Look at him!"

"Look at *who*?"

By the time she spotted the zombie, it was almost upon her, and she forgot all about high ground and the Master's path to victory.

The dreadful had been so long dead there was no clothing left on it and only enough flesh to hold some of the bones together. It had no arms, no legs—just a rib cage, neck, and skull stitched over with stringy cords of old skin.

It humped its way toward Mary like a massive, rabid inchworm. A *fast* one.

Mary whipped up her flintlock and fired, and one of the unmentionable's shoulders exploded in a shower of powderized bone.

The rest of the unmentionable kept coming.

"Run!" Kitty shouted. "Let the Master handle it!"

"Yes!" Lydia threw in. "Our tree's full, but there are plenty of others for you!"

The Master himself said nothing. He was sure to be watching, though. Sure to be judging. And Mary intended to pass the test.

She threw aside her pistol and drew her katana just as the dreadful reached her, and she sidestepped and sliced downward simultaneously.

The unmentionable lost its other shoulder. What was left slithered around to snap at Mary's heels.

A clumsy attempt at a Leaping Leopard nearly broke her ankles, but it also took her out of range just in time.

"Ooooo, nice jump," Lydia said. She whipped a throwing star into the top of the dreadful's head, yet it didn't even seem to notice.

"Climb, Mary, climb!" Kitty called out. "Before the zombie

charges again!"

"Oh, Kitty—you, too, now?" Mary widened her stance and brought up her sword. "A lady says *unmentionable*."

The dreadful wriggled toward her again. Just as it jerked its head up for a chomp out of her shin, she plunged her sword through its mouth, skewering it straight down the spine. Yet still the creature wouldn't die, and it writhed wildly and bit at the blade of the katana, chipping off shards of its own jaw.

Mary walked over to the tree her sisters were sitting in and bashed the zombie against the trunk until what was left of its brain had been smeared like blackberry jam across the rough bark. At last, the unmentionable stopped moving.

"Mary, that was . . . astonishing."

Kitty leapt down from her branch.

"Yes," Lydia said, dropping to the ground beside her. "But did you have to beat out the thing's brains? I am *not* picking my throwing star out of that mess."

Mary paid them no heed. Neither their praise nor their censure meant anything to her. There was only one person who mattered.

She looked up at Master Hawksworth.

He watched her from on high for what seemed like a long, long time. And then, at last, he spoke.

"Well done, Mary Bennet. Your sword work was sloppy, however, and that Leaping Leopard? Shameful! We must return to the dojo at once for more practice."

"Ohhhh, back to the dojo already?" Lydia moaned.

Kitty kicked at the dirt. "We didn't even make it to Netherfield. I want to see more soldiers!"

Yet Mary silently rejoiced.

"Well done," the Master had said. Well done! For him this was gushing, raving, even *fawning*.

Perhaps Geoffrey Hawksworth was revealing his true self at last.

IT HUMPED ITS WAY TOWARD MARY LIKE A MASSIVE, RABID INCHWORM.

CHAPTER 28

CAPTURING A DREADFUL, it turned out, was the easy part. Getting it to go where one wanted—that was nearly impossible.

Dr. Keckilpenny's custom-built zombie net fit over the unmentionable's head and upper torso snugly enough, pinning its arms to its sides. But the only way to get the creature to do anything other than hurl itself, snarling, at the nearest sign of life was to push or pull it by the attached rod. And even with Elizabeth and the doctor pushing and pulling together, the dreadful was almost too strong for them, and either they or it were continually being jerked this way or that. Accordingly, their path through the forest was a staggering zigzag, and twice the unmentionable jerked the net pole from their hands and ran madly in some random direction only to crash into a tree and collapse.

Eventually, the trio stumbled into view of the sentry stationed on the road, and it was only much shouting of "We're alive! Still! Really! Believe us!" that spared them another greeting from his Brown Bess.

"I think you might want to fetch the lieutenant and a few of your mates, Private Johnson!" Dr. Keckilpenny called out when the man finally lowered his musket.

"Jones," Elizabeth corrected.

"Sorry! *Jones!*"

The dreadful lunged at the sound of the doctor's voice, scratching wildly with its gray fingers.

"If you could hurry, it would be appreciated!" Elizabeth added.

Jones scampered off.

Within minutes, he was back with Lt. Tindall and a small squad of soldiers. The lieutenant came striding up tight lipped and hard eyed, but most of his men slinked cringingly behind him, looking only slightly less reluctant to go where they were told than the dreadful was.

"I didn't believe it, but I see it's true." Lt. Tindall drew his sword. "All right, then . . . release it and stand back. I'll finish it for you."

"If our intention had been to finish it, we could have easily done that ourselves," Elizabeth replied. The words felt good until the dreadful thrust itself at her, nearly knocking her over. Fortunately, she managed to retain her footing and, in the process, her dignity (or whatever dignity one can have when being jostled by a zombie in a butterfly net).

"Perhaps I should explain, Lieutenant," Dr. Keckilpenny said.

"There is no 'perhaps' about it."

"No, I suppose not. Well, here's the gist of it . . ."

When the doctor was through outlining his intentions—that the "gentleman in question" was to be held prisoner in order to "accommodate certain vital experiments"—Lt. Tindall's response required but one word and a suitable scowl to go with it.

"Abominable!"

"There is little 'perhaps' about that, either, I suppose," said Dr. Keckilpenny. "But do remember: The War Office has given me carte blanche, and I should think you'd at least want to consult with your commanding officer before contravening orders that have come down to you from so very high."

The lieutenant devoted a long moment to grinding his perfect, pearly white teeth before speaking again.

"All right, then. You may keep the wretched thing on three conditions. One, it is to be sequestered out of sight. Two, all possible steps will be taken to ensure that it does not escape. And three, at the first sign that it is in *any* way endangering *anyone*, it will be destroyed."

"Done, done, and done!" Dr. Keckilpenny said. "In fact, I can accommodate your first two provisos in one fell swoop. Just wait till you see my laboratory!"

Soon enough, that's just what the lieutenant and the others were doing—though the doctor's "laboratory" turned out to be nothing more than Netherfield's largest, draftiest attic. Dr. Keckilpenny had found it, he explained, while exploring the house that morning, not letting anything so prosaic as a locked door keep him from getting inside.

"Medical student, remember?" he'd said when Elizabeth asked where he'd learned the fine art of lock-picking. "Every morgue or cemetery has its . . . well. Let's let that lie, shall we? This way, everyone, this way! Allow me to present the pièce de résistance!"

He swept his long arms out toward a particularly gloomy, cobwebbed corner. Hanging from the wall was a pair of thick, black iron chains, each ending in manacles.

"What in heaven's name?" Lt. Tindall muttered.

"I imagine some mad maiden aunt or idiot son spent many a year up here," Dr. Keckilpenny said. "It's what one does in the best families, I've found. You're not considered a true aristocrat until you've got at least one daft relation howling away up in the attic. How fortunate for us that the penthouse, as it were, is currently untenanted."

"Yes," the lieutenant drawled. "How very."

Still, despite his obvious reluctance, Lt. Tindall ordered his men to unpack the doctor's prize, the zombie having been brought into the house stuffed in a trunk so as not to alarm the servants or the other soldiers. (This precaution met with only partial success, as "Dr. Keckilpenny's equipment" kept moaning, kicking, and scratching as it was carried inside and up the stairs.) After a few frantic minutes of tugging and shoving with the zombie net, the soldiers had the dreadful chained in place.

"I'm going to keep a guard posted outside the door at the bottom of the stairs, with his musket loaded," Lt. Tindall said as his men hurried down the staircase. He turned to leave, as well, then stopped and faced Elizabeth. "Miss Bennet," he drew in a deep breath, "if you're still interested in musketry instruction, I would be happy to have our Sergeant Meadows see to it."

He couldn't quite pull off the "happy" without a quiver in his voice, nor could he completely erase the look of distaste upon his face. He managed to jut out an elbow, though, bowing slightly as he offered to escort her outside.

Elizabeth shook her head. "Thank you, Lieutenant. Perhaps another time."

Lt. Tindall dropped his arm.

"Suit yourself," he said, spinning crisply on his heel and marching to and down the stairs.

Elizabeth actually felt a little sorry for him as she watched him go. The man was still a starchy martinet, but at least he'd tried.

"Thank you for staying, Miss Bennet," Dr. Keckilpenny said. He was eyeing Elizabeth with a strange intensity, as if she were an experiment yielding unexpected—yet pleasing—results. "It's an honor being chosen over the company of Sergeant Meadows and a Brown Beth."

"Brown *Bess*. And . . . well, I . . . I just have so many questions."

That was certainly true enough. Some of them Elizabeth couldn't even find words for.

She turned away from the doctor's stare and found herself looking into another.

The zombie was straining against its chains, wide eyes fixed on her. The creature seemed calm, though, as if it had accepted its captivity. It didn't thrash, didn't grimace, didn't bite at the gag the soldiers had tied around its mouth to keep its screams from escaping the trunk. It almost could have passed for a living man—a youngish, not altogether unhandsome one out sleepwalking or staggering around drunk—if not for the putrid smell, the dingy tint of its skin, and the viscous black fluid that trickled from its ears and nose and mouth. Whoever he'd been, he hadn't died violently, that much was obvious. No zombie had cursed him with a bite or scratch. The strange plague had awakened him from his grave.

"A fine specimen, isn't he?" Dr. Keckilpenny said. "But I wonder how in the world we're going to get him undressed."

"Excuse me?"

The doctor nodded in the general direction of the unmentionable's pants. "Those clothes of his—they'll have to go. We don't want him in the wormy old things he was buried in. He needs to be in something more . . . aliveish."

And finally one of the questions in Elizabeth's mind became refreshingly obvious, with obvious words to match.

"Doctor, what are you up to?"

Dr. Keckilpenny grinned. "It is a joy hearing you ask that. It can be so lonely being the only one thinking these things! May I have permission to babble?"

"Always, so long as it's not about the weather."

"I knew it! I *knew* it! A kindred spirit!"

To Elizabeth's great surprise, the doctor took her by the shoulders and shifted her a few steps to the left. When she was directly before the trunk they'd used to haul up the zombie, he pushed down gently until she was seated atop it. Then he stepped back and clapped his hands together.

"In the old days, during The Troubles, many men of science studied the zombies, yes. But always the goal was the same: How to destroy them? What are their weaknesses? How best to fight them? No one stopped to ask, 'Why do they want to eat us?'"

"I suspect no one bothered asking because the dreadfuls were not inclined to reply."

Dr. Keckilpenny stomped a foot and thrust a pointed finger toward the ceiling, yet he never lost his broad, almost manic smile.

"That is an assumption! What if the zombies *would* tell us, if only they could? It's clear some part of the mind survives in them. *Exempli gratia*: They're drawn to places where they can find food, that is, people—roads and homes and the like. There are eyewitness accounts of them using rudimentary tools, such as rocks or logs, to break through windows and doors. And they were known to flee when faced with superior numbers of well-armed men—proof that the instinct for self-preservation lives on. And if they retain that, who knows what else might still reside in those rotting heads of theirs?"

The doctor had been waving and thrusting wildly with his right index finger, and now he brought it up to give a hard *tap-tap-tap* to the side of his forehead.

"The answers we need are here." *Tap-tap-tap* again. "The answers are *always* here! Even the zombies know it. What is the one thing they hunger for above all else? Brains! They're trying to regain that which they have lost. I propose to help them find it again. And then, no matter how far the plague might spread this time, it won't matter, for we shall have peace!"

"Because we'll be able to *talk* to them?"

"Because—" Dr. Keckilpenny's finger wilted, and the rest of him wilted with it. "Something like that. We'll have to see where it all leads. But of this much I'm certain: Understanding a problem is the only way to solve it. You do agree, don't you?"

"Well. It sounds . . ."

The doctor's eyes widened. "Mad?"

"Reasonable," Elizabeth finished.

Dr. Keckilpenny smiled.

And mad, Elizabeth thought. Yet she liked the young man's smile too much to wipe it away.

"So," she said, "how do you propose to begin? Aside from chaining your subject to a wall, that is."

The doctor turned and took a few steps toward the dreadful. It pushed all its weight toward him, its shackled arms stretched out straight to the sides, turning its body into a great leaning T.

"We shall treat him like a man. Remind him that he *is* a man. And every man's sense of self starts in the same place. With his name. Miss Bennet, allow me to introduce . . . Mr. Smith."

"Mr. Smith?"

"Yes, Mr. Smith. It's as good a guess as any. One in ten Englishmen is named Smith, you know."

"I don't believe we have quite so many in Hertfordshire."

"Well, now you have one more. Isn't that right, Mr. Smith?"

"Hrrrrrrrrrrrrrr," Mr. Smith said.

"Excellent! Your turn, Miss Bennet. Tell him you're glad to make his acquaintance."

Elizabeth tried to force a smile, thinking the doctor was joking. But then he rolled his hands in the air and said, "Go on."

Elizabeth looked into the zombie's eyes. It was still staring at Dr. Keckilpenny, who'd stopped just a few steps beyond the thing's reach. There seemed to be more . . . life to it now. Not intelligence, certainly, but awareness, perhaps. Awareness of what, though?

She cleared her throat.

"Pleased to meet you."

Yet she wasn't—and she wasn't alone in that.

"Pleased to meet you, *Mr. Smith*," the doctor was prodding when footsteps clunked up the stairwell behind them, and they both turned to find Mr. Bennet joining them in the attic, a look of revulsion upon his face.

"What the devil is going on here?"

"Father, you're back! Has Jane returned, as well?"

Mr. Bennet nodded without taking his eyes off Mr. Smith. "She's in the library with Lord Lumpley making plans for tomorrow. The spring ball is to be held here instead of Pulvis Lodge, and there is much to be done."

"The ball? Here? Mrs. Goswick agreed to that?"

"She will if the baron gets his way, and getting his way is the one thing he's good at, I suspect. But enough about the ball. Would someone kindly explain the meaning of *that*?"

Even if Mr. Bennet hadn't been pointing at the looming figure chained to the wall, there would have been no question what *that* was.

"*He*," Dr. Keckilpenny said with a smile of almost paternal pride, "is Mr. Smith."

Mr. Bennet gaped at him.

Before, Elizabeth had fancied the doctor and her father would get along famously, both being intelligent men with a penchant for irony. Alas, things were not off to the start she had hoped for.

"Lizzy," her father said, "who is this young man and is he quite sane?"

Elizabeth launched into introductions and explanations, and it helped smooth things over—somewhat—that Dr. Keckilpenny was the man who'd saved her life not long before. Still, Mr. Bennet never quite shook the look of perturbed perplexity with which he'd arrived.

"Well, one thing is clearer, at least," he said to Elizabeth after hearing of the doctor's plans. "Lieutenant Tindall told me I'd find you up here tilting at putrid windmills. Now I know what he meant." He turned to Dr. Keckilpenny and shook his head. "It's been tried before, you know."

"Has it really?" The doctor mused a moment, then shrugged. "Well, not recently. And not by me."

Mr. Bennet cocked an eyebrow at that, then slowly approached the dreadful who was now leaning toward him, fingers clawing listlessly at the air.

"I don't recognize this man."

"Should you?" Dr. Keckilpenny asked.

"Yes." Mr. Bennet looked first at the doctor and then, not seeing realization dawn, at his daughter. "I should."

"Because the body's so fresh, so well dressed," Elizabeth said. "He was given a proper burial, but not in Meryton."

Mr. Bennet nodded. "I think I should hurry Lord Lumpley along with Mrs. Goswick. And I suddenly find there are certain other arrangements I must see to, as well. Lizzy—if you would assist me?"

He took his leave of the doctor with a nod, then headed for the stairs.

"Good-bye, Dr. Keckilpenny." Elizabeth went up on her tiptoes to peer past him. "Good-bye, Mr. Smith."

Both looked strangely bereft.

"Until we meet again," the doctor said.

"Hrrrrrrrrrrrrrr," said Mr. Smith.

Elizabeth suspected they were saying more or less the same thing.

CHAPTER 29

FOR HER YOUNGEST SISTERS, it would've been a dream come true. Sleeping in a plush four-poster bed in a plush bedroom the size of a barn in the plush manor house of a plush nobleman. Yet for Jane Bennet, it was neither dream nor nightmare, for she wasn't sleeping at all. She was lying on her back, staring up at the canopy stretched out above her, thinking.

She thought about the ball she'd be attending the next day—and how humiliating it would be when only Lord Lumpley dared dance with those social lepers, the Bennet girls. She thought about how persistent the baron had been when they'd paid a call on the Goswicks that afternoon— and how it had been his seemingly offhand remark about their daughter Julia's "London friend, Mr. Schwartz" that convinced the couple to put the spring ball in his hands. She thought about her father's rather anxious good-bye to her that evening, and how he'd looked truly distressed only after she'd told him not to worry about her, as Lord Lumpley had been a perfect host so far and, she hoped, might still grow into the role of sober, responsible squire.

But mostly she thought about how much she missed Elizabeth. There could be no dash across the hall for comfort and wisdom here. It would be a long dash indeed to find anyone she knew at all, for Jane had been quartered (for propriety's sake, the baron explained) in a deserted wing of the house far from the other guests. Lt. Tindall and Capt. Cannon (how wonderfully cheerful the man had been when returning from his "reconnoiter" that afternoon!) had been given rooms downstairs on the opposite side of the grand foyer, along with Ensign Pratt and the company surgeon, a crusty old campaigner named Dr. Thorne. The rest of the soldiers were in tents out on the lawn, the only exceptions being Right Limb and Left Limb (who slept in the captain's room, though in what arrangement Jane couldn't guess) and a single guard dozing in a chair outside "Dr. Keckilpenny's sanitarium" (as Papa had cryptically called it).

So she was alone—as alone as she'd ever been, except when out walking or riding by herself. Certainly, she'd never felt more alone. And it wasn't a feeling she liked.

Of what importance were her feelings, though? So she'd been ruined socially. So no matter what the baron might do, she'd never make a match with a gentleman of the sort she admired most—a true *gentle man*, as warm and soft and pliant as a puppy's fuzzy belly. So it would only be cold, hard warriors like Master Hawksworth who'd look twice at a woman who wore the sword, except to gape or sneer. So . . . what of it? It would be pure, selfish vanity to think of all that when the unmentionables might be on the rise again.

But, oh, how she longed for love! How she longed for kisses! How she longed for . . . the rest of it. Whatever that looked like.

Yet none of this was to be hers. She would be forever denied, forever alone.

There was a soft knock on the door.

For a moment, Jane was torn between her nunchucks and her dirk. The dirk won.

"Yes?" Jane said, lifting the dagger by the tip of the blade.

A woman answered.

"Are you awake, Miss?"

Jane could guess how Elizabeth might reply to that: "Not unless I'm talking in my sleep." (Jane wasn't without wit herself. It just rarely seemed charitable to wield it, and charity for Jane always came first.)

"Yes, I am," she said.

Her bedroom was blessed with its own hearth, and by the orange glow of the dying embers within, she saw the knob on the door begin to turn.

"I brought you something, Miss."

As the door swung slowly open, a new light spread into the room—the dull yellow gleam of a candle. It sat upon a tray being carried by a roly-poly young chambermaid.

On one side of the candle was a decanter of amber liquid. On the other was a single crystal goblet.

Jane slipped the dagger back under her pillow before the girl spotted it. She didn't want it spreading through the household staff that she was the sort of person who'd pull a knife on a servant.

"Thank you. That is so kind," she said. "What is it?"

The maid toddled over to a table and set down her tray. "Our Mr. Belgrave—he's His Lordship's steward, you know—he was worried you might have trouble sleeping, this being your first night in a strange place. So he sent up a splash of medicinal brandy. The baron swears by it. Always does the trick when he's having trouble abed."

The girl made an abrupt hiccup of amusement not unlike Lydia and Kitty's chirpy "La!"

"Shall I bring you a glass?" she asked, already reaching for the brandy.

"Well, I don't usually—"

"Oh, but tonight's different, isn't it? Hardly usual." The maid half filled the goblet, then turned and started toward Jane with it. "Go on. Do yourself a kindness." She didn't stop coming until she was pushed up against the side of the bed with the glass practically thrust under Jane's nose. "Just a little nip, and before long you'll be having such sweet, sweet dreams."

"But I—"

"Oh, go onnnnnnnnnnn."

Jane took the goblet and sipped.

The maid smiled.

"Good, good. Now how about a nice big gulp to bring the Sandman calling?"

"Mmmmmmmm," Jane said.

She tried to hand the goblet back to the chambermaid, but the girl backed away, still grinning.

"Oh, you keep that for now. Drink your fill, and there's plenty more over there if you want it."

"Mmm mmm," Jane said, nodding.

"Good night, then, Miss. And if there's anything you need, just ring. Someone will get it up for you quick."

"Mmm mmm!"

Jane waved as the maid slipped out the door. Then she leaned forward and spat the brandy back in the glass.

Not only did she not care for spirits in general, the one brandy she'd ever tried had struck her as particularly repulsive. To her surprise, the baron's was even worse. He was well off enough to afford only the best, yet there was a gritty quality to the drink the girl had brought, and a faint aftertaste of licorice.

Jane got out of bed and walked the goblet across the room.

Now, where was I? she thought as she settled the glass on the tray beside the decanter. *Oh, yes. Alone. Forever.*

Something thumped directly above her head, and she whipped into the sumo stance so quickly she knocked the carafe of brandy into the fireplace. The glass shattered, there was a burst of here-and-gone flame, and a billow of black, spice-scented smoke plumed into the room.

Jane didn't even notice. She was staring at the ceiling.

There was another thump, then a pause, then—so muffled they were little more than a drone, at first—words. Jane had to strain to make them out.

"Down, Mr. Smith! Smithy, *down*!" a man seemed to be saying. "Bad zombie! Bad, bad zombie!"

Jane assumed she wasn't hearing correctly.

There was one more thump, then silence. Jane stood there, staring up, still in her stance, for a long, long time.

She heard nothing more from above, though eventually she did detect the creak of a floorboard just outside her door. She waited for the chambermaid to come barging back in with a glass of milk or a bed warmer or some other unwanted succor she'd insist on foisting on her. Yet no one entered, no one knocked.

The floorboard creaked again.

Jane picked up the nearest weapon—a mace she'd left propped up against the table—and slipped silently across the room. With a sudden jerk and a half-hearted battle cry, she yanked the door open and brought the mace up high.

Lt. Tindall threw up an arm to block her blow. "It's just me! It's just me!"

He was standing outside the door in full uniform.

"I do beg your pardon!" Jane lowered both her mace and her gaze, and she felt her cheeks flushing with a blush she prayed it was too dark for the handsome young officer to see. "I heard a noise and . . . oh, Lieutenant, I'm so sorry!"

"There is no need for you to apologize, Miss Bennet. The fault is entirely mine. If I hadn't been dawdling out here in the hall like a fool . . ."

Jane peeped up quizzically.

"I couldn't bring myself to knock, you see," the lieutenant explained. "I knew it was most improper, coming to a young lady's room like this. Yet still, I felt compelled to assure myself of your safety." He looked down at Jane's mace, and his expression soured. "I suppose I need not have bothered."

"Yet you did," Jane said. "And your consideration touches me deeply. I know that you put great stock in what is proper, so for you to come here, at night, on my account . . . I . . . I find it quite admirable, actually. It was a fine thing to do. The gesture of a *true* gentleman!"

This last ejaculation used up Jane's meager store of forwardness, and she could say no more. Lt. Tindall seemed truly pleased to see her so overcome, however. The pinched look to his face faded away, and his eyes seemed to gleam brighter than the dim light could account for.

"That anyone would wish to extinguish such delicacy . . . ," he began. Then he, too, couldn't go on, and he took his leave with a muttered "Good night" and a bow so deep it brought his head almost even with Jane's knees.

Jane returned to her bed and lay down, though she knew she may as well be doing *dand-baithaks* for the Master. Sleep would be coming no time soon. Now she had the lieutenant to think of, too.

That morning, he'd made his disapproval of her plain, and the rebuke hurt her deeply. What salve it was—and what a puzzlement—to find that he harbored such concern for her. And such tenderness. He seemed so stern, so stiff, yet perhaps this was but the shield he wielded to protect a vulnerable, more sensitive self. With a little careful coaxing, maybe that gentler spirit could be drawn out from—

There was a soft, shushing sort of sound and what might have been the squeak of a hinge, and one of the shadows in the darkest part of the room began moving toward the bed. By the time Jane realized it was Lord Lumpley, she already had her dagger at his throat.

"Ah, you are awake, I see," the baron croaked. "So very, very awake."

"My Lord! I'm sorry! I didn't know it was you!"

Jane scurried back to the bed, tossed her dirk on the pillow, and snatched up a dressing gown to cover the white chemise in which she slept.

As she pulled her nightgown on, Lord Lumpley averted his eyes. (A little. Until he thought Jane wasn't looking.)

"Perhaps I did doze off," Jane said. "I didn't even notice you come in."

"Oh, that shouldn't surprise you. Netherfield has been in my family for years. I know where all the squeaky floorboards and rusty hinges are!"

"Still . . ." Jane peered into the gloom across the room. "What were you doing over there, if I may ask?"

"Of course, you may—and I pray you'll forgive me the unpardonable liberty I was taking. It's just that I misplaced my favorite . . ."

The baron must have been awfully tired himself, Jane thought, for he had to think a moment before dredging up the word he sought.

". . . Bible," he finally said. "I keep some of my most cherished volumes in this room, so—seeing as you were surely asleep—I thought I'd just pop in and look for it. Abominably overfamiliar, I know, but we barons are generally allowed our little eccentricities."

When he wasn't eyeing Jane, Lord Lumpley had been eyeing the room, as if searching for something—the Bible, Jane assumed. His gaze finally settled on the goblet the maid had left. It had tipped over when Jane knocked the carafe into the fire, and the pool of brandy around it sparkled dully in the firelight.

"I see that someone brought you my favorite sleeping draft," the baron said. "Pity it spilled."

"Oh! Yes! I'm sorry. I forgot all about it. And I'm afraid I broke the decanter, too. So careless of me."

Lord Lumpley waved away Jane's apologies with a strained smile. "Think nothing of it. I'll have someone sent along to tidy up . . . and to bring you another glass of brandy, of course."

"That's really not necessary, My Lord."

"But I insist." The baron bowed. "*Au revoir*, Miss Bennet."

"Good night, My Lord."

When the door was closed again, Jane shrugged off her dressing gown and climbed back into bed, certain now that she'd never fall asleep. Not only was a maid on her way, there was even more to think about now.

The baron. Lizzy and Father seemed to consider the man barely one step up from a dreadful—and perhaps even less preferable, as hosts go. Yet he'd been nothing but polite and attentive all day. Yes, it was beyond brazen, his creeping into a young lady's bedchamber. But how different was that, really, from what Lt. Tindall had done? And hadn't it been motivated by the most admirable of interests?

Though, come to think of it, Lord Lumpley had left without any Bible, nor had he mentioned where he was off to search for it next. Strange how thoroughly he seemed to forget about it once he'd offered his excuse for being in the room.

It wasn't often Jane acknowledged the possibility of duplicity. It was so much simpler, so much *nicer*, to take everyone at his or her word without complicating matters with guile or suspicion. Yet could it be, she wondered, that the baron had indeed been doing just what the lieutenant had—assuring himself of her well-being—because he was . . . oh, it was embarrassing simply to think it!

Was he really in love with her?

Even sitting alone in bed, Jane looked down and blushed.

A thump on the door roused her from her reverie. The chambermaid was already back with a new decanter of brandy, it seemed, and Jane, feeling guilty about the mess she'd made for the girl, hopped out of bed to let her in.

The girl Jane found standing outside wasn't the servant she'd expected, though. She wasn't a servant at all, in fact.

Nor was she alive.

It was a dreadful, long dead but fresh from the grave to judge by the black earth still caked to its dress and withered flesh and patchy blonde hair. In spots—the tips of the fingers, on and around the teeth no longer covered by lips or gums—the dirt had been smeared away with something new: a paste of jellied brain.

The unmentionable's hands were flapping at waist level, gaze tilted downward, as if the creature had been fumbling clumsily with the doorknob. When it looked up and saw Jane frozen pop-eyed before it, it hissed like an angry cat and lunged forward.

Jane ducked to the side and gave the thing a shove as it hurtled past.

But the dreadful stumbled only a few steps before it whipped around and charged again, hands slashing.

Jane hopped onto her bed, grabbed one of the posts, and launched herself up atop the canopy frame. She meant to try a Panther's Bound down again, hopefully within grabbing range of one of the weapons strewn about the room—a battle axe propped up beside the bedside table was particularly tantalizing. The unmentionable didn't give her time, though. It began jumping up swiping at her, tearing down ragged strips of cloth as Jane scuttled this way and that to avoid its raking nails.

Looking down on the zombie's upturned, hideously decayed face, Jane thought she saw a flash of something familiar—although with no nose or mouth or eyelids to go by, and the ears dangling from flaps of loose flesh like grisly jewelry, recognition was impossible. Still, Jane began to feel she might have known this girl.

If only she'd stop jumping around for a second. If only she'd stop trying to kill her. . . .

"Oooo, I hope I'm not interrupting any-AHHHHHH!"

Both Jane and the dreadful turned toward the doorway. Standing there, the tray in her hands loaded with another bottle of brandy, was the plump chambermaid.

The unmentionable rushed toward her with a snarl. So shocked was the girl she didn't even turn to flee but simply stood there, motionless, as if calmly offering the thing a drink.

Jane flipped down from the canopy, snatched up the battle-axe, and used all her momentum to bring the blade down into the zombie's skull.

The chop split the dreadful down the middle like a rotted-out log.

The two halves splayed out on the floor at the chambermaid's feet.

"Ahh . . . ahh . . . ahh . . . ," the maid spluttered, too breathless even to scream. Her hands were shaking so violently the decanter danced around on her tray, rattling and sloshing and threatening to topple over.

Jane tried to think of something comforting to say. To her surprise—and vague consternation—she realized that she needed no comfort herself, and in fact she found it difficult, for once, to commiserate with someone who did.

She searched for words another moment, then put down her axe and placed a firm hand on the girl's trembling, fleshy-soft arm.

"Why don't you take that back downstairs?" she said, nodding down at the tray. "I don't even like brandy, you know."

CHAPTER 30

ELIZABETH AND MR. BENNET spoke not a word to each other until they were almost back to Longbourn. The parting with Jane had been painful for each of them, Elizabeth knew, yet she couldn't bring herself to console her father in any way. Leaving her sister at Netherfield for the night was no better than abandoning her in a nest of vipers, and if he felt guilty about that, well, that was the least he could do after the fact. So they'd stalked toward home side by side, each scanning the opposite side of the lane, hand on hilt, saying nothing.

It was Elizabeth who finally broke the silence.

"Zombie droppings?" she asked, jutting her chin out at a glistening red mound of pulp beside a low stone wall just off the road.

Mr. Bennet crossed over to kneel down beside it.

"Zombie droppings," he said.

"Fresh?"

"Fresh."

Mr. Bennet stood up and swiftly carried on toward Longbourn. Yet as he did so, he finally defended himself against the rebuke his daughter had never put into words—because she didn't have to.

"The stakes we play for are the highest, and if I must put up my own flesh and blood as collateral, I will do so."

"You *have* done so," Elizabeth said.

"Yes. And you, my favorite, I would gladly sell into a sultan's harem if it gave the living even the slightest advantage over the dead."

They walked a little farther without speaking or looking at each other.

"Of course," Mr. Bennet eventually said, "I would fully expect to find you on my doorstep the next morning with the sultan's head on a pike."

Elizabeth glanced over at her father and found him watching her with a sheepish smile. She didn't quite smile back, but she did allow the tight, hard line of her mouth to loosen just a bit.

"Is that what you expect to find when you awake tomorrow?" she said.

"I hope not. Not tomorrow, at any rate." Mr. Bennet looked away again. "If Jane could stay her hand at least a day, it would suit my plans better."

"And which plans are those, exactly?"

"Ah," Mr. Bennet said, nodding ahead. "It appears someone has been anxiously awaiting our return."

By the pink-gold glow of twilight, Elizabeth could see a lone figure standing to the side of the lane just where it curved past Longbourn's front lawn.

A big, brawny figure that put a flutter in her stomach.

Master Hawksworth was watching their approach silently, motionless. All the same, he somehow projected an air of nervous anticipation. It reminded Elizabeth of a chained dog, of all things—a pet sensing its owner's approach yet unable to dart up for the pat on the head it yearned for.

Which made no sense. It was supposed to be *she* who craved *his* approval. Who was the Master here, after all?

Elizabeth assumed it was the presence of her father that held Hawksworth back, and indeed he addressed himself only to Mr. Bennet as they approached.

"It is good you chose to return before nightfall, Oscar Bennet," the Master said. He'd relaxed as they drew near, spreading his legs and clasping his hands behind his back and studiously composing his features until they were so immutably cool they could have been chipped from a block of ice. "Today we encountered The Enemy again not two hundred paces from this very spot."

"Did you, now? Where were you going?"

There was a pause before Master Hawksworth answered.

"To the west along the lane. The dreadfuls seem drawn to that stretch of road, and I thought it time to take the young ones out of the dojo, into the field. Their performance was . . . not bad."

"I'm not surprised," Mr. Bennet said, nodding in a wry, knowing way that called into question what it was that didn't surprise him.

Elizabeth fought to keep her face as frozen as Master Hawksworth's.

He'd been heading toward Netherfield Park when he "encountered The Enemy." Toward *her*.

"Come," Mr. Bennet said. "Let us retire to my library, and you may tell me the whole story. I have much to tell you, as well." He started for the house, then slowed a moment and added as an obvious afterthought: "If that meets with your approval, Master."

"It does." For the first time, Master Hawksworth let his gaze settle fully on Elizabeth. "As for you, Elizabeth Bennet—"

"Yes, it will be an early night for her," Mr. Bennet cut in. "You should be in bed within the hour, Lizzy, and I want you sleeping in late come morning, too. You have quite a day before you." He looked at the Master and spoke in a voice that seemed less to state a fact than issue a command. "She's coming out tomorrow. At a ball at Netherfield." Then he smiled and went on lightly, "A pity she hasn't had time to practice her dancing lately. But then again, I always found even the liveliest quadrille to be child's play after mastering the Way of the Panther."

"Coming out?" Master Hawksworth said. "Indeed, you do have much to explain, Oscar Bennet."

He spoke sternly, like a man reserving judgment on some possible folly he could squelch with a single word, should he choose. Yet the look he gave Elizabeth before disappearing into the library with her father seemed doleful and thwarted. Longing, one could call it . . . and Elizabeth both did and didn't want to.

The library door was still swinging shut when Elizabeth's sisters descended on her, Lydia and Kitty each taking an arm and dragging her into the drawing room demanding news of the day while Mary walked behind sharing some of her own.

"I slew an unmentionable this afternoon. The Master seemed quite pleased."

"Oh, hush. No one wants to hear about that," Mrs. Bennet said from her chaise longue. She sounded more affectionate than annoyed, though, and there was a look of contented ease upon her face that Elizabeth hadn't seen in a long, long time. "Lizzy's back—that's what matters."

Mrs. Bennet turned her head and pushed an uncharacteristically rosy cheek upward, signaling Elizabeth to come plant a kiss upon it, which she did.

"You must tell us all the news from Netherfield. Jane and Lord Lumpley are getting along famously, I trust."

"Well, there was nothing *in*famous about it. Though I don't doubt the baron would change that, if he could."

Mrs. Bennet waved a languid hand in the air and replied with a simple "Ohhhhhhh."

"And Jane told me some of our neighbors were less than convivial when she and His Lordship went into the village together this morning."

Mrs. Bennet shrugged. "They'll come around. We have a nobleman's patronage. That more than compensates for the little quirks your father has foisted upon you."

Elizabeth could scarcely believe how at ease her mother seemed. It was almost as though some other woman had slipped into Mrs. Bennet's skin—for which Elizabeth was glad, since this other woman was altogether more pleasant to be around.

"Perhaps you're right, Mamma," she said. "We'll certainly see that put to the test tomorrow. The spring ball is no longer to be held at Pulvis Lodge. It will be at Netherfield—and the Bennets are once again welcome."

Mrs. Bennet's newfound tranquility was obliterated in an instant.

"I knew it, I knew it, I knew it!" she cried. "At last, our luck has changed for the better! We are redeemed! *We are redeemed!*"

Kitty and Lydia had hopped to their feet squealing with glee, and Mrs. Bennet actually jumped up and took them each by the hand and joined in. If there'd been a maypole handy, Elizabeth thought, they would've begun prancing around it.

This near-hysterical excitement carried on through the rest of the evening, with Mrs. Bennet and her two youngest daughters giddily debating the merits of this gown or these gloves or that or the other way of wearing one's hair. Elizabeth herself could only work in the occasional opinion (quite often getting no further than "I think that's—" before being overruled by her mother) while Mary simply curled up in a corner with her history book and flintlock and gun oil and left the hullabaloo to the others.

Eventually, however, Elizabeth was allowed to string enough words together to tease out the details of her sisters' day with the master. He'd seemed restless and preoccupied, she was told, and he even let them end their training early so he could "patrol the grounds."

"Of course, 'the grounds' turned out to be a patch of clover down by the road," Kitty giggled.

"And it wasn't unmentionables he was patrolling for!" Lydia chimed in. "It was his pet student!"

"You don't know that," Mary grumbled from the corner. As usual, no one paid any attention.

"Never you mind that Hawksworth," Mrs. Bennet told Elizabeth. "He might be fine for teaching you the Strutting Rooster or the Preening Peacock or what have you, I don't know. But it's men of consequence you need to set your sights on, not long-haired savages who eat raw fish and live in a garden shed. Just take that smart young Lieutenant Tindall, for instance. He comes from good stock, that one. I can sniff them out like a pig finds truffles. It's a good thing I'll be with you tomorrow night to steer you toward the quality catches."

"Yes, Mamma," Elizabeth sighed. "If I find myself in any doubt as to the truffles, I'll simply turn to my pig."

Mrs. Bennet nodded firmly. "You do that."

Somewhere in the midst of all this, Master Hawksworth finished his meeting with Elizabeth's father and slipped out of the house.

"All right, all right—to bed with you," Mr. Bennet said, shooing Lydia and Kitty from Elizabeth's room (where they'd been helping her prepare for the ball by arguing about which of them looked better in her jewelry). "You, too, Mrs. Bennet. You know anything you decide tonight will be reversed in the light of day, anyway. Let the poor girl get her rest."

Yet there was little that was restful about the long night that followed. Elizabeth told herself it was concern for Jane that kept her up, and indeed that was what her sleepy, half-dreaming mind dwelled on most. It was almost as though she welcomed the worry, though, for she found herself shifting to it whenever certain other thoughts threatened to take root.

If she should wonder why Master Hawksworth fixated on her so, she reminded herself that her sister was perhaps in peril just a few miles away.

If she should find herself dizzied by the swirl of her own uncertain feelings for the Master—attraction shunted aside by respect giving way to . . . something else?—she anchored herself with Jane.

Even if she should dwell too long upon Dr. Keckilpenny and his mad experiments and his open mind and his infectious smile, she pushed it aside in favor of Jane.

Only once, to her surprise, did thoughts of the ball occupy her, and even then there was a curiously inert quality to her musings. Coming out was supposed to change everything—childhood would end, a new future would unfold—yet Elizabeth couldn't seem to make herself care anymore. Not with the dreadfuls likely to be in *everyone's* future.

Once again, it was Jane she turned to, hoping her sister's night was passing more peacefully than her own.

Eventually, Elizabeth gave up on sleep entirely. A faint orange glimmer had appeared around her curtains, and she rose and went to them and drew them aside.

Dawn was breaking, bringing the day that would, supposedly, make her a lady. A woman. As she stood there, staring out at the light that crept across the landscape, chasing back the shadows, another shape—that of her own face—slowly sharpened in the glass of the windowpane. At first, it was just a blur between her and the world, but with time and more light it became a reflection almost as clear as in a mirror.

"Good morning," Elizabeth said to herself. "My, but don't you look a fright."

And then there was movement down below, and suddenly Elizabeth was looking through the glass once more.

Master Hawksworth was walking off toward the stables with his katana at his side and his warrior's bedroll slung over his back.

Elizabeth threw on her dressing gown and dashed from the room, down the stairs and out the door.

"Master! Master, wait!"

Master Hawksworth stopped but didn't turn around.

"Master?" Elizabeth said, coming closer. As she walked across the grass, her bare feet were quickly covered with cold morning dew she barely even noticed. "Are you going somewhere?"

The Master finally faced Elizabeth. When he saw she was in her nightclothes, he looked, for a moment, shocked—and then as though he might actually smile.

"No, Elizabeth Bennet. I am merely preparing for an important day. Your father and I have much we must do."

"Then I should be doing it, too," Elizabeth said. "All of us, I mean. Me and Mary and Kitty and Lydia. If it's so important, we must every one of us do what we can."

At last, the Master really did smile. It looked horribly small on such a big man, though, and it barely amounted to more than a slight, fleeting curl of the lips.

"You are an example for us all, Elizabeth Bennet. But no. Your father wanted you and your sister, Jane Bennet, to have this day for your country dance. It is, perhaps, the last chance for any of us to taste such unfettered pleasure. So I gave my consent."

"You are growing soft, Master."

It was meant as a jest, not reproof. Yet Master Hawksworth winced.

"No. It's not that. The truth is, I've *always*—" He cut himself off and started to turn away again, then stopped with his side to Elizabeth, his fists clenched. "I have a shameful secret, Elizabeth Bennet. I believe your father suspects, yet I dare not speak of it aloud, even to you . . . though in you I have found my only hope of overcoming it."

Elizabeth started toward him again. "Master . . . *Geoffrey* . . . what is it?"

She reached out, about to take one of his hands in hers.

"Ahh, Lizzy," Mr. Bennet said as he came around the side of the house. He had a crossbow in his hands and a look of mild surprise on his face. "I thought I told you to sleep in. And here I find you on the lawn in your night things with the sun not up half an hour? Such shameful disregard for your father's wishes! If it weren't your special day, it'd be *dand-baithaks* till noon. Am I right, Master?"

Master Hawksworth stiffened—back and legs straightening, chest puffing out, chin jutting—until he looked like something out of a Grecian courtyard.

Mr. Bennet had the gaze of a Gorgon, it seemed: It had turned the man to stone.

"Indeed," the Master said. "You rose early, too, Oscar Bennet."

"Not at all. I never went to bed. 'Eternal vigilance'—that is my credo now."

Mr. Bennet and Master Hawksworth shared a long, silent look.

"Shall I have Hill bring out some hot coffee?" Elizabeth said. "You both seem to have fallen asleep standing up."

"Not a bad idea, Lizzy. But it's one, I'm afraid, for which we have not the time." Mr. Bennet stepped swiftly up to Hawksworth and then swept past him, bound for the stables. "Come, Master. We must away to Meryton to collect Ensign Pratt and his men. We'll need their help if we're to see our plans through."

"What of *my* help?" Elizabeth said. "Surely, there is some part in your plans for me."

Her father stopped and turned toward her, nodding gravely. For the first time, Elizabeth noticed a red smear high up on his left cheek, and his hands and cuffs were speckled with tiny dots, as from a spray of crimson liquid.

He hadn't just been watching for dreadfuls that night. He'd met with at least one.

"Of course. There is a task of vital importance that you and only you can undertake," he said to her. "Go back into the house, go up to your room," Mr. Bennet cocked an eyebrow, then grinned, "and lay out your best gown. Then let your mother and sisters spend the next twelve hours fussing over your hair. After that, you are to travel to Netherfield and dance the night away in the company of your sister Jane and whatever respectable gentlemen the two of you might coax into your webs."

Mr. Bennet looked up at the second-floor windows—and the three young faces peering down from them—and threw his arms wide.

"On this, Elizabeth's special day, I release all of my daughters! From this moment on, you are not warriors! You are again young ladies! Revel in it however you would!"

And with that he left.

CHAPTER 31

"REVEL IN IT however you would." That's how Elizabeth's father told her to spend the day of her coming out. Which was cruelly ironic, since it was he who'd cast a pall over the ball and all her preparations for it.

Mr. Bennet's sudden, strange change of heart about his daughters—releasing them from their training just as the peril of the dreadfuls seemed about to peak—plagued Elizabeth the whole day. Was he doing them one last kindness before calamity struck? Was he shunting his loved ones out of harm's way? Or was he simply trying to come between her and . . . ?

Oh, bosh! There was nothing to come between.

Right?

Elizabeth's misery was compounded by her mother's bliss. If something made Mrs. Bennet happy, it was virtually guaranteed to be a disaster in the making. And Mrs. Bennet had never seemed happier.

She hummed as she and Lydia pinned up Elizabeth's hair and wove in pearl beads and ribbon. She sang as she and Kitty laid out the necklace, earrings, bracelets, and brooch with which Elizabeth would soon be festooned. She giggled as she and Mary played tug-of-war with Elizabeth's bodice, the mother pulling down in favor of "display," the daughter pulling up in defense of "decorum." And when all her labors were done and Elizabeth was at last a vision of loveliness—or Mrs. Bennet's vision of loveliness, at least, for Elizabeth had taken no more of a role in her own dressing than would a porcelain doll—she laughed and clapped her hands and declared her to be "radiant, entrancing . . . why, almost as pretty as Jane!"

To Elizabeth's relief, Mrs. Bennet was alone in her oblivious good spirits. It was nothing new to see Mary moping around looking sour, but eventually even Lydia and Kitty lost interest in their mother's fussing over Elizabeth. By midafternoon, they were half-heartedly sparring with *yari* spears out on the front lawn. For weeks, the girls had longed for a day without training, a day they could devote to gossip and mischief and dreams of their own balls and gentleman callers. And now that they finally had such a day, they seemed so bored they'd welcome a horde of unmentionables with open arms.

Elizabeth was tempted to grab a spear and join them, and her restlessness grew so acute she asked her mother again and again if they might set out for Netherfield early so as to check on Jane. Yet Mrs. Bennet poohpoohed the idea every time. "His Lordship doesn't need us barging in just as he's getting to know your sister," she'd say. Eventually, however—when she had been stuffed into the last of the various layers a lady must keep between herself and all others—Mrs. Bennet announced that they'd be leaving Longbourn ahead of schedule, after all. Her old acquaintance Capt. Cannon had extended an invitation for a tour of his encampment, she said, and now seemed the perfect time to accept his gracious offer.

Soon after, she and Elizabeth were waving good-bye to Mary, Kitty, Lydia, and Mrs. Hill as the Bennets' carriage rolled off. It was a bright, warm day, yet though Mrs. Bennet prattled on about its beauty, for Elizabeth the sunshine merely meant the shadows of the surrounding woods were all the darker and more impenetrable by comparison. Indeed, she couldn't stop staring off into the trees and bracken, and several times she thought she caught a blurry flurry of movement and a whiff of putrescence upon the air. Once, when turning her head, she even got a glimpse of a small, childlike figure peering back at her from behind a tree. But by the time Elizabeth again focused on the spot where it had been, she saw nothing, and she could but conclude it had been a phantasm conjured up by her own overstoked imagination. All the same, her palms itched, and the back of her neck tingled with something that should have been dread, but was not.

As they neared Netherfield Park, they could hear the occasional *pop* of a distant gunshot, and when they rounded the final bend before the main drive they found themselves confronted not by a single sentry but a picket line of five, all with their muskets raised.

"Halt!" one of the soldiers shouted.

The driver pulled back hard on the reins and the horses reared, nearly sending Elizabeth and Mrs. Bennet flying out of their seat.

"Hello again, Private Jones!" Elizabeth called out. "Perhaps you might remind your friends that unmentionables don't make a habit of traveling by coach."

"Hasn't anyone told you there's to be a ball tonight?" Mrs. Bennet added. "You can't stand out here waving guns at the cream of Hertfordshire!"

The soldiers lowered their Brown Besses and made way for the Bennets' carriage.

"Begging your pardon, Madam." Pvt. Jones started to tip his black, tall-peaked cap, then seemed to realize this wasn't something soldiers were supposed to do. "It's just everyone's a bit on edge around here. We've had three more of *them* on the grounds, y'see—and one even slipped through the lines last night and got into the house, though no one can guess how."

Mrs. Bennet gasped.

"Was anyone hurt?" Elizabeth asked.

The soldier shrugged. "They don't share the details with the likes of us. We're not even supposed to know that—"

"Go on! *Go on!*" Elizabeth snapped at the driver, and with a crack of the whip the carriage jerked off toward the house. Elizabeth jumped out and ran inside before the wheels had even stopped turning.

The baron's gray, wraithlike steward, Belgrave, appeared out of nowhere to block her path as she crossed the foyer.

"May I help you?"

"My sister. Miss Jane Bennet. I must see her at once."

Belgrave took on the dead-eyed look of quiet condescension peculiar to servants in manor houses. "I don't know if that's possible."

"*Why*? Is she—"

"Lizzy? Is everything all right?"

Elizabeth looked up and saw Jane and Lord Lumpley standing side by side at the top of the stairs.

She heaved a sigh of relief, which turned to a cringe of embarrassment when her mother popped through the door after her.

"Ah, *there* you are, Jane!" Mrs. Bennet said. She paused for a hurried curtsy. "So sorry to barge in like this, My Lord, but the soldiers out front put us in an absolute tizzy with their foolish gossip! I should have known they were talking nonsense. Just look at this house! Why, it seems a shame even to walk on the floors, they gleam so. No dirty old dreadfuls here. They wouldn't match the décor, I imagine. La! Well, what are you waiting for, dear? Come down and give your mother a kiss before you show her the ballroom."

"Yes, Mamma." Jane turned to the baron and, to Elizabeth's surprise, managed to look him square in the eye. "If it pleases His Lordship?"

Lord Lumpley beamed benevolence. "Of course. I think I can survive a little while without my Amazon. I need to retire to my chambers, at any rate; we've been so busy with the preparations for the ball, I've barely left myself two hours to get properly dressed." The baron offered Elizabeth a smile then turned to Mrs. Bennet and, though the smile withered, at least managed to suppress his grimace. "If you need anything, please don't hesitate to ask my man Belgrave."

He took his leave with a shallow bow to Lizzy and Mrs. Bennet and an "Until tonight" to Jane.

"Ooooo," Mrs. Bennet cooed when Jane joined them at the bottom of the stairs. "You've got your hooks in deep, I can see. I always knew you'd marry above us, but who could have guessed how very high?"

"Mamma, *please*," Elizabeth said. Though Belgrave had departed not long after his master, she couldn't help feeling he lingered behind somehow, unseen yet unmistakably present, like a musty smell or a draft of cold air. "Keep your voice down."

She might as well have been Mary for all the mind her mother paid her.

"Is Lord Lumpley to thank for all these pretty baubles, then? As if your beauty didn't shine brightly enough already. Tonight it shall be blinding!"

Blushing, Jane put a hand to the gold, gemstone-studded choker around her neck. Elizabeth had never seen it before. New, too, were her sister's earrings and kid gloves and dancing slippers. The gown, though, was one Jane had brought with her from Longbourn (as was, of course, the sword that slightly crumpled the skirt on one side).

"His Lordship let me borrow a few things that his cousin, Lady Wellaway, left behind after her last visit," Jane explained. "He rather insisted on it, actually."

Elizabeth didn't care for the color on her sister's cheeks or the hint of a curl to her lips, but whatever they might mean, that could wait.

"Jane, *was* a dreadful loose in the house last night?"

Jane nodded, her face falling. "No one knows how it got inside. It killed one of the servants and a soldier before I, well, I rather split it in two."

"Oh!" Mrs. Bennet huffed. "Can't we talk about something else? Who put up your hair, dear? They did simply marvelous work with the curls!"

"Was it a male?" Elizabeth asked. "Fairly fresh?"

"Just the opposite. It was a girl, quite decomposed."

"And would you just look at those beautiful bangles," Mrs. Bennet said. "Do they belong to Lady Wellaway, too?"

"A *girl?* So it wasn't—"

Elizabeth caught herself just in time.

"So it wasn't Mr. Smith?" she'd been about to say. She could just imagine explaining "Mr. Smith" to her mother. Mrs. Bennet was desperate for her daughters to meet eligible males, but Elizabeth suspected even she had her standards.

"Have you seen Dr. Keckilpenny this morning?" she asked instead.

"Yes," Jane said. "I finally met the good doctor at breakfast."

Elizabeth let out a breath she didn't even know she'd been holding.

"He didn't stay to eat with us," Jane went on. "He simply loaded a plate in the kitchen and went back to the attic. The cook said all he took were pastries and desserts—along with some uncooked kidneys and tripe." She shook her head. "A strange young man. Nice, of course. But strange."

"Doctors," Mrs. Bennet snorted. "They're all strange, if you ask me. Who'd want to spend all their time around *sick people*? And I've never known a one who had more than four hundred a year. Now, solicitors, there's a sensible bunch. Or, better yet, barristers. Or—"

"Tell me, Jane," Elizabeth said, cocking an eyebrow. "Were there any other unwelcome callers in the night?"

For once, Jane looked as if she would have preferred pursuing her mother's line of conversation.

"Yes . . . in a way . . . but it wasn't like *that*." She dropped her voice to a whisper. "The baron's not as bad as you think, Lizzy."

"Believe me, Jane: He's not as good as *you* think," Elizabeth replied. "No one is."

Yet Jane looked unconvinced.

Soon after, Cuthbert Cannon and his Limbs came rolling/striding in, and it was quickly decided that the captain would see to Mrs. Bennet's entertainment while Elizabeth helped Jane prepare for the ball. It was a somewhat surprising arrangement: Capt. Cannon surely had better things to do, and Mrs. Bennet was passing up the chance to do worse by insinuating herself into the baron's household or playing Cupid for her daughters. Yet Elizabeth was too grateful to be free of her mother (and the constant danger of shame she posed) to ponder long on the oddness of it all.

She spent the next hours with her sister seeing to various last-minute details on Lord Lumpley's behalf. Jane had been appointed the baron's proxy, apparently, and it fell to her to make the final decisions on the placement of the orchestra, the arrangement of the card tables, the tartness of the punch, the ratio of grapes to apples in the fruit bowl, etcetera. In addition to being a great honor, this was a great responsibility. Everything in the ballroom and the drawing room and the long portrait-lined gallery connecting them had to be just so, and one servant after another came to Jane for direction, or simply glared at the upstart girl who dared to play mistress for the day.

Yet through it all Jane remained her usual agreeable, serene self. Elizabeth, however, found each new triviality rubbing her nerves more raw. What should she care about the desperate shortage of oysters or how to keep the Lumbards from mixing with their mortal enemies the Maydestones? Especially when she could look out any of the huge windows in that wing of the house and see soldiers drilling with muskets, hammering boards together into what looked like shields, marching up the road bound for who knew where or what?

"Oh, sod the Cotswold!" she finally snapped when Jane took a little too much time deliberating over the proper arrangement of the cheese plate. "And sod the ruddy Wensleydale, too!"

"Lizzy!"

Elizabeth clapped her hands over her mouth, hardly believing what had just popped from it.

"Oh, Jane. Forgive me, please," she said when she could finally trust herself to speak again. "It's just ... I find myself feeling so ... so ... "

Whatever she was feeling, it didn't come to her in anything so simple as a single word, and she had to get at her meaning another way.

"You're supposed to be the baron's bodyguard, not his master of ceremonies. For heaven's sake, can't we leave these trifles to Belgrave and the other servants?"

Jane reached out and gently took one of Elizabeth's hands in her own.

"Don't think I'm not frustrated, as well, Lizzy. Papa, Master Hawksworth, little Ensign Pratt, Lieutenant Tindall—they're all out there in harm's way so that we might stand here trying to keep the Stilton as far as possible from the Brie. It was our father's wish that this be so, however, and we can only assume there is some intent behind it, for how often has he made decisions unwisely or without due consideration?"

"You mean other than when he married Mother?"

Jane gave her sister another reproachful look.

"Yes, I know. You're right, of course," Elizabeth sighed. "I just wish I knew what Father was up to and why he felt it necessary to be so secretive about it."

"I suspect we'll have answers to both those questions soon." Jane gave Elizabeth's hand a squeeze, then turned back to the cheese plate. "Now, I'm beginning to incline to your way of thinking on the Cotswold. It's altogether too bold, isn't it? Perhaps we could have someone check the larder for a block of Gloucester."

Presently, Lord Lumpley returned with what proved to be impeccable timing: He came downstairs *after* all the necessary arrangements had been made and just *before* the arrival of the first guests. Elizabeth thought he actually looked rather good in his black coat and breeches and silvery silk vest, though he moved with a stiff-backed stiltedness that suggested his corset strings had been pulled especially tight for this night. Mrs. Bennet and Capt. Cannon reappeared then, as well, both of them looking cheery and flushed from their tour of the grounds.

This, then, was the de facto receiving line when Belgrave escorted the Goswicks into the ballroom. Mr. Goswick was actually able to bluff out an almost-convincing show of gratitude to the baron for "assuming patronage of the ball." But Mrs. Goswick and her daughter Julia—who, like Elizabeth, was to have her coming out that night—looked as though they could barely resist pinching their noses.

"You've taken off your scimitars, I see," Mrs. Goswick sniffed to Elizabeth and Jane. "Well ... I suppose they would get in the way during the dancing, wouldn't they?"

She led her daughter and husband off to the opposite side of the room, where they could keep company with the only truly respectable people present. Themselves.

More familiar faces soon followed, and the expressions upon them quickly grew quite familiar: strained graciousness for Lord Lumpley and Capt. Cannon, ill-concealed disdain for all the rest. Even Elizabeth's own aunt and uncle, Mr. and Mrs. Philips, were less than warm, and the couple quickly scurried away to the refreshments table, where they pretended to admire the tasteful arrangement of the cheeses.

"So this is to be my coming out," Elizabeth said to her sister. "It appears our neighbors would have preferred it had I stayed in."

"Don't worry, Lizzy. The mood will brighten once the music starts. Then you'll need a card to keep track of all the gentlemen asking for a turn around the floor."

Yet when the baron called for a Scotch Reel—which he proceeded to lead with Jane as his partner—no one came to Elizabeth to ask for a dance or offer an introduction to a willing partner. Even her mother, to her horror, was soon whirling this way and that with Capt. Cannon, his Limbs and wheelbarrow scattering the other dancers (when not crushing their toes).

"He's a blackguard, you know," someone said, and Elizabeth turned to find an eligible gentleman at her side at last—an eligible gentleman who was staring enviously at her sister and Lord Lumpley as they pranced, hand in hand, down the line.

"I do know it, Lieutenant Tindall," Elizabeth said. "But my sister insists on seeing the best in everyone, including those who have none."

"That is what makes her so special. Even the savagery your father has subjected her to could not snuff the light that shines within her lovely heart. She may parody a man when she straps on a sword, but without it she is everything any Englishwoman could hope to be."

"How flattering," Elizabeth said dryly. "For my sister."

The lieutenant nodded without taking his eyes off Jane. He cut quite a figure in his red regimentals, and Elizabeth could see Mrs. Goswick and her daughter across the room watching him with nearly the same intensity he focused on her sister.

"She represents everything I fight for," Lt. Tindall said. "I have vowed not to allow any harm to befall her."

"Oh? I hope you won't construe this as a criticism, but if that's true, why are you here attending a ball instead of outside hunting dreadfuls?"

This *was* a criticism, of course, and it came out even more sharply than Elizabeth had intended. So sharp, in fact, that the lieutenant winced as if stung and finally faced her fully.

"Night has fallen, Miss Bennet. There is little my men can do but guard the roads and the manor house—and that they are doing already. I will rejoin them in time. For now, however, there is danger of a different sort to be dealt with right here."

He turned back toward the dance floor and grimaced at the sight of Jane and the baron's carefree smiles.

"I intend to have the next dance with your sister . . . and however many more after that I can," he said. "May God strike me down dead if I allow her to be his partner twice in a row."

Elizabeth stared at the young officer a moment, amazed by how handsome, how pure hearted, how incredibly *thick* he was. She looked around the room at the other men and saw none to match the lieutenant on the first two counts, and many who far surpassed him on the last.

She was supposed to be introducing herself this night, making herself known to society. Yet she felt, instead, that society was making itself known to her.

Somewhere outside lurked a menace as close to pure evil as God or Satan could possibly produce, and only a few brave souls—men like her father and Geoffrey Hawksworth—were out in the darkness to face it. Meanwhile, here were Hertfordshire's leading lights laughing and skipping in circles under the glimmer of crystal chandeliers.

"Why are you at a ball instead of out hunting dreadfuls?" she'd asked the lieutenant. And it was a good question. For everyone.

Especially herself.

"Excuse me," she said. "I find there's something I've forgotten to attend to."

Lt. Tindall turned to her just enough to offer a perfunctory bow. His gaze never left Jane.

As she walked from the ballroom, Elizabeth was acutely aware how her sudden departure must look. "There goes poor, perverse, ruined Elizabeth Bennet—snubbed by every man in the place, now she flees to cry her tears of humiliation alone." And the beautiful thing about it was that she didn't care.

"Belgrave," she said, though the man was nowhere in sight. "Belgrave."

She didn't need to say it a third time. He appeared at her side, matching her stride for stride.

"Yes, Miss Bennet?"

"There is a package in my family's carriage. Beneath the backseat. Would you send someone out for it, please?"

"Right away, Miss."

The servant fell away, then somehow managed to beat Elizabeth to the foyer.

He was waiting for her with the package in his hands. It was long and narrow, wrapped in rough hessian.

Elizabeth took it and cradled it and folded back the burlap covering, gazing down like the Madonna on her wrapped katana.

"Thank you, Belgrave," she said. "I won't be needing anything else."

CHAPTER 32

ELIZABETH HAD ONE CALL to make before she went out to find Master Hawksworth and her father and whatever dreadfuls they'd managed to find. There was someone she wished to say hello to and, depending on how things went, perhaps good-bye as well.

The guard outside the door to the attic was as quick to level a Brown Bess as Pvt. Jones, only he had even more reason to do so. Elizabeth could deduce as much from the dark stains the maids hadn't quite managed to scrub from the floor and wall.

"Good evening," she said, and that was enough for the soldier to lower his musket, sighing with relief. No passwords were needed to tell friend from foe in this war. *Any* word—that was enough.

"Evening, Miss. Here to see His Queerness, are you?"

"Dr. Keckilpenny. Yes."

"Need an escort up?"

"No," Elizabeth said firmly. "That's quite all right."

"Suit yourself. It certainly suits me. Oooo, the awful sounds his pet makes. If I had to actually *see* the thing . . . "

The soldier shivered, then stepped aside to let Elizabeth pass.

Halfway up the dimly lit stairwell, she began to hear some of those sounds the man had mentioned. Groaning, grunting, the clomping of heavy footfalls.

Only, when Elizabeth reached the top of the steps, she saw it wasn't "Mr. Smith" making the noise at all.

"Daaaaaaaaaaaaaaaaaance," Dr. Keckilpenny said as he spun and capered about the attic. "Dance. Dance!" He waved his arms in time to the muffled waltz filtering up through the floorboards. "Muuuuuuuuuuuuu-uuusic. Music. Music!"

Mr. Smith watched him from a few feet away, black drool dripping from his open mouth, arms swept back to the sides, straining against his chains.

"Grrrrrrrrrrrrrrrr," he said.

"No, Smithy. Muuuuuuuuuuuuusic. Daaaaaaaaaaaaance."

Dr. Keckilpenny threw his gangly form into a slipshod arabesque and performed a wobbly spin that left him staring, eyes wide, at Elizabeth.

"Oh! Miss Bennet! What a wonderful surprise! And here I was just thinking of you."

"Really? I'm honored that the mere thought of me should make you want to dance."

Dr. Keckilpenny put on one of his sideways-crescent grins. "You're not far off there, actually. May I tell you about it? What I was thinking, I mean?"

When Elizabeth didn't answer straightaway, his smile sagged.

"Of course, you may," Elizabeth said. "I need to be elsewhere tonight, but I can certainly delay my departure long enough to hear why a dignified man like yourself should wish to perform ballet for a dreadful."

"Dignified? And here I thought we were getting to know each other so well." The doctor held out his hands toward the chest in which Mr. Smith had been hauled up to the attic. "Please, have a trunk."

Elizabeth walked to the chest and took a seat atop it.

Mr. Smith swayed in her direction.

"Grrrrrrrrrrrrrrrrrr."

"No, Mr. Smith. Girrrrrrrrrrrrrrrl," Dr. Keckilpenny said. "Or, I suppose, young laaaaaaaaaaaaaady."

Mr. Smith made a sound that was part snarl, part wail and not "girl" or "lady" in any way whatsoever.

The doctor sighed.

"You see how it's been . . . and this is Smithy at his best. Last night he was positively wild. Flinging himself at me, shrieking, yowling. One minute he was being a perfect gentleman, as zombies go, the next it was nothing but snort snarl slobber howl."

"Was that around the time the other unmentionable got loose in the house?"

Dr. Keckilpenny tapped a long finger against his chin. "Now that you mention it, it was. Most curious. I wonder if they can sense each other's presence. By smell, perhaps?"

"I hear you lost your guard."

"Yeeeeesss," the doctor drawled, still tapping away, eyes squinting up at nothing. "Pity, that. Good thing I didn't step out for a midnight snack or I'd have *been* one." He clapped his hands together and focused on Elizabeth again. "But that's neither here nor there. I was about to tell you about Mr. Smith's re-Anglification."

"His what?"

"Re-Anglification! That's what I call my process. Or plan to call it. If it works."

Dr. Keckilpenny darted over to a dark corner of the room. On the floor was a jumble of assorted bric-a-brac, and the doctor knelt down next to it.

"Mr. Smith isn't just a dead man, Miss Bennet. He's a dead *Englishman*. And if—as we've discussed before—some part of his mind still survives, then this is how it might be reached, and even revived."

Dr. Keckilpenny began grabbing dishes and holding them up to display their contents.

"Trifle. Currant scones. Cup of tea. Good! Mangled viscera? Bad." He pointed at a small stack of books. "Shakespeare. Milton. Dr. Johnson. Good!" He reached out for a plate covered with a stained napkin, then changed his mind and simply pointed at it. "Body parts? Bad . . . when they're not attached." He swung his finger to a pile of framed portraits. "The king. The prime minister. The Prince Regent. Good! Sort of." He gestured at a sealed jar in which a loaflike mass floated in brackish brine. "Brains? Bad bad *bad*."

"Grrrrrrrrrrrr," Mr. Smith said.

"Grrrrrrrrrrrr, bad," Dr. Keckilpenny replied. "Words, good!"

"Grrrrrrrrrrrrrrrrrrrrrrrrrrrr."

"I hope you'll forgive the observation," Elizabeth said. "But Mr. Smith doesn't strike me as any more English than when we captured him."

The doctor nodded sadly. "Yes, I know. He's definitely responding to something, though. The last hour, he's seemed more alert. Aware.

Almost perky."

Elizabeth looked at the hollow-eyed thing leaning toward her groaning. "Perky?"

The doctor nodded again, this time with excitement. "I think it might be the music. It hath charms to soothe a savage breast, you know, and you won't find many breasts more savage than a zombie's. That's what got me thinking about you, Miss Bennet. If the *sound* of a waltz could stir something in Mr. Smith, just think what the *sight* of one might do."

"I don't understand. What has that got to do with—"

Dr. Keckilpenny started walking toward Elizabeth. She knew what he was going to say before he said it.

What she didn't know was how she would reply.

The doctor offered her his hand. "Miss Bennet, may I have this dance?"

Elizabeth said nothing, but she did take his hand and stand.

Dr. Keckilpenny walked her out to the center of the room, then slipped his right hand around her waist while lifting her left hand up high.

"A waltz," he said, his voice as soft as she'd ever heard it. "How like the count to choose something so risqué for a country dance."

"The baron," Elizabeth corrected as the two of them began to move in time to the muted music of the ball. There was a little warble to her voice that surprised her.

She should have been out dreadful-stalking with Master Hawksworth. That's where she'd intended to be. So why was she letting Dr. Keck-ilpenny spin her in sweeping circles around an attic?

"Grrrrruh!" Mr. Smith barked. "Grrrrrrruh!"

"That's progress, perhaps," the doctor said. "What are you trying to tell us, Smithy? Are you asking for the next dance?" He looked down into Elizabeth's eyes in a way that made her dizzy. Or maybe that was just the waltz. "Well, you can't have it."

Mr. Smith's gruff, yapping growls grew louder, and he began to struggle, stamping his feet and straining harder against his chains.

"GRRRRRUH!" MR. SMITH BARKED. "GRRRRRRRRUH!"

"I do believe he's jealous," Elizabeth said. "The way you're holding me, he probably thinks you intend to devour me."

"Not a bad theory, Miss Bennet. Shall we put it to the test?"

And he pulled her tightly to his chest and leaned in and kissed her.

Instantly, entirely by instinct, Elizabeth broke his hold with the Wings of the Phoenix, an upward sweep of the arms that sent him flying back into the nearest wall.

The doctor let out an "Oof," then stumbled forward, off balance. When he regained his footing he gaped at Elizabeth, looking as much puzzled as hurt.

"Have I offended you? It was purely in the interest of scientific inquiry." He cocked his head and furrowed his brow. "I think."

"Doctor, I . . . I don't know what to say."

But someone did.

"Buh ruh," Mr. Smith said. "Buh ruh!"

Dr. Keckilpenny burst out laughing. "Did you hear that? We did it! We did it, Miss Bennet! He said . . . something!"

He took a step toward Elizabeth as if he intended to hug her or take her hands in his, but then he suddenly stopped and spun toward Mr. Smith again.

"Oh. Right. Sorry. Well well well."

"Buh ruuuuuh!" Mr. Smith brayed. "Buuuuuuh ruuuuh!"

His struggles grew more frantic even as his words—whatever they were—grew louder.

"It's just like last night, when he went into his frenzy," Dr. Keckilpenny said. "Only with the 'buh ruh,' now. I wonder if—"

"Doctor, listen. The music."

"What of it? I don't even hear . . . oh."

The music had stopped.

Elizabeth whirled around and shot down the stairs. When she got through the door at the bottom, she found the sentry gone.

From down the hall, toward the master staircase and the foyer beneath, she could hear a great commotion: murmuring, shouting, the shuffling of many feet.

Elizabeth unsheathed her katana and sprinted toward the sound.

"What is the meaning of this?" she heard Lord Lumpley roar.

"Isn't it obvious?" a familiar (and very welcome) voice replied just as she reached the top of the main stairs. "We're crashing your party, My Lord."

Down below, Elizabeth could see her father and Master Hawksworth squared off against the baron and Jane as a teeming stream of people flowed around them into the house.

There was Mr. Maleeny, the blacksmith, with his family; Mr. and Mrs. Littlefield, who ran the local bakery; Mr. Lawes, the carpenter, with his sons Humphrey and Giles; the McGregors, who sold lamp oil and perfume; the Calders and the Masons and the Crowells and many more. All of them tradesmen or tradesmen's kin. And they weren't even coming in the servants' entrance.

"Blast you, Bennet!" Lord Lumpley railed. "You can't do this!"

"I think that you'll find, very soon, that it's done," Mr. Bennet said. "And just in time, too. We aren't the only uninvited guests who'll be calling on Netherfield tonight, I'm afraid."

"So they're here?" Capt. Cannon called out. What with the throng clogging the entrance hall, his Limbs couldn't maneuver him any closer than a doorway on the other side of the room.

"Yes," Mr. Bennet said to him, and Elizabeth heard a sudden, barely suppressed fury in his voice. "The hordes are descending at last, Captain. Not five minutes behind us are dreadfuls beyond number."

"What should we do?" Elizabeth asked.

Mr. Bennet looked up at her and, seeing the katana in her hands, smiled.

Master Hawksworth looked up at her and, seeing Dr. Keckilpenny step up close behind her, frowned.

"Oh, tonight's the easy part," Mr. Bennet said. "All we must do is survive."

CHAPTER 33

OSCAR BENNET'S OLD DREAM, the one about his daughters fighting beside him in the honorable warrior way, was about to come true at last. He knew that when the moment arrived, however, only part of him would be able to appreciate it. The other part—the vast majority of him, in fact—would be too busy trying to keep his entrails inside his own stomach. So he paused to savor the moment now.

They were all lined up with him before the manor house: Mary, Kitty, and Lydia, who'd left Longbourn to track him down as he'd swept through the countryside forging his little diaspora; Jane, there over the objections of Lord Lumpley (who didn't wish to be parted from his bodyguard) and Lt. Tindall (who insisted that his troops could do what needed to be done without endangering "those whose dainty hands should never have been soiled by instruments of war"); and finally Elizabeth, standing at the end of the line with Geoffrey Hawksworth quite literally looming up behind her, just as he'd loomed a little too large all through her training.

Mr. Bennet had his doubts about them all. Yet when he'd announced that the Bennets would be the last line of defense, guarding the front door while Capt. Cannon's soldiers nailed wooden slats over the windows, his daughters' only hesitation before following him outside was to collect their favorite weapons.

Long ago, he'd broken his vow to the Order to raise his children in the warrior way. They seemed poised to redeem his honor now, though. He could die a happy man. And very soon, he might.

It started with the occasional blast and flash of gunfire out by the road, where Lt. Tindall had stretched out his own thin skirmish line. The screaming followed, some human, some not, and not long after came the lieutenant's far-off cries: "Stand your ground!" and "Hold fast!" and finally "Hold, damn you! Hold!" Then the soldiers started streaming back across the long, moonlit lawn. One by one and two by two they came, all of them sprinting wild-eyed toward the Bennets and the house.

"Lieutenant Tindall," Jane said, taking a hesitant step toward the road.

Elizabeth stepped with her. "Perhaps we should—"

"No," Mr. Bennet said. "The Enemy will come to us in its own good time. There is no reason to rush, and every reason not to." He looked back over his shoulder at the little figure pacing nervously before a group of frantically hammering soldiers. "How much longer?"

"A few minutes," Ensign Pratt squeaked. "If only this bloody house didn't have so many bloody windows!"

"Language," Mr. Bennet chided.

"Sorry, Sir. My apologies to the ladies."

Lydia leaned in close to Kitty and whispered something, and they both giggled. Mr. Bennet found it comforting, somehow. The two of them would still be gossiping and laughing as they crossed the River Styx.

The first of the fleeing soldiers rushed past and darted through the front door.

"They have sent boys to do the work of warriors," Master Hawksworth grumbled.

"Yes. It has been known to happen," Mr. Bennet said. He pointed at a far corner of the lawn. "Ahhh, the guests of honor arrive at last."

One of the men running toward them had a peculiar, herky-jerky quality to his stride, and his head was bent so far to the side it appeared to be resting horizontally atop his right shoulder. As he came nearer, it became clear he wasn't dressed as a soldier. He was chasing one.

Mr. Bennet brought up his crossbow, took a moment to squint down the stock, and squeezed the trigger. The bolt shot across the lawn and buried itself in the dreadful's forehead with an audible *thunk*.

"It appears the first kill of the night goes to me," Mr. Bennet said as the unmentionable tumbled to the ground. "Sorry to be selfish."

Within moments, there were zombies enough for all. Some ran from the shadows, some staggered, some crawled. Some were men, some women, some children. Some wore ragged shrouds, some bloody clothing, some absolutely nothing. Yet they all had one thing in common: They were headed toward the house.

"Remember your training, and we shall triumph!" Master Hawksworth bellowed, waving his sword above his head. "Battle cries, warriors! Battle cries!"

The girls brought up their katanas and screamed in unison.

"HAA-IEEEEEEEEEEEEEE!"

"Yes, yes," Mr. Bennet said. "Haiee."

He'd never put much stock in battle cries, actually, but they did seem to help the beginners. And his daughters, inexperienced as they were, showed no sign they might turn and flee inside as the soldiers had. They looked frightened, of course, with pinched, pale faces and wide eyes. Yet their feet were planted firmly in battle-ready stances, and their weapons didn't waver.

Mr. Bennet nodded his approval, then turned back to the wave of death sweeping toward them. The swiftest dreadfuls were but a dozen strides away now, and he brought one down with another bolt before handing his bow to a soldier as he flew past blubbering hysterically.

"Put this in the house for me, there's a good lad."

He drew his sword just in time to slice the head off a zombie wearing the black robe and mortarboard of a university don.

"The Hawk and the Dove, Master?" he heard Elizabeth say, and he spared a glance her way, curious to see how Hawksworth reacted.

The Master was doubled up with his hands wrapped around his right leg.

"Ahhhh! My knee! Again! Blast!"

It had been the same earlier that day, when they'd spotted their first small herd of unmentionables. Hawksworth's "old sparring injury" had hobbled him, for a time.

"Master!" Mary cried, and she put a bullet through a dreadful's head and cleaved another's in two to reach the young man's side. "Do you need help?"

Hawksworth swiveled, grimacing, and began limping toward the door. "I will be fine. But, alas, I'm useless to you now! Try to carry on without me!"

"Go, all of you!" someone shouted. "For God's sake, get inside!"

Mr. Bennet turned back toward the lawn. Lt. Tindall was weaving wildly up the gravel drive, all of his attention on Jane even as one unmentionable after another swiped and lunged at him.

Mr. Bennet started toward him, but a brief encounter with another mindless, slobbering don proved to be a distraction. By the time a second mortarboarded head was at his feet, Jane and Elizabeth were already on either side of Lt. Tindall, rushing with him toward the house along a newly made lane of crania, arms, and torsos.

Mr. Bennet's chest went tight with pride even as he beheaded a groaning old woman with her intestines hanging out through a hole in her nightgown.

"Finished in the back!" he heard Capt. Cannon call out.

"Finished in the front!" Ensign Pratt yelped.

"Capital," Mr. Bennet said. "Girls, I do believe a retreat is in order."

Unmentionables kept coming at them as they backed toward the door, with more continuing to step out of the woods. There were too many to count—at least while chopping away at a new neck every few seconds—but Mr. Bennet thought he spotted at least half a dozen clad in red jackets and white cross belts.

The second he and the girls were inside, soldiers slammed the door shut and began nailing up boards to hold it in place.

Lydia and Kitty sheathed their swords and fell into each other's arms, laughing. It wasn't their usual giddy, frivolous tittering, though. They were laughs of disbelief and relief to find themselves still alive.

A hand settled lightly on Mr. Bennet's forearm.

"Papa?" Jane said. "How did we do?"

Mr. Bennet glanced at Master Hawksworth, who was sitting, legs spread out, back propped against a wall. Both Elizabeth and Mary were leaning in over him.

"You were splendid," Mr. Bennet said to Jane. "But there are tests yet for you to face."

"What?" Capt. Cannon said. "Limbs! Pace!"

Right Limb and Left Limb began wheeling him around the foyer so he could scowl at panting, shame-faced soldiers.

"I'd say your daughters have already proved themselves more warrior than many another here."

"If I'd had more men, it would have looked different," Lt. Tindall protested. "So many were held back in the house."

"One doesn't fight dreadfuls in the dark, Lieutenant," Capt. Cannon snapped. "When we face them again on the battlefield, it will be on our terms. Now, let us see to the—"

"I would have words with you, Cannon," Mr. Bennet said. "Alone."

"Limbs. Halt."

The two men looked into each other's eyes a moment. Mr. Bennet's were full of rage; the captain's, remorse.

"Limbs, to my chambers. Lieutenant, see to it there's a man—or a lady—at every window and door. It's going to be a long night."

The pounding began before he'd even finished. One fist thumped against the door, then another smashed into a window, then another started in, and another and another and another until the whole house rattled and seemed to shudder. Some of the villagers packed into the rooms nearby screamed in terror, and their cries were answered by screeches from just outside.

"We must have calm!" Capt. Cannon roared. "The next person I hear shrieking will be put outside with the other banshees!"

The screaming stopped, for a time. As the captain and Mr. Bennet moved off into the north wing, they approached the room where Dr. Thorne, the company's gruff old duffer of a surgeon, was seeing to the wounded.

"You're lucky, boy. That's not a bad scratch at all," the doctor was saying as they passed by. "You'll only lose the arm up to the elbow."

Mr. Cummings could be heard offering comfort by reading haltingly from his *Book of Common Prayer*. It seemed to be a selection from the table of contents, however, and it was soon drowned out by the sound of sawing and all the attendant lamentations.

When they reached the bedroom Capt. Cannon had commandeered for his headquarters, the soldiers guarding the windows were dismissed and Left Limb and Right Limb positioned in their place. The captain was left in the middle of the room in his cart. Mr. Bennet, although offered a seat, chose to stand directly before him.

"Are you sure you want your men to hear this?" Mr. Bennet said, nodding at the Limbs.

"By necessity, I have no secrets from them."

"So they know already that which has been withheld from me?"

Capt. Cannon nodded slowly, head hanging. "They do."

"Then you have grievously insulted me, Captain. When you first arrived in Hertfordshire, I greeted you as a comrade. Yet you were deceiving me from the very beginning."

"Yes. And how it has weighed on me!" the captain cried out in anguish. "You are a good man, Bennet, and I have treated you shamefully. I welcome the opportunity to expunge some of my guilt by acknowledging my dishonor now." He took in a deep, shuddering breath before going on. "Your suspicions are correct. I have been wooing your good lady wife."

Mr. Bennet nodded impatiently, opened his mouth, and then froze, utterly dumbstruck.

A softly wheezed "What?" was all he could get off his lips.

"Prudence was the one true love of my life," Capt. Cannon went on. "The one love Fate allowed me before I became as you find me. When I saw her again, it was as if parts of me that were long dead suddenly sprang to life again. I became, in those precious moments I could be with her, some semblance of my younger self . . . my *whole* self, so long lost to—"

Mr. Bennet held up a hand.

"Wait, wait, wait," he said. "*What?*"

The captain blinked at him. "You didn't suspect?"

"No! I was talking about the dreadful hordes. You've known all along that the strange plague has spread far beyond Meryton. As far as I know, we're the *last* to see its return, not the first. It's why the War Office could spare only one company of new recruits commanded by callow youths and an officer who has, to be blunt, seen better days. It's why some of the unmentionables I saw tonight obviously came from Cambridge and companies of soldiers other than your own. It's why you already had your men preparing boards for the windows and doors. It's why the mails and hackney coaches haven't been . . . my God, *really?* You've been dillydallying with Mrs. Bennet?"

"Yes. Courting her with all my heart."

"When you knew we were probably all about to die?"

"In which case there would be no opportunity later."

"But . . . *why?*"

"As I said. Because I love her. And should you fall in the days ahead and I survive, I fully intend to claim the happiness that chance has denied me the last twenty years."

"You assume Prudence would marry you?"

"Can you truly say you have been so attentive and loving a husband she would stay in mourning all her remaining days?"

Mr. Bennet gaped at the man a moment, put a hand to the side of his head as if to assure himself it was still there, then waved his confusion away and tried to focus on what he thought mattered most.

"Why didn't you tell me about the dreadfuls?"

"Orders. The War Office was desperate to avoid a panic in the Home Counties. You remember The Troubles. People try to flee, the roads become clogged, the dreadfuls descend, and before long you've got one thousand zombies where before you had one hundred."

"Yes, yes, I remember. Tell me——"

Mr. Bennet had a dozen more questions he wished to ask, but he realized they all really came down to one thing.

"Is there any hope for us?"

It was a question that could be answered with a yes or a no, of course, and Mr. Bennet found it instructive—if not encouraging—that Capt. Cannon didn't use either word.

"The North is overrun. If you didn't have friends in the War Office, even my one company of untrained London urchins would not have been sent to your aid. Lord Paget is moving a battalion over from Suffolk to reinforce the capital—to think anyone was worried about Napoleon at a time like this!—but I can't say for certain where he is at the moment. Assuming he hasn't met with disaster already, however, his column *might* be in or near Hertfordshire, and if we could get word to him somehow he *might* decide to send reinforcements."

"'Might,' 'somehow,' and 'might' again," Mr. Bennet said. "It is little to pin our lives on."

Capt. Cannon shrugged. "Yet it is something."

Mr. Bennet nodded, then sucked in a long, deep breath.

"You know that my code of honor demands your death," he said.

"Of course. And *you* know that, shamed though I might be to have betrayed the trust of a worthy man, a soldier does not face death without defending himself. My Limbs stand ready to act as my seconds."

"Of course."

Something began scratching at the planks over the nearest window.

"And yet," Mr. Bennet said, "this does not strike me as an opportune time for a duel."

"Nor I."

The scratching grew louder and was soon joined by the sound of clumsy pawing from another pair of hands.

"I propose, then, a gentleman's agreement," Mr. Bennet said. "For now, we will continue to work together. If we are both alive in two days' time, however, we may do our utmost to kill each other."

"Done. Right Limb, shake the man's hand."

And so they shook.

CHAPTER 34

EVENTUALLY, ELIZABETH TIRED of chopping off limbs and wandered away from her post. Mary had relieved her an hour before, yet she'd lingered by the window with her anyway, shouting "Breach!" and hacking away every time a plank popped free. By the time a soldier rushed over to nail the board back in place, the pile of splotchy, tatter-fleshed arms under the sill would have grown taller by at least two.

"Interesting. That one looks like it came from a blackamoor," Mary said at one point. "Or do you think that's just the way he was decaying?"

"I'm done," Elizabeth mumbled, and she simply walked off.

Just getting out of the room and down the hall was a challenge, crowded as the lower floor was: Lord Lumpley had insisted that "the uninvited" stay downstairs while the upper floor remained reserved for him and his guests. (The ballroom had been abandoned straight off, for its long rows of broad, tall windows made it impossible to defend.)

Yet the villagers cleared a path for Elizabeth as best they could, and those who weren't huddled up weeping or asleep nodded tight-lipped encouragement. Some even thanked her. They'd seen what she and her sisters had done to help hold the dreadfuls back. No one looked at them as pariahs now. They were saviors.

It was the same when Elizabeth went up to the second floor (to escape the constant pounding and the choking smell of fear and death downstairs, she told herself). The very people who'd snubbed her hours before were offering her grim smiles and the occasional "Well done" or "Good show." They were currying her favor now, and it sickened her.

Her father would understand her weariness and disgust, but he was in conference with Capt. Cannon and Lt. Tindall, planning an "action" for the next morning (assuming they lasted out the night). She knew where Jane was—just down the hall, posted outside Lord Lumpley's bedchamber door. There was no use talking to her at such a time, however. Jane was too pure-hearted to appreciate bitterness.

And then there was Master Hawksworth. Once, she would have thought that he, a proud warrior, would understand. But he'd hobbled off to stand guard in some far corner of the house, and Elizabeth found she lacked the will to seek him out. She had many questions for the Master—and little stomach for the likely answers. Easier to simply escape.

She kept going up until there was no higher to climb.

Mr. Smith noticed her first.

"Buh ruhzzzzz!" he said. "Buh ruhzzzzz!"

"And good evening to you."

Dr. Keckilpenny was half-dozing on the floor, his head against his trunk. At the sound of Elizabeth's voice, though, he hopped up smiling, instantly alert.

"Miss Bennet! I was hoping you would return to my little aerie sooner or later!" He started toward her but stopped after just one stride, his smile taking on a stiff, frozen quality. "As you can see, I've made quite a bit of progress with our subject."

"You have?"

"Indeed!"

"Buh ruhzzzzzz," said Mr. Smith. "Buh ruhzzzzz!"

"Did you hear that, Miss Bennet? 'Buh ruhz' instead of just 'Buh ruh.' And all it took was another three hours of intensive re-Anglification. Why, at this rate, I'll have him speaking complete sentences by . . . oh, the early twenty-first century, at the latest."

Mr. Smith was, as usual, pulling against his chains, his arms back, as he writhed and kicked and snapped his teeth at Elizabeth.

"Do you really think this can be of any help to us now?" she asked.

Dr. Keckilpenny shrugged. "I think it is what I can best contribute."

"I assume Dr. Thorne could still use some help with the wounded."

"He has an orderly and a clergyman assisting him already. With one to cart away the spare parts and the other to usher out the souls, I really don't see what good I could do."

"You might do much. There will be more sick soon, even if the dreadfuls don't break in tonight. The air downstairs is fetid and growing worse by the minute, and what food and drink are left will soon be gone."

For what seemed like the first time since Elizabeth met him, the doctor stopped smiling.

"Yes, well, I'll do what I can about that when the time comes. Until then, my work remains here."

Elizabeth wasn't sure what she'd come up to the attic to say, but somehow that didn't matter now. She was speaking to a different Dr. Keckilpenny than she'd once known. Or perhaps simply a truer one.

"You know, Doctor," she said, "I'm beginning to think you can't be bothered with any problem that isn't hypothetical. It's as if you exist nowhere but in your own head."

Dr. Keckilpenny's grin returned. It was askew, though—so slanted it was almost half smile, half frown.

"My favoritest place," he said, tapping a finger against his forehead. "Though I like it infinitely better when I'm not up here alone."

"Elizabeth Bennet?" a voice called out, and heavy footsteps sounded on the stairs. "Elizabeth Bennet, are you there?"

Master Hawksworth stepped into the attic.

He then immediately jumped out of the attic—or several steps back down the stairwell, at least.

"Is that a . . . ?" he said, gaping at Mr. Smith.

"Yes," Dr. Keckilpenny said. "It is *a*. A chained *a*. You have nothing to fear from him."

The Master scowled and stomped slowly to the top of the stairs again, favoring his left leg. "You are Bertram Cuckilpony?"

"Oh, my. He's even worse than I am!" the doctor scoffed. "It's Keckilpenny. And even mangling my name, Sir, you have me at a disadvantage. You would be . . . ?"

Hawksworth spread his legs and put his hands on his hips. "Elizabeth Bennet's master."

"Her *what*? Goodness gracious, this isn't America. You make it sound as though you own her."

"Master Hawksworth is my instructor in the deadly arts," Elizabeth said, moving between the two men.

Dr. Keckilpenny nodded and looked the Master up and down. "Ahhhh. That explains the physique, I suppose. Though why anyone should want to be all swollen up like a Frenchman's balloon, I don't know."

"Better to be swollen than as spindly as a dried-out twig," Master Hawksworth sneered back.

"Buh ruhzzzz," Mr. Smith moaned, hungrily ogling the Master's physique. "Buh ruhzzzzzz!"

Master Hawksworth snapped into a Striking Viper pose. "Did that thing just *speak*?"

Before anyone could answer, there was a loud thump across the room. Another quickly followed, and Dr. Keckilpenny's trunk rocked and scooted a few inches across the floor.

"Doctor," Elizabeth said, "do you have any idea why your luggage would be moving?"

"Oh, yes. That's Westlake. Or was it Eastbrook? Whichever, he's the guard who was killed in the house the other night. Capt. Cannon let me keep him as sort of a spare, in case Mr. Smith didn't work out. It appears he's reporting for duty."

Elizabeth stared at the doctor, aghast.

Master Hawksworth began edging toward the stairwell.

"Come, Elizabeth Bennet. Let us leave this lunatic to his obscenities."

"My work won't seem so obscene when it saves your life."

"Ha!" the Master spat. "What will save us is strength, not the devilry of warped meddlers."

"Ha *ha*! What will save us is ingenuity, not the brute force of bloodthirsty simpletons!"

"I can show you what brute force is capable of," Master Hawksworth said, even as he kept sliding toward the stairs.

"I'm sure you could. I would expect no more nor less from the likes of you. The only thing that surprises me is that Miss Bennet would choose to be your pupil."

"Buh ruhzzz! Buh ruhzzz!" Mr. Smith said.

"You stay out of this," Dr. Keckilpenny snapped.

"Whether you like it or not, I am Elizabeth Bennet's master, whereas you, to her, are nothing." Master Hawksworth turned to Elizabeth and held out his hand. "Come. We are leaving."

"Pah! The Elizabeth Bennet I know bows to no master save her own mind. And in that, I am something a buffoon like you could never be: her equal."

Master Hawksworth curled his hand into a fist and stepped toward Dr. Keckilpenny. "I warn you. Do not insult me."

"You're right. Why should I bother when you make an ass of yourself with no assistance from me?"

The Master bent his knees and curled his hands like claws, beginning a Panther's Pounce.

He never finished it. Elizabeth's kick sent him flying halfway across the attic.

"Stop it! Both of you!" She planted herself between the men again. "You're acting like children!"

With stunned slowness, Master Hawksworth pushed himself up off the floor. Yet it wasn't anger Elizabeth saw upon his face when he turned to look at her. It was something approaching wonder—almost *worship*.

"Elizabeth Bennet, you are a marvel," he said. "I will not pretend to command you again. Instead, I will ask you. I will beg you. Please. Leave now. With me. *Stay* with me. I need you. There is a hole in my heart . . . a hole only you can fill."

"If there's a hole in you anywhere, it's in your head," Dr. Keckilpenny declared. "Clearly, Miss Bennet intends to stay up here. With me."

"Oh!" Elizabeth cried out. She flung up her hands, and it was as if a dam within her burst, and everything she'd been holding back came pouring out. "The holes in you both are so vast I think it would take the two of you together to make one whole man!" She swung a sharp glare on Hawksworth. "You! You came to us as a Master, yet you've not mastered your own fear! You can jump, you can strike poses, you can do *dand-baithaks* by the score. But there is one thing you cannot or will not do: fight! Oh, maybe you can work up the courage to thrash some helpless weakling."

"Hey," Dr. Keckilpenny said.

"But when have you willingly faced a worthy foe?" Elizabeth went on. "You never sparred with my father in the dojo. Never even sparred with *me*! And you always seemed to disappear or go conveniently lame when it was time to deal with *zombies*."

The Master flinched, and Elizabeth knew she would never think of him as "Master" again.

"Your 'shameful secret' is obvious to me now, as it should have been all along," she said. "You are a coward, Geoffrey Hawksworth."

Hawksworth lowered his head and said nothing.

Elizabeth turned to Dr. Keckilpenny and found him eyeing his rival looking altogether too smug.

"And you. Do you know what you are?"

"Mad?" the doctor ventured.

"Yes! Mad! And cold, despite all your jokes. You treat the dead as your playthings, and the living—they don't enter into the equation at all! Not so long as you've got your toys in your ivory tower!"

"Precisely!" Dr. Keckilpenny began brightly. "And all that's left to make it paradise is a suitable playm—"

The heart for quips left him before he could even finish the word, and he sighed and slumped and said, "Oh, it's hopeless, isn't it?"

"You look for hope in the wrong place. Both of you," Elizabeth said. She felt spent now, empty. "What each of you lacks I cannot give you ... and would not if I could."

She turned and started down the stairs, hoping she'd reach the bottom before the tears came.

She did.

After a long, still moment, Master Hawksworth left the attic, as well. It was obvious he wasn't going after Elizabeth, however. He simply had no choice but to follow in her footsteps.

"Buh ruhz," groaned Mr. Smith. "Buuuuuh ruhhhhhzzzzzzzzz."

Dr. Keckilpenny slouched over and slumped back atop his chest, which was now rattling so fiercely it was scratching the floorboards.

"No, Smithy. Not 'buuuuh ruhhhhzz,'" he said. "The word is *damn*."

CHAPTER 35

"ELIZABETH."

At the sound of her name, she left the blackness. She'd been sleeping but not dreaming, as with the dead—the restful dead, anyway.

She saw her haggard father kneeling beside her, sucked in a lungful of the malodorous air, heard the banging and scraping on the window boards and the raspy, incoherent cries outside. And she longed for oblivion again as memory returned.

She'd spent hours—it seemed like days—fighting back one break-through after another. Sometimes with her father, sometimes with her sisters, sometimes with soldiers or servants or men from the village. Never with Master Hawksworth. Whatever battles he was or wasn't fighting, he was facing them without her.

She couldn't remember falling asleep, nor did she recall crawling under the dining room table with the mothers nestling sleeping or weeping children. Yet here she was.

"Come with me," her father said softly. "It begins soon."

Elizabeth was too groggy to even ask what "it" was. She simply got up and followed.

Lydia and Kitty, she found, were passed out together atop the table, while Mary was slumped, drooling on herself prodigiously, against a grandfather clock in the hallway.

"Papa?" Elizabeth said.

Mr. Bennet just put a finger to his lips and shook his head. He was letting her sisters sleep. But why not her?

The soldiers were gone from their positions along the hall, and when Elizabeth and her father reached the foyer, she saw why. The whole company was packed in there together, bayonets affixed to their Brown Besses. Ensign Pratt was at the back, his cherubic face as round and pale as a full moon. In front, by the door, was Capt. Cannon in his wheelbarrow, turned to face his men.

". . . been telling yourselves you're not ready for all this," he was saying. "Because you lack training. Because you lack experience. Poppy-cock! What does that count against what you *are*. Englishmen! And not just that. Londoners! Young, tough ones who've already faced on the streets of Spitalfields and Camden and Limehouse foes more implacable, more cunning, more tenacious than any mere shambling rotter! Footpads, sneak thieves, pimps, degenerates—now *those* are fiends to fear! So you're not good at marching. So you don't know a field marshal from a major general from the company cook. I don't care, and neither should you. Because by God, you boys already know how to fight! And mark my words: This day, you *shall!*"

The soldiers were cheering as Elizabeth and her father started up the stairs. When the Bennets were about halfway up, the captain noticed them and said something to his Limbs, who stood beside him looking weary and grim.

Right Limb looked up at Mr. Bennet and saluted.

Elizabeth's father nodded solemnly as he carried on up the staircase.

"Papa, what is going on?" Elizabeth asked.

"You will soon see, my dear. I have arranged for box seats."

The rooms on the second floor were overflowing with huddled guests from the ball, all still in their mussed finery. Though Elizabeth didn't see her mother, she knew she was among them somewhere. Mrs. Bennet's snores were quite distinctive.

Up ahead, toward the end of the hall, Elizabeth saw Lt. Tindall speaking earnestly to her sister Jane.

". . . honor-bound to do all I can to protect your person . . . and your purity," Elizabeth heard him say as she and her father walked up. His back was to them, and so absorbed was he in his own words that he didn't notice their approach.

Jane was blushing and looking away.

Mr. Bennet cleared his throat.

The lieutenant turned around.

"Oh. Is it time?"

"I believe so," Mr. Bennet said. "Good luck, Lieutenant."

"We have daylight, we have muskets, we have the element of surprise. We won't need luck."

The young officer offered Mr. Bennet and Elizabeth a bow, turned back to Jane and boldly kissed her hand, then pivoted and marched off toward the staircase.

"There goes a brave man," Mr. Bennet said to Jane, and he continued watching her for a long moment even after she'd replied with a simple "Yes."

"Is His Lordship ready?" he finally said.

"He should be. He asked if I could come in and help him with his stockings perhaps half an hour ago. He was almost fully dressed then."

Mr. Bennet cocked his right eyebrow. "Almost?"

Elizabeth cocked her left. "Help him with his stockings?"

"Yes. His dressers are all downstairs guarding the . . ." Jane flushed pink again. "I said no!"

"Of course, you did," Mr. Bennet said. "Now, perhaps we should—"

The nearest door swung open.

"Would you have a look at these breeches, Miss Bennet?" Lord Lumpley said, his attention fixated (as usual) on his own nether regions. "They seem puffy in all the wrong . . . oh. Good morning, Mr. Bennet. Miss Bennet. I didn't realize the moment had arrived."

"It has," Mr. Bennet said.

"I see. You may as well step in, then. We wouldn't want to miss it, would we?"

The baron moved back to let the Bennets into his large—and, to Elizabeth, sickeningly empty—bedchamber. Every other part of the house was packed near to bursting, yet His Lordship had been allowed to keep an entire room to himself. Elizabeth knew there was good reason: The night before, he'd complained more about the invasion of the lower classes than the damned, and concessions had to be made. Yet it still rankled that his room was now filled with nothing more than some furniture, scattered clothes, and a few poorly concealed bottles of gin.

"I drew these back a crack to have some light to see by," the baron said, walking over to a set of long, emerald green drapes. "I wasn't up to taking a good look out, though. Not before I'd had my morning tea and toast."

"I'm afraid we ran out of water for tea some time ago," Mr. Bennet said. "The food's all gone, as well."

"Oh?" Lord Lumpley pouted, then shrugged. "Well, there's nothing to hold us back then, is there?"

He drew the curtains aside, revealing a pair of glass doors. Just beyond was a shallow balcony and, beyond that, Netherfield's long front lawn bathed in the crimson light of dawn. When the baron opened the doors, a sound like a thousand moans or the lowing of a vast herd of cattle swept into the room.

The four of them stepped onto the balcony.

Scattered here and there over the grounds were dozens of ragged, staggering figures—easily two hundred in all, if not three. It was easy to tell the first wave of sorry stricken from their victim recruits. Half the dreadfuls looked moldy and rotten, and they hobbled on legs that had barely enough flesh to hold the bones together. The other half one could have almost taken for living, so natural was the pallor of their skin. Their faces were slack and often blood smeared, however, and many had gaping cavities where their organs had once been.

When they saw Lord Lumpley and the Bennets, they began drifting toward the balcony, some of them shrieking or gnashing their teeth.

"My God," the baron gasped. "Just look what they've done to the topiary."

Elizabeth tore her horrified gaze away from the unmentionables just long enough to point it at him.

"Surely, Captain Cannon doesn't think he can just march out and kill so many unmentionables," she said. "His men are outnumbered at least three to one."

"The captain doesn't intend to kill them all," Mr. Bennet replied. "He merely seeks to distract them. He very wisely had the stables sealed last night in addition to the main house. Captain Cannon plans to draw the main horde off so that someone can get inside and—presuming the dreadfuls haven't already broken in to feast upon the horses—saddle a mount. That someone would then ride west to look for a battalion of the king's army on the march from Suffolk. If all goes well, a rescue

SCATTERED HERE AND THERE OVER THE GROUNDS WERE DOZENS OF
⸳GGED, STAGGERING FIGURES—EASILY TWO HUNDRED IN ALL, IF NOT THREE.

party might very well reach Netherfield before we've either starved or been eaten."

"*If* all goes well," Elizabeth said.

Her father nodded. "Very, very well."

There was a great mass of yowling dreadfuls clustered beneath the balcony now, and looking down at them Elizabeth saw a few familiar faces scowling back.

"Not Mrs. Ford!" Jane exclaimed. "And all the Elliots and Dr. Long, too? Oh! And what a beautiful child!"

Staring straight up at them with large, round, gray-rimmed eyes was a little girl not much younger than Lydia. She neither screamed nor moaned but instead merely gazed at them plaintively, as if hoping someone might come down to play with her. The blood smeared around her mouth and hands, however, made it plain the kind of games she would have preferred.

"We could only reach so many in time. And even then, some refused to come with us," Mr. Bennet said, practically shouting now to be heard over the din of the dreadfuls.

He reached beneath his cutaway coat, produced a flintlock pistol and said something to Elizabeth she couldn't quite hear.

"What?"

"I said, 'The diversion for the diversion has gone on long enough!'"

He pointed the pistol at the sky but then changed his mind, leaned over the balcony, and aimed at the little girl.

"Why waste a bullet when it might offer deliverance?"

Both Elizabeth and Jane started to say something, but neither got out a full word.

Their father pulled the trigger, and the zombie child toppled over backward. For a moment, Elizabeth could still see its pure-white dress beneath the milling feet of the other dreadfuls, but before long even that was blotted out by the throng.

A flurry of movement caught Elizabeth's eye, and she looked up to find that the front doors of the house had been opened. The soldiers were charging out through them, hurling themselves like a great red lance bound for the heart of the lawn. Lt. Tindall led the charge, while Capt. Cannon was at the center of the column, his cart swerving and tipping treacherously as the Limbs maneuvered it around and over the bloody cornucopia of body parts and well-gnawed bones left over from the night before.

With a deafening roar, the zombies turned and hurtled after them.

"Why aren't we out there, too?" Elizabeth asked. "We should be joining the battle, not watching it."

Her father glanced over at her and, worn and worried as he was, managed to look almost pleased at the same time.

"The deadly arts have their place, but volley fire—that's what will do the greatest damage to a herd. Get them clumped up together on an open plain, and you can mow down dozens like so many weeds."

The soldiers had stopped now and were trying to form themselves into a box—four lines facing outward, each two rows deep, the first kneeling, the second standing. The unmentionables gave them little time to arrange themselves, however, running in madly no matter how torn and mangled they might be, and the lines wavered and broke into chaos each time they almost seemed set.

"They can't even get into formation to fire," Elizabeth said. "If we were with them—"

Mr. Bennet shook his head, eyes still fixed on his daughter. "Your sisters and I are being held in reserve, at the captain's insistence. But a volunteer did go along. . . . "

"Oh, Lizzy. Look!"

Jane thrust a finger toward the soldiers, and Elizabeth saw a swirl of black and pink twisting and twirling within their ranks. It bounced away from a break in the line straight into another before flipping itself over a dreadful's head, spinning then springing then spinning again.

"Master Hawksworth!"

Elizabeth grabbed the balcony railing as if about to vault herself over and into the fray.

Her father made no move to stop her.

"If anything goes wrong," he said, "we are the last line of defense for every soul in this house."

"Lizzy, you mustn't," Jane began, but Mr. Bennet silenced her with a raised hand and a hard stare. Then he looked at Elizabeth again.

She let go of the railing.

There was a staccato blast from out on the battlefield, and the men there sent up a "Huzzah!" They'd got off their first volley, and twenty dreadfuls went down at once.

"'If anything goes wrong,'" Lord Lumpley scoffed. "Look at that! We probably won't need any reinforcements at all!"

Half the fallen zombies got back up and immediately began lumbering toward the lines again.

"Well," the baron mumbled, "not many, at least."

Mr. Bennet was still watching Elizabeth.

Elizabeth was still watching Hawksworth.

She recognized most of the moves—the Bounding This and the Leaping That and the Soaring What-Have-You. They were all jumps and twirls and rolls, and they were beautiful, marred only by a rushed, uncontrolled sloppiness whenever Hawksworth had to actually throw a punch to escape a dreadful's grasp.

He never so much as unsheathed his katana.

"He's not bad, but he's not good, either," Mr. Bennet said. "He moves well, yet he has no fire for a fight. He never has, I'd say. His master obviously sent him to us because all the more, ah, ardent warriors were needed elsewhere. Why do you think he couldn't admit that to us?"

"Pride," Elizabeth said.

"Perhaps," said her father.

The soldiers sent up another cheer even as more unmentionables poured out of the woods and around the sides of the house. A huge black stallion was galloping up the drive, headed for the road. On its back was what looked like a red-clad leprechaun holding on for dear life.

"Ensign Pratt?" Elizabeth asked.

Mr. Bennet nodded. "The lad's small enough to ride at Ascot. It was thought the younger ones, like him, would have the best chance."

"Oh, no!" Jane cried.

There were dreadfuls all along the drive, and a big, burly, fresh one had grabbed hold of the horse's tail. Its grip seemed utterly unbreakable: Though the zombie lost its footing, it didn't let go, and it was soon being towed toward the road, chewing on the stallion's tail the whole time.

The horse slowed, then stopped and reared, and Ensign Pratt was thrown from the saddle. He scrambled to his feet just in time to dodge the dreadful that had grabbed his steed. It was after *him* now, and other unmentionables began closing in from all sides.

But they weren't alone.

Geoffrey Hawksworth came bouncing out of the soldiers' square, careening over and around scores of dreadfuls. He was headed for Ensign Pratt.

As Elizabeth watched him, she found her heart pounding, her skin atingle. Hawksworth had been looking to her to teach him courage. Yet he'd had it within himself all along. All he'd needed was the right moment to take action and be redeemed. And that moment had arrived.

Hawksworth was closing the remaining distance at a sprint. Elizabeth kept waiting for him to draw his katana, begin hacking off heads, but instead he just raced up to Ensign Pratt . . . then dashed *past* him, to his horse.

He threw himself onto the stallion's back and snatched up the reins. As he galloped off, a dozen unmentionables converged on the ensign. A moment later, they were going their separate ways again, each with its face buried in a hand or a foot or a gob of oozing innards.

Hawksworth never looked back. When he reached the road, he turned the horse west and dug in his heels.

Elizabeth leaned against the banister again, this time because she needed the support.

So much for redemption. . . .

"Egad," Mr. Bennet muttered. "Even I thought better of him than that."

Lord Lumpley leaned against the banister, too. "He can't send anyone back for us. You realize that, don't you? Even if he finds Lord Paget, he'll just tell him we're all dead."

Jane gaped at him. "Why would he do that?"

The baron hacked out a bitter laugh. "There's really not an evil bone in your body, is there?"

"We saw what he did," Elizabeth explained. "We know his shame."

She watched Hawksworth and his horse become a black speck on the horizon and then disappear behind distant trees. Far, far too late she'd recognized the fault within the man—perhaps because all that was outward about him was so very pleasing. It was a mistake she would never make again.

She turned back to the battle.

Clouds of thick, white powder smoke were drifting up over the field now, for the soldiers on two sides of the square were firing off volleys regularly, and the corpses—the still ones, that is—were heaped up before them to such a height they formed a makeshift rampart as high as a man's chest. The troops in the other two lines, however, were fighting off zombies by hand, and more of the undead were pressing in on them all the time. If the odds had been three to one when the battle began, they were easily six to one now.

"It was all for naught," Elizabeth said. "Why don't they retreat into the house?"

Her answer came as the scream of a horse off to the left. The rider no doubt screamed as well, but this was drowned out—and it couldn't have lasted long, anyway. The soldier was quickly pulled from the saddle, and within seconds he was butchered as efficiently (if not as tidily) as in the most modern abattoir. The proceeds were divided among a score of ravenously gorging unmentionables.

No one else made it out of the stables.

The soldiers fought on, buying time for a deliverance that didn't come. They lasted much longer than Elizabeth would have predicted, but they couldn't last forever. Eventually, one of the lines buckled completely, and zombies poured into the center of the square. The other three lines dissolved soon after, the red of the soldiers' uniforms—and spurting blood—mixing with the dirty-shroud brown and decaying green and gray of the dreadfuls.

Elizabeth saw Capt. Cannon's Limbs ripped away and devoured.

She saw him trying to fight off unmentionables with head butts until his stomach was ripped open and his steaming bowels stuffed into furiously working mouths before he'd even stopped writhing.

And she saw Lt. Tindall facing the house, staring at Jane beside her as he put a flintlock to the side of his head and pulled the trigger. He was keeping his word: They wouldn't find him pounding on a window the next morning, ravenous for the very thing he'd died to protect.

Jane turned away with a sob.

Elizabeth placed a hand on her sister's shoulder.

Lord Lumpley bolted from the balcony and out through the bedroom.

"Seal the doors!" he cried as he flew down the hall. "Seal the doors!"

"No!"

Elizabeth started after him.

Her father caught her by the arm.

"He's right," he said. "Damn him."

He let Elizabeth go.

She ran out to the hall, but she wasn't trying to stop the baron now.

"How many made it back?" she asked when she reached the top of the staircase.

Down in the foyer, men were busy nailing boards across the front doors again. None of them had the heart to answer. Not that they needed to.

There wasn't a red coat in sight.

CHAPTER 36

THERE WAS NO DIVISION between upstairs and downstairs now. There couldn't be, with the soldiers gone. Everyone was needed at a window or door with a gun or a sword or a knife or a poker or even just a leg from a broken chair. Tradesman, yeoman, gentleman, seamstress, fishwife, farmwife, lady—they all fought side by side, for surely the dreadfuls would be equally democratic. They would eat anyone and everyone.

For a time, at least, the unmentionables had full stomachs (those that still had them), and the assaults on the house tapered off while they enjoyed their picnic on the lawn. When the attacks began again, they were sporadic and easily beaten back. At first.

By nightfall, however, the onslaught was once again relentless, and hardly five minutes went by without a board somewhere giving way. It took Elizabeth nearly half an hour just to walk down a hallway with a bust of the Prince Regent—which she intended to drop onto the zombies from a second-story window—for every few steps she had to set down the prince and pull out her sword and add to the collection of freshly severed limbs lined up along the wainscoting. One would-be intruder was particularly persistent, managing to squirm its way inside even after all but its head and chest and left arm had been sliced away. A woman in a tattered yellow ball gown smashed a chamber pot into its face as it slithered after Elizabeth, slowing it for a moment. When it whirled on the lady, hissing, Elizabeth was finally able to slice through the top of its skull, and its brain-filled crown fell forward onto the floor looking like a hairy

NIGHTFALL, HOWEVER, THE ONSLAUGHT WAS ONCE AGAIN RELENTLESS.

bowl of porridge.

Elizabeth sheathed her katana and looked up at the woman who'd helped her—and was shocked to find that it was Mrs. Goswick.

"Thank you," Elizabeth said.

Mrs. Goswick shook her head. "No. Thank *you*, Miss Bennet."

When Elizabeth finally got the Prince Regent upstairs and out a window, she was only mildly disappointed that it was too dark to see the damage he did down below. It was a cloudy, moonless night, sparing her the sight of the zombie host ringing them in. At last count, it had been nearly a thousand strong.

"Do you think he made it?" Mary asked, stepping up to the window with a large, lumpy satchel. She reached in, pulled out a blue croquet ball, and hurled it down into the darkness. "The Master, I mean?"

Elizabeth helped herself to one of the balls and threw it out the window with all her strength. A second later, there was a sharp *clunk* followed by the sound of something heavy falling to the ground.

"Does it really matter?" Elizabeth said.

Mary started to toss out a mallet but seemed to change her mind when she found its heft to her liking. She leaned it against the wall, then pulled out a ball and whipped it into the night.

There was another *clunk*, and a zombie wailed.

"I suppose not," Mary said.

She and Elizabeth kept throwing croquet balls until they were all gone, at which time Mary announced that she was off to look for loose bricks. She took the mallets with her to hand out downstairs.

Elizabeth lingered a moment at the window, wondering if she might take advantage of a quiet moment to slip up to the attic and, if not apologize to Dr. Keckilpenny, at least assure herself of his well-being. She still felt a fondness for the man, despite the things she'd said the last time she'd seen him, and a part of her longed to put any awkwardness between them to rest.

But then someone screamed "They're coming through the wall!"

and she was running for the stairs with her sword in her hand.

It turned out to be a small hole—little more than a crack in the plaster just big enough for four broken, bloody fingers to wriggle into the drawing room. But it was going to get bigger.

"They're scratching away the mortar between the building stones," Mr. Bennet announced. "When they get enough of it out, they'll be able to pull out the stones themselves."

"And the walls with them," Elizabeth said.

Her father nodded, then hacked off the wriggling fingers.

"Lizzy," he said, "bring Lord Lumpley, Mr. Cummings, and Dr. Thorne to the front hall, if you would. Your sister Jane, as well, if she's not with His Lordship. There's a difficult decision before us, I'm afraid, and I'd prefer if it were made in council."

Minutes later, there they all were, gathered before the main doors even as the dreadfuls outside kept knocking upon it in their clumsy, insistent way.

"Gentlemen," Mr. Bennet said, "we are running out of time."

He spoke loudly, obviously not just addressing the baron, the vicar, and the doctor but everyone scattered around the foyer and lining the halls nearby.

"Oh, my goodness! Running out of time, you say?" Lord Lumpley widened his eyes and slapped his hands to his round cheeks. "Whatever could make you jump to such a conclusion?"

"If it's the food supply you're thinking of, Mr. Bennet, I've an idea about that," said Dr. Thorne. (It was fitting that he should bring up food, actually, as his blood-smeared surgeon's apron made him look like a particularly sloppy butcher. Which, in a way, is what he was.) "We've actually got all the meat we could possibly need, if we just looked at it as the dreadfuls do. At least a dozen of my patients died of shock after I removed a tainted limb, and of course I immediately took the next step and removed their heads, as well. The plague won't take hold in them—so why just toss the bodies out a window?"

"Wh-what? You can't possibly m-m-mean—!" Mr. Cummings blubbered. He'd lost his *Book of Common Prayer* in a tussle with an unmentionable and had taken, for the sake of comfort, to clutching a book he'd
picked at random from the baron's library: *Justine, or Good Conduct Well
Chastised* by the Marquis de Sade. "It's unnnnnnnnthinkable!"

The doctor shrugged. "If it'll keep me from starving to death, I'll do
more than think it."

"It's not actually starvation I was thinking of, Doctor," Mr. Bennet
said. "We have another, more immediate problem."

A look of discomfited surprise came over Dr. Thorne of the type
that's common among people who find that the previous minute's conversation should be, and would if it could be, unspoken.

"Oh?" he said limply. "Do tell."

Mr. Bennet obliged, explaining that the dreadfuls were capable of
taking the house apart stone by stone and had, in fact, begun to do so.
Many gasped at the news, and Mr. Bennet paused a moment, waiting for
their clamorings and murmurs to fade before carrying on again.

"They will get through. It is inevitable. So, as time is not on our
side, nor are numbers, we must press the last advantage we have."

Lord Lumpley scoffed. "I wasn't aware we had any in the first place."

"I believe the advantage my father alludes to doesn't apply equally
to all of us," Elizabeth said, and she quoted an observation Dr. Keckilpenny had once made to her about the unmentionables: "They're thick
as bricks."

Mr. Bennet nodded. "We can safely assume they have no idea how
many people are in this house. If we let them overrun it—or think they've
overrun it—they might well wander off again never knowing they left
survivors behind."

"And where will these supposed survivors be?" Dr. Thorne asked.
"Hiding in the cupboards?"

"Something like that." Mr. Bennet turned to the baron. "Tell me—
how extensive is your wine cellar?"

"Vast. I have the largest selection of clarets, ports, and brandies in the Home Counties."

"That's not quite what I meant," Mr. Bennet said.

Belgrave appeared at his master's side as if stepping out from behind a mote of dust. "The cellar has been permanently sealed. Remember, My Lord?"

"What do you mean, it's been sealed?" Mr. Bennet asked.

"It flooded," said Belgrave.

"It caved in," said Lord Lumpley.

One or the other might have been believed if they hadn't spoken at the same time—and if someone else hadn't spoken up, as well.

"It did nothing of the kind!" declared a woman guarding the front doors. She was a stout old cook from the baron's own kitchens, and in one hand she held a frying pan splattered with brains and chips of bone. "The cellar was always kept under lock and key, but the other day someone broke down the door. *That's* why his nibs there had it boarded up. Flood. Ha!"

"When was all this?" Mr. Bennet asked.

"Why, right after that Z-O-M-B-Y got into the house."

"Belgrave, sack this woman at once," Lord Lumpley said.

"You are dismissed, Mrs. Hutchinson."

"Ho! Like I care now!" The cook looked over at Mr. Bennet while waggling her pan at Belgrave. "Always it was this one alone who was allowed down there, and then all of a sudden the cellar's shut up altogether? And kept that way even with a swarm of bogies at the door and no better place to hide? If you ask me, there's something tricksy about the whole thing."

"She's right!" one of the baron's dressers called out.

"Ask them *why* the cellar's sealed!" added another.

"Ask why the door was broken down!"

Other servants joined in with "Yes!" and "Ask them!"

"What is this, the damned French Revolution?" Lord Lumpley

roared. "Mind your place!"

Belgrave looked like he wanted to slip behind another mote of dust.

"I'm with them," a man said, and as he stepped into the entrance hall, a dozen hushed voices whispered his name.

Jonathan Ward.

Emily Ward's father.

"What's in the cellar . . . My Lord?

"Or is it more a question of who?" Elizabeth said. She wasn't looking at Mr. Ward or Lord Lumpley or Belgrave. She was looking at Jane.

Her sister was standing just behind and to the right of the baron, still playing the faithful bodyguard, staying true to their father's pact with the nobleman even after all they'd been through. On her face now, however, was a look of horror equal to the one she'd worn when she first saw Emily Ward dragging her rotting carcass from the water.

Another monster was being revealed to her: the one directly before her. And she wasn't the only one seeing it for the first time. A wave of angry mutters and exclamations of dismay spread first through the foyer then down the halls along each wing, until it seemed the whole house was abuzz.

"This conversation has become highly insulting, not to mention utterly insane," Lord Lumpley said.

Mr. Bennet shook his head sadly. "Once again, I find I am a fool. I ascribed to mere lechery what should have suggested a far deeper flaw. In your case, a deeper *evil*." He turned to Mr. Ward. "I examined your daughter's body the day she . . . returned. I would prefer to say this privately—or not at all, ever—but I think it should be known: Emily Ward was with child when she died. I didn't get to see the girl dreadful who attacked my daughter here the other night—it was burned before I could do so. But I suspect I would have found her condition the same as poor Miss Ward's." He pointed an unblinking stare at Belgrave, and with his cocked head and cold eyes, he took on the look of a bird of prey watching something soft and furry scurrying through the grass. "And I presume there were others? Buried down in the cellar before you simply started throwing them in the lake?"

"This is madness!" Lord Lumpley bellowed.

Belgrave edged away from him, mumbling under his breath.

"What was that?" Mr. Bennet demanded, taking a step toward him. "Pray, speak up!"

"He told me to do it," Belgrave said, jerking his head at the baron. "Whenever another one popped up to make trouble."

"What rot! I never told you to *kill* anyone!"

"You said to get rid of them. Permanently."

"Yes! Exactly! That's not kill, is it?"

"You knew."

"I most certainly did not! I just knew they stopped pestering me."

"Yes—until the next one came along. There was always a next one." Belgrave glanced past the baron. At Jane. "There always would be. You couldn't help yourself."

Elizabeth could hear no more. She moved toward Lord Lumpley not knowing if she intended to simply strike him or break his neck, though either would be preceded by the Fulcrum of Doom.

Mr. Ward started stalking the baron's way at the same moment.

"They've lost their minds!" Lord Lumpley cried. "Jane—protect me!"

He took a step back, starting to put himself behind his guardian angel. He was stopped by something long and straight and slick red that shot from his body just above the pelvis.

It was a katana, coated with blood. The blade jerked upward, into the baron's belly, then zigzagged down again.

Lord Lumpley blinked.

"Jane . . . ?"

Then he slid forward off the sword and was dead before he hit the floor.

Though the zombies kept moaning and banging away outside, every living thing was hushed and still. Only Jane made any noise, first with her heavy breathing, then the moist *shhhhhhhhhhh* as she slid her katana back into its scabbard.

The silence was finally broken by a smattering of uncertain applause.

"I don't th-think that waaaaas c-called for," Mr. Cummings said, but the clapping just grew a little louder.

The only other dissenting voice belonged to Jane's own mother, who'd let loose with a disappointed "Ohhh!" as the favorite of all her daughters' suitors was carved up like a roast duck.

Belgrave, of course, had a less than enthusiastic reaction, as well: He simply started running. He seemed to have lost his senses, for he dashed toward what looked like solid wall—part of the paneling that ran along the underside of the staircase. When he reached it, however, a section of it slid back at his touch, revealing a black passageway into which he started to disappear.

There was a series of raps in quick succession—*thup-thup-thup*—and the tails of Belgrave's topcoat were pinned to the wall by three throwing stars.

"La!" Lydia snorted from across the hall. "I *knew* these silly things would come in handy sooner or later!"

Mr. Bennet grabbed Belgrave by the shirt collar before he could shrug free of his sleeves and escape.

"A secret passage, eh? Would there be more of these?"

"Oh, yes, Sir!" Mrs. Hutchinson said. "All through the house. We weren't supposed to know about them, but we used to hear Belgrave and His Lordship slinking around in the walls like rats."

"Capital, capital," Mr. Bennet said. "Belgrave, you have just won yourself a temporary reprieve. Mary, Kitty, Lydia—if you would be so good as to find the cellar and tidy it up in whatever way you find necessary. Elizabeth—you might want to attend to your elder sister. She's looking a touch peaked."

Indeed, Jane was staring at her handiwork—*filet de noble*—looking pale. Elizabeth hurried to her side expecting to arrive the same moment as the inevitable tears. Yet Jane's eyes, though wide and full of confusion, remained dry.

"I was beginning to believe he actually cared for me . . . that perhaps he wasn't the scoundrel you made him out to be. How could I have been so very, very wrong?"

"He thought he could take advantage because you have a good heart."

"*Had* a good heart, perhaps." Jane nodded at the baron's crumpled, bloody form. "People with good hearts don't do things like that."

"Oh, Jane—your heart is still good. It's just that it's strong now, too. Hardened. Armored." Elizabeth took her sister by the hand. "The heart of a warrior."

Jane looked into Elizabeth's eyes.

"Yes," she said, speaking in the firm, unwavering way of someone making a vow. "And nothing shall ever pierce it again."

"Ummm . . . should I have that beheaded and taken up to one of the windows?" a maid asked meekly, pointing at her former employer. "It might keep some of the unmentionables happy for a moment or two."

"Breach! Breach!" someone shouted from the south wing.

Jane and Elizabeth and Mr. Bennet all started toward the sound of the call, but they weren't needed: A cluster of men and women jumped in together to hack and slash at the zombie soldier trying to wiggle its way through a fresh gap in the plaster. Within a few seconds, the dreadful was in pieces and the hole in the wall blocked off with an upended chest of drawers.

"You were right, Father," Elizabeth said. "We can't keep them out forever."

Mr. Bennet nodded. "The time has come, I think, to stop trying."

CHAPTER 37

FIRST, THE THREE YOUNGEST Bennet girls had to clear the wine cellar of its dreadfuls. (There were two still squirming like worms from the packed-dirt floor, their progress slowed by the quicklime that had apparently eaten away most of their connective tissue.) Then it was time to clear the wine cellar of both its wines and its many rows of wine racks—all of which proved excellent fodder for zombie bombardment once it was hauled up to the second floor. After that, the packing began.

They started with the walls. The house, it was quickly discovered, was a Swiss cheese of secret passages and hidden vaults. With Belgrave's reluctant help—which turned quite a bit less reluctant whenever Jane was in the vicinity—dozens of people were soon tucked away out of sight.

Which meant there were that many fewer to fight back the unmentionables breaking through. And there were steadily fewer still as more and more people were sent into the cellar to join the children and the elderly and the wounded already there. Eventually, there was no one left guarding the windows and doors at all, and the cellar was stuffed wall to wall.

"Time for you to go in, too," Mr. Bennet said to his daughters. "Seal the door from the inside, as we discussed, and I'll put the false wall in place out here. It won't be pleasant down there in the dark, I'm sure, but the air holes should—where do you think you're going?"

Lydia and Kitty were hurrying off down the hall, toward the sound of splintering wood and phlegmy moans.

"Our friends from outside are letting themselves in a trifle early!" Lydia called over her shoulder.

"We'll just go and ask them to wait!" Kitty added.

They were drawing their swords as they darted around a corner.

"There's no time for that now!" Mr. Bennet called after them.

"Well, there's a *little* more time than you might have thought," Elizabeth said.

"We're not going down there, you know," said Jane.

Mary hefted one side of the wood panel that had been hastily fitted to hide the landing before the cellar door. "This is really quite heavy, Papa. Together on the count of three . . . ?"

Mr. Bennet looked at her, then Jane, then Elizabeth, and despite the bags under his eyes and the deep sadness within them, he seemed to be on the verge of cracking a smile. And perhaps he would have, if a familiar voice hadn't called out from the darkness below.

"Mr. Bennet! You march those girls in here this instant!" Mrs. Bennet demanded. "You're not going to leave me down in this filthy hole all alone!"

"Did you hear that?" one of the maids grumbled from under the stairs, where she stood stuffed in with the rest of the household staff. "The silly cow thinks she's all alone."

"Farewell, Mrs. Bennet. I . . . "

Whatever Mr. Bennet had been about to say went unsaid, and he instead stomped down the steps, met his wife at the bottom, and kissed her. Then he turned and marched back out of the attic, leaving Mrs. Bennet sobbing in the arms of her sister Philips.

When he reached the landing again, he couldn't meet his daughters' gazes: For once, *he* was the one blushing and looking away.

"Come now, all together," he said, grabbing one side of the false wall. "One . . . two . . . lift!"

There was a distant clatter of boards falling to the floor just as he and the girls got the panel in place, and an otherworldly yowl echoed through the halls.

"That would be in the north wing, by the sound of it," said Mr.

Bennet. "Jane, run along and greet the new arrivals, hmm? I'll join you shortly. Mary, go see what's keeping Lydia and Kitty. And you—"

He turned toward Elizabeth and took in a deep breath as her sisters darted away. It almost seemed as if he was waiting for them to get out of earshot.

"We will be retreating to the attic at the first opportunity," he said. "It is essential no unmentionables see us go up there, so it's difficult to say when that opportunity might arrive. Hopefully, it will be a matter of minutes. When we get there, we will lock the door behind us and hope for the best. There can be nothing in that attic that might give us away, however. Even the slightest disturbance would spell our doom."

"So Dr. Keckilpenny's captives—"

"Must be dealt with. And I thought it best that you do the dealing."

"Of course, Father. It will be done."

Mr. Bennet nodded just once, wordless, and headed for the north wing. Elizabeth went to the stairs.

She was barely aware of the steps under her feet, and the grunts and thumps and hammering from the halls below went unheard. All she could think of was Dr. Keckilpenny and what she could—and couldn't—say to him.

She'd tried to see him the day before, during a brief lull between breaches. She'd found the door to the attic locked, and she lacked the nerve to knock. She'd laughed about it to herself as she'd gone back downstairs to face another onslaught. The dreadfuls she could face. But a man for whom her feelings were . . . *complicated*? That she ran from.

Only she couldn't run from it now.

The door to the attic was still locked. She rapped on it firmly.

"Dr. Keckilpenny! It's Elizabeth Bennet! I need to speak to you!"

There was no answer from the other side of the door. No sound at all.

Elizabeth knocked again.

"Doctor! Please! It's urgent!"

Still nothing.

Elizabeth could hear the noises from downstairs. Shrieks and the scuffling of feet.

She pounded on the door with both fists.

"Dr. Keckilpenny! Are you there? Are you all right? Answer me!"

When there was no response, Elizabeth stepped back for a kick that she hoped would break open the door. She knew it was worse than futile: Damage the knob and lock, and the room beyond would be useless as a hiding place. But what choice was there?

And she had to know about the doctor. Would it end with him so embittered toward her that he'd actually leave her to the dreadfuls? Or could it be that he wasn't up there at all? Perhaps he'd engineered his own escape, abandoned them, just like Master Hawksworth.

The thought of the Master gave her the rage she needed. No lock was going to stop her. She swiveled on her right foot and drew up her left just as steps started down the stairs on the other side of the door.

A moment later, the key rattled in the lock, and the door opened. Not wide. Just a crack. Then the footsteps began again. And by the time Elizabeth was inside, at the bottom of the stairs, Dr. Keckilpenny was nearly at the top.

He hadn't said a word to her.

It was words she'd always liked best about the man. He had so many, and never quite the ones she expected. She found herself longing for a few of them even now, as the sound of fighting grew louder from the ground floor and she climbed to the attic with her hand on her sword.

Mr. Smith spoke to her first.

"Buh ruhz," he growled. "Buh ruhz!"

He was in his usual position, standing with arms thrown back behind him as he strained against the shackles that held him in place. He was noticeably more decayed, however, his skin blotchy and bloated, peeling away here and there to reveal glistening sinew and bone beneath. A family of flies had discovered him, it seemed, for the right side of his face was aswarm with maggots.

"Buh ruhzzzzzz . . . buh ruhzzzzz."

"Good day to you, Mr. Smith. And you, as well, Doctor. I must admit, I'm disappointed to find your pupil's vocabulary unexpanded."

Elizabeth winced at her own words. Death was at their door—quite literally—and here she was chattering away like it was just another guest come for high tea.

She stepped toward Mr. Smith.

"Yes, alas, our friend's diction is no better," Dr. Keckilpenny said, his own voice weary and rough. "Yet I find that I understand him now, all the same."

Elizabeth stopped. "You do?"

There was only one small window in the attic, set high near the arching rafters, and the doctor was standing directly beneath it. The rays of sunlight caught only the topmost curls of his unkempt hair, leaving the rest of him little more than a faint gray silhouette.

"Perfectly," he said. "I've already done some of your work for you. Hadn't you noticed?"

He spread out his hands and cocked his head, and it took Elizabeth a moment to work out what he was referring to.

"Your trunk . . . the dead soldier . . . "

The doctor nodded. "Gone. I dragged him down to the second floor and pushed him out a window last night. I've overheard enough talk in the hall to know that sort of thing's all the rage. And seeing as I didn't need a spare anymore—"

A chill rippled across Elizabeth's shoulders. "What do you mean you were doing my work for me?"

"You've been sent to kill my subjects, haven't you?" Dr. Keckilpenny said. "I'm afraid, if you mean to see it through, you'll have to kill me as well."

Elizabeth laughed joylessly, and her fingers suddenly felt slick on the hilt of her katana, her grip unsure.

"Oh, come now, Doctor! Histrionics don't suit you. You must face this with cold logic, as befits a man of science. Your experiment has run its course, and now necessity demands—"

"So that's truly how you see me?" the doctor cut in. "A creature of unfeeling intellect without the passion even for a little melodrama when faced with his own failure? *Failures*, I should say because, by gad, the plural is called for here. No wonder you said I was . . . what was it? Only half a good man?"

Elizabeth was glad, at that moment, that she couldn't make out the doctor's face in the gloom of the room. She was sure to see pain she'd put there herself. And that pained *her*.

"I owe you an apology, Doctor. I spoke far too harshly."

"Indeed, you greatly underestimated me. I am, at the very least, two-thirds of a good man, if not even three-quarters." Dr. Keckilpenny chortled at his own joke, but the sound quickly turned into a snort of disgust. "I am an arrogant ass. I came here with the temerity to think I would accomplish what no one else could. All I ended up doing was what so very, very many have done before me."

"What do you mean?"

"Well, for one thing, I went and lost my heart. Who'd have thought I even had one to begin with? It was my mind people always thought I was losing. And then . . . I guess you could say I lost all the rest of me as well."

The doctor stepped closer, shrugging off his cutaway coat as he came. His movements were stiff, deliberate, and as he moved forward into the light Elizabeth could see how pale and sweaty was his face.

He stopped a few feet from her, dangerously close to Mr. Smith. Yet the dreadful paid no attention to him. Its hungry gaze stayed only on her.

Dr. Keckilpenny tossed his coat aside and began rolling up the right sleeve of his shirt. It was stained reddish black, and once it was up over the elbow, Elizabeth could see why.

She gasped.

His upper arm was bloody and mangled, with a chunk ripped away as large as her fist. The flesh ringing the wound had turned purple, and the rest of the arm was as gray and mottled as marble.

"When?" was all Elizabeth could say.

"Not long after our little talk up here with Master Hercules or Lord Samson or whatever his name is. My better—or at least bigger—half. I was trying to interest Smithy in a game of whist and I grew careless, and the in-grate bit me. After all I've done for him! I suppose I could've gone down to see Dr. Thorne about it. I find I've grown rather attached to my limbs, though, ho ho, and the survival rate of the doctor's patients hardly inspires confidence. And, well, I suppose my pride wouldn't allow—"

A deafening crash echoed up the stairwell, followed by frenzied shouts and a long, piercing screech.

"Buh ruhz!" Mr. Smith howled as if in answer, and he tried to charge at Elizabeth, his feet slapping and sliding over the floorboards even as he went nowhere. "Buuuuhhhhhh ruuuuuuuhhhhzzzzzz!"

"Yes, yes—the lady has them in abundance, and quite luscious they are, too," Dr. Keckilpenny said. "'Brains,' he's saying, Miss Bennet. Buh-rain-uhz. I know it because I can hear the call, as well, though the plague hasn't fully taken me yet. It's really a rather delicious irony: It was your mind I was attracted to from the beginning. My longing's just growing a little too literal."

There was more commotion downstairs, and Elizabeth heard her father shout "Quadrangle of Death, if you please! Very nice!"

"It's time," Dr. Keckilpenny said, and he straightened his shoulders and lifted his head high. "I'd prefer it if you attended to me first."

"Doctor . . . Bertram . . . I can't—"

There was a sickening *riiiiiiiip*, and Mr. Smith barreled across the room. He'd freed himself from his chains—by freeing himself of his arms. They plopped to the floor still in the sleeves of his moldy coat as he charged at Elizabeth.

"Brrrrrrrrrraaaaaaaiiiiinnnnnsss!"

Elizabeth jumped back knowing she wouldn't get the katana from its sheath in time. But then Mr. Smith suddenly had arms again—two long, thin ones, wrapped tight around his body from behind, dragging him to a halt.

"Do it!" Dr. Keckilpenny shouted. "Do it now!"

Mr. Smith turned his head and bit a huge, pulpy hunk from the man's shoulder.

The doctor screamed but managed to hold on.

"What you feel doesn't matter, Elizabeth! What you think doesn't matter! Just do!"

She took off both their heads with one swing.

There wasn't much blood left in Mr. Smith, but the same couldn't be said of Dr. Keckilpenny. A geyser sprayed the room as he fell, and Elizabeth's gown was dyed bright red.

Her father and sisters came up the stairs a moment later, moving quickly but quietly, the door behind them again closed and locked.

"Oh, Lizzy," Jane said when she saw the bodies lying near the top of the steps. "What—"

Mr. Bennet shushed her.

"Don't speak," he whispered. He paused to look all the girls in the eye, lingering longest on Lydia and Kitty. "Don't move. Don't make a sound. Our lives depend upon it."

And so they all stood there, utterly still, surrounded by silence.

Lydia and Kitty stared at each other, seeming to carry on a conversation purely through grimaces, shrugs, and waggling eyebrows.

Mary closed her eyes, her face blank and tranquil, as if she were rereading a favorite book in her head.

Jane and Mr. Bennet stared at Elizabeth.

She stared at nothing.

She was facing the window at the far end of the attic, looking directly into a light she didn't really see. Even if they survived, she knew, a part of her had died and could never be resurrected. The part of her that would hesitate. The part that knew mercy. Perhaps the part that could fall in love.

She'd be better off without it. Just look at the men who'd loved her and Jane. All dead or ruined.

A world with zombies in it had no tolerance for softness or sentiment. The dreadfuls infected everything just by virtue of existing. To live in their world, one had to become like them. Dead inside.

So be it.

Something shuffled past the attic door. Then another something, moving faster. There were groans and more footsteps and the sounds of furniture being clumsily overturned.

"Mmm-hmm!" said Lydia, jerking her head at the stairs.

Mr. Bennet glared at her and put a finger to his lips.

"Mmm-hmm!" she said again, pointing downward.

Kitty's eyes went wide, and she started pointing, too. "Mmm-hmm mmm-hmm!"

"Oh, no," Jane murmured.

Dr. Keckilpenny's blood had flowed over the floorboards to the stairs. The first step down was coated with it. The second, as well. The third and fourth and fifth, all progressively less. Yet a single scarlet trickle was still steadily working its way toward the bottom of the stairwell.

If they tried to stop it, to blot it up with a handkerchief or the hem of a skirt, they would surely be heard. All they could do was watch as it dripped down another step . . . then another . . . then another. . . .

All the way to—and finally under—the door.

Footfalls suddenly stopped in the hall.

The knob rattled. The wood shook.

The pounding began.

"Well," Mr. Bennet said, "there you have it."

Kitty began to whimper, but Lydia silenced her with a simple "Oh, don't start in with that."

"At least this way, our ruse will be more convincing," Jane said. "The dreadfuls will find people alive in the house. Once they're done up here, it's doubly likely they'll go away again satisfied."

"Oh, hurrah—I get to satisfy a zombie!" Lydia rolled her eyes and stamped a foot. "Hmph!"

"We won't really let them, um," Mary blinked, then swallowed, "*eat* us, will we, Papa?"

"We won't *let* them do anything, child. We will fight. We certainly won't take the easy way out, if that's what you're asking." Mr. Bennet gave each of his daughters another long look. "You will die warriors, all of you. You've already passed the test that proves it: You *chose* to come out and face death with me. And in the choosing is the being."

"That's why you released us from our training the day of the ball," Elizabeth said. "You wanted to see what choice we would make."

Mr. Bennet nodded proudly. "Mary, Lydia, and Kitty came and found me as I helped with the evacuation of the village. And the next time I saw you, your sword was back at your side."

"And what of me?" Jane asked. "I was dancing with the baron when you arrived with the dreadfuls at your heels."

"Yes. But weren't you just doing your duty as you understood it— staying close to the man you'd been told to protect? When it became obvious that man was unworthy of your protection, you removed it as only a true warrior would."

Jane seemed relieved even as the banging on the door grew louder.

"I wanted to be certain you wouldn't make the same mistake I did," Mr. Bennet said, gazing at Jane, then Elizabeth. "Twenty years ago, I chose a passing fancy over my own honor. You have proved yourselves stronger than that. Stronger than I was . . . and am. I'm certain you would have become far greater—"

The door's top panel splintered, and a bloody stump popped through. It was followed by clawing hands that ripped frantically at the wood, tearing it apart, splintered shard by splintered shard.

As the Bennets stepped back, spreading out across the attic, giving themselves room to fight, Elizabeth allowed herself one last glance at all her sisters. With them, at least, there could still be love, and she felt lucky, in a way, to die surrounded by it.

She was smiling when she looked again toward the top of the stairs and braced for the ghoulish faces that would appear there any second.

"Let's make a game of it, shall we?" she said. "Whoever kills the most, wins."

"I will kill twenty!" Lydia declared.

"I will kill thirty!" Kitty countered.

Mary paused for a moment of sober calculation.

"I will kill thirty-two," she said.

"I will kill as long as I must," said Jane.

"And I will kill as long as I can," said Elizabeth.

The door gave way.

The whole house shook.

"What—" Lydia began.

The booms came then, so many of them in such quick succession they could have been rolling beats on some monstrous drum. Screams followed—high, whistling, eerie, neither human nor zombie.

"I can't believe it," Mr. Bennet said, and he burst into raucous laughter. "To hear it again *now*, after all these years! The most beautiful sound in creation!"

Elizabeth wasn't sure which sound he meant, for others were rising up from downstairs. Howls and screeches and the pounding of what sounded like a thousand feet.

The dreadfuls were fleeing.

"To a window! To a window!" Mr. Bennet cried, scampering toward the stairs.

The girls looked at each other in utter confusion, then ran after their father. He led them, casually beheading the small handful of unmentionables still in the hall, to the baron's bedchamber.

The whole world convulsed again as his daughters joined him on the balcony. And when the roars and screams came a second later, they

MR. BENNET GAVE EACH OF HIS DAUGHTERS A LONG LOOK.
"YOU WILL DIE WARRIORS, ALL OF YOU."

could see now what caused them.

A line of cannons was spread along the eastern edge of Netherfield Park, and they spat not just smoke and flame but black blurs that shot across the grounds and through the dreadful horde, hurling ragged chunks of flesh in every direction.

"Chain shot!" Mr. Bennet hooted happily. He jumped up and down and clapped his hands as a company of mounted soldiers swept around the side of the house and tore through the retreating unmentionables, trampling them and kebabing them on long lances and beheading them with their sabers. "And dragoons! Oooo, and look over there! Lurking in the trees! *Ninjas!* Ah, it's just like the old days . . . the few good ones we had, anyway. There weren't many, but I tell you they were just . . . like . . . this!"

"So word of our plight somehow got through to the king's army, after all," Jane said.

Her father nodded. "Bless my soul. It's almost enough to make a tired old man believe in a loving and merciful God."

Within minutes, a herd hundreds if not thousands strong was more than halved, and the survivors were scattering in every direction. The ones that kept to the open fields were quickly overrun by the dragoons, while scores fleeing into the woods were decapitated by razor wire. The few who turned away in time were cut down by black-clad ninjas pouncing down from overhanging branches.

"That's it, then?" Elizabeth said, still too stunned to trust her sense of relief. "Just like that? It's over?"

"Oh, dear me, no. Quite the opposite." Mr. Bennet swept a hand out over the gory diorama before them. "This is no happy ending we have here. It's merely a hopeful beginning."

He turned his back on the scene below, and Elizabeth thought she caught a glimmer of the old, sly Oscar Bennet gleam in his eye.

"Now," he said to her, "shall we let your mother out of the cellar, or go join the fun before it's over?"

They joined the fun.

EPILOGUE

ENSIGN OSILLBURY approached the lady cautiously. It wasn't that he was scared of her, exactly. It was just . . .

All right, he *was* scared of her. Terrified, actually. Simply looking at her made his stomach do things that put sweat on his brow, and hearing her name gave him a creepy chill like centipedes running up his arms.

Surely, though, there should be no shame in that, given the things he'd seen her do—and the even worse things the men whispered she was capable of.

He stomped his feet as he came up the hill toward her, went out of his way to snap a few twigs, and when he was still about thirty feet off he cleared his throat for good measure. It wasn't wise to startle the lady. Not if one wanted to keep one's brains inside one's skull.

"What?" she said. The word came out quick and hard and cold. Like everything about her.

She was atop her great white stallion observing the battle below through a spyglass. The unmentionables had been routed, yet you'd hardly have guessed it from the look of distaste on her face.

Then again, she *always* looked like that—as if she were about to sneeze, or had a pickle tucked under her tongue.

Even though she wasn't looking at him, Ensign Osillbury saluted. Just to be safe.

"We found survivors in the house, Ma'am. Dozens, perhaps hundreds. It's really quite miraculous."

"But?"

"Lord Lumpley wasn't among them. They say he fell to the sorry stricken days ago."

"Hmm. The Prince Regent will be disappointed, no doubt." The lady finally lowered her telescope, though she still didn't bother looking at Ensign Osillbury. "*I* care not one whit. Tell Captain Ramsey: We rejoin Lord Paget's column directly. We have wasted enough time here as it is."

"Yes, Ma'am! Right away, Ma'am!"

The young officer had to jump out of her way as she spun her horse and charged downhill toward the road. It didn't pay to come between the lady and London. The man who'd brought word of Lord Lumpley's plight could attest to that. Rumor held that the lady had relations in the besieged capital—a daughter, some said; others, a nephew—and Lord Paget's order to divert to this remote corner of Hertfordshire had been met with displeasure, to say the least.

"Oh." The lady turned her mount and jerked her chin at the box that sat on the hilltop, near where she'd been watching the battle. "Have my ninjas attend to *him*."

And with that Lady Catherine de Bourgh, defender of the realm and head of the Order of the Ever Watchful, whirled away again and galloped off.

Ensign Osillbury started to hustle after her, but a hissing whisper stopped him.

"Please . . . *pleasssssssse* . . . "

The ensign turned and walked warily up the hill again. It wasn't fear that slowed him this time. He wasn't scared of the box's contents. He just didn't like looking at them. No one did.

The box was about three feet high and open in front, almost like a child's casket at a wake. As Ensign Osillbury knelt down beside it, he was careful to position himself at an angle so as not to look straight on at the bandage-wrapped homunculus strapped inside. All he could see was one of the stumps Lady Catherine had created with her own sword.

The man's arms and legs had been riddled with bloody bites when he'd come riding into camp, and after learning the lady was there with

Lord Paget, he'd insisted on seeing her immediately, doctors be damned. The two knew each other, it seemed—the man had been some sort of student of hers. And when they were through talking, the lady had declared that she'd spare her disciple a trip to the surgery.

Those who saw it swore there'd been no mercy in her eyes, however. It was more like fury.

"Yes, sir?"

"Do you know," the man wheezed, "among the survivors . . . was there a . . . a Miss Elizabeth Bennet?"

"I don't know, Sir. Though, come to think of it, there were some young ladies tearing through the unmentionables rather like Lady Catherine herself, and I think I might have heard someone refer to them as 'the Bennet girls.'"

"Ohhh . . . thank . . . you."

Ensign Osillbury got the impression the man was speaking not to him but to Him.

"Umm, will you be all right up here, Sir? By yourself? While I go get someone to fetch you down?"

There was a moist, sticky rustle, and it took the ensign a moment to realize the man was trying to nod.

"I'll . . . be fine. I must accustom myself to waiting . . . for the help of others. Only . . . would you turn me a little more . . . toward the house?"

"Of course, Sir."

The soldier stepped behind the box—he was more than happy to do so—and shifted it a little to the left.

"That's fine. Thank you."

"Very good, Sir. I'll just, uhh, be off, then."

And Ensign Osillbury hurried away, leaving the man in the box there alone, watching for Miss Elizabeth Bennet—and practicing his waiting.

Quirk Classics

Visit www.quirkclassics.com
Masters of Our Public Domain